HORNBLOWER
& THE *ATROPOS*

Books by C. S. Forester

Novels

PAYMENT DEFERRED

BROWN ON RESOLUTION

PLAIN MURDER

DEATH TO THE FRENCH

THE GUN

THE AFRICAN QUEEN

THE GENERAL

THE EARTHLY PARADISE

THE CAPTAIN FROM CONNECTICUT

THE SHIP

THE SKY AND THE FOREST

RANDALL AND THE RIVER OF TIME

THE NIGHTMARE

THE GOOD SHEPHERD

The 'Hornblower' novels in chronological order

MR MIDSHIPMAN HORNBLOWER

LIEUTENANT HORNBLOWER

HORNBLOWER AND THE 'HOTSPUR'

HORNBLOWER AND THE CRISIS

HORNBLOWER AND THE 'ATROPOS'

THE HAPPY RETURN

A SHIP OF THE LINE

FLYING COLOURS

THE COMMODORE

LORD HORNBLOWER

HORNBLOWER IN THE WEST INDIES

Omnibus Volumes

THE YOUNG HORNBLOWER   CAPTAIN HORNBLOWER, R.N.

ADMIRAL HORNBLOWER

History

THE NAVAL WAR OF 1812   HUNTING THE BISMARCK

Travel

THE VOYAGE OF THE 'ANNIE MARBLE'   THE 'ANNIE MARBLE' IN GERMANY

Autobiography

LONG BEFORE FORTY

Biography

NELSON

Plays

U 97

NURSE CAVELL

(with C. E. Bechofer Roberts)

Short Stories

THE MAN IN THE YELLOW RAFT

GOLD FROM CRETE

Miscellaneous

MARIONETTES AT HOME   THE HORNBLOWER COMPANION

For Children

POO-POO AND THE DRAGONS

C. S. FORESTER

Hornblower and the 'Atropos'

London

MICHAEL JOSEPH

First published in Great Britain by
MICHAEL JOSEPH LTD
52 Bedford Square
London, W.C.1
NOVEMBER 1953
SECOND IMPRESSION BEFORE PUBLICATION
THIRD IMPRESSION JUNE 1954
FIRST PUBLISHED IN GREENWICH EDITION 1957
REPRINTED AUGUST 1961
REPRINTED DECEMBER 1964
REPRINTED JULY 1968
REPRINTED JUNE 1970
REPRINTED MARCH 1975

© 1953 by C. S. Forester

7181 0175 8

Printed in Great Britain by Hollen Street Press Limited at Slough, and bound by James Burn at Esher

hension that might be expected of an Oriental bridegroom affianced to a veiled bride—that was not a simile that it would be wise to mention to Maria, though.

Now they were gliding down the summit level of the canal; the cutting was growing deeper and deeper, so that the echo of the sound of the horses' hoofs came ringing from the rocky banks. Round the shallow curve must surely be Sapperton Tunnel.

'Hold hard, Charlie!' suddenly yelled the steersman. A moment later he sprang to the after towline and tried to cast it off from the timber head, and there was wild confusion. Shouts and yells on the towpath, horses whinnying, hoofs clattering. Hornblower caught a glimpse of the lead horse leaping frantically up the steep slope of the cutting—just ahead of them was the castellated but gloomy mouth of the tunnel and there was no other way for the horse to turn. The *Queen Charlotte* lurched hideously against the bank to the accompaniment of screams from the second-class cabin; for a moment Hornblower was sure she would capsize. She righted herself and came to a stop as the towlines slackened; the frantic struggles of the second horse, entangled in two towlines, ended as it kicked itself free. The steersman had scrambled on to the towpath and had dropped the after line over a bollard.

'A pretty kettle o' fish,' he said.

Another man had shown up, running down the bank from the top whence spare horses looked down at them, whinnying. He held the heads of the *Queen Charlotte's* horses, and near his feet lay Charlie, the boatman-postillion, his face a mask of blood.

'Get ye back in there!' bellowed the steersman to the women who were all scrambling out of the second-class cabin. 'All's well. Get ye back! Once let them loose on the country'—he added to Hornblower—'and they'd be harder to catch than their own chickens.'

'What is it, Horatio?' asked Maria, standing at the door of the first-class cabin with the baby in her arms.

'Nothing to alarm yourself about, my dear,' said
Hornblower. 'Compose yourself. This is no time for
agitation.'

He turned and looked at the one-handed steersman, who
bent down to examine Charlie; taking a hold of the breast of
his coat with his steel hook he hauled up, but Charlie's head
only hung back helplessly, the blood running over his cheeks.

'Not much use out of Charlie,' said the steersman, letting
him drop with a thump. As Hornblower stooped to look he
could catch the reek of gin three feet from the bleeding
mouth. Half stunned and half drunk—more than half of
both for that matter.

'We've the tunnel to leg through,' said the steersman.
'Who's up at the Tunnel House?'

'Ne'er a soul,' replied the man with the horses. 'The trade
all went through in the early morning.'

The steersman whistled.

'You'll have to come wi' us,' he said.

'Not I,' said the horseholder. 'I've sixteen horses—eighteen
with these two. I can't leave 'em.'

The steersman swore a couple of astonishing oaths—
astonishing even to Hornblower, who had heard many in
his time.

'What d'you mean by "legging" through the tunnel?
Hornblower asked.

The steersman pointed with his hook at the black, for-
bidding tunnel mouth in the castellated entrance.

'No towpath through the tunnel, o' course, Captain,' he
said. 'So we leaves our horses here an' we legs through. We
puts a pair o' "wings" on the bows—sort o' catheads, in a
way. Charlie lies on one an' I lies on the other, wi' our heads
inboard an' our feet agin the tunnel wall. Then we sort o'
walks, and we gets the boat along that way, and we picks up
another pair o' horses at the south end.'

'I see,' said Hornblower.

'I'll souse this sot wi' a couple o' buckets o' water,' said
the steersman. 'Mebbe it'll bring him round.'

'Maybe,' said Hornblower.

But buckets of water made no difference to the unconscious Charlie, who was clearly concussed. The slow blood flowed again after his battered face had been washed clean. The steersman produced another couple of oaths.

'The other trade'll be coming up arter you,' said the horseholder. ' 'Nother couple o' hours, mebbe.'

All he received in reply was a further series of oaths.

'We have to have daylight to run the Thames staunches,' said the steersman. 'Two hours? We'll only just get there by daylight if we go now.'

He looked round him, at the silent canal cut and tunnel mouth, at the chattering women in the boat and the few doddering old gaffers along with them.

'Twelve hours late, we'll be,' he concluded, morosely.

A day late in taking up his command, thought Hornblower.

'Damn it,' he said, 'I'll help you leg through.'

'Good on ye, sir,' said the steersman, significantly dropping the equalitarian 'captain' for the 'sir' he had carefully eschewed so far. 'D'ye think you can?'

'Likely enough,' said Hornblower.

'Let's fit those wings,' said the steersman, with sudden decision.

They were small platforms, projecting out from either bow.

'Horatio,' asked Maria, 'whatever are you doing?'

That was just what Maria *would* ask. Hornblower was tempted to make use of the rejoinder he had heard used once in the *Renown*, to the effect that he was getting milk from a male ostrich, but he checked himself.

'Just helping the boatman, dear,' he said patiently.

'You don't think enough of your position,' said Maria.

Hornblower was by now a sufficiently experienced married man to realize the advantages of allowing his wife to say what she liked as long as he could continue to do as he liked. With the wings fitted he and the steersman on board, and the horseholder on the bank, took their places along the

side of the *Queen Charlotte*. A strong united shove sent the
boat gliding into the cut, heading for the tunnel.

'Keep 'er goin', sir,' said the steersman, scrambling forward to the port side wing. It was obvious that it would be
far easier to maintain gentle way on the boat than to progress
in fits and starts of alternate stopping and moving. Hornblower hurried to the starboard side wing and laid himself
down on it as the bows of the boat crept into the dark
tunnel. Lying on his right side, with his head inboard, he
felt his feet come into contact with the brick lining of the
tunnel. He pressed with his feet, and then by a simple backwards walking motion he urged the boat along.

'Hold hard, sir,' said the steersman—his head was just
beside Hornblower's—'there's two miles an' more to go.'

A tunnel two miles long, driven through the solid rock of
the Cotswolds! No wonder it was the marvel of the age. The
Romans with all their aqueducts had achieved nothing to
compare with this. Farther and farther into the tunnel they
went, into darkness that increased in intensity, until it was
frightfully, astonishingly dark, with the eye recording nothing
at all, strain as it might. At their entrance into the tunnel
the women had chattered and laughed, and had shouted to
hear the echoes in the tunnel.

'Silly lot o' hens,' muttered the steersman.

Now they fell silent, oppressed by the darkness, all except
Maria.

'I trust you remember you have your good clothes on,
Horatio,' she said.

'Yes, dear,' said Hornblower, happy in the knowledge that
she could not possibly see him.

It was not a very dignified thing he was doing, and not at
all comfortable. After a few minutes he was acutely aware of
the hardness of the platform on which he was lying; nor was
it long before his legs began to protest against the effort
demanded of them. He tried to shift his position a little, to
bring other muscles into play and other areas of himself into
contact with the platform, but he learned fast enough that

it had to be done with tact and timing, so as not to disturb the smooth rhythm of the propulsion of the boat—the steersman beside him grunted a brief protest as Hornblower missed a thrust with his right leg and the boat baulked a little.

'Keep 'er goin', sir,' he repeated.

So they went on through the darkness, in the strangest sort of mesmeric nightmare, suspended in utter blackness, utterly silent, for their speed was not sufficient to raise a ripple round the *Queen Charlotte's* bows. Hornblower went on thrusting with his feet, urging his aching legs into further efforts; he could tell by the sensations conveyed through the soles of his shoes that the tunnel was no longer brick-lined—his feet pressed against naked rock, rough and irregular as the tunnellers' picks and gunpowder had left it. That made his present employment more difficult.

He became aware of a slight noise in the distance—a low muttering sound, at first so feeble that when he first took note of it he realized that he had been hearing it already for some time. It gradually increased in volume as the boat crept along, until it was a loud roaring; he had no idea what it could be, but as the steersman beside him seemed unconcerned he decided not to ask about it.

'Easy a minute, sir,' said the steersman, and Hornblower, wondering, rested his aching legs, while the steersman, still recumbent, fumbled and tugged beside him. Next moment he had dragged a tarpaulin completely over both of them, except for their feet protruding from under the edges. It was no darker under the tarpaulin than outside it, but it was considerably stuffier.

'Carry on, sir,' said the steersman, and Hornblower recommenced pushing with his feet against the wall, the roaring he had heard before somewhat muffled by the tarpaulin. A trickle of water volleyed loudly on the tarpaulin, and then another, and he suddenly understood what the roaring was.

'Here it comes,' said the steersman under the tarpaulin.

An underground spring here broke through the roof of

the tunnel and tumbled roaring into the canal. The water fell down on them in deafening cataracts. It thundered upon the roofs of the cabins, quite drowning the cries of the women within. The weight of its impact pressed the tarpaulin upon him. Then the torrent eased, fell away to trickles, and then they were past it.

'Only one more o' those,' said the steersman in the stuffy darkness beside him. 'It's better arter a dry summer.'

'Are you wet, Horatio?' asked Maria's voice.

'No, dear,' said Hornblower, the simple negative having the desired cushioning effect and smothering further expostulation.

Actually his feet were wet, but after eleven years at sea that was not a new experience; he was much more concerned with the weariness of his legs. It seemed an age before the next trickling of water and the steersman's 'Here it comes' heralded the next deluge. They crawled on beyond it, and the steersman, with a grunt of relief, dragged the tarpaulin from off them. And with its removal Hornblower, twisting his neck, suddenly saw something far ahead. His eyes were by now accustomed to the darkness, and in that massive darkness, incredibly far away, there was something to be seen, a minute something, the size apparently of a grain of sand. It was the farther mouth of the tunnel. He worked away with his legs with renewed vitality. The tunnel opening grew in size, from a grain of sand to a pea; it assumed the crescentic shape to be expected of it; it grew larger still, and with its growth the light increased in the tunnel by infinitesimal gradations, until Hornblower could see the dark surface of the water, the irregularities of the tunnel roof. Now the tunnel was brick-lined again, and progress was easier—and seemed easier still.

'Easy all,' said the steersman with a final thrust.

It seemed unbelievable to Hornblower that he did not have to work his legs any more, that he was emerging into daylight, that no more underground springs would cascade upon him as he lay suffocating under a tarpaulin. The boat slowly slid out of the tunnel's mouth, and despite its slow progress, and despite the fact that outside the sun shone with only wintry brilliance, he was quite blinded for a while. The chatter of the passengers rose into a roar almost comparable with the sound of the underground spring upon the tarpaulin. Hornblower sat up and blinked round him. There was a horseholder on the towpath with a pair of horses; he caught the line the steersman tossed to him and between them they drew the boat to the bank. Many of the passengers were leaving at this point, and they began to swarm out at once with their packages and their chickens. Others were waiting to board.

'Horatio,' said Maria, coming out of the first-class cabin; little Horatio was awake now and was whimpering a little.

'Yes, my dear?'

Hornblower was conscious of Maria's eyes taking in the disorder of his clothes. He knew that Maria would scold him, brush him down, treat him with the same maternal possessiveness as she treated his son, and he knew that at the moment he did not want to be possessed.

'One moment, dear, if you will pardon me,' he said, and stepped nimbly out on to the towpath, joining himself to the conversation of the steersman and the horseholder.

'Ne'er a man here,' said the latter. 'An' you won't find one before Oxford, that I'll warrant you.'

In reply the steersman said much the same things as he had said to the other horseholder.

'That's how it is, an' all,' said the horseholder philosophically, 'you'll have to wait for the trade.'

'No spare men here?' asked Hornblower.

'None, sir,' said the steersman, and then, after a moment's hesitation, 'I suppose, sir, you wouldn't care to drive a pair o' horses?'

'Not I,' answered Hornblower hastily—he was taken sufficiently by surprise by the question to make no attempt to disguise his dismay at the thought of driving two horses in the manner of the injured Charlie; then he saw how to recover his dignity and keep himself safe from Maria's ministrations, and he added: 'But I'll take the tiller.'

'O' course you could, sir,' answered the steersman. 'Not the first time you've handled a tiller. Not by a long chalk. An' I'll drive the nags, me an' my jury fist an' all.'

He glanced down at the steel hook that replaced his missing hand.

'Very well,' said Hornblower.

'I'm grateful to you, sir, that I am,' said the steersman, and to emphasize his sincerity he swore a couple more oaths. 'I've a contract on this here v'yage—that's two chests o' tea for'rard there, first o' the China crop for Lunnon delivery. You'll save me pounds, sir, an' my good name as well. Grateful I am, by ——'

He emphasized his sincerity again.

'That's all right,' said Hornblower. 'The sooner we start the sooner we arrive. What's your name?'

'Jenkins, sir.' Tom Jenkins, the steersman—now to be the postillion—tugged at his forelock, 'main topman in the old *Superb*, Cap'n Keates, sir.'

'Very well, Jenkins. Let's start.'

The horseholder tended to the business of attaching the horses' towlines, and while Jenkins cast off the bow-line, Hornblower cast off the stern one and stood by with a single turn round the bollard; Jenkins climbed nimbly into the saddle and draped the reins about his hook.

'But, Horatio,' said Maria, 'whatever are you thinking about?'

'About arriving in London, my dear,' said Hornblower, and at that moment the whip cracked and the towlines tightened.

Hornblower had to spring for the stern sheets, line in hand, and he had to grab for the tiller. Maybe Maria was still expostulating, but if she were, Hornblower was already far too busy to hear anything she said. It was impressive how quickly the *Queen Charlotte* picked up speed as the horses, suddenly breaking into a trot, pulled her bows up on to her bow wave. From a trot they changed to a canter, and the speed seemed fantastic—far faster, to Hornblower's heated imagination, now that he was at the helm instead of being a mere irresponsible passenger. The banks were flying by; fortunately in this deep cut of the summit level the channel was straight at first, for the steering was not perfectly simple. The two towlines, one at the bow and one at the stern, held the boat parallel to the bank with the smallest use of the rudder—an economic employment of force that appealed to Hornblower's mathematical mind, but which made the feel of the boat a little unnatural as he tentatively tried the tiller.

He looked forward at the approaching bend with some apprehension, and as they neared it he darted his eyes from bank to bank to make sure he was holding in mid-channel. And round the bend, almost upon them, was a bridge— another of these infernal canal bridges, built for economy, with the towpath bulging out under the arch, so that it was hard to sight for the centre of the greatly narrowed channel. Maria was certainly saying something to him, and little Horatio was undoubtedly yelling like a fury, but this was no moment to spare them either a glance or a thought. He steadied the boat round the bend. The hoofs of the lead horse were already ringing on the cobbles under the bridge. God! He was over too far. He tugged the tiller across. Too far the other way! He pushed the tiller back, straightening the boat on her course even as her bows entered the narrows. She turned, very nearly fast enough—her starboard quarter, just where he stood, hit with a solid thump against the elbow of the brick-faced canal side, but she had a thick rope rubbing strake there—presumably to meet situations of this sort—which cushioned the shock; it was not violent enough to throw the passengers off their benches in the cabin, although it nearly threw Hornblower, crouching low under the arch, on to his face. No time to think, not even though little Horatio had apparently been bumped by the shock and was now screaming even more wildly in the bows; the canal was curving back again and he had to guide the *Queen Charlotte* round the bend.

Crack-crack-crack-crack—that was Jenkins with his whip—was not the speed already great enough for him? Round the bend, coming towards them, there was another canal boat, creeping peacefully along towed by a single horse. Hornblower realized that Jenkins' four whip cracks were a signal, demanding a clear passage. He hoped most sincerely and fervently that one would be granted, as the canal boat hastened down upon the barge.

The bargee at the tow horse's head brought the beast to a standstill, edging him over into the hedge beside the towpath; the bargee's wife put her tiller over and the barge swerved majestically, with her residual way, towards the reeds that lined the opposite bank; so between horse and barge the tow-rope sank to the ground on the towpath, and into the water in a deep bight. Over the tow-rope cantered Jenkins' horses, and Hornblower headed the passage boat for the narrow space between the barge and the towpath. He could guess that the water beside the path was shallow; it was necessary to steer the passage boat to shave the barge as closely as possible, and in any case the bargee's wife, accustomed to encountering skilled steersmen, had only left him the minimum of room. Hornblower was in a fair way towards panic as the passage boat dashed forward.

Starboard—meet her. Port—meet her. He was giving these orders to himself, as he might to his coxswain; like a streak of lightning through the dark confusion of his mind flashed the thought that although he might give the orders he could not trust his clumsy limbs to execute them with the precision of a skilled helmsman. Into the gap now; the stern was still swinging and at the last moment he got the tiller over to check her. The barge seemed to flash by; out of the tail of his eye he was dimly aware of the bargee's wife's greeting, changing to surprise as she noted that the *Queen Charlotte* was being steered by a man quite unknown to her. Faintly to his ear came the sound of what she said, but he could distinguish no word—he had no attention to spare for compliments.

They were through, in that flash, and he could breathe again, he could smile, he could grin; all was well in a marvellous world, steering a passage boat at nine miles an hour along the Thames and Severn Canal. But that was another yell from Jenkins; he was checking his horses, and there was the grey tower of a lock-house ahead. The gates were open, the lock-keeper standing by them. Hornblower steered for them, greatly helped by the *Queen Charlotte's* abrupt reduction in speed as her bow wave passed ahead of her. Hornblower grabbed for the stern rope, leaped for the bank, and miraculously kept his footing. The bollard was ten feet ahead; he ran forward and dropped a loop over it and took the strain. The ideal method was to take nearly all the way off the boat, let her creep into the lock, and stop her fully at the next bollard, but it was too much to hope that he could at his first attempt execute all this exactly. He let the line slip through his hands, watching the boat's progress, and then took too sudden a pull at it. Line and bollard creaked; the *Queen Charlotte* swung her bows across the lock to bump them against the further side, and she lay there half in and half out, helpless, so that the lock-keeper's wife had to run along from the farther gates, lean over, shove the bows clear while seizing the bow-line, and, with the line over her sturdy shoulder, haul the boat the final dozen yards into the lock—a clear waste of a couple of minutes. Nor was this all, for, as they had now passed the summit level, this was a downward lock, and Hornblower had not readied his mind for this transition. He was taken by surprise when the *Queen Charlotte* subsided abruptly, with the opening of the gate paddles, along with the emptying water, and he had only just time to slack away the stern-line, or else the boat might have been left hanging on it.

'Ee, man, you know little about boats,' said the lock-keeper's wife, and Hornblower's ears burned with embarrassment. He thought of the examination he had

passed in navigation and seamanship; he thought of how
often he had tacked a monstrous ship of the line in heavy
weather. That experience was not of much use to him here
in inland Gloucestershire—or perhaps it was Oxfordshire by
now—and in any case the lock was empty, the gates opening,
the towlines tightening, and he had to leap down six feet or
more in a hurry into the already moving stern, remembering
to take the stern-line down with him. He managed it,
clumsily as ever, and he heard the lock-keeper's wife's hearty
laugh as he glided on below her; and she said something
more, too, but he could pay no attention to it, as he had to
grab for the tiller and steer the hurrying boat out under the
bridge. And when he had first paid for their passages he had
pictured to himself the leisurely life of the canal boatman!

And, heavens and earth! Here was Maria beside him
having made her way aft through the second-class cabin.

'How can you let these people be so insolent to you, dear?'
she was asking. 'Why don't you tell them who you are?'

'My dear——' began Hornblower, and then stopped.

If Maria could not see the incongruity of a naval captain
mishandling a canal boat it was hopeless to argue. Besides,
he had no attention to spare for her, not with those cantering
horses whisking the *Queen Charlotte* along like this.

'And this all seems very unnecessary, dear,' went on Maria.
'Why should you demean yourself like this? Is there all this
need for haste?'

Hornblower took the boat round a bend—he congratu-
lated himself that he was getting the feel of the tiller now.

'Why don't you answer me?' went on Maria. 'And I have
our dinner waiting for us, and little Horatio——'

She was like the voice of conscience—for that matter that
was exactly what she was.

'Maria,' snapped Hornblower. 'Get for'rard! Get for'rard,
I say. Go back to the cabin.'

'But, my dear——'

'Get for'rard!'

Hornblower roared this out—here was another barge

approaching and he could spare no time for the niceties of married life.

'You are very heartless,' said Maria, 'and in my condition, too.'

Heartless, maybe, but certainly preoccupied. Hornblower pulled the tiller over, and Maria put her handkerchief to her eyes and flounced—as much of a flounce as was possible to her as she was—back into the second-class cabin again. The *Queen Charlotte* shot neatly down the gap between the barge and the towpath, and Hornblower could actually spare enough attention to acknowledge with a wave of his hand the greeting of the bargee's wife. He had time, too, now, for a prick of conscience about his treatment of Maria, but only a momentary one. He still had to steer the boat.

II

THERE was still plenty of daylight when they came out
into the Thames valley and Hornblower, looking down
to starboard, could see the infant river—not such an
infant at its winter level—running below. Every turn and
every lock brought the canal nearer to the stream, and at last
they reached Inglesham, with Lechlade church steeple in
view ahead, and the junction with the river. At Inglesham
lock Jenkins left his horses and came back to speak to
Hornblower.

'There's three staunches on the river next that we have to
run, sir,' he said.

Hornblower had no idea what a staunch was, and he very
much wanted to know before he had to 'run' them, but at
the same time he did not want to admit ignorance. Jenkins
may have been tactful enough to sense his difficulty; at least
he gave an explanation.

'They're dams across the river, sir,' he told Hornblower.
'At this time o' year, with plenty of water, some o' the
paddles are kept out for good, at the towpath end o' the
staunch. There's a fall o' five or six feet.'

'Five or six feet?' repeated Hornblower, startled.

'Yes, sir. 'Bout that much. But it isn't a real fall, if you
know what I mean, sir. Steep, but no more.'

'And we have to run down it?'

'Yes, sir. It's easy enough, sir—at the top, leastways.'

'And at the bottom?'

'There's an eddy there, sir, like as you'd expect.
But if you hold her straight, sir, the nags'll take you
through.'

'I'll hold her straight,' said Hornblower.

' O' course you will, sir.'

'But what the devil do they have these staunches on the river for?'

'They keeps back the water for the mills—an' the navigation, sir.

'But why don't they have locks?'

Jenkins spread his hand and his hook in a gesture of ignorance.

'Dunno, sir. There's locks from Oxford down. These 'ere staunches are a plague. Takes six horses to get the old *Queen Charlotte* up 'em, sometimes.'

Hornblower's thinking about the subject had not yet progressed as far as thinking about how the staunches were passed up-river; and he was a little annoyed with himself at not having raised the point. But he managed to nod sagely at the information.

'I daresay,' he said. 'Well, it doesn't concern us this voyage.'

'No, sir,' said Jenkins. He pointed down the canal. 'The first 'un is half a mile below Lechlade Bridge, there. It's well over on the port side. You can't miss it, sir.'

Hornblower hoped he was right about that. He took his place in the stern and seized the tiller with a bold attempt to conceal his misgivings, and he waved to the lock-keeper as the boat moved rapidly out of the lock—he was adept enough by now to be able to spare attention for that even with a gate to negotiate. They shot out on to the surface of the young river; there was plenty of current running in their direction—Hornblower noted the eddy at the point—but the speed of the horses gave them plenty of steerage-way.

Lechlade Bridge just ahead of them—the staunch was half a mile beyond, Jenkins said. Although the air was distinctly cold now Hornblower was conscious that his palms, as they rested on the tiller, were distinctly damp. To him now it appeared a wildly reckless thing to do, to attempt to shoot the staunch inexperienced as he was. He would prefer—infinitely prefer—not to try. But he had to steer through the arch of the bridge—the horses splashed fetlock deep there—

and then it was too late to do anything about his change of mind. There was the line of the staunch across the stream, the gap in it plainly visible on the port side. Beyond the staunch the surface of the river was not visible because of the drop, but above the gap the water headed down in a steep, sleek slope, higher at the sides than in the middle; the fragments which floated on the surface were all hurrying towards it, like people in a public hall all pressing towards a single exit. Hornblower steered for the centre of the gap, choking a little with excitement; he could feel the altered trim of the boat as her bows sank and her stern rose on the slope. Now they were flying down, down. Below, the smooth slope narrowed down to a point, beyond which and on each side was the turbulent water of the eddy. He still had steerage way enough to steer down the point; as he felt the boat answer the helm he was momentarily tempted to follow up the mathematical line of thought presented by that situation, but he had neither time nor really the inclination. The bows hit the turbulent water with a jar and a splash; the boat lurched in the eddy, but next moment the towlines plucked them forward again. Two seconds' careful steering and they were through the eddy and they were gliding over a smooth surface once more, foam-streaked but smooth, and Hornblower was laughing out loud. It had been simple, but so exhilarating that it did not occur to him to condemn himself for his earlier misgivings. Jenkins looked back, turning in his saddle, and waved his whip, and Hornblower waved back.

'Horatio, you *must* come and have your dinner,' said Maria. 'And you have left me alone all day.'

'Not long before we reach Oxford now, dear,' said Hornblower—he was just able to conceal the fact that he had temporarily, until then, forgotten the existence of his wife and child.

'Horatio——'

'In a little while, dear,' said Hornblower.

The winter evening was closing round them, the light mellowing while it faded over ploughland and meadow, over the pollard willows knee-deep in the stream, over the farm-houses and cottages. It was all very lovely; Hornblower had the feeling that he did not want this moment ever to end. This was happiness, as his earlier feelings of well-being changed to something more peaceful, just as the surface of the river had changed below the eddy. Soon he would be back in another life again, plunged once more into a world of cruelty and war—the world he had left behind in the tidewater of the Severn and would meet again in the tide-water of the Thames. It was symbolic that it should be here in the centre of England, at the midpoint of his journey, that he should reach this momentary summit of happiness. The cattle in the fields, the rooks in the trees—were they part of this happiness? Possibly, but not certainly. The happiness came from within him, and depended on even more transi-tory factors than those. Hornblower breathed the evening air as though it were divine poetry, and then he noticed Jenkins waving to him from his saddle and pointing with his whip, and the moment was over, lost for ever.

That was the next staunch at which Jenkins was pointing. Hornblower steered boldly for it, without a moment of nervousness; he steadied the boat on her course above it, felt the heave and sudden acceleration as she topped the slope, and grinned with delight as she shot down it, hit the eddy below, and emerged as before after a brief period of indecision. Onward, down the river, through the gathering night. Bridges; another staunch—Hornblower was glad it was the last; there had been much point to what Jenkins had said about needing daylight in which to run them—villages, churches. Now it was quite dark, and he was cold and weary. The next time Maria came aft to him he could address her sympathetically, and even share her indignation that Oxford was so far away. Jenkins had lighted candle-lanterns; one hung on the collar of the lead horse and the other from the cantle of the saddle of the horse he rode. Hornblower, in the stern sheets of the *Queen Charlotte*, saw the specks of light dancing on the towpath—they gave him

an indication of the turns the river was making, and just
enabled him to steer a safe course, although twice his heart
was in his mouth as the side of the boat brushed against the
reeds at the river bank. It was quite dark when Hornblower
felt the boat slow up suddenly with the easing of the towlines, and in response to Jenkins' quiet hail he steered the
boat towards a lantern-lit landing-stage; ready hands took
the lines and moored the boat, and the passengers began to
swarm out.

'Captain—sir?' said Jenkins.

That was not the way he had used the word 'captain' at
their first acquaintance. Then it had been with an equalitarian gibe; now he was using the formula and the intonation
that would be used by any member of a ship's company
addressing his captain.

'Yes?' said Hornblower.

'This is Oxford, sir, and the relief is here.'

In the wavering lantern light Hornblower could see the
two men indicated.

'So now I can have my dinner?' he asked, with gentle
irony.

'That you can, sir, an' it's sorry I am that you have had to
wait for it. Sir, I'm your debtor. Sir——'

'Oh, that's all right, Jenkins,' said Hornblower testily. 'I
had my own reasons for wishing to get to London.'

'Thank'ee, sir, and——'

'How far to London now?'

'A hunderd miles to Brentford, sir, by the river. You'll be
there at the first light. How'll the tide be then, Jem?'

'Just at the flood,' said the member of the relief crew
holding the whip. 'You can take water there, sir, an' be at
Whitehall Steps in an hour.'

'Thank you,' said Hornblower. 'I'll say good-bye to you,
then, Jenkins.'

'Good-bye, sir, and thank'ee agen for a true gennelman.'

Maria was standing by the bows of the boat, and even in
the dim light Hornblower thought he could detect reproach

in her attitude. But it was not immediately apparent in her words.

'I've found you a hot supper, Horatio,' was what she said.

'By Jingo!' said Hornblower.

Standing on the quay were a few boys and young women come to sell food to the river travellers. The one who caught Hornblower's eye was a sturdy lad with a keg, clearly containing beer, on a barrow, and Hornblower realized that he was consumed with thirst even more acutely than with hunger.

'That's what I want,' he said. 'Give me a quart.'

'On'y pints, sir,' said the boy.

'Two pints then, you lubber.'

He emptied the first wooden piggin without an effort, without even taking breath, and started on the second, before he remembered his manners. He had honestly been so consumed with thirst that he had forgotten them completely.

'How about you, dear?' he asked Maria.

'I think I'd like half a pint,' said Maria—Hornblower could have guessed at her reply beforehand; Maria would think it was a sign of a lady to drink beer only by the half pint.

'On'y pints, sir,' said the boy again.

'Well, give the lady a pint and I'll finish it,' said Hornblower, his second piggin two-thirds empty.

'All aboard!' called the new steersman. 'All aboard!'

'That'll be a shilling, sir,' said the boy.

'Fourpence a pint for this beer!' marvelled Maria.

'Cheap at the price,' said Hornblower. 'Here, boy.'

Out of sheer lightness of heart he gave the boy a florin, and the boy spun it in the air delightedly before putting it in his pocket. Hornblower took the piggin from Maria's hand and drained it and tossed it to the boy.

'All aboard!'

Hornblower stepped down into the boat and elaborately handed Maria down too. He was taken a little aback to find that the *Queen Charlotte* had acquired some more first-class passengers either here or farther back along their route. There were two or three men and half a dozen women sitting in the cabin lit by the light of a lamp; little Horatio was asleep in one corner. Maria was fluttered; she wanted to speak about domestic subjects, but was self-conscious about it in the presence of strangers. She whispered what she had to say, while her hands now and then gesticulated towards the stony-faced strangers to indicate how much more she would have said if there were no fellow passengers.

'That was two shillings you gave the boy, dear,' she said. 'Why did you do it?'

'Just lunacy, my dear, lunacy,' said Hornblower, speaking lightheartedly but not so far from the truth.

Maria sighed as she looked at this unpredictable husband of hers who could throw away a shilling, and talk about lunacy in the hearing of strangers without dropping his voice.

'And here's the supper I bought,' said Maria, 'while you were talking to the men. I hope it's still hot. You've not had a bite all day, and by now the bread and meat I brought for dinner will be stale.'

'I'll eat whatever there is, and more,' said Hornblower, with more than a quart of beer inside his otherwise empty stomach.

Maria indicated the two wooden platters awaiting them on the bench beside little Horatio.

'I got out our spoons and forks,' explained Maria. 'We leave the platters on board here.'

'Excellent,' said Hornblower.

There were two sausages on each platter, embedded in masses of pease pudding, still steaming. Hornblower sat down with his platter on his lap and began to eat. Those were beef sausages, naturally, if they were not mutton or possibly goat or horse, and they apparently were made from the purest gristle. The skins were as tough as their contents. Hornblower stole a sideways glance at Maria, eating with apparent contentment. He had hurt her feelings several times to-day and he could not bear to do it again; otherwise he would have pitched those sausages over the side into the river where possibly the fish could deal with them. But as it was he made a valiant effort to eat them. By the time he had started the second he decided it was beyond him. He made his handkerchief ready in his left hand.

'We'll be at the first lock any moment,' he said to Maria, with a gesture of his right hand calling her attention to the dark window. Maria tried to peer out, and Hornblower flipped the second sausage into his handkerchief and stuffed it into his side pocket. He caught the eye of the elderly man sitting nearly opposite him across the narrow cabin. This individual had been sitting muffled up in great coat and scarf, his hat pressed down low on his forehead, grouchily keeping watch from under his eyebrows at every movement the Hornblowers had made. Hornblower gave him an elaborate wink in reply to the astonishment which replaced the grouchy old gentleman's bad-tempered curiosity. It was not a con-spiratorial wink, nor did Hornblower attempt the hopeless task of trying to pretend that he stuffed hot greasy sausages into his pocket every day of his life; the wink simply dared the old gentleman to comment on or even think about the remarkable act. He applied himself to finishing off the pease pudding.

'You eat so fast, dear,' said Maria. 'It cannot be good for your stomach.'

She herself was struggling desperately with her own sausages.

'I'm hungry enough to eat a horse,' said Hornblower. 'Now I'll start on our dinner, stale or not.'

'I am delighted,' said Maria. 'Let me——'

'No, dear. Sit still. I'll look after myself.'

Hornblower took the food parcel and opened it.

'Quite excellent,' he said, with his mouth full of bread and meat.

At every moment he was making amends to Maria for his cavalier treatment of her during the day. The larger the meals he ate, the more appetite he evinced, the better Maria was pleased. A little gesture like helping himself to his own dinner gratified her absurdly. He could give her so much happiness; he could hurt her so easily.

'I regret having seen so little of you during the day, dear,' he said. 'It was my loss. But if I had not helped with the working of the boat we should still be at Sapperton Tunnel.'

'Yes, dear,' said Maria.

'I would have liked to point out the scenery to you as we passed it,' went on Hornblower, battling with the self-contempt that his hypocrisy was arousing. 'I trust you enjoyed it even so?'

'Not nearly as much as if you had been with me, dear,' said Maria, but gratified beyond all measure. She darted glances at the other women in the cabin to detect the envy they must feel on account of her having such a wonderful husband.

'The boy was good?' asked Hornblower. 'He ate his pap?'

'Every bit of it,' answered Maria proudly, looking down at the sleeping child. 'He was inclined to whimper at times, but now he is sleeping happily.'

'If it had been two years from now that we made this journey,' said Hornblower, 'how interested he would have been! He would have helped with the lines, and I could have taught him to hold the tiller.'

Now he was not being hypocritical at all.

'He showed a lively interest even now,' said Maria.

'And what about his little sister?' asked Hornblower. 'Did she behave well?'

'Horatio!' said Maria, a little scandalized.

'I hope not badly, dear,' said Hornblower, smiling away her embarrassment.

'No, excellently,' admitted Maria.

They were gliding into a lock; Hornblower heard the rattle of the paddles being let down behind them.

'You made very little progress with your sausages, dear,'

he said. 'Let me dispose of them while you tackle some of this bread and meat, which is really delicious.'

'But, dear——'

'I insist.'

He took Maria's platter and his own, and stepped out into the bows of the boat in the darkness. It was the work of a moment to give the platters a quick rinse overside; the work of another moment to drop overside the sausage from his pocket, and he returned with the dripping platters to a Maria both scandalized and delighted at the condescension of her husband in thus doing menial work.

'Too dark to enjoy any scenery,' he said—already the boat was moving out of the lock—'Maria, my dear, when you have completed your supper I will endeavour to make you as comfortable as is possible for the night.'

He bent over the sleeping child while Maria repacked the remains of the supper.

'Now, my dear.'

'Horatio, really you should not. Horatio, please, I beg of you——'

'No need for a hat at this time of night. Let's have it off. Now there's plenty of room for you on the bench. Put your feet up here. No need for shoes either. Not a word, now. Now a pillow for your head. The bag will make a good foundation. Comfortable like that? Now, the coat over you to keep you warm. There, now sleep well, my dear.'

Maria was carried away by his masterful attentions so that she could not protest. She had lain still for a full two minutes before she opened her eyes again to ask what he was doing for his own comfort.

'I shall be supremely comfortable, my dear. I'm an old campaigner. Now close those eyes again, and sleep in peace, my dear.'

Hornblower was by no means supremely comfortable, although he had often spent worse nights, in open boats, for instance. With Maria and the child lying on the thinly-cushioned bench he had necessarily to sit upright, as the

other passengers were doing. What with the lamp and the
breathing of all those people in the cramped little cabin the
air was stuffy; his legs were cramped, the small of his back
ached, and the part on which he sat protested against bearing
his weight unrelieved. But it was only one night to live
through, after all. He crammed his hands into his pockets
and settled himself again, while the boat went on down the
river through the darkness, stopping at intervals at the locks,
bumping gently against the walls, gliding forward again. He
knew nothing, naturally, of the river between Oxford and
London, so he could not guess where they were at any time.
But they were heading downstream and towards his new
command.

Lucky he was to have a command, he told himself. Not a
frigate, but a sloop so big—twenty-two guns—as to justify
having a captain and not a commander. It was the best that
could be hoped for, for the man who a month ago was the
six hundred and first captain out of the six hundred and two
on the list. Apparently Caldecott, the previous captain of the
Atropos, had broken down in health while fitting her out at
Deptford, which accounted for his unexpected summons
thither to replace him. And the orders had no sooner reached
him than the news of Nelson's victory at Trafalgar had
arrived in England. Since that time no one had had a thought
save for Nelson and Trafalgar. The country was wild with
delight at the destruction of Villeneuve's fleet, and in the
depths of sorrow at Nelson's death. Nelson—Trafalgar—
Nelson—Trafalgar—no column in a newspaper, no momentary gossip with a stranger, but contained those names. The
country had been lavish with its rewards. A state funeral was
promised for Nelson; for the Navy there were peerages and
knighthoods and promotions. With the re-creation of the
rank of Admiral of the Red twenty new admirals had been
promoted from the top of the captains' list; two captains
had fallen at Trafalgar, and two more had died; so that
Hornblower was now the five hundred and seventy-seventh
captain in seniority. But at the same time promotion had

been lavish among the commanders and lieutenants. There were forty-one new captains on the list—there was something gratifying in the thought that now he was senior to forty-two captains. But it meant that now there were six hundred and nineteen captains seeking employment, and even in the vast Royal Navy there were not enough vacancies for all those. A hundred at least—more likely a hundred and fifty—would be on half-pay awaiting employment. That was as it should be, one might think. That proportion not only made allowance for sickness and old age among the captains, but also made it unnecessary to employ those who had been proved to be inefficient.

Unless the inefficient had friends in high places; then it would be the friendless and the unfortunate who languished on half-pay. Hornblower knew himself to be friendless, and even though he had just been congratulating himself on his good fortune he always thought himself ultimately doomed to misfortune. He was on his way to take over a ship that someone else had fitted out, with officers and men he knew nothing of; those facts were sufficient basis on which his gloomy pessimism could build itself.

Maria sighed and turned herself on the bench; Hornblower crept down to her to rearrange the heavy coat over her body.

B

III

A T Brentford, in the early light of the winter's morning, it was cold and damp and gloomy. Little Horatio whimpered ceaselessly; Maria was uncomfortable and weary, as she stood beside Hornblower while her trunk and Hornblower's two sea chests were being hoisted out of the boat.

'Is it far to Deptford, my dear?' she asked.

'Far enough,' said Hornblower; between Brentford and Deptford lay the whole extent of London and much more besides, while the river on which they were to travel wound sinuously in wide curves, backwards and forwards. And they had arrived late, and the tide would barely serve.

The wherrymen were soliciting for his custom.

'Boat, sir? Sculls, sir? Oars, sir?'

'Oars,' said Hornblower.

It cost twice as much for a wherry rowed by two oarsmen as for one rowed by a single man with sculls, but with the ebbing tide it was worth it. Hornblower helped Maria and the baby down into the stern-sheets and looked on while the baggage was handed down.

'Right, Bill. Give way,' said stroke-oar, and the wherry shot away from the slip out on to the grey river.

'Ooh,' said Maria, a little afraid.

The oars ground in the rowlocks, the boat danced on the choppy water.

'They say the old King's fair mazed, sir, at Lord Nelson's death,' said stroke, with a jerk of his hand towards Kew, across the river. 'That's where he lives, sir. In the Palace there.'

'Yes,' said Hornblower; in no mood to discuss the King or Lord Nelson or anyone else.

The wind was brisk and westerly; had it been easterly the river would have been far more choppy, and their progress would be delayed, so there was something at least to be said in favour of this grey world.

'Easy, 'Arry,' said bow, and the wherry began to round the bend.

'Hush, baby. Don't you like the nasty boat?' said Maria to little Horatio, who was making it plain that Maria had guessed at the truth of the matter.

'Nipper's cold, likely,' volunteered stroke.

'I think he is,' agreed Maria.

The boatman and Maria fell into conversation, to Hornblower's relief; he could immerse himself in his thoughts then, in his hopes and his apprehensions—the latter predominating—about his ship that awaited him down river. It would only be an hour or two before he would go on board. Ship, officers and crew were all unknown to him.

'The Dook lives there, ma'am,' said the boatman, through little Horatio's yells, 'an' you can see the Bishop's Palace through the trees.'

This was Maria's first visit to London; it was convenient that they should have a loquacious boatman.

'See the pretty houses,' said Maria, dancing the baby in her arms. 'Look at the pretty boats.'

The houses were getting thicker and thicker; they shot bridge after bridge, and the boat traffic on the river was growing dense, and suddenly Hornblower became aware they were at London's edge.

'Westminster, ma'am,' said the boatman. 'I used to ply on the ferry here until they built the bridge. A ha'penny toll took the bread out of the mouths of many an honest boatman then.'

'I should think so, indeed,' said Maria, sympathetically. By now she had forgotten the dignity of her position as a captain's wife.

'White'all Steps, ma'am, and that 'ere's the Strand.'

Hornblower had taken boat to Whitehall Steps often, during those bitter days of half-pay when he was soliciting employment from the Admiralty.

'St Paul's, ma'am.'

Now they were really within the City of London. Hornblower could smell the smoke of the coal fires.

'Easy, 'Arry,' said bow again, looking back over his shoulder. Boats, lighters, and barges covered the surface of the river, and there was London Bridge ahead of them.

'Give way, 'ard,' said bow, and the two oarsmen pulled desperately through a gap in the traffic above the bridge. Through the narrow arches the tide ran fast; the river was piled up above the constriction of the bridge. They shot down through the narrow opening.

'Goodness!' said Maria.

And here was the greatest port in the world; ships at anchor, ships discharging cargo, with only the narrowest channel down the centre. North country collier brigs, Ramsgate trawlers, coasters, grain ships, with the grey Tower looking down on them.

'The Pool's always a rare sight, ma'am,' said stroke. 'Even wi' the war an' all.'

All this busy shipping was the best proof that Bonaparte across the water was losing his war against England. England could never be conquered while the Navy dominated the sea, strangling the continental powers while allowing free passage to British commerce.

Below the Pool lay a ship of war, idly at anchor, topmasts sent down, hands at work on stages overside painting. At her bows was a crude figurehead of a draped female painted in red and white; in her clumsily carved hands she carried a large pair of gilded shears, and it was those which told Hornblower what the ship was, before he could count the eleven gunports aside, before they passed under her stern and he could read her name, *Atropos*. He choked down his excitement as he stared at her, taking note of her trim and her lines, of the petty officer of the anchor watch—of everything that in that piercing moment he could possibly observe.

'*Atropos, twenty-two*,' said stroke-oar, noting Hornblower's interest.

'My husband is captain of her,' said Maria proudly.

'Indeed, sir?' answered stroke, with a new respect that must have been gratifying to Maria.

Already the boat was swinging round; there was Deptford Creek and Deptford Hard.

'Easy!' said bow. 'Give way again. Easy!'

The boat rasped against the shore, and the journey from Gloucester was over. No, not over, decided Hornblower preparing to disembark. There was now all the tedious business before them of getting a lodging, taking their baggage there, and settling Maria in before he could get to his ship. Life was a succession of pills that had to be swallowed. He paid the boatman under Maria's watchful eye; fortunately a riverside lounger came to solicit custom, and produced a barrow on which he piled the luggage. Hornblower took Maria's arm and helped her up the slippery Hard as she carried the baby.

'Glad I'll be,' said Maria, 'to take these shoes off. And the sooner little Horatio is changed the better. There, there, darling.'

Only the briefest walk, luckily, took them to the 'George.' A plump landlady received them, running a sympathetic eye over Maria's condition. She took them up to a room while a maid under her vigorous urgings sped to get hot water and towels.

'There, my poppet,' said the landlady to little Horatio.

'Ooh,' said Maria, sitting down on the bed and already beginning to take off her shoes.

Hornblower was standing by the door waiting for his sea chests to be brought up.

'When are you expecting, ma'am?' asked the landlady.

It seemed not a moment before she and Maria were discussing midwives and the rising cost of living—the latter

subject introduced by Maria's determination to chaffer over
the price of the room. The potman and the riverside
lounger carried the baggage up and put it down on the
floor of the room, interrupting the discussion. Hornblower
took out his keys and knelt eagerly at his chest.

'Horatio, dear,' said Maria, 'we're speaking to you.'

'Eh—what?' asked Hornblower absently over his shoulder.

'Something hot, sir, while breakfast is preparing?' asked
the landlady. 'Rum punch? A dish o' tea?'

'Not for me, thank you,' said Hornblower.

He had his chest open by now and was unpacking it
feverishly.

'Cannot that wait until we've had breakfast, dear?' asked
Maria. 'Then I could do it for you.'

'I fear not, ma'am,' said Hornblower, still on his knees.

'Your best shirts! You're crumpling them,' protested
Maria.

Hornblower was dragging out his uniform coat from
beneath them. He laid the coat on the other chest and
searched for his epaulette.

'You're going to your ship!' exclaimed Maria.

'Of course, my dear,' said Hornblower.

The landlady was out of the room and conversation could
run more freely.

'But you must have your breakfast first,' expostulated
Maria.

Hornblower made himself see reason.

'Five minutes for breakfast, then, after I've shaved,' he
said.

He laid out his coat on the bed, with a frown at its creases,
and he unlatched the japanned box which held his cocked
hat. He threw off the coat he was wearing and undid,
feverishly, his neckcloth and stock. Little Horatio decided
at that moment to protest again against a heartless world,
and Hornblower unrolled his housewife and took out his
razor and addressed himself to shaving while Maria attended
to the baby.

'I'll take Horatio down for his bread and milk, dear,' said Maria.

'Yes, dear,' said Hornblower through the lather.

The mirror caught Maria's reflection, and he forced himself back into the world again. She was standing pathetically looking at him, and he put down his razor, and took up the towel and wiped the lather from his mouth.

'Not a kiss since yesterday!' he said. 'Maria, darling, don't you think you've been neglecting me?'

She came to his outheld arms; her eyes were wet, but the gentleness of his voice and the lightness of his tone brought a smile to her lips despite her tears.

'I thought I was the neglected one,' she whispered.

She kissed him eagerly, possessively, her hands at his shoulders, holding him to her swollen body.

'I have been thinking about my duty,' he said to her, 'to the exclusion of the other things I should have thought about. Can you forgive me, dearest?'

'Forgive!' the smile and the tears were both more evident as she spoke. 'Don't say that, darling. Do what you will— I'm yours, I'm yours.'

Hornblower felt a wave of real tenderness rise within him as he kissed her again; the happiness, the whole life, of a human creature depended on his patience and his tact. His wiping off of the lather had not been very effective; there were smears of it on Maria's face.

'Sweetness,' he said, 'that makes you my very dearest possession.'

And while he kissed her he thought of *Atropos* riding to her anchor out there in the river, and despised himself as a hypocritical unfaithful lover. But his concealment of his impatience brought its reward, for when little Horatio began to wail again it was Maria who drew back first.

'The poor lamb!' she said, and quitted Hornblower's arms to go and attend to him. She looked up at her husband from

where she bent over the child, and smiled at him. 'I must see
that both of these men of mine are fed.'

There was something Hornblower had to say, but it called
for tact, and he fumbled in his mind before he found the
right way to say it.

'Dearest,' he said. 'I do not mind if the whole world
knows I have just kissed you, but I fear lest you would be
ashamed.'

'Goodness!' said Maria, grasping his meaning and hurrying to the mirror to wipe off the smears of lather. Then she
snatched up the baby. 'I'll see that your breakfast is ready
when you come down.'

She smiled at him with so much happiness in her face,
and she blew him a kiss before she left the room. Hornblower turned again to renew the lather and prepare himself
for going on board. His mind was full of his ship, his wife,
his child, and the child to be. The fleeting happiness of
yesterday was forgotten; perhaps, not being aware that he
was unhappy now, he could be deemed happy to-day as well,
but he was not a man with a gift for happiness.

With breakfast finished at last he took boat again at the
Hárd to go the short distance to his ship; as he sat in the
stern-sheets he settled his cocked hat with its gold loop and
button, and he let his cloak hang loose to reveal the epaulette
on his right shoulder that marked him as a captain of less
than three years' seniority. He momentarily tapped his
pocket to make sure that his orders were in it, and then sat
upright in the boat with all the dignity he could muster. He
could imagine what was happening in *Atropos*—the master's
mate of the watch catching sight of the cocked hat and the
epaulette, the messenger scurrying to tell the first lieutenant,
the call for sideboys and bosun's mates, the wave of nervousness and curiosity that would pass over the ship at the news
that the new captain was about to come on board. The
thought of it made him smile despite his own nervousness
and curiosity.

'Boat ahoy!' came the hail from the ship.

The boatman gave an inquiring glance at Hornblower, received a nod in return, and turned to hail back with a pair of lungs of leather.

'*Atropos!*'

That was positive assurance to the ship that this was her captain approaching.

'Lay her alongside,' said Hornblower.

Atropos sat low in the water, flush-decked; the mizzen chains were within easy reach of Hornblower where he stood. The boatman coughed decorously.

'Did you remember my fare, sir?' he asked, and Hornblower had to find coppers to pay him.

Then he went up the ship's side, refusing, as far as his self-control would allow, to let the incident fluster him. He tried to conceal his excitement as he reached the deck amid the twittering of the pipes, with his hand to his hatbrim in salute, but he was not capable of seeing with clarity the faces that awaited him there.

'John Jones, First Lieutenant,' said a voice. 'Welcome aboard, sir.'

Then there were other names, other faces as vague as the names. Hornblower checked himself from swallowing in his excitement for fear lest it should be noticed. He went to some pains to speak in a tone of exactly the right pitch.

'Call the ship's company, Mr Jones, if you please.'

'All hands! All hands!'

The cry went through the ship while the pipes twittered and squealed again. There was a rush of feet, a bustling and a subdued murmur. Now there was a sea of faces before him in the waist, but he was still too excited to observe them in detail.

'Ship's company assembled, sir.'

Hornblower touched his hat in reply—he had to assume that Jones had touched his hat to him, for he was not aware of it—and took out his orders and began to read.

'Orders from the Commissioners for executing the

office of Lord High Admiral of Great Britain and Ireland, addressed to Captain Horatio Hornblower of His Majesty's Navy.

'You are hereby required——'

He read them through to the end, folded them, and returned them to his pocket. Now he was legally captain of the *Atropos*, holding a position of which only a court martial —or an Act of Parliament—or the loss of the ship—could deprive him. And from this moment his half-pay ceased and he would begin to draw the pay of a captain of a sixth-rate. Was it significant that it was from this moment the mists began to clear from before his eyes? Jones was a lantern-jawed man, his close-shaven beard showing blue through his tan. Hornblower met his eyes.

'Dismiss the ship's company, Mr Jones.'

'Aye aye, sir.'

This might have been the moment for a speech, Hornblower knew. It was even customary to make one. But he had prepared nothing to say; and he told himself it was better to say nothing. He had it in mind that he would give a first impression of someone cold and hard and efficient and unsentimental. He turned to the waiting group of lieutenants; now he could distinguish their features, recognize that they were distinct individuals, these men whom he would have to trust and use for years in the future; but their names had escaped him completely. He had really heard nothing of them in those excited seconds after arriving on the quarterdeck.

'Thank you, gentlemen,' he said to them. 'We shall know each other better soon, I do not doubt.'

There was a touching of hats and a general turning away of them all except Jones.

'There's an Admiralty letter waiting for you, sir,' said the latter.

An Admiralty letter! Orders! The key to the future, which would reveal what was to be their fate—the words which might despatch him and the *Atropos* to China or

Greenland or Brazil. Hornblower felt his excitement surge up again—it had hardly subsided in any case. Once more he checked himself from swallowing.

'Thank you, Mr Jones. I'll read it as soon as I have leisure.'

'Would you care to come below, sir?'

'Thank you.'

The captain's quarters in the *Atropos* were as minute as Hornblower had expected; the smallest possible day-cabin and night-cabin. They were so small that they were not bulkheaded off from one another; a curtain was supposed to be hung between them, but there was no curtain. There was nothing at all—no cot, no desk, no chair, nothing. Apparently Caldecott had made a clean sweep of all his belongings when he left the ship. There was nothing surprising about that, but it was inconvenient. The cabin was dark and stuffy, but as the ship was newly out of dry dock she had not yet acquired all the manifold smells which would impregnate her later.

'Where are these orders?' demanded Hornblower, brusque with his suppressed excitement.

'In my desk, sir. I'll fetch 'em at once.'

It could not be too quickly for Hornblower, who stood under the little skylight awaiting Jones' return. He took the sealed package into his hand and stood holding it for a moment. This was an instant of transition. The journey of the last twenty-four hours had been a longer period, but of the same kind—an interval between one kind of activity and another. The next few seconds would eventually transform the *Atropos* from an idle ship in the Thames to an active ship at sea, lookouts at the mastheads, guns ready for action, peril and adventure and death only just over the horizon if not alongside. Hornblower broke the seal—the foul anchor of the Admiralty, the most inappropriate emblem conceivable for a nation that ruled the sea. Looking up, he met Jones' eyes, as the first lieutenant waited anxiously to hear what their fate was to be. Hornblower knew now that

he should have sent Jones away before breaking the seal, but
it was too late now. Hornblower read the opening lines—he
could have announced beforehand what would be the first
six words, or even the first twelve.

You are hereby requested and required, immediately
upon receipt of these orders——

This was the moment; Hornblower savoured it for one
half of one second.

——to wait upon Henry Pallender, Esq., Blue Mantle
Pursuivant at Arms, at the College of Heralds——

'God bless my soul,' said Hornblower.
'What is it, sir?' asked Jones.
'I don't know yet,' answered Hornblower.

——there to consult with him upon the arrangements
to be made for the funeral Procession by water of the late
Vice-Admiral Lord Viscount Nelson——

'So that's it,' said Hornblower.
'It's *what*, sir?' asked Jones, but Hornblower could not
spare the time at present to enlighten him.

——You will take upon yourself, by the authority of
these orders, the command of all officers, seamen, and
Royal Marines to be engaged in the Procession aforesaid,
likewise of all vessels, boats and barges belonging to the
Cities of London and Westminster and to the City
Companies. You will issue all the orders necessary for
the Procession to be conducted in a seaman-like manner.
You will, by your consultations with Henry Pallender,
Esq., aforesaid, ascertain the requirements of Ceremonial
and Precedence, but you are hereby charged, upon your
peril, to pay strict attention to conditions of Tide and
Weather so that not only may Ceremonial be observed,
but also that no Danger or Damage may be incurred by

the boats, barges, and vessels aforesaid, nor by their Crews and Passengers.

'Please, sir. *Please*, sir,' said Jones.

His thoughts came back into the little cabin.

'These are orders for me personally,' he said. 'Oh—very well, you can read them if you wish to.'

Jones read them with moving lips and finally looked up at Hornblower with a bewildered expression.

'So the ship stays here, sir?' he asked.

'She certainly does. She is from this moment the flagship of the funeral procession,' said Hornblower. 'I shall need a boat and boat's crew at once. Oh yes, pen and paper to send a message to my wife.'

'Aye aye, sir.'

'See there's a good petty officer in the boat. She'll be waiting a good deal ashore.'

'Aye aye, sir. We're having men run every day.'

Of course desertion could be a very serious problem in a ship anchored here in the river, within swimming distance of shore and innumerable boats plying about, with the whole City of London close at hand into which a deserter might disappear. And there could be the question of liquor being surreptitiously sold on board from shore boats. And Hornblower had been on board for a full ten minutes and he was no wiser about the things he most wanted to know—about how *Atropos* was manned and officered, what she lacked, what was her material condition—than he had been yesterday. But all the problems with which he was so anxious to deal must for the moment be shelved, to be dealt with at intervals when this new strange duty permitted. The mere question of the furnishing of his cabin might demand more attention than he could spare at present. Hornblower knew from the newspaper he had read yesterday that Nelson's body was at the Nore, awaiting a fair wind before being brought up to Greenwich. Time was pressing, and there were orders in hundreds to be written, he did not doubt.

And so the moment of transition was over. If he had been allowed a thousand guesses as to what his orders would contain, he would never have thought of this particular duty. He could laugh about it if it were not so serious. He could laugh in any case, and he did. After a moment's glance of surprise Mr Jones decided that he should laugh too, and did so, obsequiously.

IV

'BLACK breeches?' asked Hornblower, startled.
'Of course. Black breeches and stockings, and mourning bands,' said Mr Pallender solemnly.

He was an aged man, and although the top of his head was bald he wore the remainder of his white hair long, clubbed at the nape of his neck in a thick short queue tied with black ribbon. He had pale blue eyes, rheumy with age, and a thin pointed nose which in the chill of the room bore a small drop at its reddish tip—perhaps always bore one.

Hornblower made a note on the sheet of paper before him regarding the black breeches and stockings and mourning bands. He also made a mental note that he would have to obtain these things for himself as well, and he wondered where the money was coming from to do it.

'It would be best,' went on Mr Pallender, 'if the procession were to pass through the City at midday. Then the populace will have plenty of time to assemble, and the apprentices can do a morning's work.'

'I can't promise that,' said Hornblower. 'It depends on the tide.'

'The tide, Captain Hornblower? You must realize that this is a ceremonial in which the Court—His Majesty himself—is deeply interested.'

'But it has to depend on the tide all the same,' said Hornblower. 'And even on the winds too.'

'Indeed? His Majesty will be most provoked if his ideas are scouted.'

'I see,' said Hornblower.

He thought of remarking that although His Majesty ruled the waves he had no more control over the tides than had his illustrious predecessor King Canute, but he thought

better of it. Mr Pallender was not the type to appreciate
jokes about the limitations of the royal power. Instead
Hornblower decided to imitate Mr Pallender's solemnity.

'Since the actual day of the ceremonial hasn't yet been
decided upon,' he said, 'it might be possible to choose such
a day as the tide serves best.'

'I suppose so,' conceded Mr Pallender.

Hornblower made a note of the necessity of immediately
consulting the tide-tables.

'The Lord Mayor,' said Mr Pallender, 'will not be present
in person, but his representative will.'

'I understand.'

There would be some small relief in not being responsible
for the person of the Lord Mayor, but not much, seeing that
the eight most senior admirals in the Navy were going to be
present, and were going to be his responsibility.

'Are you sure you won't try a little of this brandy?' asked
Mr Pallender, giving the decanter a little push.

'No, thank you.'

Hornblower had no desire at all to drink brandy at this
time of day; but now he knew what gave Mr Pallender's nose
that reddish tip. Mr Pallender sipped appreciatively before
going on.

'Now as regards the minute guns——'

Along the processional route apparently there were fifteen
points at which minute guns were to be fired, and His
Majesty would be listening to see that they were properly
timed. Hornblower covered more paper with notes. There
would be thirty-eight boats and barges in the procession, to
be assembled in the tricky tideway at Greenwich, marshalled
in order, brought up to Whitehall Steps, and dispersed again
after delivering over the body to a naval guard of honour
assembled there which would escort it to the Admiralty to
lie there for the night before the final procession to St Paul's.

'Can you tell me, sir,' asked Hornblower, 'what kind of
vessel these ceremonial barges are?'

He regretted the question as soon as he asked it; Mr

Pallender showed surprise that any man should not be familiar with ceremonial barges, but as for knowing how handy they were in choppy water, or even how many oars aside they rowed, that was of course more than could be expected of Mr Pallender. Hornblower realized that the sooner he took one over, and rowed it over the course of the procession in the appropriate tidal conditions, timing every stage, the better. He went on adding to his pages of notes while Mr Pallender went on with what to him was most important—the order of precedence of the boats; how the whole College of Heralds would be present, including Norroy King of Arms and himself, Blue Mantle Pursuivant; the Royal Dukes and the Admirals; the formalities to be observed at the embarkation and the landing; the Chief Mourner and the train-bearer, the pall-bearers and the Family of the Deceased.

'Thank you, sir,' said Hornblower at last, gathering up his notes. 'I will begin these preparations at once.'

'Greatly obliged, I'm sure, sir,' said Mr Pallender, as Hornblower took his leave.

This was an operation as elaborate as Abercrombie's landing on the Egyptian coast—and in the Mediterranean there were no tides to complicate arrangements. Thirty-eight boats with their crews and oarsmen; guards of honour; mourners and officials; there would be a thousand officers and men at least under Hornblower's command. And Hornblower's heart sank a little when he was able to take one of the barges from the hands of the workmen who were attaching the insignia to it in Deptford Yard, and conduct his own trials with it. It was a vast clumsy vessel, not much smaller and no more manageable than a cargo lighter. Forward in the open bows she pulled twelve oars; from midships aft she was covered with a vast canopy of solid construction, exposing an enormous area to the wind. The barge allotted to the conveyance of the Body (Mr Pallender had made that capital letter quite obvious in their discussion) was being so covered with plumes that she would catch the wind like a frigate's mainsail. There must be lusty oarsmen detailed to the task of rowing that barge along—and it would be best to have as nearly as complete a relief available as possible, hidden away under the canopy. But as she would head the procession, with the other boats taking station upon her, he must be careful not to overdo that. He must time everything exactly—up with the flood tide, arriving at Whitehall Steps precisely at slack water so that the complicated manœuvres there could be carried out with the minimum of risk, and then back with the ebb, dispersing barges and crews along the route as convenient.

'My dear,' said Maria to him, in their bedroom at the 'George,' 'I fear I have little of your attention at present.'

'Your pardon, dear?' said Hornblower, looking round from the table at which he was writing. He was deep in plans for issuing a solid breakfast to a thousand men who would have small chance of eating again all day.

'I was telling you that I spoke to the midwife to-day. She seems a worthy woman. She will hold herself free from to-morrow. As she lives only in the next street there is no need for her to take up residence here until the time comes, which is fortunate—you know how little money we have, Horatio.'

'Yes, dear,' said Hornblower. 'Have those black breeches of mine been delivered yet?'

It was a perfectly natural step from Maria's approaching confinement to Hornblower's black breeches, *via* the question of money, but Maria resented her husband's apparent heartlessness.

'Do you care more for your breeches than for your child?' she asked, '—or for me?'

'Dearest,' answered Hornblower. He had to put down his pen and rise from his chair to comfort her. 'I have much on my mind. I can't tell you how much I regret it at this moment.'

This was the very devil. The eyes not only of London but of all England would be on that procession. He would never be forgiven if there was any blunder. But he had to take Maria's hands in his and reassure her.

'You, my dear,' he said, smiling into her eyes, 'are my all in all. There is nothing in my world as important as you are.'

'I wish I could be sure,' said Maria.

He kissed the hands he held.

'What can I say to make you sure?' he asked. 'That I love you?'

'That would be pleasant enough,' said Maria.

'I love you, dear,' he said, but he had not had now a smile from her as yet, and he went on, 'I love you more dearly even than my new black breeches.'

'Oh!' said Maria.

He had to labour the point to make sure that she understood he was both joking and tender.

'More dearly than a thousand pair of black breeches,' he said. 'Could any man say more?'

She was smiling now, and she took her hands from his and laid them on his shoulders.

'Is that a compliment for me to treasure always?' she asked.

'It will always be true, my dear,' he said.

'You are the kindest of husbands,' she said, and the break in her voice showed that she meant it.

'With the sweetest of wives,' he answered. 'And now may I go on with my work?'

'Of course, darling. Of course. I fear I am selfish. But—but—darling, I love you so. I love you so!'

'There, there,' said Hornblower patting her shoulder. Perhaps he felt as strongly over this business as Maria did, but he had much else to feel strongly about. And if he mismanaged these ceremonial arrangements the child to come might go on short commons with him on half-pay for life. And Nelson's body was at this very moment lying in state at Greenwich, and the day after to-morrow was the date fixed for the procession, with the tide beginning to flood at eleven, and there was still much to be done. He was glad to

get back to the writing of his orders. He was glad to go back
on board *Atropos* and plunge into business there.

'Mr Jones, I'd be glad if you'd call the midshipmen and
master's mates. I need half a dozen who can write a fair
round hand.'

The cabin of the *Atropos* took on the appearance of a
schoolroom, with the midshipmen sitting on mess stools at
improvised tables, with inkwells and pens, copying out
Hornblower's drafts of the orders, and Hornblower going
from one to another, like a squirrel in a cage, answering
questions.

'Please, sir, I can't read this word.'

'Please, sir, do I start a new paragraph here?'

It was one way of finding out something of the junior
officers, of distinguishing them as individuals out of what
had been so far a formless mass of officers; there were the
ones who appealed for help at every turn, and the ones who
could make deductions from the context; there were the
stupid ones who wrote orders that made nonsense.

'Damn it, man,' said Hornblower. 'Would anyone out of
Bedlam say a thing like that—far less write it?'

'That's what it looked like, sir,' said the midshipman
stubbornly.

'God help us all,' said Hornblower in despair.

But that was the man who wrote a very clear hand; Hornblower put him on to the task of writing the beginnings of
each letter.

H.M.S. *Atropos* at Deptford
Jan 6th 1806
Sir
    By virtue of the powers entrusted to me by the Lords
Commissioners of the Admiralty——

Other men could carry on from there, with a saving of
time. The ninety different written orders with their duplicates
were written at last, and distributed by midnight; crews and
petty officers had been found from various sources for every

boat that was to take part in the procession, rations allotted
to them, their place in the line clearly stated—'You will take
the seventeenth position, immediately after the barge of the
Commander-in-Chief at the Nore and immediately preceding
that of the Worshipful Company of Fishmongers.'

The final arrangements were made with Mr Pallender at
two in the morning of the day of the procession, and Hornblower, yawning, could think of nothing else to be done.
Yes, there was a final change to be made.

'Mr Horrocks, you will come with me with the Body in
the first barge. Mr Smiley, you'll command the second with
the Chief Mourner.'

Horrocks was the stupidest of the midshipmen and Smiley
the brightest—it had been natural to reserve the latter for
himself, but now he realized how stupid Horrocks was, and
how necessary it was to keep him under his own eye.

'Aye aye, sir.'

Hornblower fancied Smiley looked pleased at thus escap-
ing from the direct supervision of his captain, and he pricked
that bubble.

'You'll have nine admirals and four captains as passengers,
Smiley,' he said. 'Including Admiral of the Fleet Sir Peter
Parker and Lord St Vincent.'

Smiley did not look nearly as pleased at that.

'Mr Jones, have the longboat with the hands at Greenwich
Pier at six o'clock, if you please.'

'Aye aye, sir.'

'And call away the gig for me now.'

'Aye aye, sir.'

'I'll be at the "George" until five. Send any messages there.'

'Aye aye, sir.'

He still had a personal life; Maria was very near her time
now.

On deck there was a brisk westerly wind harping in the
rigging, gusty, Hornblower noted. The barges would call for
careful handling unless it dropped considerably. He stepped
down into the gig.

'Make for Deptford Hard,' he ordered the coxswain, and clasped his coat close tightly round him, for the cabin of the *Atropos* had been hot with lamps and candles and many people. He walked up the Hard and knocked at the door of the 'George'; from the window at the side there was a faint light showing and the window of their room above was illuminated. The door opened to reveal the landlady.'

'Oh, it's you, sir. I thought it was the midwife. I've just sent Davie for her. Your good lady——'

'Let me by,' said Hornblower.

Maria was walking about the bedroom in her dressing-gown; two candles illuminated the room, and the shadows of the bed-tester and the other furniture moved in sinister fashion as Hornblower opened the door.

'Darling!' said Maria.

Hornblower came towards her, his hands held out.

'I hope all is well with you, dear,' he said.

'I think so. I—I hope so. It has only just begun,' said Maria.

They kissed.

'Darling,' said Maria. 'How good of you to come here. I—I was hoping I should see you again before—before—my time came.'

'Not good of me,' said Hornblower. 'I came because I wanted to come. I wanted to see you.'

'But you are so busy. To-day is the day of the procession, is it not?'

'Yes,' said Hornblower.

'And our child will be born to-day. A little girl, dear? Or another little boy?'

'We'll know soon,' said Hornblower. He knew which Maria wanted. 'Whichever it is we'll love her—or him.'

'That we shall,' said Maria.

The last syllable was jerked out of her more forcibly than necessary, and Maria's face took on an expression of preoccupation.

'How is it, dearest?' asked Hornblower, concerned.

'Only a pain,' said Maria, smiling—forcing a smile, as Hornblower well knew. 'They are not coming close together yet.'

'I wish I could help,' said Hornblower, in the manner of uncounted millions of fathers.

'You have helped by coming to me, my darling,' said Maria.

A bustle outside the door and a knock heralded the entrance of the midwife and the landlady.

'Well, well,' said the midwife. 'So it has began, has it?'

Hornblower looked her over carefully. She was not neat—no none could be expected to be in those conditions—but she was at least sober, and her gap-toothed smile was kindly.

'I'll have a look at you, ma'am,' said the midwife, and then, with a sidelong glance, 'Gentlemen will retire.'

Maria looked at him. She was trying so hard to appear unconcerned.

'I'll see you again, dear,' said Hornblower, trying equally hard.

Outside the bedroom the landlady was cordial in her offers of hospitality.

'How about a go of brandy, sir? Or a glass o' rum, hot?'

'No, thank you,' said Hornblower.

'The young gennelman's sleeping in with one o' the maids now,' explained the landlady. 'He didn't cry, no, not a sound, when we carried him in. A fine little fellow he is, sir.'

'Yes,' said Hornblower. He could smile at the thought of his little son.

'You'd better come into the coffee-room, sir,' said the landlady. 'There's still what's left of the fire there.'

'Thank you,' said Hornblower, with a glance at his watch. God, how time was passing!

'Your good lady will be all right,' said the landlady maternally. 'It'll be a boy, as sure as fate. I can tell by the way she was carrying.'

'Perhaps you'll be right,' said Hornblower, and he looked

at his watch again. He really must start preparations for the
day.

'Now see here, please,' he said, and then he paused, as he
made his mind clear itself of its preoccupation with Maria,
and of its deadly fatigue. He began to list the things he
needed from the bedroom upstairs, ticking them off on his
fingers as he told them to the landlady. The black breeches
and stockings, the epaulette and the best cocked hat, the
sword and the mourning band.

'I'll get 'em, sir. You can dress in here—no one won't
disturb you, not at this time o' night.'

She came back later with her arms full of the things
Hornblower had asked for.

'A marvel that I should forget this was the day of the
Funeral, sir,' she said. 'No one hasn't talked o' nothing else
along the river not for the last week. There's your things,
sir.'

She looked closely at Hornblower in the candlelight.

'You'd better shave, sir,' she went on. 'You can use my
husband's razor if yours is in the ship.'

One mention of maternity, it seemed, turned all women
into mothers.

'Very well,' said Hornblower.

Later he was dressed and looking at his watch again.

'I must leave now,' he said. 'Will you find out if I can see
my wife?'

'I'll tell you now you can't, sir,' said the landlady. 'Not if
you can hear what I can hear.'

Much of what Hornblower felt must have shown in his
expression, for the landlady went on——

'It'll all be over in a hower, sir: whyn't you wait a bit?'

'Wait?' repeated Hornblower, looking at his watch again.
'No, I can't do that. I'll have to go.'

The landlady lighted the candle of his lantern at that on
the coffee-room mantel.

'Lord a mercy,' she said. 'You look just the picture. But
it's cold out.'

She fastened the button of his coat close at his neck.

'Can't have you catching cold. There! Don't you worry, now.'

Good advice, thought Hornblower, walking down the slope towards the river again, but as difficult to act upon as most good advice. He saw the light of the gig at the water's edge, and a sudden movement of shadowy figures there. The gig's crew must have appointed one of its members to keep watch for his lantern, while the others snatched what sleep they could in the exceedingly uncomfortable spaces of the gig. But however uncomfortable they were, they were better off than he was. He felt he could sleep on the bobstay of the *Atropos* if only he had the chance. He got into the gig.

'Down river,' he ordered the coxswain.

At Greenwich Pier it was still dark, no sign as yet of the late January dawn. And the wind was blowing steadily from the west, downstream. It would probably freshen as the day went on. A loud challenge halted him as he walked down the pier.

'Friend,' said Hornblower, opening his cloak for his lantern to show his uniform.

'Advance and give the countersign!'

'The Immortal Memory,' said Hornblower—he had chosen that countersign himself; one detail out of a thousand details of the day before.

'Pass, friend. All's well,' said the sentry.

He was a private in the Blackheath Militia; during the time the Body had been lying in state at Greenwich there had had to be guards posted at all points to prevent the public from straying into areas where they were not wanted. The Hospital was lighted up; there was already bustle and excitement there.

'The Governor's dressing now, sir,' said a wooden-legged lieutenant. 'We're expecting the quality at eight.'

'Yes,' said Hornblower. 'I know.'

It was he who had drawn up the time-table; the national, naval, and civic dignitaries were to come by road from

London, to accompany the Body back by water. And here
was the Body, in its coffin, the trestles on which it lay concealed by flags and trophies and heraldic insignia. And here
came the Governor, limping with his rheumatism, his bald
head shining in the lamplight.

'Morning, Hornblower.'

'Good morning, sir.'

'Everything settled?'

'Yes, sir. But the wind's blowing very fresh from the
west. It'll hold back the flood.'

'I feared as much.'

'It will delay the boats, too, of course, sir.'

'Of course.'

'In that case, sir, I'd be obliged if you would do all you can
to see that the Mourners leave in time. There'll be little to
spare, sir.'

'I'll do my best, Hornblower. But you can't hurry an
Admiral of the Fleet. You can't hurry Lord St Vincent.
You can't hurry a Lord Mayor—not even his representative.'

'It will be difficult, I know, sir.'

'I'll do my best, Hornblower. But they have to have their
bite of breakfast.'

The Governor gestured towards the next room where,
under the supervision of the wooden-legged lieutenant,
seamen with black scarves round their necks were laying out
a meal. There were cold pies, there were hams, there were
cold roasts of beef being assembled on the buffet; silver was
being set out on the dazzling white cloth. At the smaller
buffet a trusted petty officer was setting out decanters and
bottles.

'A bite and a glass of something?' asked the Governor.

Hornblower looked as always at his watch.

'Thank you, sir. I've three minutes to spare.'

It was gratifying to have a meal when he expected to have
none; it was gratifying to gulp down slices of ham which
otherwise would have gone down the throat of an Admiral
of the Fleet. He washed the ham down with a glass of water,

to the ill-concealed amazement of the petty officer at the wine buffet.

'Thank you, sir,' he said to the Governor. 'I must take my leave now.'

'Good-bye, Hornblower. Good luck.'

At the pier now it was almost dawn—light enough to satisfy the Mohammedan definition of being able to distinguish a black thread from a white. And the river was alive now with boats. From upstream the wind carried down the sound of the splash of oars and sharp naval commands. Here was the *Atropos'* longboat, with Smiley and Horrocks in the stern; here were the boats from the guardship and the receiving ship; measured tread on the pier heralded the arrival of another contingent of seamen. The day was beginning in earnest.

Really in earnest. The thirty-eight boats had to be manned and arranged in their correct order, stretching a mile downstream. There were the fools who had mislaid their orders, and the fools who could not understand theirs. Hornblower dashed up and down the line in the gig, that watch of his continually in and out of his pocket. To complicate matters, the grog sellers, anticipating a good day's business, were already out and rowing along the line, and they obviously had effected some surreptitious sales. There were red faces and foolish grins to be seen. The ebb was still running strongly, with the wind behind it. Horrocks, in the state barge that was to carry the Body, completely misjudged his distances as he tried to come alongside. The clumsy great boat, swept round by the wind and borne by the tide, hit the pier on her starboard quarter with a resounding crash. Hornblower on the pier opened his mouth to swear, and then shut it again. If he were to swear at every mishap he would be voiceless soon. It was enough to dart a glance at the unhappy Horrocks. The big raw-boned lout wilted under it; and then turned to rave at the oarsmen.

These ceremonial barges were heartbreaking boats to manage, admittedly. Their twelve oars hardly sufficed to control their more than forty feet of length, and the windage of the huge cabin aft was enormous. Hornblower left Horrocks struggling to get into his station, and stepped down into his gig again. They flew downstream; they toiled up. Everything seemed to be in order. Hornblower, looking over the side from the pier when he landed again, thought he could detect a slacking of the ebb. Late, but good enough. High and clear from the Hospital came the notes of a trumpet. Tone-deaf as he was, the notes meant nothing to him. But the sound itself was sufficient. The militia were forming up along the road from the Hospital to the pier, and here came the dignitaries in solemn procession, walking two by two, the least important leading. The boats came to the pier to receive them, in inverted order of numbers—how hard that had been for Hornblower to impress upon the petty officers commanding—and dropped back again downstream to wait, reversing their order. Even now there was a boat or two out of correct order, but this was not a moment for trifles. The dignitaries on the pier were hustled into even inappropriate boats without a chance of protesting. More and more important were the dignitaries advancing on to the pier—here were the Heralds and Pursuivants, Mr Pallender among them. And here at last was the Chief Mourner, Admiral of the Fleet Sir Peter Parker, with Blackwood bearing his train, and eight other admirals with—as the drill-book stated—melancholy aspects; perhaps their aspects would be melancholy even without the drill-book. Hornblower saw them down into their boat, all of them. The tide had turned, and already the flow was apparent. Minutes would be precious now.

The shattering boom of a gun from not far away made Hornblower start, and he hoped nobody would notice it. That was the first of the minute guns, that would boom on from now until the Body reached its next temporary resting-place at the Admiralty. For Hornblower it was the signal that the Body had started from the Hospital. He handed Sir Peter Parker into the barge. A loud order from the militia colonel,

and the troops reversed their arms and rested on them.
Hornblower had seen them doing that drill every available
minute during the last two days. He reversed his own sword
with as much military precision as he could manage—a
couple of days ago Maria, coming into the bedroom at the
'George,' had caught him practising the drill, and had laughed
immoderately. The mourners' barge had shoved off, and
Horrocks was gingerly bringing his up to the pier. Hornblower watched from under his eyebrows, but now that the
wind was against the tide it was not such a difficult operation.
The band approached; all tunes were dreary to Hornblower,
but he gathered that the one they were playing was drearier
than most. They wheeled to the right at the base of the pier,
and the seamen drawing the gun-carriage, stepping short,
with bowed heads, came into view behind them. Hornblower
thought of the long line of boats struggling to keep position
all down the reach, and wished they would step out, although
he knew such a wish was nonsense. The monotonous booming of the minute gun marked the passage of valuable time.
Up to the pier's end came the carriage. It was a tricky
business to transfer the coffin from the gun-carriage to the
top of the state barge; Hornblower caught some of the words
whispered, savagely, by the petty officer supervising the
operation, and tried not to smile at their incongruity. But
the coffin was put safely in place, and quickly lashed into
position, and while the wreaths and flags were being arranged
to conceal the lashings Hornblower advanced to the barge.
He had to make himself step short, with his back bowed and
the melancholy aspect on his face, his reversed sword under
his right arm, and he strove to maintain the attitude while
making the wide stride from the pier on to the stern of the
barge behind the canopy.

'Shove off!' he ordered, out of the side of his mouth. The
minute guns bellowed a farewell to them as the barge left
the pier, the oar-blades dragging through the water before
she gathered way. Horrocks beside him put the tiller over,
and they headed out for midstream. Before they straightened

on their course Hornblower, his head still bowed, was able to steal a sideways glance downstream at the waiting procession. All seemed to be well; the boats were bunched in places, crowded in others, with the effort of maintaining station in difficult weather conditions, but once everyone was under way it would be easier.

'Slow at first,' he growled to Horrocks, and Horrocks translated the order to the rowers; it was necessary to give the boats time to take up station.

Hornblower wanted to look at his watch. Moreover, he realized that he would have to keep his eye continually on his watch, and he certainly could not be pulling it out of his pocket every minute. The foot of the coffin was there by his face. With a quick movement he hauled out both watch and chain, and hung them on the end handle, the watch dangling conveniently before his nose. All was well; they were four minutes late, but they still had a full eleven minutes in reserve.

'Lengthen the stroke,' he growled to Horrocks.

Now they were rounding the bend. The shipping here was crowded with spectators, so was the shore, even as far from London as this. The *Atropos* had her yards manned by the remnant of her crew, as Hornblower had ordered. He could see that out of the tail of his eye; and as they approached the clear sharp bang of her aftermost nine-pounder took up the tale of minute guns from the one at Greenwich. All well, still. Of all the ungrateful duties a naval officer ever had to perform, this one must be the worst. However perfect the performance, would he receive any credit? Of course not. Nobody—not even the Admiralty—would stop and think how much thought and labour were necessary to arrange the greatest water procession London had ever seen, on one of the trickiest possible tideways. And if anything went wrong there were hundreds of thousands of pairs of eyes ready to observe it, and hundreds of thousands of pairs of lips ready to open in condemnation.

'Sir! Sir!'

The curtains at the after end of the cabin had parted; an anxious seaman's face was peering out, from where the reserve rowers lay concealed; so anxious was the speaker that he put out his hand to twitch at Hornblower's black breeches to call attention to himself.

'What is it?'

'Sir! We've sprung a leak!'

My God! The news chimed in with his thoughts with perfectly devilish accuracy of timing.

'How bad?'

'Dunno, sir. But it's up over the floorboards. That's 'ow we know. Must be making pretty fast, sir.'

That must have been when Horrocks allowed the barge to crash against the pier. A plank started. Up over the floorboards already? They would never get to Whitehall Steps in time, then. God, if they were to sink here in the middle of the river! Never, never, *never*, would England forgive the man who allowed Nelson's coffin to sink, unceremoniously, in Thames mud beside the Isle of Dogs. Get in to shore and effect repairs? With the whole procession behind them—God, what confusion there would be! And without any doubt at all they would miss the tide, and disappoint the waiting thousands, to say nothing of His Majesty. And to-morrow was the final ceremony, when the Body would be carried from the Admiralty to St Paul's—dukes, peers, the royal family, thousands of troops, hundreds of thousands of people were to take part in or to watch the ceremonies. To sink would be disaster. To stop would be disaster. No; he could get into shore and effect repairs, causing to-day's ceremony to be abandoned. But then they could get the Body up to the Admiralty to-night, enabling to-morrow's funeral to be carried out. It would ruin him professionally, but it was the safest half-measure. No, no, no! To hell with half-measures.

'Mr Horrocks!'

'Sir!'

'I'll take the tiller. Get down in there. Wait, you fool, and listen to me. Get those floorboards up and deal with that leak. Keep bailing—use hats or anything else. Find that leak and stop it if you can—use one of the men's shirts. Wait. Don't let all the world see you bailing. Pitch the water out here, past my legs. Understand?'

'Er—yes, sir.'

'Give me the tiller, then. Get below. And if you fail I'll have the hide off you, if it's the last thing I do on earth. Get below.'

Horrocks dived down through the curtains, while Hornblower took the tiller and shifted his position so as to see forward past the coffin. He had to let his sword drop, and of course had had to abandon his melancholy aspect, but that was no hardship. The westerly wind was blowing half a gale now, right in their teeth; against the tide it was raising a decided chop on the water—spray was flying from the bows and now and then the oar-blades raised fountains. Perhaps it was a fitting homecoming for the dead hero whose corpse lay just before him. As they came to the bend a fresher gust set them sagging off to leeward, the wind acting powerfully on all the top hamper in the stern.

'Put your backs into it!' shouted Hornblower to the rowers, throwing much of his dignity to the wind, although he was the leading figure in the procession.

The rowers clenched their teeth, snarling with the effort as they tugged at the oars, dragging the obstinate barge by main force forward. Here the wind, acting directly against the tide, was raising some quite respectable rollers, and the barge plunged over them, bows up, bows down, stagger, and heave, like a fishing smack in a gale at sea, lurching and plunging; it was hard to stand upright in her, harder to hold her on her course. And surely—surely—Hornblower was conscious of the water on board cascading forward and back as she plunged. With the ponderous coffin stowed so high up he was nervous about the stability of the absurd craft. Inch by inch they struggled round the bend, and once round it the massed shipping on the north side gave them a lee.

'Haven't you got those floorboards up, Mr Horrocks?' said Hornblower, trying to hurl the words down into the cabin without stooping in the sight of the crowds.

He heard a splintering crash at that moment, and Horrocks' face emerged between the curtains.

'They were all nailed down tight here,' he said. 'I had to prise 'em up. We're down by the stern an' we'd have to bail from here, anyways.'

What with the coffin and the auxiliary rowers they would, of course, be down by the stern.

'How much water?'

'Nigh on a foot, I should say, sir.'

'Bail like hell!'

Horrocks' nose had hardly been withdrawn from between the curtains when a hatful of water shot out past Hornblower's legs, and was followed by another and another and another. A good deal of it soused Hornblower's new black breeches. He cursed but he could not complain. That was Bermondsey on the Surrey shore; Hornblower glanced at his watch dangling from the coffin. They were dropping very slightly behind time, thanks to this wind. Not dangerously, though. They were not nearly in as much danger of missing the tide as they were of sinking in mid-river. Hornblower shifted position miserably in his soaking breeches and glanced back. The procession was keeping station well enough; he could see about half of it, for the centre of it was just now fighting round the bend he had already negotiated. Ahead lay another bend, this time to starboard. They would have a head-wind there again.

So indeed they had. Once more they plunged and staggered over the rollers. There was one moment when the barge put her bows down and shipped a mass of water over them—as much must have come in as Horrocks had been able by now to bail out. Hornblower cursed again, forgetting all about the melancholy aspect he should maintain. He could hear and feel the water rolling about in her as she plunged. But the hatfuls of water were still flying out from between the

C

curtains, past—and on to—Hornblower's legs. Hornblower
did not worry now about the effect on the crowd of the
sight of the funeral barge bailing out; any seamen among
the crowd, seeing that rough water, would appreciate the
necessity for it without making allowance for a leak. They
fought their way round the bend; for a few desperate
moments it seemed as if they were making no progress at all,
with the oar-blades dragging through the water. But the gust
was succeeded by a momentary lull and they went on again.

'Can't you plug that leak, Mr Horrocks?'

''Tain't easy, sir,' said Horrocks, putting his nose out
again. 'There's a whole plank stove in. The tree-nails at the
ends are on'y just holding, sir. If I plug too hard——'

'Oh, very well. Get on with the bailing again.'

Make for the shore? Over there, beside the Tower? That
would be a convenient place. No, damn it. Never. Bail,
bail, bail. Steer a course that gave them the utmost advantage
from the flood and from the lee afforded by the shipping—
that calculation was a tricky one, something to occupy his
mind. If he could spare a moment to look round he could
see the thousands of spectators massed along the shores. If
he could spare a moment—God, he had forgotten all about
Maria! He had left her in labour. Perhaps—most likely—
the child was born by now. Perhaps—perhaps—no, that
did not bear thinking about.

London Bridge, with its narrow arches and the wicked
swirls and eddies beyond. He knew by the trials he had made
two days ago that the oars were too wide for the arches.
Careful timing was necessary; fortunately the bridge itself
broke most of the force of the wind. He brought the tiller
over and steadied the barge as best he could on a course
direct for the arch's centre.

'Now, pull!' he bellowed to the oarsmen; the barge swept
forward, carried by the tide and the renewed efforts of the
oarsmen. 'In oars!'

Fortunately they did it smartly. They shot into the arch,
and there the wind was waiting for them, shrieking through

the gap, but their way took them forward. Hornblower measured their progress with his eye. The bows lurched and began to swing in the eddy beyond, but they were just clear enough even though he himself was still under the arch.

'Pull!' he yelled—under the bridge he had no fear of being seen behaving without dignity.

Out came the oars. They groaned in their rowlocks. The eddy was turning her—the oars were dragging her forward —now the rudder could bite again. Through—with the eddeis left behind.

The water was still cascading out through the curtains, still soaking his dripping breeches, but despite the rate at which they were bailing he did not like the feel of the barge at all. She was sluggish, lazy. The leak must be gaining on them, and they were nearing the danger point.

'Keep pulling!' he shouted to the rowers; glancing back he saw the second barge, with the Chief Mourners, emerging from the bridge. Round the bend to sight the churches in the Strand—never did shipwrecked mariner sight a sail with more pleasure.

'Water's nearly up to the thwarts, sir,' said Horrocks.

'Bail, damn you!'

Somerset House, and one more bend, a shallow one, to Whitehall Steps. Hornblower knew what orders he had given for the procession—orders drawn up in consultation with Mr Pallender. Here the funeral barge was to draw towards the Surrey bank, allowing the next six barges in turn to come alongside the Steps and disembark their passengers. When the passengers had formed up in proper order, and not until then, the funeral barge was to come alongside for the coffin to be disembarked with proper ceremony. But not with water up to the thwarts—not with the barge sinking under his feet. He turned and looked back to where Smiley was standing in the stern-sheets of the second barge. His head was bowed as the instructions stated, but fortunately the coxswain at the tiller noticed, and nudged Smiley to call his attention. Hornblower put up his hand with a gesture to

stop; he accentuated the signal by gesturing as though
pushing back. He had to repeat the signal before Smiley
understood and nodded in reply. Hornblower ported his
helm and the barge came sluggishly round, creeping across
the river. Round farther; no; with that wind, and with the
flood slacking off, it would be better to come alongside
bows upstream. Hornblower steadied the tiller, judging his
distances, and the barge crept towards the Steps.

'Easy all!'

Thank God, they were alongside. There was a Herald at
Arms, tabard and all, standing there with the naval officer
in command of the escort.

'Sir!' protested the Herald, as vehemently as his melancholy aspect allowed, 'You're out of your order—you——'

'Shut your mouth!' growled Hornblower, and then, to the
naval officer, 'Get this coffin ashore, quick!'

They got it ashore as quickly as dignity would permit;
Hornblower, standing beside them, head bowed, sword
reversed again, heaved a genuine sigh of relief as he saw,
from under his lowered brows, the barge rise perceptibly in
the water when freed from the ponderous weight of the
coffin. Still with his head bowed he snapped his orders.

'Mr Horrocks! Take the barge over to the jetty there.
Quick. Get a tarpaulin, put it overside and plug that leak.
Get her bailed out. Give way, now.'

The barge drew away from the Steps; Hornblower could
see that Horrocks had not exaggerated when he said the
water was up to the thwarts. Smiley, intelligently, was now
bringing the Mourners' barge up to the Steps, and Hornblower, remembering to step short, moved out of the way.
One by one they landed, Sir Peter Parker with Blackwood
bearing his train, Cornwallis, St Vincent. St Vincent, labouring on his gouty feet, his shoulders hunched as well as his
head bent, could hardly wait to growl his complaints, out
of the corner of his mouth as he went up the Steps.

'What the devil, Hornblower?' he demanded. 'Don't you
read your own orders?'

Hornblower took a few steps—stepping slow and short—alongside him.

'We sprung a leak, sir—I mean, my lord,' he said, out of the corner of his mouth in turn. 'We were nigh on sinking. No time to spare.'

'Ha!' said St Vincent. 'Oh, very well then. Make a report to that effect.'

'Thank you, my lord,' said Hornblower.

He halted again, head bowed, sword reversed, and allowed the other mourners to flow on past him. This was extemporized ceremonial, but it worked. Hornblower tried to stand like a statue, although no statue he had ever seen was clothed in breeches streaming with wet. He had to repress a start when he remembered again about Maria. He wished he knew. And then he had more difficulty in repressing another start. His watch! That was still dangling on the coffin, now being put into the waiting hearse. Oh well, he could do nothing about that at the moment. And nothing about Maria. He went on standing in his icy breeches.

V

THE sentry at the Admiralty was worried but adamant.
'Pardon, sir, but them's my orders. No one to pass,
not even a Admiral, sir.'

'Where's the petty officer of the guard?' demanded
Hornblower.

The petty officer was a little more inclined to listen to
reason.

'It's our orders, sir,' he said, however. 'I daren't, sir. You
understand, sir.'

No naval petty officer gladly said 'no' to a Post Captain,
even one of less than three years' seniority.

Hornblower recognized a cocked-hatted lieutenant passing
in the background.

'Bracegirdle!' he hailed.

Bracegirdle had been a midshipman along with him in
the old *Indefatigable*, and had shared more than one wild
adventure with him. Now he was wearing a lieutenant's
uniform with the aiguillettes of a staff appointment.

'How are you, sir?' he asked, coming forward.

They shook hands and looked each other over, as men
will, meeting after years of war. Hornblower told about his
watch, and asked permission to be allowed in to get it.
Bracegirdle whistled sympathetically.

'That's bad,' he said. 'If it was anyone but old Jervie I'd
risk it. But that's his own personal order. I've no desire
to beg my bread in the gutter for the rest of my days.'

Jervie was Admiral Lord St Vincent, recently become
First Lord of the Admiralty again, and once Sir John Jervis
whose disciplinary principles were talked of with bated
breath throughout the Navy.

'You're his flag-lieutenant?' asked Hornblower.

'That's what I am,' said Bracegirdle. 'There are easier appointments. I'd exchange for the command of a powder hulk in Hell. But I only have to wait for that. By the time I've gone through my period of servitude with Jervie that'll be the only command they'll offer me.'

'Then I can say good-bye to my watch,' said Hornblower.

'Without even a farewell kiss,' said Bracegirdle. 'But in after years when you visit the crypt of St Paul's you will be able to look at the hero's tomb with the satisfaction of knowing that your watch is in there along with him.'

'Your humour is frequently misplaced, Mr Bracegirdle,' replied Hornblower, quite exasperated, 'and you seem to have forgotten that the difference in rank between us should invite a more respectful attitude on the part of a junior officer.'

Hornblower was tired and irritated; even as he said the words he was annoyed with himself for saying them. He was fond of Bracegirdle, and there was still the bond of perils shared with him, and the memory of lighthearted banter in the days when they were both midshipmen. It was not good manners, so to speak, to make use of his superior rank (which only good fortune had brought him) to wound Bracegirdle's feelings—as undoubtedly he had, and merely to soothe his own. Bracegirdle brought himself stiffly to attention.

'I beg your pardon, sir,' he said. 'I allowed my tongue to run away with me. I hope you will overlook the offence, sir.'

The two officers eyed each other for a moment before Bracegirdle unbent again.

'I haven't said yet how sorry I am about your watch, sir,' he said. 'I'm genuinely sorry on your account. Really sorry, sir.'

Hornblower was about to make a pacific reply, when another figure appeared behind Bracegirdle, huge and ungainly, still in gold-laced full dress, and peering from under vast white eyebrows at the two officers. It was St

Vincent; Hornblower touched his hat and the gesture informed Bracegirdle that his superior was behind him.

'What's the young man so sorry about, Hornblower?' asked St Vincent.

Hornblower explained as briefly as he could, with hardly a stumble this time over saying 'my Lord.'

'I'm glad to see Mr Bracegirdle was carrying out my orders,' said St Vincent. 'We'd have the Admiralty chock a block with sightseers in a moment otherwise. But you have my personal permission, Captain Hornblower, to pass the sentries.'

'Thank you, my lord. I am most grateful.'

St Vincent was about to hobble on his way when he checked himself and looked more acutely than ever at Hornblower.

'Have you been presented to His Majesty yet, young Hornblower?'

'No sir—my lord.'

'You should be. Every officer should show his respect to his king. I'll take you myself.'

Hornblower thought about his wife, about the new baby, about his ship at Deptford, about his wet uniform which would have to be pressed into incredible smartness before he could show it at court. He thought about the rich, and the great, and the powerful, who frequented courts, and knew he would be out of place there and would be unhappy every minute he was compelled to appear there. It might be possible to make an excuse. But—but it would be a new adventure. The distasteful aspects about which he had been thinking were really so many challenges, which he felt spurred to meet.

'Thank you, my lord,' he said, searching in his mind for the words appropriate to the subject, 'I should be most honoured, most deeply obliged.'

'Settled, then. To-day's Monday, isn't it? Levee's on Wednesday. I'll take you in my coach. Be here at nine.'

'Aye aye, sir—my lord.'

'Pass Captain Hornblower through, Mr Bracegirdle,' said St Vincent, and hobbled on his way.

Bracegirdle led Hornblower through to where the coffin stood on its trestles, and there, sure enough, the watch still hung on the end handle. Hornblower unhooked it with relief and followed Bracegirdle out again. There he stood and offered his hand to Bracegirdle in farewell; as they clasped hands Bracegirdle's expression was one of hesitant inquiry.

'Two bells in the forenoon watch the day after to-morrow, then, sir,' he said; there was the faintest accent on the 'forenoon.'

'Yes, I'll see you then,' said Hornblower.

His other responsibilities were crowding in upon him, and he turned and hurried back to Whitehall Steps. But as he walked, with his mind busily engaged in planning his activities for the next two days, that slight stress came back into his mind. Bracegirdle had relieved him of one small extra worry—by to-morrow at the latest he would have been in painful doubt as to whether his appointment with St Vincent had been for the morning or the evening.

At the Steps the ebb was already running full; there were broad strips of mud visible on either side of the river. Over at the Lambeth jetty the funeral barge could be seen with Horrocks and his men completing their task of getting a tarpaulin over the bottom of the boat. The other boats which had taken part in the procession were clustered here, there, and everywhere, and it was with pleasure that Hornblower saw his own gig clinging to the steps below him. He climbed down into it, picked up his speaking trumpet, and plunged into the business of dispersing the craft in accordance with the scheme he had laid down in his previous orders. The wind was blowing as briskly as ever, but now that the tide had turned the water was more smooth, and the only new difficulty he encountered was the great number of small craft that now were pulling about the river, bearing sightseers to a closer inspection of the ceremonial vessels.

Aldermen and City Companies, Heralds at Arms and

Admirals, had all landed and gone home to their respective dinners, and the January darkness had hardly closed in before Hornblower dismissed the last of his charges at Greenwich and, getting back into his gig, was able with relief to give the order to pull for Deptford Hard. He climbed wearily up to the 'George,' cold and hungry and fatigued. That busy day seemed to stretch back in his memory for a week at least—except that he had left Maria in labour only that morning.

He came walking into the 'George,' and the first face that he caught sight of was the landlord's—a shadowy figure with whom he was scarcely acquainted, in this house where the landlady assumed all the responsibility.

'How's my wife?' demanded Hornblower.

The landlord blinked.

'I don't rightly know, sir,' he said, and Hornblower turned away from him impatiently and ran up the stairs. He hesitated at the bedroom door, with his hand on the handle; his heart was beating fast. Then he heard a murmur of voices within and opened the door. There was Maria in bed, lying back on the pillows, and the midwife moving about by the window. The light of a candle faintly illuminated Maria's face.

'Horry!' said Maria; the glad surprise in her voice accounted for her use of the diminutive.

Hornblower took her hand.

'All well, dearest?' he asked.

'Yes,' said Maria.

She held up her lips to be kissed, but even before the kiss was completed she was turning her eyes towards the wicker basket which stood on a small table beside the bed.

'It's a little girl, darling,' she said. 'Our little girl.'

'And a fine little babby too,' added the midwife.

Hornblower walked round the bed and peered into the basket. The blanket there concealed a diminutive figure— Hornblower, grown accustomed to playing with little Horatio, had forgotten how tiny a thing was a new-born baby—and a minute red face, a sort of caricature of humanity, was visible on the little pillow. He gazed down upon it; the little lips opened and emitted a squall, faint and high-pitched, so that little Horatio's remembered cries were lusty bellows by comparison.

'She's beautiful,' said Hornblower, gallantly, while the squalling continued and two minute clenched fists appeared above the edge of the blanket.

'Our little Maria,' said Maria, 'I'm sure her hair is going to curl.'

'Now, now,' said the midwife, not in reproof of this extravagant prophecy but because Maria was trying to lift herself in bed to gaze at the child.

'She has only to grow up like her mother,' said Hornblower, 'to be the best daughter I could wish for.'

Maria rewarded him with a smile as she sank back on the pillow again.

'Little Horatio's downstairs,' she said. 'He has seen his sister.'

'And what did he think of her?'

'He cried when she did,' said Maria.

'I had better see how he is,' suggested Hornblower.

'Please do,' said Maria, but she extended her hand to him again, and Hornblower bent and kissed it.

The room was very warm with a fire burning briskly in the grate, and it smelt of sickness, oppressive to Hornblower's lungs after the keen January air that had filled them all day.

'I am happy beyond all measure to see you so well, dear,' said Hornblower, taking his leave.

Downstairs as he stood hesitating in the hall the landlady popped her head out from the kitchen.

'The young gennelman's in here, sir,' she said, 'if you don't mind stepping in.'

Little Horatio was sitting up in a high-chair. His face lit up with a smile as he caught sight of his father—the most flattering experience Hornblower had ever known—and he bounced up and down in his chair and waved the crust he held in his fist.

'There! See him smile 'cause his daddy's come home!'
said the landlady; then she hesitated before she put forward
a suggestion which she knew to verge on the extravagant.
'His bedtime's coming soon, sir. Would you care to play
with him until then, sir?'

'Yes,' said Hornblower.

'There, baby!' said the landlady. 'Daddy's going to play
with you. Oops-a-daisy, then. The bar parlour's empty now,
sir. This way, sir. Emily, bring a candle for the captain.'

Little Horatio was in two minds, once he found himself on
the parlour floor, as to which of two methods of progression
was most satisfactory to a man almost a year old. On hands
and knees he could make prodigious speed, and in any
direction he chose. But on the other hand he could pull himself upright by clinging to the leg of a chair, and the radiant
expression on his face when he did so was proof of the
satisfaction this afforded him. Then, having let go of the
chair, provided he had already been successful in the
monstrous effort necessary to turn away from it, he could
manage to take a step towards his father; he was then compelled to stop and sway perilously on widely separated feet
before taking another step, and it was rarely that he could
accomplish a step before sitting down on the floor with
something of a bump. And was it possible that the mono-
syllable he said so frequently—'Da' it sounded like—was an
attempt to say 'Daddy?'

This was happiness again, fleeting, transient, to have his
little son tottering towards him with a beaming smile.

'Come to Daddy,' said Hornblower, hands outstretched.

Then the smile would turn to a mischievous grin, and
down on his hands and knees went young Horatio, gallop-
ing like lightning across the room, and gurgling with delirious
joy when his father came running after him to seize him and
swing him into the air. Simple and delightful pleasure; and
then as Hornblower held the kicking gurgling baby up at
arm's length he had a fleeting recollection of the moment
when he himself had hung suspended in the mizzen rigging

on that occasion when the *Indefatigable's* mizzen mast fell when he was in command of the top. This child would know peril and danger—and fear; in later years. He would not let the thought cloud his happiness. He lowered the baby down and then held him at arm's length again—a most successful performance, judging by the gurgles it elicited.

The landlady came in, knocking at the door.

'That's a big man,' she said, and Hornblower forced himself not to feel self-conscious at being caught enjoying the company of his own child.

'Dunno what come over me, sir,' went on the landlady. 'I clear forgot to ask if you wanted supper.'

'Supper?' said Hornblower. The last time he had eaten was in the Painted Hall at Greenwich.

'Ham an' eggs?' asked the landlady. 'A bite o' cold beef?'

'Both, if you please,' said Hornblower.

'Three shakes of a duck's tail an' you'll have 'em,' said the landlady. 'You keep that young feller busy while I get it.'

'I ought to go back to Mrs Hornblower.'

'She'll do for another ten minutes without you,' said the landlady, briskly.

The smell of bacon and eggs when they came was heavenly. Hornblower could sit down with appetite while Emily bore little Horatio off to bed. And after bacon and eggs, cold beef and pickled onions, and a flagon of beer—another simple pleasure, that of eating his fill and more, the knowledge that he was eating too much serving as a sauce to him who kept himself almost invariably within bounds and who looked upon over-indulgence usually with suspicion and contempt. With his duty carried out successfully to-day he had for once no care for the morrow, not even when the day after to-morrow would see him engaged in the rather frightening experience of attending the King's levee. And Maria had come safely through her ordeal, and he had a little daughter who would be as adorable as his little son. Then he sneezed three times running.

VI

'WHITEHALL Steps,' said Hornblower, stepping down into his gig at Deptford Hard.

It was convenient having his gig for use here; it was faster than a wherryman's boat and it cost him nothing.

'Give way!' said the coxswain.

Of course it was raining. The westerly wind still blew and bore with it to-day flurries of heavy rain, which hissed down on the surface of the river, roared on the tarpaulins of the wretched boat's crew, and rattled loudly on the sou'wester which Hornblower wore on his head while he sheltered his cocked hat under his boat cloak. He sniffed lamentably. He had the worst cold he had ever experienced, and he needed to use his handkerchief. But that meant bringing a hand out from under his cloak, and he would not do that—with the boat cloak spread round him like a tent as he sat in the stern-sheets, and with the sou'wester on top, he could hope to keep himself reasonably dry as far as Whitehall if he did not disturb the arrangement. He preferred to sniff.

Up the river, through the rain; under London Bridge, round the bends he had come to know so well during the last few days. He cowered in misery under his boat cloak, shuddering. He was sure he had never felt so ill in his life before. He ought to be in bed, with hot bricks at his feet and hot rum-and-water at his side, but on the day when the First Lord was going to take him to the Court of St James's he could not possibly plead illness, not even though the shivers ran up and down his spine and his legs felt too weak to carry him.

The Steps were slippery where the tide had receded from them; in his weak state he could hardly keep his footing as he climbed them. At the top, with the rain still beating down, he put his appearance to rights as well as he could. He rolled up the sou'wester and put it in the pocket of his cloak, put on his cocked hat, and hurried, bending forward into the driving rain, the hundred and fifty yards to the Admiralty. Even in the short time that took him his stockings were splashed and wet, and the brim of his cocked hat was filled with water. He was glad to stand before the fire in the Captain's Room while he waited until Bracegirdle came in with the announcement that His Lordship was ready for him.

'Morning, Hornblower,' said St Vincent, standing under the portico.

'Good morning, my lord.'

'No use waiting for a smooth,' growled St Vincent, looking up at the rain and eyeing the distance between him and his coach. 'Come on.'

He hobbled manfully forward. Hornblower and Bracegirdle advanced with him. They had no cloaks on— Hornblower had left his at the Admiralty—and had to wait in the rain while St Vincent walked to the coach and with infinite slowness hauled himself into it. Hornblower followed him and Bracegirdle squeezed in after him, perching on the turn-down seat in front. The coach rumbled forward over the cobbles, with a vibration from the iron-rimmed wheels that found an echo in the shudders that were still playing up and down Hornblower's spine.

'All nonsense, of course, having to use a coach to St James's from the Admiralty,' growled St Vincent. 'I used to walk a full three miles on my quarterdeck in the old *Orion*.'

Hornblower sniffed again, miserably. He could not even congratulate himself on the fact that as he felt so ill he knew almost no qualms about his new experience which was awaiting him, because, stupefied by his cold, he was unable even to indulge in his habitual self-analysis.

'I read your report last night, Hornblower,' went on St Vincent. 'Satisfactory.'

'Thank you, my lord.' He braced himself into appearing

intelligent. 'And did the funeral at St Paul's go off well
yesterday?'

'Well enough.'

The coach rumbled down the Mall.

'Here we are,' said St Vincent. 'You'll come back with
me, I suppose, Hornblower? I don't intend to stay long.
Nine in the morning and I haven't done a third of my day's
work yet.'

'Thank you, my lord. I'll take station on you, then.'

The coach door opened, and Bracegirdle nimbly stepped
out to help his chief down the steps. Hornblower followed;
now his heart was beating faster. There were red uniforms,
blue and gold uniforms, blue and silver uniforms, in evidence
everywhere; many of the men were in powder. One powdered
wig—the dark eyes below it were in startling contrast—
detached itself and approached St Vincent. The uniform
was black and silver; the polished facets of the silver-hilted
sword caught and reflected the light at a myriad points.

'Good morning, my lord.'

'Morning, Catterick. Here's my protégé, Captain Horatio
Hornblower.'

Catterick's keen dark eyes took in every detail of Hornblower's appearance in one sweeping glance, coat, breeches,
stockings, sword, but his expression did not change. One
might gather he was used to the appearance of shabby naval
officers at levees.

'His Lordship is presenting you, I understand, Captain.
You accompany him into the Presence Chamber.'

Hornblower nodded; he was wondering how much was
implied by that word 'protégé.' His hat was in his hand, and
he made haste to cram it under his arm as the others did.

'Follow me, then,' said St Vincent.

Up the stairs; uniformed men on guard on the landings;
another black and silver uniform at the head of the stairs;
a further brief exchange of sentences; powdered footmen
massed about the doorway; announcements made in a
superb speaking voice, restrained but penetrating.

'Admiral the Right Honourable Earl St Vincent. Captain Horatio Hornblower. Lieutenant Anthony Bracegirdle.'

The Presence Chamber was a mass of colour. Every possible uniform was represented there. The scarlet of the infantry; light cavalry in all the colours of the rainbow, be-frogged and be-furred, cloaks swinging, sabres trailing; heavy cavalry in jack boots up to the thigh; foreign uniforms of white and green; St Vincent carried his vast bulk through them all, like a battleship among yachts. And there was the King, seated in a throne-like chair with a lofty back; it was an odd surprise to see him, in his little tie-wig, looking so exactly like his pictures. Behind him stood a semi-circle of men wearing ribbons and stars, blue ribbons, red ribbons, green ribbons, over the left shoulder and over the right; Knights of the Garter, of the Bath, of St Patrick, these must be, the great men of the land. St Vincent was bending himself in clumsy obeisance to the King.

'Glad to see you, my lord, glad to see you,' said the latter. 'Haven't had a moment since Monday. Glad all went well.'

'Thank you, sir. May I present the officer responsible for the naval ceremonial?'

'You may.'

The King turned his eyes on Hornblower; light blue eyes, prominent, but kindly.

'Captain Horatio Hornblower,' said St Vincent, and Hornblower did his best to bow, as his French emigre dancing teacher had tried to teach him ten years before, left foot forward, hand over his heart. He did not know how far down to bend; he did not know how long to stay there when he had bent. But he came up again at last, with something of the sensation of breaking the surface of the water after a deep dive.

'What ship, sir? What ship?' asked the King.

'*Atropos*, *twenty-two*, Your Majesty.'

Sleepless during the previous night Hornblower had imagined that question might be put to him, and so the answer came fast enough.

'Where is she now?'

'Deptford, Your Majesty.'

'But you go to sea soon?'

'I—I——' Hornblower could not answer that question, but St Vincent spoke up for him.

'Very shortly, sir,' he said.

'I see,' said the King. 'I see.'

He put up his hand and stroked his forehead with a gesture of infinite weariness before recalling himself to the business in hand.

·'My great-nephew,' he said, 'Prince Ernst—did I speak to you about him, my lord?'

'You did, sir,' answered St Vincent.

'Do you think Captain Hornblower would be a suitable officer for the duty?'

'Why yes, sir. Quite suitable.'

'Less than three years' seniority,' mused the King, his eyes resting on Hornblower's epaulette. 'But still. Harmond!'

'Your Majesty.'

A glittering figure with ribbon and star came gliding forward from the semi-circle.

'Present Captain Hornblower to His Serene Highness.'

'Yes, Your Majesty.'

There was a smile in the pale blue eyes.

'Thank you, Captain,' said the King. 'Do your duty as you have done it, and your conscience will always be clear.'

'Yes, Your Majesty,' said Hornblower.

St Vincent was bowing again; Hornblower bowed. He was aware of the fact that he must not turn his back upon the King—that was almost the sum of his knowledge of court ceremonial—and he found it not so difficult to withdraw. Already there was a line formed of people waiting their turn to reach the royal presence, and he sidled away from them in St Vincent's wake.

'This way, if you please,' said Harmond, directing their course to the farther side of the room. 'Wait a moment.'

'His Majesty's service makes strange bedfellows

sometimes,' said St Vincent as they waited. 'I hardly
expected you would be saddled with this, Hornblower.'

'I—I have not yet understood,' said Hornblower.

'Oh, the Prince is——'

'This way, if you please,' said Harmond, appearing
again.

He led them towards a diminutive figure who awaited
them with composure. A young man—no, only a boy—wearing an outlandish uniform of gold and green, a short gold-
hilted sword at his side, orders on his breast, and two more
hanging from his neck. Behind him towered a burly figure
in a more moderate version of the same uniform, swarthy,
with fat pendulous cheeks. The boy himself was handsome,
with fair hair falling in ringlets about his ears, frank blue
eyes and a nose slightly turned upwards. The burly figure
stepped forward, intercepting the approach of the group to
the boy. Harmond and he exchanged glances.

'Presentations should be made to me first,' said the burly
figure; he spoke thickly, in what Hornblower guessed to be a
German accent.

'And why, sir?' asked Harmond.

'By the fundamental law of Seitz-Bunau only the High
Chamberlain can make presentations to His Serene
Highness.'

'Yes?'

'And I, sir, am the High Chamberlain. As you know.'

'Very well, sir,' said Harmond with resignation. 'Then
may I have the honour to present—Admiral the Right
Honourable Earl St Vincent; Captain Horatio Hornblower;
Lieutenant Anthony Bracegirdle.'

Hornblower was about to bow, but out of the tail of his
eye he caught sight of St Vincent still holding himself
ponderously erect, and he restrained himself.

'To whom have I the honour of being presented?' asked
St Vincent, coldly. It appeared as if St Vincent entertained
some prejudice against Germans.

'Doctor Eisenbeiss,' said Harmond.

'His Excellency the Baron von Eisenbeiss, High Chamberlain and Secretary of State to His Serene Highness the Prince of Seitz-Bunau,' said the burly man, in further explanation. 'It is with much pleasure that I make your acquaintance.'

He stood meeting St Vincent's eyes for a moment, and then he bowed; St Vincent bowed only after Eisenbeiss had begun to bow; Hornblower and Bracegirdle followed his example. All four of them straightened up at the same moment.

'And now,' said Eisenbeiss, 'I have the honour to present——'

He turned to the Prince and continued his speech in German, apparently repeating his first words and then mentioning the names in turn. The little Prince gave a half bow at each name, but as St Vincent bowed low—nearly as low as he had bowed to the King—Hornblower did likewise. Then the Prince spoke in German to Eisenbeiss.

'His Serene Highness says,' translated the latter, 'that he is delighted to make the acquaintance of officers of His Majesty's Navy, because it is His Highness's will that he should make war against the French tyrant in their company.'

'Tell His Serene Highness,' said St Vincent, 'that we are all delighted, too.'

The translation was made, and the Prince produced a smile for each of them. Then there was an uncomfortable moment as they looked at each other. Finally Eisenbeiss said something again to the Prince, received a reply, and then turned to the group.

'His Serene Highness,' he announced, 'says that he will not detain you longer.'

'Hm'ph,' said St Vincent, but he bent himself once more in the middle, as did the others, and then they withdrew themselves, backwards and sideways, from out of His Serene Highness's presence.

'Damned upstart whippersnapper,' mumbled St Vincent to himself, and then added, 'At any rate, our duty's done. We can leave. Follow me over to that door.'

Down below loud bawling by a footman in the courtyard brought up the Earl's coach again, and they climbed in, Hornblower utterly dazed by reason of his cold, the excitement he had been through, and his puzzlement about the incident in which he had taken part.

'Well, that's your midshipman, Hornblower,' said St Vincent. His voice was so like the rumbling of the iron tyres over the cobbles that Hornblower was not sure that he had heard aright—especially as what St Vincent had said was so strange.

'I beg your pardon, my lord?'

'I've no doubt you heard me. I said that's your midshipman—the Prince of Seitz-Bunau.'

'But who is he, my lord?'

'One of those German princes. Boney chased him out of his principality last year, on his way to Austerlitz. Country's brimful of German princes chased out by Boney. The point is that this one's the King's great-nephew, as you heard.'

'And he's to be one of my midshipmen?'

'That is so. He's young enough to learn sense, not like most of 'em. Most of 'em go in the army. On the staff, God help the staff. But now the navy's fashionable—first time since the Dutch Wars. We've been winning battles, and God knows the soldiers haven't. So all the ne'er do well young lords join the Navy nowadays instead of the Light Dragoons. It was His Majesty's own idea that this young fellow should do the same.'

'I understand, my lord.'

'It won't do him any harm. *Atropos* won't be any palace, of course.'

'That's what I was thinking, my lord. The midshipmen's berth in *Atropos*——'

'You'll have to put him there, all the same. Not much room in a flush-decked sloop. If it were a ship of the line he might berth by himself, but if it's to be *Atropos* he'll have to take what comes. And it won't be caviar and venison, either. I'll send you orders on the subject, of course.'

'Aye aye, my lord.'

The coach was grinding to a stop at the Admiralty; some-one opened the door, and St Vincent began to heave himself out of his seat. Hornblower followed him in under the portico.

'I'll bid you good-bye, then, Hornblower,' said St Vincent, offering his hand.

'Good-bye, my lord.'

St Vincent stood looking at him from under his eyebrows.

'The Navy has two duties, Hornblower,' he said. 'We all know what one is—to fight the French and give Boney what for.'

'Yes, my lord?'

'The other we don't think about so much. We have to see that when we go we leave behind us a Navy which is as good as the one in which we served. You've less than three years' seniority now, Hornblower, but you'll find you'll grow older. It'll seem you've hardly had time to look round before you'll have forty-three years' seniority, like me. It goes fast enough, I assure you. Perhaps then you'll be taking another young officer to present him at the Palace.'

'Er—yes, my lord.'

'Choose carefully, Hornblower, if it ever becomes your duty. One can make mistakes. But let them be honest mistakes.'

'Yes, my lord.'

'That's all.'

The old man turned away without another word, leaving Hornblower with Bracegirdle under the portico.

'Jervie's in a melting mood,' said Bracegirdle.

'So it seems.'

'I think he wanted to say he had his eye on you, sir.'

'But he had an anchor out to windward all the same,' said Hornblower, thinking of what St Vincent had said about the chance of one making mistakes.

'Jervie never forgives, sir,' said Bracegirdle, seriously.

'Well——'

Twelve years of service in the Navy had gone far to make Hornblower, on occasions, fatalist enough to be able to shrug off that sort of peril—at least until it was past.

'I'll take my boat cloak, if you please,' he said, 'and I'll say good-bye, and thank you.'

'A glass of something? A cup of tea? A mouthful to eat, sir?'

'No, thank you, I'd better shove off.'

Maria was waiting for him at Deptford, longing to hear about his visit to Court and his presentation to the King. Maria had been wildly excited when Hornblower had told her what he was going to do. The thought that he was going to meet face to face the Lord's anointed was almost too much for her—the midwife had come forward with a warning that all this excitement might bring on a fever. And he had not merely been presented to the King, but the King had actually spoken to him, had discussed his professional career with him. Besides, he was to have a real Prince as a midshipman on board his ship—a dispossessed prince, admittedly, but to counter-balance that was the fact that the prince was a great-nephew of the King, related by blood to the Royal Family. That would delight Maria as much as his presentation at Court.

She would want to know all about it, who was there (Hornblower found himself wishing he had been able to identify a single one of the figures who had stood behind the throne) and what everyone was wearing—that would be easier, as there had been no women present, of course, at the levee, and practically everyone had been in uniform. He would have to be careful in his account, as it was possible to hurt Maria's feelings. Hornblower himself fought for his country; it might be better said that he fought for the ideals of liberty and decency against the unprincipled tyrant who ruled across the Channel; the hackneyed phrase 'for King and Country' hardly expressed his feelings at all. If he was ready to lay down his life for his King that really had no

reference to the kindly pop-eyed old gentleman with whom
he had been speaking this morning; it meant that he was
ready to die for the system of liberty and order that the old
gentleman represented. But to Maria the King was representative of something other than liberty and order; he had
received the blessing of the Church; he was somebody to
be spoken about with awe. To turn one's back on the King
was to Hornblower a breach of good manners, something
damaging, in some degree, to the conventions which held the
country together in the face of its imminent peril; but to
Maria it would be something very close to sacrilege. He
would have to be careful not to speak too lightly of the old
gentleman.

And yet (the gig was carrying him through the Pool now,
under the walls of the Tower) Hornblower had to admit it
to himself that Maria's views about his service in the Navy
were not on as lofty a plane as his own. To Maria it was a
gentlemanly trade; it gave her a certain social status to
which she otherwise would not have attained, and it put
food into the mouth of her precious child—children, now
that little Maria was born. But self-sacrifice for a cause; the
incurring of danger beyond the dictates of duty; honour;
glory; these were conceptions that Maria cared little about.
She was in fact rather inclined to turn up her nose at them
as purely masculine notions, part of an elaborate game or
ritual devised by men to make them feel superior to and
different from women whose self-respect and sublime
certainty of superiority needed no such puerile bolstering.

It was a surprise to Hornblower to find that the gig was
now passing the *Atropos* as she lay at the edge of the stream.
He should have been all eyes to see that all was well with her
and that the officer of the watch had been on the alert to
detect the gig as she came down the river; as it was Hornblower merely had time to acknowledge the salute of
Lieutenant Jones as the gig left the ship behind. There was
Deptford Dock, and beside it the enormous activities of the
Victualling Yard. From a sailing barge lying beside the jetty

a gang of men were at work driving a herd of pigs up into the yard, destined for slaughter and salting down to feed the Navy.

'Eyes in the boat, there!' growled the coxwain.

One of the gig's crew had made a *sotto voice* joke about those pigs, evidently. It was hard to believe, even with this evidence before their eyes, that the unrecognizable, wooden hard chunks of matter that were issued from the brine barrels to the men at sea, really came from decent respectable animals like those there. Hornblower's sympathies were with his men. The coxswain was putting his tiller over to bring the gig up to Deptford Hard. Hornblower disembarked, to walk up to the 'George,' to where his family was awaiting him. He would sit by Maria's bed and tell her about the pageantry of the Court of St James's. He would hold his little daughter in his arms; he would play with his little son. It might well be for the very last time; at any moment his orders would come, and he would take *Atropos* to sea. Battle, storm, shipwreck, disease—what were the chances that he would never come back again? And if ever he did the squalling baby he was leaving behind would be a trim little miss playing with her dolls; little Horatio would be at least starting with slate and pencil writing his letters and figures; he might be beginning to decline mensa and learning the Greek alphabet. And he himself? He hoped he would be able to say he had done his duty; he hoped that those weaknesses of which he was so conscious would not prevent him from achieving something of which his children might be proud.

VII

So it was to be the Mediterranean. Hornblower sat in his canvas chair in his cabin in *Atropos*, re-reading the orders which had come for him.

Sir—
I am commanded by the Lords Commissioners of the Admiralty——

He was to prepare himself with the utmost diligence ready to proceed to Gibraltar, and there he was to call for orders which the Vice-Admiral Commanding in the Mediterranean might send to him there. In the event that no such orders should be forthcoming, he was to ascertain where the Vice-Admiral was likely to be found, and to proceed with the same diligence to put himself under the Vice-Admiral's orders.

That must be Cuthbert Collingwood—Lord Collingwood now that he had received his peerage after Trafalgar. The fleet that had won the battle there—or such ships of it as were still seaworthy—had been sent into the Mediterranean after the battle, he knew. The destruction of the French and Spanish fleets outside Cadiz had definitely established British command of the Atlantic, so now the Navy was carrying its ponderous weight into the Mediterranean to head off there any moves that Bonaparte might make now that Austerlitz had given him command of Continental Europe. Austerlitz——Trafalgar. The French army——and the Royal Navy. The one might be balanced against the other. There was no corner of Europe whither French troops might not march—as long as there was land for them to march on; there was no corner of the sea where British ships might not bring their influence to bear—as long as there was water in which they could float. In the landlocked Mediterranean with its peninsulas and islands sea power could best confront land power. The bloody and seemingly endless conflict between tyranny and liberty would be fought out there. He would play his part in it. The Secretary to the Lords Commissioners signed himself 'your obedient humble servant,' but before he did so he went on to say that Their Lordships rested assured that *Atropos* was ready for immediate departure, so that on receipt of final orders and of the last minute despatches which would be entrusted to her she would be able to leave at once. Hornblower and his ship, in other words, were being put on notice of instant readiness.

Hornblower felt a slight feeling of apprehension, a sensation of gooseflesh at the back of his neck. He did not believe that his ship was prepared in all respects to leave at a moment's notice.

Hornblower lifted up his voice in a call to the sentry outside his door.

'Pass the word for Mr Jones.'

He heard the cry repeated in the 'tween decks like an echo, as he sat on with the orders in his hands. It was only a few moments before Mr Jones came in hastily, and it was only when he arrived that Hornblower realized that he had not prepared himself to give the necessary orders and make the necessary inquiries. As a result Hornblower found himself compelled to look Jones over without speaking. His mind was sorting out his thoughts without reacting at all to the reports his eyes were making to it, but Hornblower's steady stare discomposed the unfortunate Jones, who put his hand up nervously to his face. Hornblower saw a dab of dry lather in front of Jones's right ear, and as the lieutenant's gesture recalled him to himself he noticed something more; one lantern cheek was smooth and well shaved, while the other bristled with a fair growth of black beard.

'Pardon, sir,' said Jones, 'but your call caught me half shaved, and I judged it best to come at once.'

'Very well, Mr Jones,' said Hornblower; he was not sorry that Jones had something to explain away while he himself

was not ready with the definite orders that a good officer
should be able to issue.

Under that embarrassing stare Jones had to speak again.

'Did you want me, sir?'

'Yes,' said Hornblower. 'We are under orders for the
Mediterranean.'

'Indeed, sir?' Mr Jones's remarks did not make any great
contribution to the progress of the conversation.

'I want your report on how soon we can be ready for
sea.'

'Oh, sir——'

Jones put his hand up to his face again; perhaps it was as
long as it was because of his habit of pulling at his chin.

'Are stores and water complete?'

'Well, sir, you see——'

'You mean they are not?'

'N—no, sir. Not altogether.'

Hornblower was about to ask for an explanation, but
changed his approach at the last second.

'I won't ask why at present. How short are we?'

'Well, sir——' The wretched Jones entered into a hurried
statement. They were twenty tons of water short. Bread,
spirits, meat——

'You mean that with the Victualling Yard only across the
river you have not kept the ship complete with stores?'

'Well, sir——' Jones tried to explain that he had not
thought it necessary to draw supplies from day to day.
'There was plenty of other work for the hands, sir, fitting
out.'

'Watch bills? Station bills?'

These were the lists that allocated the hands to their duties
and quarters in the ship.

'We're twenty topmen short, sir,' said Jones pitifully.

'All the more reason to make the most of what we have.'

'Yes, sir, of course, sir.' Jones sought desperately in his
mind for excuses for himself. 'Some of our beef, sir—it—it
isn't fit to eat.'

'Worse than usual?'

'Yes, sir. Must be some of an old batch. Real bad, some of it.'

'In which tier?'

'I'll ask the purser, sir.'

'You mean you don't know?'

'No, sir—yes, sir.'

Hornblower fell into deep thought again, but as once more he did not take his eyes from Jones's face that did not help the delinquent first lieutenant to recover his equanimity. Actually Hornblower was condemning himself. During the few days he had held command of the *Atropos* he had been hard at work on the details of Nelson's funeral, and then he had been preoccupied with his own family affairs, but all that was no excuse. The captain of a ship should be aware at every moment of the state of his command. He was savagely angry with himself. He hardly knew his officers' names; he could not even estimate what sort of fight *Atropos* could put up—and yet he would not have to go very far down the river to find his ship likely to be in action.

'What about the gunner's stores?' he asked. 'Powder? Shot? Wads? Cartridges?'

'I'll send for the gunner, sir, shall I?' asked Jones. He was desperate at all this revelation of his own inadequacies.

'I'll see 'em all in a minute,' said Hornblower. 'Purser, gunner, bos'n, cooper, master's mate.'

These were the subordinate heads of department responsible through the first lieutenant to the captain for the proper functioning of the ship.

'Aye aye, sir.'

'What the devil's that noise?' asked Hornblower pettishly. For some minutes now there had been some sort of altercation on the quarterdeck over their heads. Strange voices were making themselves heard through the skylight.

'Shall I find out, sir?' asked Jones eagerly, hoping for some distraction. But as he spoke there was a knock at the cabin door.

'This'll tell us,' said Hornblower. 'Come in!'

Midshipman Horrocks opened the door.

'Mr Still's respects, sir, an' there are some gentlemen come on board with an Admiralty letter for you, sir.'

'Ask them to come here.'

It could only be trouble of one sort or another, Hornblower decided, as he waited. One more distraction at a moment when he was about to be desperately busy. Horrocks ushered in two figures, one large and one diminutive, wearing glittering uniforms of green and gold—Hornblower had last seen them only yesterday at the Court of St James's, the German princeling and his bear-leader. Hornblower rose to his feet, and Eisenbeiss stepped forward with an elaborate bow, to which Hornblower replied with a curt nod.

'Well, sir?'

Eisenbeiss ceremoniously handed over a letter; a glance showed Hornblower that it was addressed to him. He opened it carefully and read it.

> *You are hereby requested and required to receive into your ship His Serene Highness Ernst Prince of Seitz-Bunau, who has been rated as midshipman in His Majesty's Navy. You will employ your diligence in instructing His Serene Highness in his new profession as well as in continuing his education in readiness for the day which under Providence may not be far distant, when His Serene Highness will again assume the government of his hereditary dominions. You will also receive into your ship His Excellency the Baron Otto von Eisenbeiss, Chamberlain and First Secretary of State to His Serene Highness. His Excellency was until recently practising as a surgeon, and he has received from the Navy Office a warrant as such in His Majesty's Navy. You will make use of His Excellency's services, therefore, as Surgeon in your ship while, as far as naval discipline and the Articles of War allow, he continues to act as Chamberlain to His Serene Highness.*

'I see,' he said. He looked at the odd pair in their resplendent uniforms. 'Welcome aboard, Your Highness.'

The prince nodded and smiled, clearly without understanding.

Hornblower sat down again, and Eisenbeiss began to speak at once, his thick German accent stressing his grievances.

'I must protest, sir,' he said.

'Well?' said Hornblower, in a tone that might well have conveyed a warning.

'His Serene Highness is not being treated with proper respect. When we reached your ship I sent my footman on board to announce us so that His Highness could be received with royal honours. They were absolutely refused, sir. The man on the deck there—I presume he is an officer—said he had no instructions. It was only when I showed him that letter, sir, that he allowed us to come on board at all.'

'Quite right. He had no instructions.'

'I trust you will make amends, then. And may I remind you that you are sitting in the presence of royalty?'

'You call me "sir," ' snapped Hornblower. 'And you will address me as my subordinate should.'

Eisenbeiss jerked himself upright in his indignation, so that his head came with a shattering crash against the deckbeam above; this checked his flow of words and enabled Hornblower to continue.

'As officers in the King's service you should have worn the King's uniform. You have your dunnage with you?'

Eisenbeiss was still too stunned to answer, even if he understood the word, and Horrocks spoke for him.

'Please, sir, it's in the boat alongside. Chests and chests of it.'

'Thank you, Mr Horrocks. Now, doctor, I understand you have the necessary professional qualifications to act as surgeon in this ship. That is so?'

Eisenbeiss still strove to retain his dignity.

'As Secretary of State I am addressed as "Your Excellency," ' he said.

'But as surgeon in this ship you are addressed as "doctor." And that is the last time I shall overlook the omission of the word "sir." Now. Your qualifications?'

'I am a surgeon—sir.'

The last word came out with a jerk as Hornblower's eyebrows rose.

'You have been in practice recently?'

'Until a few months ago—sir. I was surgeon to the Court of Seitz-Bunau. But now I am——'

'Now you are surgeon in H.M.S. *Atropos*, and we can leave off the farce of your being Secretary of State.'

'Sir——'

'Silence, if you please, doctor. Mr Horrocks!'

'Sir!'

'My compliments to Mr Still. I'll have these two gentlemen's baggage swayed up. They are to make immediate selection of their necessities to the extent of one sea chest each. You will be able to help them in their choice. The remainder is to leave the ship within ten minutes by the boat in which it came. Is that quite clear, Mr Horrocks?'

'Aye aye, sir. If you please, sir, there's a couple of footmen with the baggage.'

'Footmen?'

'Yes, sir, in uniforms like these,' Horrocks indicated the green and gold of the Germans.

'That's two more hands, then. Read 'em in and send 'em for'rard.'

The Navy could always use more men, and a couple of fat, well-fed footmen would make useful hands in time to come.

'But, sir——' said Eisenbeiss.

'Speak when you're spoken to, doctor. Now Mr Horrocks, you will take the prince and settle him into the midshipmen's berth. I'll introduce you. Mr Midshipman Horrocks—er, Mr Midshipman Prince.'

Horrocks automatically offered his hand, and the prince as automatically took it, displaying no immediate change at the contamination of a human touch. He smiled shyly, without understanding.

'And my compliments to the master's mate, too, Mr Horrocks. Ask him to be good enough to show the doctor where he berths for'rard.'

'Aye aye, sir.'

'Now, doctor, in half an hour I wish to see you both in the King's uniform. You can take up your duties then. There will be a court of inquiry opened at that time, consisting of the first lieutenant, the purser, and yourself, to decide whether certain hogsheads of beef are fit for human consumption. You will be secretary of that court and I want your written report by noon. Go with Mr Horrocks now.'

Eisenbeiss hesitated a moment under Hornblower's sharp glance before he turned to leave the cabin, but at the curtain his indignation overcame him again.

'I shall write to the Prime Minister, sir,' he said. 'He shall hear about this treatment of His Majesty's Allies.'

'Yes, doctor. If you contravene the Mutiny Act you'll swing at the yardarm. Now, Mr Jones, with regard to these station and quarter bills.'

As Hornblower turned to Jones to re-enter into the business of getting *Atropos* ready for sea he was conscious of feeling some contempt for himself. He could browbeat a silly German doctor effectively enough; he could flatter himself that he had dealt adequately with what might have been a difficult though petty situation. But that was nothing to be proud of, when he had to realize that with regard to his real duties he had been found wanting. He had wasted precious hours. During the last two days he had twice played with his little son; he had sat by his wife's bedside and held his little daughter in his arms, when really he should have been on board here looking after his ship. It was no excuse that it was Jones's duty to have attended to the matters under consideration; it had been Hornblower's

D

duty to see that Jones had attended to them. A naval
officer should not have a wife or children—this present
situation was the proof of that trite saying. Hornblower
found himself setting his mouth hard as he came to that
conclusion. There were still eight hours of daylight left
to-day. He began an orderly planning of those eight hours.
There were the matters that would call for his own personal
activity like appealing to the superintendent of the dockyard;
there were the matters he could safely leave to his subordinates. There was work that could be done on one side
of the ship, leaving the other side clear; there was work that
would demand the services of skilled seamen, and work that
landsmen could do. There were some jobs that could not
be started until other jobs were finished. If he was not careful
some of his officers would have to be in two places at once,
there would be confusion, delay, ridiculous disorder. But
with good planning it could be done.

Purser and gunner, boatswain and cooper, each in turn
was summoned to the after cabin. To each was allotted his
tasks; to each was grudgingly conceded a proportion of the
men that each demanded. Soon the pipes were shrilling
through the ship.

'Launch's crew away!'

Soon the launch was pulling across the river, full of the
empty barrels the cooper and his mates had made ready, to
begin ferrying over the twenty tons of water necessary to
complete the ship's requirements. A dozen men went scurrying up the shrouds and out along the yards under the urging
of the boatswain; yardarm tackles and stay tackles had to be
readied for the day's work.

'Mr Jones! I am leaving the ship now. Have that report on
the beef ready for me by the time I return from the dockyard.'

Hornblower became aware of two figures on the quarter-
deck trying to attract his attention. They were the prince and
the doctor. He ran his eye over their uniforms, the white
collar patches of the midshipman and the plain coat of the
surgeon.

'They'll do,' he said, 'your duties are awaiting you, doctor. Mr Horrocks! Keep Mr Prince under your lee for to-day. Call away my gig.'

The captain superintendent of the dockyard listened to Hornblower's request with the indifference acquired during years of listening to requests from urgent officers.

'I've the men ready to send for the shot, sir. Port side's clear for the powder hulk to come alongside—slack water in half an hour, sir. I can send men to man her too if necessary. It's only four tons that I need. Half an hour with the hulk.'

'You say you're ready now?'

'Yes, sir.'

The captain superintendent looked across at the *Atropos* lying in the stream.

'Very well. I hope what you say is quite correct, captain, for your sake. You can start warping the hulk alongside—I warn you I want her back at her moorings in an hour.'

'Thank you, sir.'

Back in the *Atropos* the cry went round the ship.

'Hands to the capstan! Waisters! Sailmakers! Loblolly boys!'

The inmost recesses of the ship were cleared of men to man the capstan bars—any pairs of arms, any stout backs, would serve for that purpose. A drum went roaring along the deck.

'All lights out!'

The cook and his mates dumped the gallery fire overside and went reluctantly to man the yardarm and stay tackles. The powder hulk came creeping alongside. She had stout sheers and wide hatchways, efficient equipment for the rapid transfer of explosives. Four tons of powder, eighty kegs of one hundredweight each, came climbing out of the hulk's holds to be swayed down the hatchways of the *Atropos*, while down below the gunner and his mates and a sweating working party toiled in near darkness—barefooted to avoid all chance of friction or sparks—to range the kegs about the magazines. Some day *Atropos* might be fighting for her life, and her life would depend on the proper arrangement of those kegs down below so that the demands of the guns on deck might be met.

The members of the court of inquiry, fresh from their investigation of the defective beef barrels, made their appearance on deck again.

'Mr Jones, show the doctor how to make his report in due form.' Then to the purser, 'Mr Carslake, I want to be able to sign your indents as soon as that report is ready.'

One final look round the deck, and Hornblower could dive below, take pen and ink and paper, and devote himself single-mindedly to composing a suitable covering letter to the Victualling Yard (worded with the right urgency and tactfully coaxing the authorities there into agreement without annoying them by too certain assumption of acquiescence) beginning: 'Sir, I have the honour to enclose——' and concluding: '——in the best interests of His Majesty's service, Your Obedient Servant——'

Then he could come on deck again to see how the work was progressing and fume for a space before Jones and Carslake appeared with the documents they had been preparing. Amid the confusion and din he had to clear his head again to read them with care before signing them with a bold 'H. Hornblower, Captain.'

'Mr Carslake, you can take my gig over to the Victualling Yard. Mr Jones, I expect the Yard will need hands to man their lighter. See to that, if you please.'

A moment to spare now to observe the hands at work, to settle his cocked hat square on his head, to clasp his hands behind him, to walk slowly forward, doing his best to look quite cool and imperturbable, as if all this wild activity were the most natural thing in the world.

'Avast heaving there on that stay-tackle. Belay!'

The powder keg hung suspended just over the deck. Hornblower forced himself to speak coldly, without excitement. A stave of the keg had started a trifle. There was a minute trail of powder grains on the deck; more were dribbling very slowly out.

'Sway that keg back into the hulk. You, bos'n's mate, get a wet mop and swill that powder off the deck.'

An accident could have fired that powder easily. The flash would pass in either direction; four tons of powder in *Atropos*, forty, perhaps in the hulk—what would have happened to the massed shipping in the Pool in that event? The men were eyeing him; this would be a suitable moment to encourage them with their work.

'Greenwich Hospital is over there, men,' said Hornblower, pointing down river to the graceful outlines of Wren's building. 'Some of us will wind up there in the end, I expect, but we don't want to be blown straight there to-day.'

A feeble enough joke, perhaps, but it raised a grin or two all the same.

'Carry on.'

Hornblower continued his stroll forward, the imperturbable captain who was nevertheless human enough to crack a joke. It was the same sort of acting that he used towards Maria when she seemed likely to be in a difficult mood.

Here was the lighter with the shot, coming along the starboard side. Hornblower looked down into it. Nine-pounder balls for the four long guns, two forward and two aft; twelve-pounder balls for the eighteen carronades that constituted the ship's main armament. The twenty tons of iron made a pathetically small mass lying in the bottom of the lighter, when regarded with the eye of a man who had served in a ship of the line; the old *Renown* would have discharged that weight of shot in a couple of hours' fighting. But this dead weight was a very considerable proportion of the load *Atropos* had to carry. Half of it would be distributed fairly evenly along the ship in the shot-garlands; where he decided to stow the other ten tons would make all the difference to *Atropos*, could add a knot to her speed or reduce it by a knot, could make her stiff in a breeze or crank, handy or awkward under sail. He could not reach a decision

about that until the rest of the stores were on board and
he had had an opportunity of observing her trim. Hornblower ran a keen eye over the nets in which the shot were
to be swayed up at the starboard fore-yardarm, and went
back through his mind in search of the data stored away
there regarding the breaking strain of Manila line—this,
he could tell, had been several years in service.

'Sixteen rounds to the load,' he called down into the
lighter, 'no more.'

'Aye aye, sir.'

It was typical of Hornblower's mind that it should spend
a moment or two thinking about the effect that would be
produced if one of those nets was to give way; the shot would
pour down into the lighter again; falling from the height of
the yardarm they could go clear through the bottom of the
lighter; with all that deadweight on board, the lighter would
sink like a stone, there on the edge of the fairway, to be an
intolerable nuisance to London's shipping until divers had
painfully cleared the sunken wreck of the shot, and camels
had lifted the wreck clear of the channel. The vast shipping
of the Port of London could be seriously impeded as a
result of a momentary inattention regarding the condition
of a cargo net.

Jones was hastening across the deck to touch his hat to
him.

'The last of the powder's just coming aboard, sir.'

'Thank you, Mr Jones. Have the hulk warped back to her
moorings. Mr Owen can send the powder boys here to put
the shot in the garlands as they come on board. '

'Aye aye, sir.'

And the gig was coming back across the river with
Carslake sitting in the stern.

'Well, Mr Carslake, how did the Victualling Yard receive
those indents?'

'They've accepted them, sir. They'll have the stores on the
quayside to-morrow morning.'

'To-morrow? Didn't you listen to my orders, Mr Carslake?

I don't want to have to put a black mark against your name. Mr Jones! I'm going over to the Victualling Yard. Come back with me, Mr Carslake.'

The Victualling Yard was a department of the Navy Office, not of the Admiralty. The officials there had to be approached differently from those of the dockyard. One might almost think the two organizations were rivals, instead of working to a common patriotic end against a deadly enemy.

'I can bring my own men to do the work,' said Hornblower. 'You needn't use your own gangs at all.'

'M'm,' said the victualling superintendent.

'I'll move everything to the quayside myself, besides lightering it over.'

'M'm,' said the victualling superintendent again, a trifle more receptively.

'I would be most deeply obliged to you,' went on Hornblower. 'You need only instruct one of your clerks to point out the stores to the officer in command of my working party. Everything else will be attended to. I beg of you, sir.'

It was highly gratifying to a Navy Office official to have a captain, metaphorically, on his knees to him, in this fashion. Equally gratifying was the thought that the Navy would do all the work, with a great saving of time-tallies to the Victualling Yard. Hornblower could see the satisfaction in the fellow's fat face. He wanted to wipe it off with his fist, but he kept himself humble. It did him no harm, and by this means he was bending the fellow to his will as surely as if he was using threats.

'There's the matter of those stores you have condemned,' said the superintendent.

'My court of inquiry was in due form,' said Hornblower.

'Yes,' said the superintendent thoughtfully.

'Of course I can return you the hogsheads,' suggested Hornblower. 'I was intending to do so, as soon as I had emptied the beef over into the tide.'

'No, please do not go to that trouble. Return me the full hogsheads.'

The working of the minds of these government Jacks-in-office was beyond normal understanding. Hornblower could not believe—although it was just possible—that the superintendent had any personal financial interest in the matter of those condemned stores. But the fact that the condemnation had taken place presumably was a blot on his record, or on the record of the yard. If the hogsheads were returned to them no mention of the condemnation need be made officially, and presumably they could be palmed off again on some other ship—some ship that might go to sea without the opportunity of sampling the stuff first. Sailors fighting for their country might starve as long as the Victualling Yard's records were unsmirched.

'I'll return the full hogsheads gladly, sir,' said Hornblower. 'I'll send them over to you in the lighter that brings the other stores over.'

'That might do very well,' said the superintendent.

'I am delighted, and, as I said, intensely obliged to you, sir. I'll have my launch over here with a working party in ten minutes.'

Hornblower bowed with all the unction he could command; this was not the moment to spoil the ship for a ha'porth of tar. He bowed himself out before the discussion could be reopened. But the superintendent's last words were:

'Remember to return those hogsheads, captain.'

The powder hulk had been warped back to her moorings; the other ordnance stores that were being taken on board seemed trifling in appearance, bundles of wads, and bales of empty serge cartridges, a couple of sheaves of flexible rammers, spare gun trucks, reels of slow-match—the multifarious accessories necessary to keep twenty-two guns in action. Hornblower sent off Midshipman Smiley with the working party promised to the Victualling Yard.

'Now I'll have those condemned hogsheads got up on deck, Mr Carslake. I must keep my promise to return them.'

'Aye aye, sir,' said Carslake.

Carslake was a bull-headed, youngish man with expression-less pale-blue eyes. Those eyes were even more expressionless than usual. He had been a witness of the interview be-tween Hornblower and the superintendent, and he did not allow his feelings to show. He could not guess whether as a purser he thoroughly approved of saving the stores to be fobbed off on another ship or whether as a sailor certain to endure privations at sea he despised Hornblower's weakness in agreeing to the superintendent's demands.

'I'll mark 'em before I return 'em,' said Hornblower.

He had thought of paint when he had been so accommo-dating towards the superintendent, but was not quite happy in his mind about it, for turpentine would remove paint fast enough. A better idea occurred to him, marvellously, at that very moment.

'Have the cook relight the fire in the galley,' he ordered. 'I'll have—I'll have a couple of iron musket ramrods heated in the fire. Get them from the armourer, if you please.'

'Aye aye, sir. If you please, sir, it's long past the hand's dinner-time.'

'When I've time for my own dinner the hands can have theirs,' said Hornblower.

He was glad that the deck was crowded so that those words of his could be overheard, for he had had the question of the men's dinner-time in his mind for some time although he was quite resolved not to waste a moment over it.

The first of the condemned hogsheads came creaking and swaying up from the hold and was lowered to the deck. Hornblower looked round him; there was Horrocks with the young prince, quite bewildered with all the continuous bustle, trailing after him.

'You'll do, Mr Horrocks. Come here,' said Hornblower. He took the chalk from beside the slate at the binnacle; and wrote with it, in large letters diagonally round the hogshead, the word 'CONDEMNED.' 'There are two irons heating in the galley fire. You and Mr Prince can spend your time

branding these hogsheads. Trace out those letters on every
one. Understand?'

'Er—yes, sir.'

'Good and deep, so there is no chance of planing it off.
Look sharp about it.'

'Aye aye, sir.'

The next lighter for the Dockyard was alongside now, at
the port side recently vacated by the powder hulk. It was full
of boatswain's stores, cordage, canvas, paint; and a weary
party of men were at work swaying the bundles up. There
seemed no end to this business of getting *Atropos* fully
equipped for sea. Hornblower himself felt as leg-weary as a
foundered horse, and he stiffened himself up to conceal his
fatigue. But as he looked across the river he could see the
Victualling Yard's lighter already emerging from the Creek.
Smiley had his men at work on the sweeps, straining to row
the ponderous thing across the ebbing tide. From the quarter-
deck he could see the lighter was crammed with the hogsheads and kegs and biscuit bags. Soon *Atropos* would be
full-gorged. And the acrid smell of the red-hot irons burning
into the brine-soaked staves of the condemned hogsheads
came to his nostrils. No ship would ever accept those stores.
It was a queer duty for a Serene Highness to be employed
upon. How had those orders read? 'You will employ your
diligence in instructing His Serene Highness in his new
profession.' Well, perhaps it was not a bad introduction to
the methods of fighting men and civilian employees.

Later—ever so much later, it seemed—Mr Jones came up
and touched his hat.

'The last of the stores are on board, sir,' he said. 'Mr
Smiley's just returning the Victualling Yard's lighter.'

'Thank you, Mr Jones. Call away my gig, please.'

Hornblower stepped down into the boat conscious of
many weary eyes on him. The winter afternoon was dissolving
in a cold and gloomy drizzle as a small rain was beginning
to fall. Hornblower had himself rowed round his ship at a
convenient distance to observe her trim. He looked at her

from ahead, from broadside on, from astern. In his mind's eye he was visualizing her underwater lines. He looked up at the spread of her lower yards; the wind would be pressing against the canvas there, and he worked out the balance of the forces involved, wind against lateral resistance, rudder versus headsails. He had to consider seaworthiness and handiness as well as speed. He climbed back on deck to where Jones was awaiting him.

'I want her more down by the head,' he announced. 'I'll have those beef casks at the for'rard end of the tier, and the shot for'rard of the magazine. Get the hands to work, if you please.'

Once more the pipes shrilled through the ship as the hands began to move the stores ranged upon the deck. It was with anxiety that Hornblower's return was awaited from his next pull round the ship.

'She'll do for the present,' said Hornblower.

It was not a casual decision, no stage-effect. The moment *Atropos* should clear the land she would be in danger, she might find herself in instant action. She was only a little ship; even a well found privateer might give her a hard battle. To overtake in pursuit; to escape in flight; to handle quickly when manœuvring for position in action; to claw off to windward should she be caught on a lee shore; she must be capable of all this, and she must be capable of it to-day, for to-morrow, even to-morrow, might be too late. The lives of his crew, his own life, his professional reputation, could hang on that decision.

'You can strike everything below now, Mr Jones.'

Slowly the littered decks began to clear, while the rain grew heavier and the night began to close in round the little ship. The tiers of great casks, down against the skin of the ship, were squeezed and wedged into position; the contents of the hold had to be jammed into a solid mass, for once at sea *Atropos* would roll and pitch, and nothing must budge, nothing must shift, lest the fabric of the ship be damaged or even perhaps the ship might be rolled completely over by the movement of an avalanche of her cargo. The Navy still thought of Sir Edward Berry as the officer who, when captain of Nelson's own *Vanguard*, allowed the masts of his ship to be rolled clear out of her in a moderate gale of wind off Sardinia.

Hornblower stood aft by the taffrail while the rain streamed down on him. He had not gone below; this might be part of the penance he was inflicting on himself for not having sufficiently supervised the management of his ship.

'The decks are cleared, sir,' said Jones, looming up in the wet darkness before him.

'Very well, Mr Jones. When everything is swabbed down the men can have their dinners.'

The little cabin down below was cold and dark and cheerless. Two canvas chairs and a trestle-table stood in the day cabin; in the night cabin there was nothing at all. The oil lamp shone gloomily over the bare planks of the deck under his feet. Hornblower could call for his gig again; it would whisk him fast enough half a mile downstream to Deptford Hard, and there at the 'George' were his wife and his children. There would be a roaring fire of sea coal, a spluttering beef steak with cabbage, a feather bed with the sheets made almost too hot to bear by the application of a warming pan. His chilled body and aching legs yearned inexpressibly for that care and warmth. But in his present mood he would have none of them. Instead he dined, shivering, off ship's fare hastily laid out for him on the trestle-table. He had a hammock slung for himself in the night cabin, and he climbed into it and wrapped himself in clammy blankets. He had not lain in a hammock since he was a midshipman, and his spine had grown unused to the necessary curvature. He was too numb, both mentally and physically, to feel any glow of conscious virtue.

VIII

Fog in the Downs, cold, dense, and impenetrable over the surface of the sea. There was no breath of air to set it stirring; overside the surface of the sea, just visible when Hornblower looked down at it from the deck, was black and glassy. Only close against the side could be detected the faintest of ripples, showing how the tide was coursing beside the ship as she lay anchored in the Downs. Condensing on the rigging overhead the fog dripped in melancholy fashion on to the deck about him, an occasional drop landing with a dull impact on his cocked hat; the heavy frieze pea-jacket that he wore looked as if it were frosted with the moisture that hung upon it. Yet it was not freezing weather, although Hornblower felt chilled through and through inside his layers of clothing as he turned back from his gloomy contemplation of the sea.

'Now, Mr Jones,' he said, 'we'll start again. We'll have topmasts and yards struck—all top hamper down and stowed away. Order "out pipes," if you please.'

'Aye aye, sir,' said Jones.

The hands had already spent half the morning at sail drill; Hornblower was taking advantage of the fogbound calm to exercise his ship's company. With so many landsmen on board, with officers unfamiliar with their divisions, this fog actually could be used to advantage; the ship could be made more of a working, fighting unit during this interval of grace before proceeding down Channel. Hornblower put his cold hand inside his coat and brought out his watch; as if the gesture had called forth the sound five bells rang out sharply from beside the binnacle, and from the thick fog surrounding them came the sound of other bells—there were many ships anchored in the Downs all about them, so many

that it was some minutes before the last sound died away;
the sand-glasses on board the ships were by no means in
agreement.

While the bells were still sounding Hornblower took note
of the position of the minute hand of his watch and nodded
to Jones. Instantly came a roar of orders; the men, already
called to attention after their brief stand-easy came pouring
aft with their petty officers urging them on. Watch in hand,
Hornblower stood back by the taffrail. From where he stood
only the lower part of the main rigging was visible; the foremast was completely hidden in fog. The hands went hurrying
up the ratlines, Hornblower watching keenly to see what
proportion of them were vague about their stations and
duties. He could have wished that he could see all that was
going on—but then if there had been no fog there would have
been no sail drill, and *Atropos* would have been making the
best of her way down Channel. Here was the Prince, hurried
along by Horrocks with a hand at his shoulder.

'Come on,' said Horrocks, leaping at the ratlines.

The Prince sprang up beside him. Hornblower could see
the bewildered expression on the boy's face. He had small
enough idea of what he was doing. He would learn, no
doubt—he was learning much even from the fact that the
blood-royal, the King's nephew, could be shoved about by
the plebeian hand of a midshipman.

Hornblower got out of the way as the mizzen topsail came
swaying down. A yelping master's mate came running up
with a small pack of waisters at his heels; they fell upon the
ponderous roll and dragged it to the side. The mizzen mast
hands were working faster than the mainmast, apparently
—the main topsail was not lowered yet. Jones, his head
drawn back so that his Adam's apple protruded apparently
by inches, was bellowing the next orders to the masthead.
A shout from above answered him. Down the ratlines came
a flood of men again.

'Let go! Haul! Lower away!'

The mizzen topsail yard turned in a solemn arc and made

its slow descent down the mast. There was an exasperating delay while the mainstay tackle was applied—organization at this point was exceedingly poor—but at last the yard was down and lying along the booms beside its fellows. The complicated and difficult business of striking the topmasts followed.

'An hour and a quarter, Mr Jones. More nearly an hour and twenty minutes. Far too long. Half an hour—half an hour with five minutes' grace; that's the longest you should ever take.'

'Yes, sir,' said Jones. There was nothing else he could say.

As Hornblower was eyeing him before giving his next orders a faint dull thud came to his ears, sounding flatly through the fog. A musket shot? A pistol shot? That was certainly what it sounded like, but with the fog changing the quality of all the sounds he could not be sure. Even if it were a shot, fired in one of the numerous invisible ships round about, there might be endless innocent explanations of it; and it might not be a shot. A hatch cover dropped on a deck —a grating being pushed into place—it could be anything.

The hands were grouped about the deck, looming vaguely in the fog, awaiting further orders. Hornblower guessed that they were sweating despite the cold. This was the way to get that London beer out of them, but he did not want to drive them too hard.

'Five minutes stand-easy,' said Hornblower. 'And, Mr Jones, you had better station a good petty officer at that mainstay tackle.'

'Aye aye, sir.'

Hornblower turned away to give Jones an opportunity to arrange his reorganization. He set himself to walk the deck to bring some life back into his cold body; his watch was still in his hand through sheer forgetfulness to replace it in his pocket. He ended his walk at the ship's side, glancing over into the black water. Now what was that floating down beside the ship? Something long and black; when Hornblower first caught sight of it it had bumped one end against the ship's side under the main chains, and as he watched it swung solemnly round, drawn by the tide, and came down towards him. It was an oar. Curiosity overcame him. In a crowded anchorage like this there was nothing very surprising about a floating oar, but still——

'Here, quartermaster,' said Hornblower. 'Get down into the mizzen chains with a line to catch that oar.'

It was only an oar; Hornblower looked it over as the quartermaster held it for his inspection. The leather button was fairly well worn—it was by no means a new oar. On the other hand, judging by the fact that the leather was not entirely soaked through, it had not long been in the water, minutes rather than days, obviously. There was the number '27' burned into the loom, and it was that which caused Hornblower to look more sharply. The '7' bore a crossbar. No Englishman ever wrote a '7' with a crossbar. But everyone on the Continent did; there were Danes and Swedes and Norwegians, Russians and Prussians, at sea, either neutrals in the war or allies of England. Yet a Frenchman or a Dutchman, one of England's enemies, would also write a '7' in that way.

And there had certainly been something that sounded like a shot. A floating oar and a musket shot made a combination that would be hard to explain. Now if they had been connected in causation——! Hornblower still had his watch in his hand. That shot—if it was a shot—had made itself heard just before he gave the order for stand-easy, seven or eight minutes ago. The tide was running at a good two knots. If the shot had caused the oar to be dropped into the water it must have been fired a quarter of a mile or so—two cables' length—upstream. The quartermaster still holding the oar was looking at him curiously, and Jones was waiting, with the men poised for action, for his next orders. Hornblower was tempted to pay no more attention to the incident.

But he was a King's officer, and it was his duty to make inquiry into the unexplainable at sea. He hesitated in inward debate; the fog was horribly thick. If he sent a boat to investigate it would probably lose itself; Hornblower had had much experience of making his way by boat in a fog-ridden anchorage. Then he could go himself. Hornblower felt a qualm at the thought of blundering about trying to find his way in the fog—he could make a fool of himself so easily in the eyes of his crew. Yet on the other hand that was not likely to be as exasperating as fuming on board waiting for a dilatory boat to return.

'Mr Jones,' he said, 'call away my gig.'

'Aye aye, sir,' said Jones, the astonishment in his voice hardly concealed at all.

Hornblower walked to the binnacle and took a careful reading of how the ship's head lay. It was the most careful reading he could possibly take, not because his comfort or his safety but because his personal dignity depended on getting that reading right. North by East half East. As the ship lay riding to her anchor bows to the tide he could be sure that the oar had come down from that direction.

'I want a good boat compass in the gig, Mr Jones, if you please.'

'Aye aye, sir.'

Hornblower hesitated before the last final order, which would commit him to a public admission that he thought there was a chance of something serious awaiting him in the fog. But not to give the order would be to strain at a gnat and swallow a camel. If that had really been a musket shot that he had heard there was a possibility of action; there was a likelihood that at least a show of force would be necessary.

'Pistols and cutlasses for the gig's crew, Mr Jones, if you please.'

'Aye aye, sir,' said Jones, as if nothing could astonish him again.

Hornblower turned back as he was about to step down into the boat.

'I shall start timing you from this moment, Mr Jones. Try to get those tops'l yards across in half an hour from now— I'll be back before then.'

'Aye aye, sir.'

The ship broke into a roar of activity as Hornblower took his place in the stern-sheets of the gig.

'I'll take the tiller,' he said to the coxswain. 'Give way.'

He steered the gig along the *Atropos* from stern to bow. He took one last look up at her bows, at her bowsprit and bobstay, and then the fog swallowed them up. The gig was instantly in a world of its own, constricted about by the walls of mist. The sounds of activity on board the ship died rapidly away.

'Pull steady!' growled Hornblower to the man at the oars. That little boat compass would be swinging about chasing its tail in ten seconds if he allowed the gig to keep anything except an exactly straight course. North by East half East.

'Seventeen,' said Hornblower to himself. 'Eighteen. Nineteen.'

He was counting the strokes of the oars; it was a rough way of estimating the progress made. At seven feet to the stroke less than two hundred strokes meant a quarter of a mile. But there was the speed of the tide to be allowed for. It would be nearer five hundred strokes—all very vague, but every possible precaution must be taken on a foolish expedition like this.

'Seventy-four, seventy-five,' said Hornblower, his eyes glued to the compass.

Even with the brisk tide running the surface of the sea was a glassy flat calm; the oar-blades, lifting from the water at the completion of each stroke, left whirlpools circling on the surface.

'Two hundred,' said Hornblower, suppressing a momentary fear that he had miscounted and that it was really three hundred.

The oars groaned on monotonously in the rowlocks.

'Keep your eyes ahead,' said Hornblower to the coxswain. 'Tell me the moment you see anything. Two sixty-four.'

It seemed only yesterday that he had sat in the stern-sheets of the jolly boat of the *Indefatigable*, rowing up the estuary of the Gironde to cut out the *Papillon*. But that was more than ten years ago. Three hundred. Three hundred and fifty.

'Sir,' said the coxswain, tersely.

Hornblower looked forward. Ahead, a trifle on the port bow, there was the slightest thickening in the fog, the slightest looming of something solid there.

'Easy all!' said Hornblower, and the boat continued to glide over the surface; he put the tiller over slightly so as to approach whatever it was more directly. But the boat's way died away before they were near enough to distinguish any details, and at Hornblower's command the men began to row again. Distantly came a low hail out of the fog, apparently called forth by the renewal of the sound of the oars.

'Boat ahoy!'

At least the hail was in English. By now there was visible the vague outlines of a large brig; from the heaviness of her spars and fast lines she looked like one of the West India packets.

'What brig's that?' hailed Hornblower in reply.

'*Amelia Jane* of London, thirty-seven days out from Barbados.'

That was a direct confirmation of Hornblower's first impression. But that voice? It did not sound quite English, somehow. There were foreign captains in the British merchant service, plenty of them, but hardly likely to be in command of a West India packet.

'Easy,' said Hornblower to the rowers, the gig glided silently on over the water. He could see no sign of anything wrong.

'Keep your distance,' said the voice from the brig.

There was nothing suspicious about the words. Any ship at anchor hardly more than twenty miles from the coast of France was fully entitled to be wary of strangers approaching in a fog. But that word sounded more like 'deestance' all the same. Hornblower put his helm over to pass under the brig's stern. Several heads were now apparent at the brig's

side; they moved round the stern in time with the gig. There
was the brig's name, sure enough. *Amelia Jane*, London.
Then Hornblower caught sight of something else; it was a
large boat lying under the brig's port quarter from the main
chains. There might be a hundred possible explanations of
that, but it was a suspicious circumstance.

'Brig ahoy!' he hailed, 'I'm coming aboard.'

'Keep off!' said the voice in reply.

Some of the heads at the brig's side developed shoulders,
and three or four muskets were pointed at the gig.

'I am a King's officer,' said Hornblower.

He stood up in the stern-sheets and unbuttoned his pea-
jacket so that his uniform was visible. The central figure at
the brig's side, the man who had been speaking, looked for a
long moment and then spread his hands in a gesture of
despair.

'Yes,' he said.

Hornblower went up the brig's side as briskly as his chilled
limbs would permit. As he stood on the deck he felt a trifle
self-conscious of being unarmed, for facing him were more
than a dozen men, hostility in their bearing, and some of
them with muskets in their hands. But the gig's crew had
followed him on to the deck and closed up behind him,
handling their cutlasses and pistols.

'Cap'n, sir!' It was the voice from overside of one of the
two men left down in the gig. 'Please, sir, there's a dead man
in the boat here.'

Hornblower turned away to look over. A dead man
certainly lay there, doubled up in the bottom of the boat.
That accounted for the floating oar, then. And for the shot,
of course. The man had been killed by a bullet from the
brig at the moment the boat was laid alongside; the brig had
been taken by boarding. Hornblower looked back towards
the group on the deck.

'Frenchmen?' he asked.

'Yes, sir.'

The fellow was a man of sense. He had not attempted a

hopeless resistance when his coup had been discovered. Although he had fifteen men at his back and there were only eight altogether in the gig he had realized that the presence of a King's ship in the immediate vicinity made his final capture a certainty.

'Where's the crew?' asked Hornblower.

The Frenchman pointed forward, and at a gesture from Hornblower one of his men ran to release the brig's crew from their confinement in the forecastle, half a dozen coloured hands and a couple of officers.

'Much obliged to you, mister,' said the captain, coming forward.

'I'm Captain Hornblower of His Majesty's ship *Atropos*,' said Hornblower.

'I beg your pardon, Captain.' He was an elderly man, his white hair and blue eyes in marked contrast with his mahogany tan. 'You've saved my ship.'

'Yes,' said Hornblower, 'you had better disarm those men.'

'Gladly, sir. See to it, Jack.'

The other officer, presumably the mate, walked aft to take muskets and swords from the unresisting Frenchmen.

'They came out of the fog and laid me alongside before I was aware, almost, sir,' went on the captain. 'A King's ship took my four best hands when we was off the Start, or I'd have made a better account of them. I only got one crack at them as it was.'

'It was that crack that brought me here,' said Hornblower shortly. 'Where did they come from?'

'Now that's just what I was asking myself,' said the captain. 'Not from France in that boat, they couldn't have come.'

They turned their gaze inquiringly upon the dejected group of Frenchmen. It was a question of considerable importance. The Frenchmen must have come from a ship, and that ship must be anchored somewhere amid the crowded vessels in the Downs. And at that rate she must be disguised as a British vessel or a neutral, coming in with the others before the wind dropped and the fog closed down. There had been plenty of similar incidents during the war. It was an easy way to snap up a prize. But it meant that somewhere close at hand there was a wolf in sheep's clothing, a disguised French privateer, probably crammed with men— she might have made more than one prize. In the bustle and confusion that would ensue when a breeze should get up, with everyone anxious to up anchor and away, she could count on being able to make her escape along with her prizes.

'When the fog closed down,' said the captain, 'the nearest vessel to us was a Ramsgate trawler. She anchored at the same time as we did. I doubt if it could be her.'

It was a matter of so much importance that Hornblower could not keep still. He turned and paced the deck for a space, his mind working rapidly. Yet his mind was not completely made up when he turned back and gave his first order in execution of the vague plan. He did not know if he would have the resolution to go through with it.

'Leadbitter,' he said to the coxswain.

'Sir!'

'Tie those men's hands behind them.'

'Sir?'

'You heard what I said.'

To bind prisoners was almost a violation of the laws of war. When Leadbitter approached to carry out his orders the Frenchmen showed evident resentment. A buzz of voices arose.

'You can't do this, sir,' said their spokesman. 'We have——'

'Shut your mouth,' snapped Hornblower.

Even having to give that order put him in a bad temper, and his bad temper was made worse by his doubts about himself. Now that the Frenchmen were disarmed they could offer no resistance in face of the drawn pistols of the British sailors. With loud protests they had to submit, as Leadbitter

went from man to man tying their wrists behind their backs.
Hornblower was hating himself for the part he had to play,
even while his calculating mind told him that he had a fair
chance of success. He had to pose as a bloodthirsty man,
delighting in the taking of human life, without mercy in his
soul, gratified by the sight of the death struggles of a fellow-
human. Such men did exist, he knew. There were gloomy
tyrants in the King's service. In the past ten years of war at
sea there had been some outrages, a few, on both sides.
These Frenchmen did not know him for what he really was,
nor did the West India crew. Nor for that matter his own
men. Their acquaintance had been so short that they had no
reason to believe him not to have homicidal tendencies, so
that their behaviour would not weaken the impression he
wished to convey. He turned to one of his men.

'Run aloft,' he said. 'Reeve a whip through the block at
the main yardarm.'

That portended a hanging. The man looked at him with a
momentary unbelief, but the scowl on Hornblower's face
sent him scurrying up the ratlines. Then Hornblower strode
to where the wretched Frenchmen were standing bound;
their glance shifted from the man at the yardarm to Hornblower's grim face, and their anxious chattering died away.

'You are pirates,' said Hornblower, speaking slowly and
distinctly. 'I am going to hang you.'

In case the English-speaking Frenchman's vocabularly did
not include the word 'hang' he pointed significantly to the
man at the yardarm. They could all understand that. They
remained silent for a second or two, and then several of them
began to speak at once in torrential French which Hornblower could not well follow, and then the leader, having
pulled himself together, began his protest in English.

'We are not pirates,' he said.

'I think you are,' said Hornblower.

'We are privateersmen,' said the Frenchman.

'Pirates,' said Hornblower.

The talk among the Frenchmen rose to a fresh height;

Hornblower's French was good enough for him to make out
that the leader was translating his curt words to his com-
panions, and they were urging him to explain more fully
their position.

'I assure you, sir,' said the wretched man, striving to be
eloquent in a strange language, 'we are privateersmen and
not pirates.'

Hornblower regarded him with a stony countenance, and
without answering turned away to give further orders.

'Leadbitter,' he said, 'I'll have a hangman's noose on the
end of that line.'

Then he turned back to the Frenchmen.

'Who do you say you are then?' he asked. He tried to
utter the words as indifferently as he could.

'We are from the privateer *Vengeance* of Dunkirk, sir. I
am Jacques Lebon, prizemaster.'

Privateers usually went to sea with several extra officers,
who could be put into prizes to navigate them back to a
French port without impairing the fighting efficiency of the
privateer, which could continue her cruise. These officers
were usually selected for their ability to speak English and
for their knowledge of English seagoing ways, and they bore
the title of 'prizemaster.' Hornblower turned back to observe
the noose now dangling significantly from the yardarm, and
then addressed the prizemaster.

'You have no papers,' he said.

He forced his lips into a sneer as he spoke; to the wretched
men studying every line in his face his expression appeared
quite unnatural, as indeed it was. And Hornblower was
gambling a little when he said what he did. If the prizemaster had been able to produce any papers the whole line
of attack would have to be altered; but it was not much of a
gamble. Hornblower was certain when he spoke that if
Lebon had had papers in his pocket he would have already
mentioned them, asking someone to dive into his pocket for
them. That would be the first reaction of any Frenchman
whose identity had been put in question.

'No,' said Lebon, crestfallen. It was hardly likely that he would have, when engaged on an ordinary operation of war.

'Then you hang,' said Hornblower. 'All of you. One by one.'

The laugh he forced himself to produce sounded positively inhuman, horrible. Anyone hearing it would be justified in thinking that he was inspired by the anticipated pleasure of watching the death struggles of a dozen men. The white-haired captain of the *Amelia Jane* could not bear the prospect, and came forward to enter into the discussion.

'Sir,' he said. 'What are you going to do?'

'I am going to attend to my own business, sir,' said Hornblower, striving to throw into his voice all the harshness he had ever heard employed by all the insolent officers he had met during his service. 'May I ask you to be kind enough to do the same?'

'But you can't be meaning to hang the poor devils,' went on the captain.

'But that is what I do mean.'

'But not in my ship, sir—not now—not without trial.'

'In your ship, sir, which you allowed to be captured. And now. Pirates taken red-handed can be hanged instantly, as you know, sir. And that is what I shall do.'

It was a stroke of good fortune that the captain should have entered into the discussion. His appearance of sick dismay and the tone of his protests were convincingly genuine—they would never have been so if he had been admitted previously to a planned scheme. Hornblower's attitude towards him was brutal, but it was for the good of the cause.

'Sir,' persisted the captain, 'I'm sure they're only privateersmen——'

'Please refrain from interfering with a King's officer in the execution of his duty. You two men, there, come here.'

The two of the crew of the gig that he indicated approached obediently. Probably they had seen hangings before, along with every kind of brutality in a brutal service. But the imminent certainty of taking personal part in a hanging obviously impressed them. There was some reluctance visible in their expressions, but the hard discipline of the service would make certain they would obey the orders of this one man, unarmed and outnumbered.

Hornblower looked along the line of faces. Momentarily he felt a horrid sickness in his stomach as it occurred to him to wonder how he would be feeling if he really was selecting a victim.

'I'll have that one first,' he said, pointing.

The bull-throated swarthy man whom he indicated paled and shuddered; backing away he tried to shelter himself among his fellows. They were all speaking at once, jerking their arms frantically against the bonds that secured their wrists behind them.

'Sir!' said Lebon. 'Please—I beg of you—I implore——'

Hornblower condescended to spare him a glance, and Lebon went on in a wild struggle against the difficulties of language and the handicap of not being free to gesticulate.

'We are privateersmen. We fight for the Empire, for France.' Now he was on his knees, his face lifted. As he could not use his hands he was actually nuzzling with his mouth against the skirts of Hornblower's pea-jacket. 'We surrendered. We did not fight. We caused no death.'

'Take this man away from me,' said Hornblower, withdrawing out of reach.

But Lebon on his knees followed him over the deck, nuzzling and pleading.

'Captain,' said the English captain, interceding once again. 'Can't you at least wait and land 'em for trial? If they're pirates it'll be proved quick enough.'

'I want to see 'em dangling,' said Hornblower, searching feverishly in his mind for the most impressive thing he could say.

The two English seamen, taking advantage of the volume of protest, had paused in the execution of their orders.

Hornblower looked up at the noose, dangling dimly but horribly in the fog.

'I don't believe for one single moment,' went on Hornblower, 'that these men are what they say they are. Just a band of thieves, pirates. Leadbitter, put four men on that line. I'll give the word when they are to walk away with it.'

'Sir,' said Lebon, 'I assure you, word of honour, we are from the privateer *Vengeance*.'

'Bah!' replied Hornblower. 'Where is she?'

'Over there,' said Lebon. He could not point with his hands; he pointed with his chin, over the port bow of the anchored *Amelia Jane*. It was not a very definite indication, but it was a considerable help, even that much.

'Did you see any vessel over there before the fog closed down, captain?' demanded Hornblower, turning to the English captain.

'Only the Ramsgate trawler,' he said, reluctantly.

'That is our ship!' said Lebon. 'That is the *Vengeance!* She was a Dunkirk trawler—we—we made her look like that.'

So that was it. A Dunkirk trawler. Her fish-holds could be crammed full of men. A slight alteration of gear, an 'R' painted on her mainsail, a suitable name painted on her stern and then she could wander about the narrow seas without question, snapping up prizes almost at will.

'Where did you say she lay?' demanded Hornblower.

'There—oh!'

Lebon checked himself as he realized how much information he was giving away.

'I can hazard a good guess as to how she bears from us,' interposed the English captain, 'I saw—oh!'

He broke off exactly as Lebon had done, but from surprise. He was staring at Hornblower. It was like the denouement scene in some silly farce. The lost heir was at last revealed. The idea of now accepting the admiration of his unwitting fellow players, of modestly admitting that he was not the

monster of ferocity he had pretended to be, irritated Hornblower beyond all bearing. All his instincts and good taste
rose against the trite and the obvious. Now that he had
acquired the information he had sought he could please
himself as long as he acted instantly on that information.
The scowl he wished to retain rested the more easily on his
features with this revulsion of feeling.

'I'd be sorry to miss a hanging,' he said, half to himself,
and he allowed his eye to wander again from the dangling
noose to the shrinking group of Frenchmen who were still
ignorant of what had just happened. 'If that thick neck were
stretched a little——'

He broke off and took a brief turn up and down the
deck, eyed by every man who stood on it.

'Very well,' he said, halting. 'It's against my better
judgment, but I'll wait before I hang these men. What was
the approximate bearing of that trawler when she anchored,
captain?'

'It was at slack water,' began the captain, making his
calculations. 'We were just beginning to swing. I should
say——'

The captain was obviously a man of sober judgment and
keen observation. Hornblower listened to what he had to say.

'Very well,' said Hornblower when he had finished.
'Leadbitter, I'll leave you on board with two men. Keep an
eye on these prisoners and see they don't retake the brig.
I'm returning to the ship now. Wait here for further orders.'

He went down into his gig; the captain accompanying him
to the ship's side was clearly and gratifyingly puzzled. It was
almost beyond his belief that Hornblower could be the
demoniac monster that he had appeared to be, and if he
were it was strange good fortune that his ferocity should
have obtained, by pure chance, the information that the
prisoners had just given him. Yet on the other hand it was
almost beyond his belief that if Hornblower had employed
a clever ruse to gain the information he should refuse to
enjoy the plaudits of his audience and not to bask in their

surprise and admiration. Either notion was puzzling. That
was well. Let him be puzzled. Let them all be puzzled—
although it seemed as if the sobered hands pulling at the
oars of the gig were not at all puzzled. Unheeding of all that
had been at stake they were clearly convinced that their
captain had shown himself in his true colours, and was a
man who would sooner see a man's death agonies than eat
his dinner. Let 'em think so. It would do no harm. Hornblower could spare them no thought in any case, with all his
attention glued upon the compass card. It would be ludicrous
—it would be horribly comic—if after all this he were to miss
Atropos on his way back to her, if he were to blunder about
in the fog for hours looking for his own ship. The reciprocal
of North by East half East was South by West half West,
and he kept the gig rigidly on that course. With what still
remained of the ebb tide behind them it would only be a few
seconds before they ought to sight *Atropos*. It was a very
great comfort when they did.

Mr Jones received Hornblower at the ship's side. A glance
had told him that the gig's crew was two men and a coxswain
short. It was hard to think of any explanation of that, and
Mr Jones was bursting with curiosity. He could not help
but wonder what his captain had been doing, out there in
the fog. His curiosity even overcame his apprehension at
the sight of the scowl which Hornblower still wore—now
that he was back in his ship Hornblower was beginning to
feel much more strongly the qualms that should have
influenced him regarding what Their Lordships might think
of his absence from his ship. He ignored Jones's questions.

'You got those tops'l yards across, I see, Mr Jones.'

'Yes, sir. I sent the hands to dinner when you didn't come
back, sir. I thought——'

'They'll have five minutes to finish their dinners. No longer
Mr Jones, if you were in command of two boats sent to
capture a hostile vessel at anchor in this fog, how would you
set about it? What orders would you give?'

'Well, sir, I'd—I'd——'

Mr Jones was not a man of quickness of thought or rapid adaptability to a new situation. He hummed and he hawed. But there were very few officers in the Navy who had not been on at least one cutting-out and boarding operation. He knew well enough what he should do, and it slowly became apparent.

'Very well, Mr Jones. You will now hoist out the long boat and the launch. You will man them and see that the boats' crews are fully armed. You will proceed North by East half East—fix that in your mind, Mr Jones, North by East half East—from this ship for a quarter of a mile. There you find a West India brig the *Amelia Jane*. She has just been recaptured from a French prize crew, and my coxswain is on board with two men. From her you will take a new departure. There's a French privateer, the *Vengeance*. She's a Dunkirk trawler disguised as a Ramsgate trawler. She is probably heavily manned—at least fifty of a crew left—and she is anchored approximately three cables' lengths approximately north-west of the *Amelia Jane*. You will capture her, by surprise if possible. Mr Still will be in command of the second boat. I will listen while you give him his instructions. That will save repetition. Mr Still!'

The despatch that Hornblower wrote that evening and entrusted to the *Amelia Jane* for delivery to the Admiralty was couched in the usual Navy phraseology.

Sir
    I have the honour to report to you for the information of Their Lordships that this day while anchored in dense fog in the Downs I became aware that it seemed likely that some disturbance was taking place near at hand. On investigating I had the good fortune to recapture the brig Amelia Jane, *homeward bound from Barbados, which was in possession of a French prize crew. From information gained from the prisoners I was able to send my first lieutenant, Mr Jones, with the boats of H.M. ship under my command, to attack the French private ship of war*

Vengeance *of Dunkirk. She was handsomely carried by Mr Jones and his officers and men, including Mr Still, second lieutenant, Messrs Horrocks and Smiley, and His Serene Highness the Prince of Seitz-Bunau, midshipmen, after a brief action in which our loss was two men slightly wounded while the French Captain, Monsieur Ducos, met with a severe wound while trying to rally his crew. The* Vengeance *proved to be a French trawler masquerading as an English fishing boat. Including the prize crew she carried a crew of seventy-one officers and men, and she was armed with one four-pounder carronade concealed under her net.*

> *I have the honour to remain,*
> *Your obed't servant,*
> *H. Hornblower, Captain.*

Before sealing it Hornblower read through this report with a lopsided smile on his face. He wondered if anyone would ever read between the lines of that bald narrative, how much anyone would guess, how much anyone would deduce. The fog, the cold, the wet; the revolting scene on the deck of the *Amelia Jane;* the interplay of emotion; could anyone ever guess at all the truth? And there was no doubt that his gig's crew was already spreading round the ship horrible reports about his lust for blood. There was some kind of sardonic satisfaction to be derived from that, too. A knock at the door. Could he never be undisturbed?

'Come in,' he called.

It was Jones. His glance took in the quill in Hornblower's fingers, and the inkwell and papers on the table before him.

'Your pardon, sir,' he said. 'I hope I don't come too late.'

'What is it?' asked Hornblower; he had little sympathy for Jones and his undetermined manners.

'If you are going to send a report to the Admiralty, sir— and I suppose you are, sir——'

'Yes, of course I am.'

'I don't know if you're going to mention my name, sir—

I don't want to ask if you are, sir—I don't want to presume——'

If Jones was soliciting a special mention of himself in the Admiralty letter he would get none at àll.

'What is it you're saying to me, Mr Jones?'

'It's only that my name's a common one, sir. John Jones, sir. There are twelve John Jones's in the lieutenants' list, sir. I didn't know if you knew, sir, but I am John Jones the Ninth. That's how I'm known at the Admiralty, sir. If you didn't say that, perhaps——'

'Very well, Mr Jones. I understand. You can rely on me to see that justice is done.'

'Thank you, sir.'

With Jones out of the way Hornblower sighed a little, looked at his report, and drew a fresh sheet towards him. There was no chance of inserting 'the Ninth' legibly after the mention of Jones's name. The only thing to do was to take a fresh sheet and write it all over again. An odd occupation for a bloodthirsty tyrant.

IX

HORNBLOWER watched with a keen eye his crew at work as they took in sail while *Atropos* came gliding into Gibraltar Bay. He could call them well-drilled now. The long beat down the Channel, the battles with the Biscay gales, had made a correlated team of them. There was no confusion and only the minimum number of orders. The men came hurrying off the yards; he saw two figures swing themselves on to the main backstays and come sliding down all the way from the masthead, disdaining to use the shrouds and ratlines. They reached the deck simultaneously and stood grinning at each other for a moment—clearly they had been engaged in a race. One was Smiley, the midshipman of the maintop. The other—His Serene Highness the Prince of Seitz-Bunau. That boy had improved beyond all expectation. If ever he should sit on his throne again in his princely German capital he would have strange memories to recall.

But this was not the time for a captain to let his attention wander.

'Let go, Mr Jones!' he hailed, and the anchor fell, dragging the grumbling hawser out through the hawsehole; Hornblower watched while *Atropos* took up on her cable and then rode to her anchor. She was in her assigned berth; Hornblower looked up at the towering Rock and over at the Spanish shore. Nothing seemed to have changed since the last time—so many years ago—that he had come sailing into Gibraltar Bay. The sun was shining down on him, and it was good to feel this Mediterranean sun again, even though there was little warmth in it during this bleak winter weather.

'Call away my gig, if you please, Mr Jones.'

Hornblower ran below to gird on his sword and to take the better of his two cocked hats out of its tin case so as to make himself as presentable as possible when he went ashore to pay his official calls. There was a very decided thrill in the thought that soon he would be reading the orders that would carry him forward into the next phase of his adventures—adventures possibly; more probably the mere dreariness of beating about on eternal blockade duty outside a French port.

Yet in Collingwood's orders to him, when he came to read them, there was a paragraph which left him wondering what his fate was to be.

> *You will take into your ship Mr. William McCullum, of the Honourable East India Company's Service, together with his native assistants, and you will give them passage when, in obedience to the first paragraph of these orders, you come to join me.*

Mr. McCullum was awaiting him in the Governor's anteroom. He was a burly, heavy-set man in his early thirties, blue-eyed and with a thick mat of black hair.

'Captain Horatio Hornblower?' There was a roll to the 'r's' which betrayed the county of his origin.

'Mr McCullum?'

'Of the Company's Service.'

The two men eyed each other.

'You are to take passage in my ship?'

'Aye.'

The fellow carried himself with an air of vast independence. Yet judging by the scantiness of the silver lace on his uniform, and by the fact that he wore no sword, he was not of a very lofty position in the Company's hierarchy.

'Who are these native assistants of yours?'

'Three Sinhalese divers.'

'Sinhalese?'

Hornblower said the word with caution. He had never heard it before, at least pronounced in that way. He suspected that it meant something to do with Ceylon, but he was not going to make a display of his ignorance.

'Pearl divers from Ceylon,' said McCullum.

So he had guessed right. But he could not imagine for one moment why Collingwood, at grips with the French in the Mediterranean, should need Ceylonese pearl divers.

'And what is your official position, Mr McCullum?'

'I am wreck-master and salvage director of the Coromandel Coast.'

That went far to explain the man's ostentatious lack of deference. He was one of those experts whose skill made them too valuable to be trifled with. He might have drifted out to India as a cabin boy or apprentice; presumably he had been treated like a menial while young, but he had learned a trade so well as now to be indispensable and in a position to repay the slights he had endured earlier. The more the gold lace he was addressing the brusquer was likely to be his manner.

'Very well, Mr McCullum. I shall be sailing immediately and I shall be glad if you will come on board with your assistants at the earliest possible moment. Within an hour. Do you have any equipment with you to be shipped?'

'Very little besides my chests and the divers' bundles. They are ready, along with the food for them.'

'Food?'

'The poor bodies'—McCullum narrowed the vowel sound until the word sounded like 'puir'—'are benighted heathen, followers of Buddha. They wellnigh died on the voyage here, never having known what it was to have a full belly before. A scrap of vegetable, a drop of oil, a bit of fish for a relish. That's what they're used to living on.'

Oil? Vegetables? Ships of war could hardly be expected to supply such things.

'I've a puncheon of Spanish olive oil for them,' explained McCullum. 'They've taken kindly to it, although it's far removed from their buffalo butter. Lentils and onions and carrots. Give them salt beef and they'll die, and that would be poor business after shipping them all round the Cape of Good Hope.'

The statement was made with apparent callousness, but Hornblower suspected that the manner concealed some consideration for his unfortunate subordinates so far from their homes. He began to like McCullum a little better.

'I'll give orders for them to be well looked after,' he said.

'Thank you.' That was the first shade of politeness that had crept into McCullum's speech. 'The poor devils have been perishing of cold here on the Rock. That makes them homesick, like, and a long way they are from home, too.'

'Why have they been sent here in any case?' asked Hornblower. That question had been striving for utterance for some time; he had not asked it because it would have given McCullum too good an opportunity to snub him.

'Because they can dive in sixteen and a half fathoms,' said McCullum, staring straight at him.

It was not quite a snub; Hornblower was aware that he owed the modification to his promise that they would be well treated. He would not risk another question despite his consuming curiosity. He was completely puzzled as to why the Mediterranean Fleet should need divers who could go down through a hundred feet of water. He contented himself with ending the interview with an offer to send a boat for McCullum and his men.

The Ceylonese when they made their appearance on the deck of the *Atropos* were of an appearance to excite pity. They held their white cotton clothes close about them against the cold; the keen air that blew down from the snow-clad Spanish mountains set them shivering. They were thin, frail-looking men, and they looked about them with no curiosity, but with only a dull resignation in their dark eyes. They were of a deep brown colour, so as to excite the interest of the hands who gathered to stare. They spared no glances for the white men, but conversed briefly with each other in high piping musical voices.

'Give them the warmest corner of the 'tween decks, Mr

Jones,' said Hornblower. 'See that they are comfortable. Consult with Mr McCullum regarding anything they may need. Allow me to present Mr McCullum—Mr Jones. I would be greatly obliged if you will extend to Mr McCullum the hospitality of the wardroom.'

Hornblower had to phrase it that way. The wardroom theoretically was a voluntary association of officers, who could make their own choice as to what members they might admit. But it would be a bold set of officers who decided to exclude a wardroom guest recommended by their captain, as Jones and Hornblower both knew.

'You must provide a cot for Mr McCullum, too, Mr Jones, if you please. You can decide for yourself where you will put it.'

It was comforting to be able to say that. Hornblower knew perfectly well—and so did Jones, as his slightly dismayed expression revealed—that in a twenty-two gun sloop there was not a square foot of deck space to spare. Everyone was already overcrowded, and McCullum's presence would add seriously to the overcrowding. But it was Jones who would have to find a way round the difficulty.

'Aye aye, sir,' said Jones; the interval that elapsed before he said it was the best indication of the involved train of thought he had been following out.

'Excellent,' said Hornblower. 'You can attend to it after we're under way. No more time to waste, Mr Jones.'

Minutes were always valuable. The wind might always shift, or drop. An hour wasted now might mean the loss of a week. Hornblower was in a fever to get his ship clear of the Gut and into the wider waters of the Mediterranean, where he would have sea room in which to beat against a head wind should a Levanter come blowing out of the East. Before his mind's eye he had a picture of the Western Mediterranean; the north-westerly blowing at present could carry him quickly along the southern coast of Spain, past the dangerous shoal of Alboran, until at Cape de Gata the Spanish coast trended away boldly to the northward. Once there he would be less restricted; until Cape de Gata was left behind he could not be happy. There was also—Hornblower could not deny it—his own personal desire to be up and doing, to find out what was awaiting him in the future, to put himself at least in the possible path of adventure. It was fortunate that his duty and his inclination should coincide in this way; one of the few small bits of good fortune, he told himself with amused grimness, that he had experienced since he had made his original choice of the career of a naval officer.

But at least he had come into Gibraltar Bay after dawn and he was leaving before nightfall. He could not be accused of wasting any time. They had rounded the Rock; Hornblower looked into the binnacle and up at the commission pendant blowing out from the masthead.

'Full and bye,' he ordered.

'Full and bye, sir,' echoed the quartermaster at the wheel.

A keen gust of wind came blowing down out of the Sierra de Ronda, laying the *Atropos* over as the trimmed yards braced the sails to catch it. Over she lay; a short steep wave came after them, the remnants of an Atlantic roller that had survived its passage through the Gut. *Atropos* lifted her stern to it, heaving jerkily in this unnatural opposition of wind and wave. Spray burst under her counter, and spray burst round her bows as she plunged. She plunged again in the choppy sea. She was only a little ship, the smallest three-masted vessel in the service, the smallest that could merit a captain to command her. The lofty frigates, the massive seventy-fours, could condescend to her. Hornblower looked round him at the wintry Mediterranean, at the fresh clouds obscuring the sinking sun. The waves could toss his ship about, the winds could heel her over, but standing there, braced on the quarter-deck, he was master of them. Exultation surged within him as his ship hurried forward into the unknown.

The exultation even remained when he quitted the deck

and descended into the cabin. Here the prospect was cheerless in the extreme. He had mortified his flesh after he had come on board his ship at Deptford. His conscience had nagged at him for the scanty hours he had wasted with his wife and children; and he had never left his ship again for a moment after he had reported her ready for sea. No farewell to Maria lying in childbed, no last parting from little Horatio and little Maria. And no purchase of cabin equipment. The 'furniture about him was what the ship's carpenter had made for him, canvas chairs, a rough-and-ready table, a cot whose frame was strung with cordage to support a coarse canvas mattress stuffed with straw. A canvas pillow, straw-filled, to support his head; coarse Navy blankets to cover his skinny body. There was no carpet on the deck under his feet; the light came from a swinging and odorous ship's lantern. A shelf with a hole in it supported a tin wash-basin; on the bulkhead above it hung the scrap of polished steel mirror from Hornblower's meagre canvas dressing-roll. The most substantial articles present were the two sea chests in the corners; apart from them a monk's cell could hardly have been more bare.

But there was no self-pity in Hornblower's mind as he crouched under the low deck beams unhooking his stock preparatory to going to bed. He expected little from this world, and he could lead an inner life of the mind that could render him oblivious to discomfort. And he had saved a good deal of money by not furnishing his cabin, money which would pay the midwife's fee, the long bill at the 'George,' and the fare for the carrier's cart which would convey Maria and the children to lodge with her mother at Southsea. He was thinking about them—they must be well on their way now— as he drew the clammy blankets over himself and rested his cheek on the rough pillow. Then he had to forget Maria and the children as he reminded himself that as the *Atropos'* junction with the fleet was so imminent he must exercise the midshipmen and the signal ratings in signalling. He must devote a good many hours to that, and there would not be

much time to spare, for the creaking of the timbers, the
heave of the ship, told him that the wind was holding
steady.

The wind continued to hold fair. It was at noon on the
sixth day that the lookout hailed the deck.

'Sail ho! Dead to loo'ard.'

'Bear down on her, Mr Jones, if you please. Mr Smiley!
Take a glass and see what you make of her.'

This was the second of the rendezvous which Collingwood
had named in his orders. Yesterday's had been barren, off
Cape Carbomara. Not a sail had been sighted since leaving
Gibraltar. Collingwood's frigates had swept the sea clear of
French and Spanish shipping, and the British Levant convoy
was not due for another month. And no one could guess
what was going on in Italy at this moment.

'Captain, sir! She's a frigate. One of ours.'

'Very well. Signal midshipman! Be ready with the private
signal and our number.'

Thank Heaven for all the signalling exercise he had been
giving during the last few days.

'Captain, sir! I can see mastheads beyond her. Looks like
a fleet.'

'Very well, Mr Jones, I'll have the gunner make ready to
salute the flag, if you please.'

'Aye aye, sir.'

There was the Mediterranean Fleet, a score of ships of the
line, moving slowly in two columns over the blue sea under
a blue sky.

'Frigate's *Maenad*, 28, sir.'

'Very well.'

Reaching out like the tentacles of a sea monster, the scouting frigates lay far ahead of the main body of the fleet, four
of them, with a fifth far to windward whence most likely
would appear ships hostile or friendly. The air was clear;
Hornblower on the quarter-deck with his glass to his eye
could see the double column of topsails of ships of the line,
close hauled, every ship exactly the same distance astern of

her predecessor. He could see the vice-admiral's flag at the foremast of the leader of the weather line.

'Mr Carslake! Have the mail-bags ready for sending off.'

'Aye aye, sir.'

His own packet of despatches for Collingwood was handy in his cabin.

'Signal midshipman! Can't you see the flagship's making a signal?'

'Yes, sir, but the flags are blowing straight away from us. I can't make them out.'

'What do you think the repeating frigate's for? Use your eyes.'

'General signal, sir. Number 41. That is "tack," sir.'

'Very well.'

As *Atropos* had not yet officially joined the Mediterranean squadron a general signal could not apply to her. Down came the signal from the flagship's yardarm; that was the executive moment. Round came the flagship's yards; round came the yards of the scouting frigates, and of the leader of the lee column. One by one, at precise intervals, the succeeding ships in the columns came round in order; Hornblower could see the momentary backing and filling of the mizzen-topsails which maintained the ships so exactly spaced. It was significant that the drill was being carried out under all plain sail, and not merely under the 'fighting sails.' There was something thrilling in the sight of this perfection of drill; but at the same time something a little disturbing. Hornblower found himself wondering, with a qualm of doubt, if he would be able to maintain *Atropos* so exactly in station now that the time had come to join the fleet.

The manœuvre was completed now; on its new tack the fleet was steadily plunging forward over the blue sea. There was more bunting fluttering at the flagship's yardarm.

'General signal, sir. "Hands to dinner." '

'Very well.'

Hornblower felt a bubbling of excitement within him as he stood and watched. The next signal would surely be for him.

'Our number, sir! Flag to *Atropos*. Take station to windward of me at two cables' lengths.'

'Very well. Acknowledge.'

There were eyes turned upon him everywhere on deck.
This was the moment of trial. He had to come down past the
screening frigates, cross ahead of what was now the weather
column, and come to the wind at the right moment and at
the right distance. And the whole fleet would be watching
the little ship. First he had to estimate how far the flagship
would progress towards his starboard hand while he was
running down to her. But there was nothing for it but to
try; there was some faint comfort in being an officer in a
fighting service where an order was something that must be
obeyed.

'Quartermaster! Port a little. Meet her. Steady as you go!
Keep her at that! Mr Jones!'

'Aye aye, sir.'

No need for an order to Jones. He was more anxious—at
least more apparently anxious—than Hornblower was. He
had the hands at the braces trimming the yards already.
Hornblower looked up at yards and commission pendant to
assure himself that the bracing was exact. They had left the
Maenad behind already; here they were passing *Amphion*,
one of the central frigates in the screen. Hornblower could
see her lying over as she thrashed to windward, the spray
flying from her bows. He turned back to look at the flagship,
nearly hull up, at least two of her three rows of checkered
gunports visible.

'Port a little! Steady!'

He resented having to give that additional order; he wished
he could have headed straight for his station with no alteration of course. The leading ship—she wore a rear admiral's
flag—of the weather column was now nearly on his port
beam. Four cables' length was the distance between the two
columns, but as his station was to windward of the flagship,
nearly on her starboard beam, he would be by no means
between the two ships, nor equidistant from them. He juggled

in his mind with the scalene triangle that could be drawn connecting *Atropos* with the two flagships.

'Mr Jones! Clue up the mizzen tops'l.' Now *Atropos* would have a reserve of speed that he could call for if necessary. He was glad that he had subjected his crew to ceaseless sail drill ever since leaving Deptford. 'Stand by the mizzen tops'l sheets.'

The reduction in the after-sail would make *Atropos* a little slower in coming to the wind; he must bear it in mind. They were fast approaching their station. His eye darted from one column of ships to the other; he could see all the starboard sides of one and all the port sides of the other. It might be useful to take sextant angles, but he would rather trust his eye in a trigonometrical problem as uncomplicated as this. His judgment told him this must be the moment. The bows were pointing at the flagship's jib-boom.

'Port your helm,' he ordered. Perhaps he was wrong. Perhaps the little ship's response would be delayed. Perhaps—— He had to keep his voice steady. 'Bring her to the wind.'

The wheel spun over. There was a nervous second or two. Then he felt the heel of the ship alter under his feet; and he saw the flagship come round on *Atropos'* port beam, and he knew *Atropos* was turning.

'Steady!'

The yards were braced up; strong arms were hauling on the tacks. A moment or two while *Atropos* regained the small amount of way she had lost through her turn; but even making allowance for that he could see that the flagship was slowly head-reaching on her.

'Mr Jones! Sheet home the mizzen tops'l.'

With the mizzen topsail drawing full they would head-reach in turn upon the flagship.

'Keep the hands at the braces there!'

Occasionally spilling the wind from the mizzen topsail would enable *Atropos* to keep her speed equal to the flagship's. Hornblower felt the wind on his neck; he looked up at the pendant and at the flagship. He was exactly to windward of her, and there was two cables' lengths between them.

'Mr Jones! You may begin the salute.'

Fifteen guns for a vice-admiral, a minute and a quarter to fire them. That might be long enough for him to regain his composure, and for his heart to resume its normal rate of beating. Now they were part of the Mediterranean Fleet, the tiniest, most insignificant part of it. Hornblower looked down the massive lines of ships ploughing along behind them, three-deckers, two-deckers, ships of a hundred guns and ships of seventy-four, the ships which had fought at Trafalgar, the roar of whose cannons had dashed from Bonaparte's lips the heady cup of world domination. On the invisibly distant Mediterranean shores that encompassed them armies might march, kings might be set up and kings might be pulled down; but it was these ships which in the end would decide the destiny of the world, as long as the men who sailed them retained their skill, as long as they remained ready to endure danger and hardship, as long as the government at home remained resolute and unafraid.

'Our number, sir! Flag to *Atropos*. "Welcome." '

'Reply to Flag. "Respectful greetings." '

Eager hands worked vigorously on the signal halliards.

'Signal "*Atropos* to Flag. Have aboard dispatches and letters for fleet." '

'Flagship acknowledges, sir.'

'Flagship's signalling again,' announced Still; from a point of vantage on the weather side he could see through his glass enough of the flagship's quarter-deck, despite the fact that she was heeling away from him, to make out that signal ratings were bending fresh flags on the halliards. The dark lumps soared up to the flagship's yardarm and broke into gaily-coloured bunting.

'General signal. "Heave to on the starboard tack." '

'Acknowledge, Mr Jones! Clue up the courses.'

Hornblower watched the hands at the clue-garnets and buntlines, the hands at the tacks and sheets.

'Signal's down, sir.'

Hornblower had already seen the first movement of descent.

'Back the mizzen tops'l. Let her come up.'

Atropos rode easily, just meeting the waves with her bow, as the sharp struggle with the wind changed to yielding acquiescence, like a girl's resistance giving way in her lover's arms. But this was no time for that sort of sentimental simile—here was another long signal from the flagship.

'General signal. "Send to"—our number, sir—"for letters." '

'Mr Carslake! Have those mail-bags on deck at once. You'll have a boat from every ship in the fleet alongside.'

It was at least a month—it might well be two—since any letters had reached the Fleet from England. Not a newspaper, not a word. Possibly some of the ships present had not yet seen the accounts in the press of the victory they had won at Trafalgar four months before. *Atropos* had brought a respite from the dreadful isolation in which a fleet at sea habitually lived. Boats would be hastening as fast as sail or oar could drive them to collect the pitifully lean mail-bags.

Another signal.

'Our number, sir. "Flag to *Atropos*. Come and report." '

'Call away my gig.'

He was wearing the shabbier of his two coats. There was just time, when he ran below to get the packets of dispatches, to change his coat, to pass a comb through his hair, and twitch his neckcloth into position. He was back on deck just as his gig touched the water. Lusty work at the oars carried him round to the flagship. A chair dangled at her side, now almost lipped as a wave rose at it, now high above the water as the wave passed on. He had to watch carefully for his chance; as it was there was an uncomfortable moment when he hung by his arms as the gig went away from under him. But he managed to seat himself, and he felt the chair soar swiftly upwards as the hands above hauled on the tackle. The pipes shrilled as his head reached the level of the

main-deck and the chair was swung in. He stepped aboard
with his hand to the brim of his hat.

The deck was as white as paper, as white as the gloves and
the shirts of the sideboys. Gold leaf gleamed in the sun, the
most elaborate Turks' heads adorned the ropework. The
King's own yacht could not be smarter than the quarter-deck
of the *Ocean*—that was what could be done in the flagship
of a victorious admiral. It was as well to remember that
Collingwood's previous flagship, the *Royal Sovereign*, had
been pounded into a mastless hulk, with four hundred dead
and wounded on board her, at Trafalgar. The lieutenant of
the watch, his telescope quite dazzling with polished brass
and pipe-clayed twine, wore spotless and unwrinkled white
trousers; the buttons on his well-fitting coat winked in the
sunshine. It occurred to Hornblower that to be always as
smart as that, in a ship additionally crowded by the presence
of an admiral and his staff, could be by no means easy.
Service in a flagship might be the quick way to promotion,
but there were many crumpled petals in the bed of roses.
The flag captain, Rotherham—Hornblower knew his name;
it had appeared in a hundred newspaper accounts of
Trafalgar—and the flag lieutenant were equally smart as
they made him welcome.

'His Lordship is awaiting you below, sir,' said the flag
lieutenant. 'Will you come this way?'

Collingwood shook hands with him in the great cabin
below. He was a large man, stoop-shouldered, with a
pleasant smile. He eagerly took the packets Hornblower
offered him, glancing at the superscriptions. One he kept in
his hands, the others he gave to his secretary. He remembered
his manners as he was about to break the seal.

'Please sit down, captain. Harkness, a glass of Madeira
for Captain Hornblower. Or there is some Marsala that I
can recommend, sir. Please forgive me for a moment. You
will understand when I tell you these are letters from my
wife.'

It was an upholstered chair in which Hornblower sat;

under his feet was a thick carpet; there were a couple of pictures in gilt frames on the bulkheads; silver lamps hung by silver chains from the deck-beams. Looking round him while Collingwood eagerly skimmed through his letters, Hornblower thought of all this being hurriedly bundled away when the *Ocean* cleared for action. But what held his attention most was two long boxes against the great stern windows. They were filled with earth and were planted with flowers—hyacinths and daffodils, blooming and lovely. The scent of the hyacinths reached Hornblower's nostrils where he sat. There was something fantastically charming about them here at sea.

'I've been successful with my bulbs this year,' said Collingwood, putting his letters in his pocket and following Hornblower's glance. He walked over and tilted up a daffodil bloom with sensitive fingers, looking down into its open face. 'They are beautiful, aren't they? Soon the daffodils will be flowering in England—some time, perhaps, I'll see them again. Meanwhile these help to keep me contented. It is three years since I last set foot on land.'

Commanders-in-Chief might win peerages and pensions, but their children, too, grew up without knowing their fathers. And Collingwood had walked shot-torn decks in a hundred fights; but Hornblower, looking at the wistful smile, thought of other things than battles—thirty thousand turbulent seamen to be kept disciplined and efficient, court-martial findings to be confirmed, the eternal problems of provisions and water, convoys and blockade.

'You will give me the pleasure of your company at dinner, Captain?' asked Collingwood.

'I should be honoured, my lord.'

It was gratifying to bring that phrase out pat like that, with hardly more than the least feeling of embarrassment.

'That is excellent. You will be able to tell me all the gossip of home. I fear there will be no other opportunity for some time, as *Atropos* will not be staying with the Fleet.'

'Indeed, my lord?'

This was a moment of high excitement, when the future was about to be revealed to him. But of course the excitement must not be allowed to appear; only the guarded interest of a self-contained captain ready for anything.

'I fear so—not that you young captains with your saucy little ships want to stay tied to a fleet's apron strings.'

Collingwood was smiling again, but there was something in the words that started a new train of thought in Hornblower's mind. Of course, Collingwood had watched the advent of the newest recruit to his fleet with a keen eye. Hornblower suddenly realized that if *Atropos* had been clumsy in taking up station, or dilatory in answering signals, his reception here might not have been so pleasant. He might be standing at attention at this moment submitting with a tight-shut mouth to a dressing-down exemplary in its drastic quality. The thought caused a little prickling of gooseflesh at the back of his neck. It reduced his reply to a not very coherent mumble.

'You have this man McCullum and his natives on board?' asked Collingwood.

'Yes, my lord.'

Only a little self-restraint was necessary to refrain from asking what the mission would be; Collingwood would tell him.

'You are not acquainted with the Levant?'

'No, my lord.'

So it was to be the Levant, among the Turks and the Greeks and the Syrians.

'You soon will be, captain. After taking my dispatches to Malta you will convey Mr McCullum to Marmorice Bay and assist him in his operations there.'

Marmorice Bay? That was on the coast of Asia Minor. The fleet and transports which had attacked Egypt some years ago had rendezvoused there. It was a far cry from Deptford.

'Aye aye, my lord,' said Hornblower.

'I understand you have no sailing master in *Atropos*.'

'No, my lord. Two master's mates.'

'In Malta you will have a sailing master assigned to you. George Turner; he is familiar with Turkish waters and he was with the fleet in Marmorice. He took the bearings when *Speedwell* sank.'

Speedwell? Hornblower raked back in his memory. She was the transport which had capsized and sunk at her anchors in a sudden gale of wind in Marmorice Bay.

'Yes, my lord.'

'She had on board the military chest of the expeditionary force. I don't expect you knew that.'

'No, indeed, my lord.'

'A very considerable sum in gold and silver coin for the pay and subsistence of the troops—a quarter of a million sterling. She sank in water far deeper than any diver in the service could reach. But as no one knew what our gallant allies the Turks might contrive by way of salvage with infinite leisure it was decided to keep the loss a secret. And for once a secret remained a secret.'

'Yes, my lord.'

Certainly it was not common knowledge that a quarter of a million in coin lay at the bottom of Marmorice Bay.

'So the Government had to send to India for divers who could reach those depths.'

'I see, my lord.'

'Now it will be your duty to go to Marmorice Bay and with the assistance of McCullum and Turner to recover that treasure.'

'Aye aye, my lord.'

No imagination could ever compass the possible range of duties of a naval officer. But it was satisfactory that the words he had just uttered were the only ones a naval officer could say in such circumstances.

'You will have to be careful in your dealings with our friend the Turk. He will be curious about your presence in Marmorice, and when he ascertains the object of your visit he may raise objections. You will have to conduct yourself according to the circumstances of the moment.'

'Aye aye, my lord.'

'You will not find all this in your orders, captain. But you must understand that the Cabinet has no wish for complications with the Turks. Yet at the same time a quarter of a million sterling in cash would be a Godsend to the Government to-day—or any day. The money is badly needed, but no offence should be offered to the Turks.'

It was necessary to steer clear of Scylla and yet not fall into Charybdis, said Hornblower to himself.

'I think I understand, my lord.'

'Fortunately it is an unfrequented coast. The Turks maintain very small forces, either military or naval, in the locality. That does not mean that you should attempt to carry off matters with a high hand.'

Not in *Atropos* with eleven popguns a side, thought Hornblower, and then he mentally withdrew the sneer. He understood what Collingwood meant.

'No, my lord.'

'Very well then, captain, thank you.'

The secretary at Collingwood's elbow had a pile of opened despatches in his hand, and was clearly waiting for a break in the conversation to give him an opportunity to intervene, and the flag lieutenant was hovering in the background. Both of them moved in at once.

'Dinner will be in half an hour, my lord,' said the flag lieutenant.

'These are the urgent letters, my lord,' said the secretary.

Hornblower rose to his feet in some embarrassment.

'Perhaps, captain, you would enjoy a turn on the quarter-deck, eh?' asked Collingwood. 'Flags here would keep you company, I'm sure.'

When a vice-admiral made suggestions to a captain and a flag lieutenant he did not have to wait long before they were acted upon. But out on the quarter-deck, pacing up and down making polite conversation, Hornblower could have wished that Collingwood had not been so thoughtful as to provide him with company. He had a great deal to think about.

X

MALTA; Ricasoli Point on the one hand and Fort St Elmo returning the salute on the other, and the Grand Harbour opening up between them; Valetta with its palaces on the promontory; gaily painted small craft everywhere; a fresh north-easterly wind blowing. That wind—the Gregale, the sailing directions called it—did not allow Hornblower any leisure at present for sightseeing. In confined waters a sailing ship before the wind always seemed pigheadedly determined to maintain her speed however much her canvas was reduced, even under bare poles. It called for accurate timing to round-to at the right moment, to take her way off her, to clue up, and drop anchor at the right moment.

Nor would there be any leisure for Hornblower, it appeared, during the few hours that he would be here. He could combine his official calls with his personal delivery of the despatches entrusted to him, which would save a good deal of time, but that saving was immediately eaten up—as the fat kine of Pharaoh's dream were eaten up by the lean kine—by the demands on his attention, and, just as the lean kine were no fatter after their meal, so he was just as busy even when his planning had saved that much time. It would be quarter-day, or as near to it as made no matter, by the time letters from Malta would reach England, so that now he could draw against his pay. Not to any great extent, of course—there were Maria and the children to be considered —but enough to provide himself with a few luxuries in this island where bread was dear and luxuries cheap. Oranges and olives and fresh vegetables—the bumboats were already awaiting permission to come alongside.

McCullum, with his salvage operations in mind, was

anxious for an indent to be made for supplies he considered
necessary. He wanted a mile of half-inch line and a quarter
mile of slow match—a fantastic demand, to Hornblower's
mind, but McCullum knew more about his business than he
did, presumably—and five hundred feet of leather 'fuse-hose,'
which was something Hornblower had hardly heard of.
Hornblower signed the indent wondering vaguely whether
the Navy Office would surcharge him with it, and turned
away to face the inevitable fact that every officer in the ship
wished to go ashore and was presenting irrefutable reasons
to Jones in favour of his so doing. If *Atropos* had been on
fire they could not be more passionately anxious to be out
of her.

And here was another complication; a note from His
Excellency the Governor. Would Captain Hornblower and
one of his officers dine at the Palace this afternoon? It would
be impossible to refuse, so no time need be wasted on debate
regarding that point—His Excellency was just as anxious as
any ordinary mortal to hear the gossip from England and to
see a new face—while there was equally no debate regarding
which officer he should take with him. His Excellency would
never forgive him if he heard who had been on board
Atropos and he had not been afforded the opportunity of
seating royalty at his table.

'Pass the word for Mr Prince,' said Hornblower, 'and the
doctor.'

It would be necessary to have the doctor to interpret to
the Prince exactly what was going to happen; the boy had
learned a good deal of English during his month on board,
but the vocabulary of the gunroom was hardly inclusive
enough to permit of discussions of vice-regal etiquette. The
Prince came in a little breathless, still twitching his uniform
into some kind of order; Eisenbeiss was breathing hard too
—he had to come the whole length of the ship and through a
narrow hatchway.

'Please explain to His Serene Highness,' said Hornblower,
'that he is coming ashore with me to dine with the Governor.'

Eisenbeiss spoke in German, and the boy gave his mechanical little bow. The use of German evoked the manners of royalty from under the new veneer of a British midshipman.

'His Serene Highness is to wear his court dress?' asked Eisenbeiss.

'No,' said Hornblower, 'his uniform. And if ever I see him again with his shoes as badly brushed as those are I'll take the cane to him.'

'Sir——' said Eisenbeiss, but words failed him. The thought of the cane being applied to his Prince struck him dumb; fortunately, perhaps.

'So that I am to wear this uniform too, sir?' asked Eisenbeiss.

'I fear you have not been invited, doctor,' said Hornblower.

'But I am First Chamberlain to His Serene Highness, sir,' exploded Eisenbeiss. 'This will be a visit of ceremony, and it is a fundamental law of Seitz-Bunau that I make all presentations.'

Hornblower kept his temper.

'And I represent His Britannic Majesty,' he said.

'Surely His Britannic Majesty cannot wish that his ally should not be treated with the honours due to his royal position? As Secretary of State it is my duty to make an official protest.'

'Yes,' said Hornblower. He put out his hand and bent the Prince's head forward. 'You might be better employed seeing that His Serene Highness washes behind his ears.'

'Sir! Sir!' said Eisenbeiss.

'Be ready and properly dressed in half an hour, if you please, Mr. Prince.'

Dinner at the Palace ran the dreary course it might be expected to take. It was fortunate that, on being received by the Governor's aide-de-camp, Hornblower was able to shuffle on to his shoulders the burden of the difficult decision regarding the presentations—Hornblower could not guess whether His Serene Highness should be presented to His Excellency or vice versa, and he was a little amused to note

Her Excellency's hurried asides when she heard the quality of her second guest; the seating arrangements for dinner needed hasty revision. So Hornblower found himself between two dull women, one of them with red hands and the other with a chronic sniff. He struggled to make polite conversation, and he was careful with his wine-glass, contriving merely to sip when the others drank deep.

The Governor drank to His Serene Highness the Prince of Seitz-Bunau, and the Prince, with the most perfect aplomb, drank to His Majesty the King of Great Britain; presumably those were the first words of English he had ever learned, long before he had learned to shout 'Vast heaving' or 'Come on, you no-sailors, you.' When the ladies had withdrawn Hornblower listened to His Excellency's comments about Bonaparte's threatening invasion of Southern Italy, and about the chances of preserving Sicily from his clutches; and a decent interval after returning to the drawing-room he caught the Prince's eye. The Prince smiled back at him and rose to his feet. It was odd to watch him receiving the bows of the men and the curtseys of the ladies with the assurance of ingrained habit. To-morrow the boy would be in the gunroom mess again—Hornblower wondered whether he was able yet to stand up for his rights there and make sure he received no more than his fair share of gristle when the meat was served.

The gig whisked them across the Grand Harbour from the Governor's steps to the ship's side, and Hornblower came on to the quarter-deck with the bos'n's mates' pipes to welcome him. He was conscious even before he had taken his hand from his hat brim that there was something wrong. He looked round him at the ship illuminated by the wild sunset the Gregale had brought with it. There was no trouble with the hands, judging by their attitudes as they stood crowded forward. The three Ceylonese divers were there in their accustomed isolation by the knight-heads. But the officers grouped aft wore an apprehensive look; Hornblower's eyes moved from face to face, from Jones to Still, the two lieutenants, to Carslake, the purser, and to Silver, the master's mate of the watch. It was Jones as senior officer who came forward to report.

'If you please, sir——'

'What is it, Mr Jones?'

'If you please, sir, there has been a duel.'

No one could ever guess what would be the next burden to be laid on a captain's shoulders. It might be an outbreak of plague, or the discovery of dry rot in the ship's timbers. And Jones's manner implied not merely that there had been a duel, but that someone had been hurt in it.

'Who fought?' demanded Hornblower.

'The doctor and Mr McCullum, sir.'

Well, somewhere they could pick up another doctor, and if the worst came to the worst they could manage without one at all.

'What happened?'

'Mr McCullum was shot through the lungs, sir.'

God! That was something entirely different, something of vital importance. A bullet through the lungs meant death almost for certain, and what was he to do with McCullum dead? McCullum had been sent for all the way from India. It would take a year and a half to get someone out from there to replace him. No ordinary men with salvage experience would do—it had to be someone who knew how to use the Ceylonese divers. Hornblower wondered with sick despair whether a man had ever been so plagued as he was. He had to swallow before he could speak again.

'Where is he now?'

'Mr McCullum, sir? He's in the hands of the garrison surgeon in the hospital ashore.'

'He's still alive?'

Jones spread despairing hands.

'Yes, sir. He was alive half an hour ago.'

'Where's the doctor?'

'Down below in his berth, sir.'

'I'll see him. No, wait. I'll send for him when I want him.

He wanted to think; he needed time and leisure to decide what was to be done. It was his instinct to walk the deck; that was how he could work off the high internal pressure of his emotions. It was only incidentally that the rhythmic exercise brought his thoughts into orderly sequence. And this little deck was crowded with idle officers—his cabin down below was of course quite useless. That was the moment when Jones came forward with something else to bother him.

'Mr Turner's come aboard, sir.'

Mr Turner? Turner? That was the sailing master with experience of Turkish waters whom Collingwood had detailed specially to service in *Atropos*. He came from behind Jones as the words were said, a wizened old man with a letter in his hand, presumably the orders which had brought him on board.

'Welcome aboard, Mr Turner,' said Hornblower, forcing himself into cordiality while wondering whether he would ever make use of Turner's services.

'Your servant, sir,' said Turner with old-fashioned politeness.

'Mr Jones, see that Mr Turner's comfortable.'

'Aye aye, sir.'

That was the only reply Jones could make, however hard of execution the order might be. But clearly Jones meditated some supplementary remark; it could be that he was going to suggest putting Turner into McCullum's quarters. Hornblower could not bear the thought of having to listen to anything of the sort while he had yet to reach a decision. It was the final irritation that roused him to the pitch of acting with the arbitrariness of a captain of the old school.

'Get below, all of you,' he snapped. 'I want this deck clear.'

They looked at him as if they had not heard him aright, and he knew they had.

'Get below, if you please,' he said, and the 'if you please' did nothing to soften the harshness of his request. 'Master's mate of the watch, see that this deck is kept clear, and keep out of my way yourself.'

They went below—this was an order from the captain who (according to the reports of his gig's crew) had barely been diverted from hanging a dozen French prisoners for no other reason than a desire to see their death struggles. So he had the quarter-deck to himself, on which to stride up and down, from taffrail to mizzen mast and back again, in the fast-fading twilight. He walked rapidly, turning with a jerk at each end, irritation and worry goading him on.

He had to reach a decision. The obvious thing to do was to report to Collingwood and await further orders. But how long would it be before any vessel left Malta with letters for Collingwood, and how long would it be before another returned? A month altogether, probably. No captain worth his salt would keep *Atropos* lying idle in Grand Harbour for a month. He could guess what Collingwood would think of a man who evaded responsibility like that. He could take *Atropos* and seek out Collingwood himself, but the same objections applied. And how would he appear in Collingwood's eyes if he were to arrive off Toulon or Leghorn or wherever the chances of war might have summoned Collingwood, at the moment when he was supposed to be two thousand miles away? No. No. It would never do. At least he had reduced two apparent possibilities to impossibilities.

Then he must proceed with his orders as if nothing had happened to McCullum. That meant he must undertake the salvage operations himself, and he knew nothing about the subject. A wave of fury passed over him as his mind dwelt on the inconvenience and loss occasioned by the duel. The idiotic Eisenbeiss and the bad-tempered McCullum. They had no business incommoding England in her struggle with Bonaparte merely to satisfy their own ridiculous passions. He himself had borne with Eisenbeiss's elephantine nonsense. Why could not McCullum have done the same? And in any event why could not McCullum have held his pistol straighter and killed the ridiculous doctor instead of getting killed himself? But that sort of rhetorical question did not get him any further with his own urgent problems; he must not think along those lines. Moreover, with a grinding feeling of guilt another consideration crept in. He should have been aware of bad blood between the people in his ship. He remembered the lighthearted way in which he had put on Jones's shoulders the responsibility for accommodating McCullum in his crowded little ship. In the wardroom the doctor and McCullum had probably got on each other's nerves; there could be no doubt about that—and presumably ashore, over wine in some tavern, the enmity had flared up and brought about the duel. He should have known about the possibility and nipped it in the bud. Hornblower scourged himself spiritually for his remissness. He experienced bitter self-contempt at that moment. Perhaps he was unfit to be captain of one of His Majesty's ships.

The thought brought about an even greater internal upheaval. He could not bear it. He must prove to himself that there was no truth in it, or he must break himself in the attempt. He must carry through that salvage operation by his own efforts if necessary. He must. He *must*.

So that was the decision. He had only to reach it for the emotion to die down within him, to leave him thinking feverishly but clearly. He must of course do everything possible to ensure success, omit nothing that could help. McCullum had indented for 'leather fuse-hose'; that was some indication of how the salvage problem was to be approached. And McCullum was not yet dead, as far as he knew. He might—no, it was hardly possible. No one ever survived a bullet through the lungs. And yet——

'Mr Nash!'

'Sir!' said the master's mate of the watch, coming at the run.

'My gig. I'm going over to the hospital.'

There was still just a little light in the sky, but overside the water was black as ink, reflecting in long, irregular lines the

lights that showed in Valetta. The oars ground rhythmically
in the rowlocks. Hornblower restrained himself from urging
the men to pull harder. They could never have rowed fast
enough to satisfy the pressing need for instant action that
seethed inside him.

The garrison officers were still at mess, sitting over their
wine, and the mess sergeant, at Hornblower's request, went
in and fetched out the surgeon. He was a youngish man, and
fortunately still sober. He stood with the candle-light on his
face and listened attentively to Hornblower's questions.

'The bullet hit him in the right armpit,' said the surgeon.
'One would expect that, as he would be standing with his
shoulder turned to his opponent and his arm raised. The
actual wound was on the posterior margin of the armpit,
towards the back, in other words, and on the level of the
fifth rib.'

The heart was on the level of the fifth rib, as Hornblower
knew, and the expression had an ominous sound.

'I suppose the bullet did not go right through?' he asked.

'No,' replied the surgeon. 'It is very rare for a pistol
bullet, if it touches bone, to go through the body, even at
twelve paces. The powder charge is only one drachm.
Naturally the bullet is still there, presumably within the
chest cavity.'

'So he is unlikely to live?'

'Very unlikely, sir. It is a surprise he has lived so long.
The hæmoptysis—the spitting of blood, you understand,
sir—has been extremely slight. Most chest wounds die of
internal bleeding within an hour or two, but in this case the
lung can hardly have been touched. There is considerable
contusion under the right scapula—that is the shoulder
blade—indicating that the bullet terminated its course there.'

'Close to the heart?'

'Close to the heart, sir. But it can have touched none of
the great vessels there, most surprisingly, or he would have
been dead within a few seconds.'

'Then why do you think he will not live?'

The doctor shook his head.

'Once an opening has been made in the chest cavity, sir, there is little chance, and with the bullet still inside the chance is negligible. It will certainly have carried fragments of clothing in with it. We may expect internal mortification, a general gathering of malignant humours, and eventual death within a few days.'

'You could not probe for the bullet?'

'Within the chest wall? My dear sir!'

'What action have you taken, then?'

'I have bound up the wound of entry to put an end to the bleeding there. I have strapped up the chest to ensure that the jagged ends of the broken ribs do no more damage to the lungs. I took two ounces of blood from the left basilar vein, and I administered an opiate.'

'An opiate? So he is not conscious now?'

'Certainly not.'

Hornblower felt hardly wiser than he had done when Jones first told him the news.

'You say he may live a few days? How many?'

'I know nothing about the patient's constitution, sir. But he is a powerful man in the prime of life. It might be as much as a week. It might even be more. But on the other hand if events take a bad turn he might be dead to-morrow.'

'But if it is several days? Will he retain his senses during that time?'

'Likely enough. When he ceases to, it is a sign of the approaching end. Then we can expect fever, restlessness, delirium, and death.'

Several days of consciousness were possible, therefore. And the faintest, remotest chance that McCullum would live after all.

'Supposing I took him to sea with me? Would that help? Or hinder?'

'You would have to ensure his immobility on account of the fractured ribs. But at sea he might perhaps even live longer. There are the usual Mediterranean agues in this island. And in addition there is an endemic low fever. My hospital is full of such cases.'

Now this was a piece of information that really helped in coming to a decision.

'Thank you, doctor,' said Hornblower, and he took his decision. Then it was only a matter of minutes to make the arrangements with the surgeon and to take his leave. The gig took him back through the darkness, over the black water, to where *Atropos*' riding light showed faintly.

'Pass the word for the doctor to come to my cabin at once,' was Hornblower's reply to the salute of the officer of the watch.

Eisenbeiss came slowly in. There was something of apprehension and something of bravado in his manner. He was prepared to defend himself against the storm he was certain was about to descend on him. What he did not expect was the reception he actually experienced. He approached the table behind which Hornblower was seated and stood sullen, meeting Hornblower's eyes with the guilty defiance of a man who has just taken another human's life.

'Mr McCullum,' began Hornblower, and the doctor's thick lips showed a trace of a sneer, 'is being sent on board here to-night. He is still alive.'

'On board here?' repeated the doctor, surprised into a change of attitude.

'You address me as "sir." Yes, I am having him sent over from the hospital. My orders to you are to make every preparation for his reception.'

The doctor's response was unintelligible German, but there could be no doubt it was an ejaculation of astonishment.

'Your answer to me is "aye aye, sir," ' snapped Hornblower, his pent-up emotion and strain almost making him tremble as he sat at the table. He could not prevent his fist from clenching, but he just managed to refrain from allowing it to pound the table. The intensity of his feelings must have had their effect telepathically.

'Aye aye, sir,' said the doctor grudgingly.

'Mr McCullum's life is extremely valuable, doctor. Much more valuable than yours.'

The doctor could only mumble in reply to that.

'It is your duty to keep him alive.'

Hornblower's fist unclenched now, and he could make his points slowly, one by one, accentuating each with the slow tap of the tip of a lean forefinger on the table.

'You are to do all you can for him. If there is anything special that you require for the purpose you are to inform me and I shall endeavour to obtain it for you. His life is to be saved, or if not, it is to be prolonged as far as possible. I would recommend you to establish an hospital for him abaft No. 6 carronade on the starboard side, where the motion of the ship will be least felt, and where it will be possible to rig a shelter for him from the weather. You will apply to Mr Jones for that. The ship's pigs can be taken for'rard where they will not discommode him.'

Hornblower's pause and glance called forth an 'aye aye, sir' from the doctor's lips like a cork from out of a bottle, so that Hornblower could proceed.

'We sail at dawn to-morrow,' he went on. 'Mr McCullum is to live until we reach our destination, and until long after, long enough for him to execute the duty which has brought him from India. That is quite clear to you?'

'Yes, sir,' answered the doctor, although his puzzled expression proved that there was something about the orders which he could not explain to himself.

'You had better keep him alive,' continued Hornblower. 'You had certainly better. If he dies I can try you for murder under the ordinary laws of England. Don't look at me like that. I am speaking the truth. The common law knows nothing about duels. I can hang you, doctor.'

The doctor was a shade paler, and his big hands tried to express what his paralysed tongue would not.

'But simply hanging you would be too good for you, doctor,' said Hornblower. 'I can do more than that, and I shall. You have a fat, fleshy back. The cat would sink deeply into it. You've seen men flogged—you saw two flogged last week. You heard them scream. You will scream at the gratings too, doctor. That I promise you.'

'No!' said the doctor—'you can't——'

'You address me as "sir," and you do not contradict me. You heard my promise? I shall carry it out. I can, and I shall.'

In a ship detached far from superior authority there was nothing a captain might not do, and the doctor knew it. And with Hornblower's grim face before him and those remorseless eyes staring into his the doctor could not doubt the possibility. Hornblower was trying to keep his expression set hard, and to pay no attention to the internal calculations that persisted in maintaining themselves inside him. There might be terrible trouble if the Admiralty ever heard he had flogged a warranted doctor, but then the Admiralty might never hear of an incident in the distant Levant. And there was the other doubt—with McCullum once dead, so that nothing could bring him to life, Hornblower could not really believe he would torture a human being to no practical purpose. But as long as Eisenbeiss did not guess that, it did not matter.

'This is all quite clear to you now, doctor?'

'Yes, sir.'

'Then my order is that you start making your arrangements now.'

It was a really great surprise to Hornblower when Eisenbeiss still hesitated. He was about to speak more sharply still, cutting into the feverish gestures of the big hands, when Eisenbeiss spoke again.

'Do you forget something, sir?'

'What do you think I have forgotten?' asked Hornblower, playing for time instead of flatly refusing to listen to any arguments—proof enough that he was a little shaken by Eisenbeiss's persistence.

'Mr McCullum and I—we are enemies,' said Eisenbeiss.

It was true that Hornblower had forgotten that. He was so

engrossed with his chessboard manipulation of human pieces
that he had overlooked a vital factor. But he must not admit it.

'And what of that?' he asked coldly, hoping his dis-
comfiture was not too apparent.

'I shot him,' said Eisenbeiss. There was a vivid gesture by
the big right hand that had held the pistol, which enabled
Hornblower to visualize the whole duel. 'What will he say
if I attend him?'

'Whose was the challenge?' asked Hornblower, still playing for time.

'He challenged me,' said Eisenbeiss. 'He said—he said I
was no Baron, and I said he was no gentleman. "I will kill
you for that," he said, and so we fought.'

Eisenbeiss had certainly said the thing that would best
rouse McCullum's fury.

'You are convinced you are a Baron?' asked Hornblower
—curiosity urged him to ask the question as well as the need
for time to reassemble his thoughts. The Baron drew himself
up as far as the deck-beams over his head allowed.

'I know I am, sir. My patent of nobility is signed by His
Serene Highness himself.'

'When did he do that?'

'As soon as—as soon as we were alone. Only His Serene
Highness and I managed to cross the frontier when
Bonaparte's men entered Seitz-Bunau. The others all took
service with the tyrant. It was not fit that His Serene Highness should be attended only by a bourgeois. Only a noble
could attend him to bed or serve his food. He had to have a
High Chamberlain to regulate his ceremonial, and a Secretary
of State to manage his foreign affairs. So His Serene Highness
ennobled me—that is why I bear the title of Baron—and
gave me the high offices of State.

'On your advice?'

'I was the only adviser he had left.'

This was very interesting and much as Hornblower had
imagined it, but it was not to the point. Hornblower was
more ready now to face the real issue.

'In the duel,' he asked, 'you exchanged shots?'

'His bullet went past my ear,' answered Eisenbeiss.

'Then honour is satisfied on both sides,' said Hornblower, more to himself than to the doctor.

Technically that was perfectly correct. An exchange of shots, and still more the shedding of blood, ended any affair of honour. The principals could meet again socially as if there had been no trouble between them. But to meet in the relative positions of doctor and patient might be something different. He would have to deal with that difficulty when it arose.

'You are quite right to remind me about this, doctor,' he said, with the last appearance of judicial calm that he could summon up. 'I shall bear it in mind.'

Eisenbeiss looked at him a little blankly, and Hornblower put on his hard face again.

'But it makes no difference at all to my promise to you. Rest assured of that,' he continued. 'My orders still stand. They—still—stand.'

It was several seconds before the reluctant answer came.

'Aye aye, sir.'

'On your way out would you please be good enough to pass the word for Mr Turner, the new sailing master?'

'Aye aye, sir.'

That showed the subtle difference between an order and a request—but both of them had to be obeyed.

'Now, Mr Turner,' said Hornblower when Turner arrived in the cabin, 'our destination is Marmorice Bay, and we sail at dawn to-morrow. I want to know about the winds we can expect at this time of year. I want to lose no time at all in arriving there. Every hour—I may say every minute is of importance.'

Time was of importance, to make the most of a dying man's last hours.

F

XI

THESE were the blue waters where history had been made, where the future of civilization had been decided, more than once and more than twice. Here Greek had fought against Persian, Athenian against Spartan, Crusader against Saracen, Hospitaller against Turk. The pentecontres of Byzantium had furrowed the seas here, and the caracks of Pisa. Great cities had luxuriated in untold wealth. Only just over the horizon on the port beam was Rhodes, where a comparatively minor city had erected one of the seven wonders of the world, so that two thousand years later the adjective colossal was part of the vocabulary of people whose ancestors wore skins and painted themselves with woad at the time when the Rhodians were debating the nature of the Infinite. Now conditions were reversed. Here came *Atropos*, guided by sextant and compass, driven by the wind harnessed to her well-planned sails, armed with her long guns and carronades—a triumph of modern invention, in short—emerging from the wealthiest corner of the world into one where misgovernment and disease, anarchy and war, had left deserts where there had been fertile fields, villages where there had been cities, and hovels where there had been palaces. But there was no time to philosophize in this profound fashion. The sands in the hour-glass beside the binnacle were running low, and the moment was approaching when course should be altered.

'Mr Turner!'

'Sir!'

'We'll alter course when the watch is called.'

'Aye aye, sir.'

'Doctor!'

'Sir!'

'Stand by for á change of course.'

'Aye aye, sir.'

McCullum's invalid bed was disposed athwart ships between Nos. 6 and 7 carronades on the starboard side; a simple tackle attached to the bed-head enabled the level of the bed to be adjusted with the change of course, so that the patient lay as horizontal as might be, whichever way the ship might be heeling. It was the doctor's responsibility to attend to that.

The watch was being called.

'Very good, Mr Turner.'

'Headsail sheets! Hands to the braces!'

Turner was an efficient seaman, despite his age. Hornblower could be sure of that by now. He stood by and watched him lay the ship close to the wind. Still came and touched his hat to Turner to take over the watch.

'We ought to raise the Seven Capes on this tack, sir,' said Turner, coming over to Hornblower.

'I fancy so,' said Hornblower.

The passage from Malta had been comfortingly rapid. They had lain becalmed for a single night to the south of Crete, but with the morning the wind had got up again from a westerly quarter. There had not been a single breath of a Levanter—the equinox was still too far off for that, apparently—and every day had seen at least a hundred miles made good. And McCullum was still alive.

Hornblower walked forward to where he lay. Eisenbeiss was bending over him, his fingers on his pulse, and with the cessation of the bustle of going about the three Ceylonese divers had returned, to squat round the foot of the bed, their eyes on their master. To have those three pairs of melancholy eyes gazing at him would, Hornblower thought, have a most depressing effect, but apparently McCullum had no objection.

'All well, Mr McCullum?' asked Hornblower.

'Not—quite as well as I would like.'

It was distressing to see how slowly and painfully the head

turned on the pillow. The heavy beard that had sprouted
over his face could not conceal the fact that McCullum was
more hollow-cheeked, more feverish-eyed, than yesterday.
The decline had been very marked; the day they sailed
McCullum had appeared hardly more than slightly wounded,
and the second day he had seemed better still—he had
protested against being kept in bed, but that night he had
taken a turn for the worse and had sunk steadily ever since,
just as the garrison surgeon and Eisenbeiss had gloomily
predicted.

Of course those had not been his only protests. McCullum
had been as angry as his muddled condition would allow
when he emerged from his narcotic to find he was under the
treatment of the man who had shot him. He had struggled
against his weakness and his bandages. It had called for
Hornblower's personal intervention—fortunately *Atropos*
was clear of the harbour mouth when McCullum regained
consciousness—to calm him down. 'It's a blackguard trick
to pursue an affair of honour after an exchange of shots,'
Hornblower had said, and 'It's the Doctor who's attending
to you, not the Baron,' and then the clinching argument
'Don't be a fool, man. There's no other surgeon within fifty
miles. Do you want to die?' So McCullum had yielded, and
had submitted his tortured body to Eisenbeiss's ministrations, perhaps deriving some comfort from the ignoble
things the doctor had to do for him.

And now all that spirit had gone. McCullum was a very
sick man. He closed his eyes as Eisenbeiss laid his hand on
his forehead. The pale lips muttered, and Hornblower,
stooping, could only hear disjointed phrases. There was
something about 'fuses under water.' McCullum was thinking, then, of the salvage operation ahead. Hornblower
looked up and met Eisenbeiss's eyes. There was deep
concern in them, and there was the least perceptible shake
of the head. Eisenbeiss thought McCullum was going to die.

'It hurts—it hurts,' said McCullum, moaning a little.

He moved restlessly, and Eisenbeiss's large powerful hands

eased him into a more comfortable position on his left side. Hornblower noticed that Eisenbeiss laid one hand, as if inquiringly, over McCullum's right shoulder-blade, and then lower down, towards the short ribs, and McCullum moaned again. There was no change in the gravity of Eisenbeiss's expression.

This was horrible. It was horrible to see this magnificently constructed creature dying. And it was equally horrible that Hornblower was aware that his deep sympathy was allayed with concern for himself. He could not imagine how he would carry through the salvage operation with McCullum dead, or even with McCullum as helpless as he was at present. He would return empty-handed, to face Collingwood's wrath and contempt. What was the use of all his endeavours? Hornblower suddenly boiled with exasperation at the duelling convention which had claimed the life of a valuable man and at the same time had imperilled his own professional reputation. Within himself he was a whirlpool of emotions conflicting with each other.

'Land! Land ho! Land on the starboard bow!'

The cry came ringing down from the fore topmast head. No one could hear it without at least a little excitement. McCullum opened his eyes and turned his head again, but Eisenbeiss, stooping over him, endeavoured to soothe him. Hornblower's place was aft, and he turned away from the bed and walked back, trying to restrain himself from appearing too eager. Turner was already there, brought up from his watch below at the cry, and by the lee bulwark the other officers were rapidly assembling in a group.

'A good landfall, sir,' said Turner.

'An hour earlier than I was led to expect,' answered Hornblower.

'The current sets northerly here with steady winds from the West, sir,' said Turner. 'We'll raise Atairo in Rhodes to port soon, and then we'll have a cross-bearing.'

'Yes,' replied Hornblower. He was aware of his shortness of manner, but only dimly aware of its cause; he was uneasy with a sailing master on board who knew more about local conditions than he did, although that sailing master had been assigned to him to save him from uneasiness.

Atropos was shouldering her way valiantly through the short but steep seas that came hurrying forward to assail her port bow. Her motion was easy; she was carrying exactly the right amount of sail for that wind. Turner put a telescope in his pocket and walked forward to ascend the main shrouds, while Hornblower stood on the weather side with the wind blowing against his sunburned cheeks. Turner came aft again, his smile denoting self-satisfaction.

'That's the Seven Capes, sir,' he said. 'Two points on the starboard bow.'

'There's a northerly set here, you say?' asked Hornblower.

'Yes, sir.'

Hornblower walked over and looked at the compass, and up at the trim of the sails. The northerly set would help, and the wind was coming from the southward of west, but there was no sense in going unnecessarily far to leeward.

'Mr Still! You can come closer to the wind than this. Brace her up.'

He did not want to have to beat his way in at the last, and he was making allowance for the danger of the current setting in on Cape Kum.

Now here was the doctor, touching his hat to demand attention.

'What is it, doctor?' asked Hornblower.

The hands were hauling on the maintack.

'May I speak to you, sir?'

That was exactly what he was doing, and at a moment by no means opportune. But of course what he wanted was a chance to speak to him in privacy, and not on this bustling deck.

'It's about the patient, sir,' supplemented Eisenbeiss. 'I think it is very important.'

'Oh, very well,' said Hornblower, restraining himself from using bad language. He led the way down into the cabin, and seated himself to face the doctor. 'Well? What do you have to say?'

Eisenbeiss was nervous, that was plain.

'I have formed a theory, sir.'

He failed, as ever, with the 'th' sound, and the word was so unusual and his pronunciation of it was so odd that Hornblower had to think for a moment before he could guess what it was Eisenbeiss had said.

'And what is this theory?'

'It is about the position of the bullet, sir,' answered Eisenbeiss; he, too, took a moment to digest what was the English pronunciation of the word.

'The garrison surgeon at Malta told me it was in the chest cavity. Do you know any more than that?'

That expression 'chest cavity' was an odd one, but the garrison surgeon had used it. It implied an empty space, and was an obvious misnomer. Lungs and heart and the great blood-vessels must fill that cavity full.

'I believe it may not be in there at all, sir,' said Eisenbeiss, clearly taking a plunge.

'Indeed?' This might be exceedingly important news if it were true. 'Then why is he so ill?'

Now that Eisenbeiss had committed himself he became voluble again. Explanations poured out of him, accompanied by jerky gestures. But the explanations were hard to follow. In this highly technical matter Eisenbeiss had been thinking in his native language even more than usual, and now he was having to translate into technical terms unfamiliar to him and still more unfamiliar to Hornblower, who grasped despairingly at one contorted sentence.

'You think that the bullet, after breaking those ribs, may have bounced off again?' he asked. At the last moment he substituted the word 'bounce' for 'ricochet' in the hope of retaining clarity.

'Yes, sir. Bullets often do that.'

'And where do you say you think it went then?'

Eisenbeiss tried to stretch his left hand far under his right armpit; his body was too bulky to permit it to go far enough to make his demonstration quite complete.

'Under the scapula, sir—the—the shoulder-blade.'

'Land ho! Land on the port bow?'

Hornblower heard the cry come down through the sky-light from above. That must be Rhodes they had sighted. Here they were heading into Rhodes Channel, and he was down below talking about ribs and scapulas. And yet the one was as important as the other.

'I can't stay down here much longer, doctor. Tell me why you think this is the case?'

Eisenbeiss fell into explanation again. He talked about the patient's fever, and about his comparative wellbeing the morning after he had been wounded, and about the small amount of blood he had spat up. He was in the full flood of his talk when a knock at the door interrupted him.

'Come in,' said Hornblower.

It was His Serene Highness the Prince of Seitz-Bunau, with a speech that he had obviously prepared carefully on his way down.

'Mr Still's respects, sir,' he said. 'Land in sight on the port bow.'

'Very well, Mr Prince. Thank you.'

It was a pity there was not time to compliment the boy on his rapid acquirement of English. Hornblower turned back to Eisenbeiss.

'So I think the bullet went round the back, sir. The skin is—is tough, sir, and the ribs are—are elastic.'

'Yes?' Hornblower had heard of bullets going round the body before this.

'And the patient has much muscle. Much.'

'And you think the bullet has lodged in the muscles of the back?'

'Yes. Deep against the ribs. Under the lower point of the scapula, sir.'

'And the fever? The illness?'

They could be accounted for, according to Eisenbeiss's

torrential explanation, by the presence of the foreign body deep inside the tissues, especially if, as was probable, it had carried fragments of clothing in along with it. It all seemed plausible enough.

'And you are trying to say that if the bullet is there and not inside the chest you might be able to extract it?'

'Yes, sir.'

Eisenbeiss showed by his manner that he knew that those words had finally committed him.

'You think that you can do that? It means using the knife?'

As soon as Hornblower finished asking the second question he was aware that it was impolitic to ask two questions at once of a man who had enough trouble answering one. Eisenbeiss had to think a long time over the phrasing of his answers.

'It means using the knife,' he said at length. 'It means a difficult operation. I do not know if I can do it.'

'But you hope you can?'

'I hope so.'

'And do you think you will be successful?'

'I do not think. I hope.'

'And if you are not successful?'

'He will die.'

'But you think he will die in any case if you do not attempt the operation?'

That was the point. Eisenbeiss twice opened his mouth and shut it again before he answered.

'Yes.'

Down through the skylight, as Hornblower sat studying Eisenbeiss's expression, came a new cry, faintly borne from the weather main-chains.

'No bottom! No bottom with this line!'

Turner and Still had very properly decided to take a cast of the lead; they were still out of soundings, as was to be expected. Hornblower brought his mind back from the situation of the ship to the decision regarding McCullum.

The latter might have some claim to be consulted on the matter, but the claim was specious. His life was his country's. A seaman was not consulted first when he was carried into the ordeal of battle.

'So that is your opinion, doctor. If you operate and fail you will only have shortened the patient's life by a few hours?'

'A few hours. A few days.'

A few days might suffice for the salvage operation; but with McCullum as sick as he was he would be no use during those few days. On the other hand there was no knowing at present whether or not he might possibly recover after those few days, without being operated on.

'What are the difficulties of the operation?' asked Hornblower.

'There are several layers of muscle there,' explained Eisenbeiss. 'Infraspinatus. Subscapularis, many of them. In each case the—the threads run in a different direction. That makes it difficult to work quickly and yet without doing great damage. And there is the big artery, the subscapular. The patient is weak already and unable to withstand much shock.'

'Have you everything you need for this operation if you carry it out?'

Eisenbeiss hunched his thick shoulders.

'The two attendants—loblolly boys, you call them, sir— are experienced. They have both served in ships in action. I have my instruments. But I should like——'

Eisenbeiss clearly wanted something he believed to be difficult to grant.

'What?'

'I should like the ship to be still. At anchor. And a good light.'

That turned the scale of the decision.

'Before nightfall,' said Hornblower, 'this ship will be at anchor in a landlocked harbour. You can make your preparations for the operation.'

'Yes, sir.' Again a pause before Eisenbeiss asked an important question. 'And your promise, sir?'

Hornblower did not have to think very long about the question as to whether Eisenbeiss would work more efficiently or not if he were faced with the certainty of flogging and hanging if he failed. The man would do all he could out of sheer professional pride. And the thought that his life was at stake might possibly make him nervous.

'I'll take my promise back,' said Hornblower. 'You'll suffer no harm, whatever happens.'

'Thank you, sir.'

'No bottom!' called the leadsman in the chains.

'Very well, then. You have until this evening to make what preparations you can.'

'Yes, sir. Thank you, sir.'

With Eisenbeiss out of the cabin Hornblower sat for hardly a moment retracing the grounds of his decision. His ship was entering Rhodes Channel and he must be on deck.

'Wind's come southerly a point, sir,' said Still, touching his hat.

The first thing, of course, that Hornblower had noticed as he came up the companion was that *Atropos* was still braced up as close to the wind as she would lie. Still and Turner had acted correctly without troubling him about it.

'Very well, Mr Still.'

Hornblower put his glass to his eye and swept the horizon. A bold, wildly rugged coast on the one hand; on the other a low sandy shore. He bent to study the chart.

'Cape Angistro to starboard, sir,' said Turner at his side. 'Cape Kum abaft the port beam.'

'Thank you.'

Everything was as it should be. Hornblower straightened up and turned his glass upon the Turkish coast. It was steep, with bold cliffs, behind which rose a chain of steeply undulating hills.

'They're only green at this time of year, sir,' explained Turner. 'The rest of the year they're brown.'

'Yes.'

Hornblower had read all he could about the Eastern
Mediterranean, and he knew something of the climatic
conditions.

'Not many people live there now, sir,' went on Turner.
'Farmers, a few. Shepherds. Little fishing villages in some of
the coves. A little coasting trade in caiques from Rhodes—
not so much of that now, sir. There's piracy in all these
waters, on account of the feuds between the Greeks and the
Turks. There's a bit of trade in honey an' timber, but
precious little.

'Yes.'

It was fortunate the wind had backed southerly, even by
so little. It eased one of the myriad complications in his
complicated life.

'Ruins a-plenty along that coast, though, sir,' droned on
Turner. 'Cities—temples—you'd be surprised.'

Ancient Greek civilization had flourished here. Over there
had stood Artemisia and a score of other Greek cities,
pulsating with life and beauty.

'Yes,' said Hornblower.

'The villages mostly stand where the old cities were,'
persisted Turner. 'Ruins all round 'em. Half the cottages
are built of marble from the temples.'

'Yes.'

In other circumstances Hornblower could have been
deeply interested, but as it was Turner was merely distraction.
There was not merely the immediate business in hand of
taking *Atropos* up into Marmorice harbour; there was the
business of how to deal with the Turkish authorities; of how
to set about the problems of salvage; there was the question
—the urgent, anxious question—as to whether McCullum
would live. There was the routine of the ship; when Hornblower looked round him he could see the hands and the
officers clustered along the ship's sides gazing out eagerly
at the shores. There were Greeks dwelling among the
Mohammedans of the mainland—that would be important

when it came to a question of keeping liquor from the men. And he would like to fill his water barrels; and there was the matter of obtaining fresh vegetables.

Here was Still with a routine question. Hornblower nodded in agreement.

'Up spirits!'

The cry went through the little ship, and when they heard it the men had no ears for any siren song from the shore. This was the great moment of the day for most of them, when they would pour their tiny issue of rum-and-water down their eager throats. To deprive a man of his ration was like barring a saint from Paradise. The speculations that went on among the men, their dealings with their rum rations, the exchanging, the buying, the selling, made the South Sea Bubble seem small by comparison. But Hornblower decided he need not vaunt himself above the herd, he need not look down with condescension at the men as if they were Circe's hogs swilling at a trough; it was perfectly true that this was the great moment of their day, but it was because they had no other moment at all, for months and for years, confined within the wooden walls of their little ship, often seeing not a shilling of money in all that time, not a fresh face, not a single human problem on which to exercise their wits. Perhaps it was better to be a captain and have too many problems.

The hands went to dinner. Cape Kum went by on the one hand and the Turkish coast on the other, the breeze freshening with the bright sunny day, and Turner droning on as the landmarks went by.

'Cape Marmorice, sir,' reported Turner.

The coast dipped here, revealing mountains more lofty close behind. Now was the time to take in sail, ready to enter. It was the time when decisive action had to be taken, too; when Atropos changed from a peaceful ship, cruising placidly along outside territorial waters, to a stormy petrel, whose entrance into a foreign harbour might send despatches hastening from embassies, and might cause cabinets to

assemble at opposite ends of Europe. Hornblower tried to
give his orders as if he had no care for the importance of the
moment.

'All hands! All hands shorten sail! All hands!'

The watch below came running to their posts. The officers,
at the call of all hands, went to their stations, the one or two
who had been dozing down below coming hastily on deck.
Courses and top gallants were got in.

'Mr Jones!' said Hornblower harshly.

'Sir!'

'Ease that sheet and take the strain off the tack! Where
did you learn your seamanship?'

'Aye aye, sir,' answered Jones rather pathetically, but he
ran up both clues smartly together.

The reprimand was deserved, but Hornblower wondered
if he would have administered it in just that way if he had
not been anxious to show that the responsibilities he was
carrying could not distract him from any detail of the
management of the ship. Then he decided bitterly that it was
unnecessary in any event; not one of those hurrying figures
on deck gave a single thought to the responsibilities of his
captain, or of what international crisis this shortening of
sail might be the preliminary.

'Red Cliff Point, sir,' said Turner. 'Passage Island. Cape
Sari over there. The east passage is better, sir—there's a
rock in the middle of the west passage.'

'Yes,' said Hornblower. There was not much detail in
the chart, but that much was clear. 'We'll take the east
passage. Quartermaster! Port your helm. Steady! Steady as
you go!'

With the wind on her quarter *Atropos* headed for the
entrance like a stag, even with her sail reduced to topsails
and headsails. The entrance became better defined as she
approached; two bold points running to meet each other
with a lofty island in between. It was obvious why Red Cliff
Point was so named; elsewhere there was a dark, straggling
growth of pine trees on capes and island, while on the

summits could just be seen the rectangular outlines of small forts.

'They don't keep those manned, sir,' said Turner. 'Gone to rack and ruin like everything else.'

'You say the east passage is absolutely clear?'

'Yes, sir.'

'Very well.'

Atropos headed in, with Hornblower giving his orders to the wheel. There was no flag flying on shore, and until one could be seen there was no question of firing a salute. From point to island the entrance extended a scant half mile, possibly less; now they could see through it, to the wide waters of Marmorice Bay, with high mountains surrounding it on nearly every side, except to the northward.

'There's the town, sir,' said Turner. 'Not much of a place.'

A white tower—a minaret—caught the afternoon sun.

'You can see the red mound behind the town now, sir.'

'Where did the *Speedwell* go down?' asked Hornblower.

'Over to port, there, sir. Right in line between the red mound and the fort on Passage Island. The fort on Ada bore sou'-sou' east half south.'

'Take the bearing now,' ordered Hornblower.

They were through the entrance now. The water was smooth, not smooth enough to reflect the blue sky. Turner was calling the bearing of the fort on Capa Ada. With his own eye Hornblower could judge the other cross-bearing. There was no harm in anchoring close to the projected scene of operations; that would attract less attention than to anchor in one place first and to move to another anchorage later. Jones took in fore and main topsails and headsails smartly enough. *Atropos* glided quietly on.

'Hard a-starboard,' said Hornblower to the quarter-master. Round came *Atropos*, the mizzen topsail helping the turn as Jones clued it up. The ship's way died away almost imperceptibly, the tiny waves lapping against her bows.

'Let go!'

The hawser rumbled out. *Atropos* swung to her anchor, in Turkish waters. The crossing of the three-mile limit, even the entrance through the Pass, had been actions that might be argued about, disavowed. But that anchor, its flukes solidly buried in the firm sand, was something of which a diplomatic note could take definite notice.

'Pass the word for the doctor,' said Hornblower.

There were many things to do; it was his duty to make contact with the Turkish authorities if they did not make contact with him. But first of all, without wasting a moment, it was necessary to make arrangements for the operation on McCullum. The man's life hung in the balance, and far more than his life.

XII

Hornblower sat waiting in his cabin. 'A few minutes' had been Eisenbeiss's estimate of the time necessary for the operation. It was necessary, Hornblower knew, to work as quickly as possible, so as to minimize the shock to the patient.

'In the old *Hannibal*, sir,' said the sickberth attendant whom Hornblower had questioned regarding his experience, 'we took off eleven legs in half an hour. That was at Algeciras, sir.'

But amputations were relatively simple. A full half of all amputation cases survived—Nelson himself had lost an arm, amputated on a dark night in a moderate storm at sea, and he had lived until a musket bullet killed him at Trafalgar. This was not an amputation. It was something which would be worse than useless if Eisenbeiss's diagnosis was incorrect and which could easily fail in any case.

The ship was very still and quiet. Hornblower knew that all his crew were taking a morbid interest in the fate of the 'poor gentleman.' They were sentimental about McCullum, lying at death's door as a result of a bullet wound he need never have received; the fact that he was going to be cut about with a knife had an unholy attraction for them; the fact that in a few minutes he might be dead, might have gone through those mysterious doors they all feared to go through, invested his personality with some special quality in their eyes. Sentries had to be posted to keep out all the sentimental, the inquisitive, and the morbid-minded among the crew, and now Hornblower could tell by the silence that his men were waiting in shuddering silence for the climax, hoping perhaps to hear a scream or a groan, waiting as they would wait to see a condemned criminal turned off the hangman's cart. He could hear the heavy ticking of his watch as he waited.

Now there were distant sounds, but sounds in the little wooden ship were susceptible to so many possible interpretations that he would not at first allow himself to think that they might arise as a result of the ending of the operation. But then there were steps and voices outside his cabin door, the sentry speaking and then Eisenbeiss, and then came a knock.

'Come in,' said Hornblower, trying to keep his voice indifferent; the first sight of Eisenbeiss as he entered was enough to tell Hornblower that all was as well as could be hoped. There was an obvious lightheartedness about the doctor's elephantine movements.

'I found the bullet,' said Eisenbeiss. 'It was where I thought—at the inferior angle of the scapula.'

'Did you get it out?' asked Hornblower; the fact that he did not correct Eisenbeiss for omitting the 'sir' was proof— if anyone had been present to notice it—that he was not as calm as he appeared.

'Yes,' said Eisenbeiss.

He laid something on the table in front of Hornblower, with a gesture positively dramatic. It was the bullet, misshapen, flattened to an irregular disc, with a raw scratch on one surface.

'That is where my scalpel cut into it,' said Eisenbeiss proudly. 'I went straight to the right place.'

Hornblower picked the thing up gingerly to examine it.

'You see,' said Eisenbeiss, 'it was as I said. The bullet struck the ribs, breaking them, and then glanced off, passing back between the bone and the muscle.'

'Yes, I see,' said Hornblower.

'And there are these as well,' went on Eisenbeiss, laying something else in front of Hornblower with the same sort of conscious pride as a conjuror at a fair bringing the rabbit out of the hat.

'Is this the wad?' asked Hornblower, puzzled, and making no attempt to pick up the horrid little object.

'No,' said Eisenbeiss, 'that is how my forceps brought it out. But see——'

Eisenbeiss's large fingers plucked the object into successive layers.

'I have looked at these through my lens. That is a piece of a blue coat. That is a piece of silk lining. That is a piece of linen shirt. And those are threads of a knitted undershirt.'

Eisenbeiss beamed with triumph.

'The bullet carried these in with it?' asked Hornblower.

'Exactly. Of course. Between the bullet and the bone these portions were cut off, as they might be between the blades of scissors, and the bullet carried them on with it. I found them all. No wonder the wound was suppurating.'

'You address me as "sir," ' said Hornblower, realizing, now that the tension had eased, that Eisenbeiss had been omitting the honorific. 'The operation was otherwise successful as well?'

'Yes—sir,' said Eisenbeiss. 'The removal of these foreign bodies and the draining of the wound brought immediate relief to the patient.'

'He did not suffer too much?'

'Not too much. The men who were ready to hold him still had hardly anything to do. He submitted with good spirit, as he promised you he would. It was well that he lay still. I feared further injury to the lung from the broken ribs if he struggled.'

'You address me as "sir," ' said Hornblower. 'That is the last time, doctor, that I shall overlook the omission.'

'Yes—sir.'

'And the patient is going on well?'

'I left him as well as I could hope—sir. I must return to him soon, of course.'

'Do you think he will live?'

Some of the triumph evaporated from Eisenbeiss's expression as he concentrated on phrasing his reply.

'He is more likely to live now, sir,' he said. 'But with wounds—one cannot be sure.'

There was always the likelihood, the unpredictable likelihood, of a wound taking a turn for the worse, festering and killing.

'You cannot say more than that?'

'No, sir. The wound must remain open to drain. When applying the sutures I inserted a bristle——'

'Very well,' said Hornblower, suddenly squeamish. 'I understand. You had better return to him now. You have my thanks, doctor, for what you have done.'

Even with Eisenbeiss gone there was no chance of quietly reviewing the situation. A knock on the door heralded the appearance of Midshipman Smiley.

'Mr Jones' compliments, sir, and there are boats heading for us from the shore.'

'Thank you. I'll come up. And if Mr Turner's not on deck tell him I want to see him there.'

Some of the gaily-painted boats in the distance were under oars, but the nearest one was under a lateen sail, lying very close to the wind. As Hornblower watched her she took in her sail, went about, and reset it on the other tack. The lateen rig had its disadvantages. On the new tack the boat would fetch up alongside *Atropos* easily enough.

'Now listen to me, Mr Turner,' said Hornblower, reaching the decision he had had at the back of his mind—overlain until now by a host of other considerations—for the last two days. 'When you speak to them you are to tell them that we are looking for a French squadron.'

'Beg pardon, sir?'

'We are looking for a French squadron. Two sail—that will do. A ship of the line and a frigate, escaped from Corfu three weeks back. The first thing you ask is whether they have touched here.'

'Aye aye, sir.'

Turner was not very clear on the point yet.

'Admiral—Admiral Harvey has sent us in for news. He's cruising off Crete looking for them with four sail of the line. Four will do. Enough force to make them respect us.'

'I see, sir.'

'You're quite sure you do?'

'Yes, sir.'

It was irksome being dependent on Turner to interpret for him. With Spanish authorities, or French, Hornblower could have conducted his own negotiations, but not with Turks.

'Remember, that's the first thing you ask, the very first. Have two French ships touched here? Then you can go on to get permission to fill the water casks. We'll buy fresh vegetables, too, and a couple of bullocks, if we can.'

'Yes, sir.'

'Keep it in your mind all the time that we're scouting for Admiral Harvey. Don't forget it for a moment, and then everything will be all right.'

'Aye aye, sir.'

The lateen boat was nearing them fast, making surprising speed with the small evening wind; there was a respectable bubble of foam under her bow. She came running close alongside and hove-to, the lateen sail flapping until they brailed up the upper portion.

'Turks, sir, not Greeks,' said Turner.

Hornblower could have guessed that without Turner's help; the boat's crew was dressed in dirty white gowns; they wore on their heads round red hats wreathed in dirty white turbans. The grey-bearded man who stood up in the stern wore a red sash about his waist, from which hung a curved sword. He hailed *Atropos* in a thin high voice. Turner hailed back; the jargon he spoke was the lingua franca of the Levant, and Hornblower tried to guess at what was being said. Italian, French, English, Arabic, Greek, all contributed to the language, he knew. It was a little strange to hear the words 'Horatio Hornblower' come clearly through the incomprehensible remainder.

'Who is this fellow?' he asked.

'The Mudir, sir. The local Jack-in-office. Harbour master —preventive officer. He is asking about our bill of health, sir.'

'Don't forget to ask about the French ships,' said Hornblower.

'Aye aye, sir.'

The shouted conversation went on; Hornblower caught
the word 'fregata' more than once. The grey-beard in the
boat extended his hands in a negative gesture and went on
to supplement it with a further sentence.

'He says there have been no French ships in here for years,
sir,' said Turner.

'Ask him if he has heard about any along the coast or in
the islands?'

The grey-beard clearly disclaimed all knowledge.

'Tell him,' said Hornblower, 'I'll give him five pieces of
gold for news of the French.'

There was something infectious in the atmosphere, in this
Oriental talk—that was the only explanation Hornblower
could think of for his using the outlandish expression 'pieces
of gold.' There was no reason why he should not have said
'guineas' to Turner. The grey-beard shook his head again;
Hornblower, looking keenly at him, fancied that the offer
impressed him nevertheless. He asked another question and
Turner answered.

'I've told him about the British squadron in the offing,
sir,' he reported.

'Good.'

There was no harm in having the Turks believe he had a
powerful force to back him up. Now the grey-beard was
gesturing with the fingers of one hand outstretched as he
answered some question of Turner's.

'He says he wants five piastres a hogshead for us to fill
our water casks, sir,' said Turner. 'That's a shilling each.'

'Tell him—tell him I'll give him half.'

The conversation continued; the western sky was beginning to redden with the sunset as the sun sank lower. At last
the grey-beard waved in farewell, and the boat turned away
and unfurled her sail to the dying wind.

'They've gone back to spread their mats for the evening

prayer, sir,' said Turner. 'I've promised him ten guineas for everything. That gives us the right to land at the jetty over there, to fill our water casks, and to buy in the market that he'll open in the morning. He'll take his share of what we pay there, you can be sure, sir.'

'Very well, Mr Turner. Mr Jones!'

'Sir!'

'With the first light in the morning I'm going to start sweeping for the wreck. I'll have the sweep prepared now.'

'Er—aye aye, sir.'

'A hundred fathoms of one-inch line, if you please, Mr Jones. Two nine-pounder shot. Have a net made for each, and attach them ten fathoms apart at equal distances from the ends of the line. Is that clear?'

'Not—not quite, sir.'

Because he was honest about it Hornblower refrained from remarking on his slowness of comprehension.

'Take a hundred fathoms of line and attach one shot forty-five fathoms from one end and another forty-five fathoms from the other end. Is that clear now?'

'Yes, sir.'

'You can get the launch and long boat into the water now, ready for the morning. They'll carry the sweep between them, dragging the bottom for the wreck. Tell off the boats' crews for duty. I want to start work at first dawn, as I said. And we'll need grapnels and buoys to mark what we find. Nothing conspicuous—planks will do, with seventeen fathoms of line to each. You understand all that?'

'Yes, sir.'

'Carry on, then, Mr Turner, report in my cabin in fifteen minutes' time, if you please. Messenger! My compliments to the doctor, and I'd like to see him in my cabin immediately.'

Hornblower felt like a juggler at a fair, keeping half a dozen balls in the air at once. He wanted to hear from the doctor how McCullum was progressing after the operation; he wanted to discuss with Turner the question of what local

authorities might be likely to be present in Marmorice to
interfere with his work there; he wanted to make all preparations for the next morning; he wanted to be ready with
his own plans for raising the treasure if McCullum was
unable to give advice; and night orders for the care of the
ship in this harbour of doubtful neutrality had to be written;
it was only late in the evening that he remembered something
else—something of which he was reminded only by a suddenly noticed feeling of emptiness inside him. He had eaten
nothing since breakfast. He ate biscuit and cold meat,
crunching the flinty fragments hurriedly at his cabin table
before hurrying on deck again into the darkness.

It was a chilly night, and the young moon had already set.
No breath of air now ruffled the black surface of the water
of the bay, smooth enough to bear faint reflections of the
stars. Black and impenetrable was the water, beneath which
lay a quarter of a million pounds sterling. It was as impenetrable as his future, he decided, leaning on the bulwark. An
intelligent man, he decided, would go to bed and sleep,
having done all that his forethought and ingenuity could
devise, and an intelligent man would worry no further for
the moment. But he had to be very firm with himself to drive
himself to bed and allow his utter weariness of body and
mind to sweep him away into unconsciousness.

It was still dark when he was called, dark and cold, but he
ordered coffee for himself and sipped it as he dressed. Last
night when he had given the time for his being called he had
allowed for a leisurely dressing before daylight, but he felt
tense and anxious as he got out of bed, much as he had felt
on other occasions when he had been roused in the night to
take part in a cutting-out expedition or a dawn landing, and
he had to restrain himself from putting on his clothes in
haphazard fashion and hurrying on deck. He forced himself
to shave, although that was an operation which had mostly
to be carried out by touch because the hanging lamp gave
almost no illumination to the mirror. The shirt he pulled on
felt clammy against his ribs; he was struggling with his

trousers when a knock at the door brought in Eisenbeiss, reporting in obedience to overnight orders.

'The patient is sleeping well, sir,' he announced.

'Is his condition good?'

'I thought I should not disturb him, sir. He was sleeping quietly, so I could not tell if he had fever nor could I examine the wound. I can wake him if you wish, sir——'

'No, don't do that, of course. I suppose it's a good symptom that he's sleeping in any case?'

'A very good one, sir.'

'Then leave him alone, doctor. Report to me if there is any change.'

'Aye aye, sir.'

Hornblower buttoned his trousers and thrust his feet into his shoes. His eagerness to be on deck overcame his self-restraint to the extent that he was still buttoning his coat as he went up the companion. On deck as well the atmosphere seemed to be charged with that feeling of impending attack at dawn. There were the dimly-seen figures of the officers, silhouetted against the sky. To the east there was the faintest illumination, a little light reaching half-way up to the zenith, so faint as almost to be unnoticed, and its colour, in its turn, was so faint a shade of pink as hardly to be called that.

'Morning,' said Hornblower in response to the touched hats of his subordinates.

In the waist he could hear orders being quietly given—just like manning the boats for a cutting-out expedition.

'Longboat's crew starboard side,' said Smiley's voice.

'Launch's crew port side.' That was the Prince's voice. He was acquiring a better accent than Eisenbeiss's.

'There's some surface mist, sir,' reported Jones. 'But it's very patchy.'

'So I see,' replied Hornblower.

'Last night we were lying two cables' lengths from the wreck as near as makes no matter, sir,' said Turner. 'We've swung during the night, with the wind dropping, but little enough.'

'Tell me when it's light enough for you to get your bearings.'

'Aye aye, sir.'

In that short time the eastern sky had changed. One might almost have said it had darkened, but perhaps that was because with the tiny increase in the general illumination the contrast was not so marked.

'You took a third bearing at the time when *Speedwell* went down, Mr Turner?'

'Yes, sir. It was——'

'No matter.'

Turner could be relied upon to manage a simple piece of business of that sort.

'I don't expect the wreck has moved an inch, sir,' said Turner. 'There's no tide here. No scour. The two rivers that run into the Bay don't set up any current you can measure.'

'And the bottom's firm sand?'

'Firm sand, sir.'

That was something to be thankful for. In mud the wreck might have sunk beyond discovery.

'How the devil did *Speedwell* come to capsize?' asked Hornblower.

'Sheer bad luck, sir. She was an old ship, and she'd been at sea a long time. The weeds and the barnacles were thick along her waterline—she wasn't coppered high enough, sir. So they were heeling her, cleaning her port side, with the guns run out to starboard and all the weights they could shift over to starboard too. It was a still day, baking hot. Then, before you could say Jack Robinson, there came a gust out of the mountains. It caught her square on the port beam and laid her over before she could pay off. The gun ports were open and the water came up over the sills. That laid her over still more—at least, that's what the court of inquiry found, sir—and with her hatchways open the water rose over the coamings and down she went.'

'Did she right herself as she sank?'

'No, sir. I looked over at her when I heard the shout, and

I saw her keel. Bottom upwards she went. Her top-masts were
snapped clean off. They came up soon enough, main and
fore top-masts still anchored to the wreck by a shroud or
two. That was a help when it came to taking the bearings.'

'I see,' said Hornblower.

Dawn was coming up fast. It actually seemed—an optical
illusion, of course—as if great arms of colour were climbing
up the sky from the eastern horizon at a pace perceptible to
the eye.

'It's light enough now, sir,' said Turner.

'Thank you. Mr Jones! You can carry on.'

Hornblower watched them go, Turner leading the way in
the gig with his instruments and compass, Still following
behind in the launch with Smiley in the longboat attached
to the launch by the sweep. Hornblower became acutely
aware that despite the cup of coffee he had drunk he wanted
his breakfast. It seemed almost against his will that he
lingered. This dead still calm at dawn was the ideal time for
an operation of this sort; it enabled the gig to take up and
maintain a position with the least possible effort. The ripples
caused by the boat's passage, slow though it was, spread far
over the glassy surface of the Bay before dying out at last.
He saw the gig stop, and clearly over the water came the
sound of Turner's voice as he spoke through his speaking
trumpet to the other boats. They jockeyed round into
position awkwardly, like two beetles tied together with a
thread, and then they paid out the sweep between them,
manœuvred awkwardly again for a moment as they laid
themselves exactly upon the correct bearing, and then the
oars began to swing rhythmically, slowly, like the pendulum
of Fate, as the boats began to sweep the area ahead of them.
Hornblower's heart beat faster despite himself, and he
swallowed with excitement. Around him the ship was beginning her normal life. Amid the peculiar patter of bare feet
on wooden planking—a sound unlike any other on earth—
the watch below were bringing their hammocks to stow in
the nettings. Swabs and holystones, buckets and pump; the

hands not at work in the boats began the eternal daily routine of washing down the decks. Not for the first time on the voyage Hornblower found himself experiencing a momentary envy of the seamen at their work. Their problems were of the simplest, their doubts were minute. To holystone a portion of planking to the whiteness demanded by a petty officer, to swab it off, to swab it dry, working in amicable companionship with friends of long standing, dabbling their naked feet in the gush of clear water—that was all they had to do, as they had done for an infinity of mornings in the past and would do for an infinity of mornings in the future. He would be glad to exchange with them his loneliness, his responsibility, the complexity of his problems; so he felt for a moment before he laughed at himself, knowing perfectly well he would be horrified if some freak of Fate forced such an exchange on him. He turned away, changing the subject of his thoughts; a generous slice of fat pork, fried to a pale brown—there had been a leg in soak for him for the past two days, and the outside cut would be not too salt now. It would smell delicious—he could almost smell it at this very moment. Holy Jerusalem, unless it was still spluttering on his plate when it was put before him despite the journey from galley to cabin he'd make someone wish he had never been born. And he would have biscuit crumbs fried with it, and he would top it off with black treacle smeared on a biscuit, thick. That was a breakfast worth thinking about.

XIII

Hornblower stood with his purse in his hand, having taken it from his sea chest where it had lain in the inner compartment. He knew exactly how many guineas there were in it, and he was trying not to wish there were more. If he were a wealthy captain he would be generous towards his ship's company, and to the wardroom and gunroom. But as it was—— He shook his head. He did not want to appear miserly or mean, but he certainly did not want to be foolish. He walked along to the wardroom door and paused there; Still caught his eye.

'Please come in, sir.'

The other officers rose from their chairs; there was nowhere for them to sit unless they sat round the table in the tiny wardroom.

'I was hoping,' said Hornblower to Carslake the purser, 'that you would be kind enough to make some purchases for me.'

'Of course, sir. Honoured, I'm sure,' said Carslake. He could say nothing else, in any case.

'A few chickens—half a dozen, say, and some eggs.'

'Yes, sir.'

'Is it the intention of the wardroom to buy fresh meat for itself?'

'Well, sir——'

That had been the subject under discussion at his entrance.

'At this time of year there might be lambs to sell. I could have one—two young ones, if they're cheap. But an ox—what am I to do with a whole ox?'

Everyone in the wardroom had been up against this problem at some time or other.

'If the wardroom decides to buy an ox I would be glad to

189

pay a quarter of the price,' said Hornblower, and the ward-room cheered up perceptibly.

A captain who bought a share in an animal would always get the best cuts—that was in the course of nature. And they had all known captains who would pay no more than their share. But with five wardroom officers Hornblower's offer was generous.

'Thank you very much, sir,' said Carslake. 'I think I can sell a couple of joints to the gunroom.'

'On advantageous terms, I trust?' said Hornblower, with a grin.

He could remember well enough as a midshipman occasions when wardroom and gunroom had gone shares in an animal.

'I expect so, sir,' said Carslake and then, changing the subject, 'Mr Turner says that it'll be goat here, mainly. Do you care for goat, sir?'

'Young kid, stewed with turnips and carrots!' said Jones. 'You can do worse than that, sir.'

Jones's lantern-jawed face was alight with appetite. These grown men, continuously fed on preserved food, were like children at a gingerbread stall at a fair with the thought of fresh meat.

'Do what you can,' said Hornblower. 'I'll eat kid or lamb, or I'll share in an ox, as you find the market provides. You know what you're buying for the crew?'

'Yes, sir,' said Carslake.

The penny-pinching clerks of a penurious government at home would scrutinize those expenditures in time. Nothing very generous could be bought for the hands.

'I don't know what vegetables we'll find, sir, at this time of year,' went on Carslake, 'winter cabbage, I suppose.'

'Nothing wrong with winter cabbage,' interposed Jones.

'Carrots and turnips out of winter store,' said Carslake. 'They'll be pretty stringy, sir.'

'Better than nothing,' said Hornblower. 'There won't be enough in the market for all we need, nor will there be until the word goes round the countryside. So much the better. Then we'll have an excuse to linger. You're going to interpret, Mr Turner?'

'Yes, sir.'

'Keep your eyes open. And your ears.'

'Aye aye, sir.'

'Mr Jones, you will attend to the water casks, if you please.'

'Aye aye, sir.'

That was the transition between the social visit and the official issuing of orders.

'Carry on.'

Hornblower went to the bedside where McCullum lay. Sailcloth pillows supported him in a position half on his side. It was a comfort to see how comparatively well he looked. The fever and its accompanying distortion of thought had left him.

'Glad to see you looking so well, Mr McCullum,' said Hornblower.

'Well enough,' answered McCullum.

He croaked a little, but his speech was almost normal.

'A full night's sleep,' said Eisenbeiss, hovering on the far side of the bed. He had already made his report to Hornblower—the wound showed every sign of healing, the sutures had not at least as yet caused undue inflammation, and the draining where the bristle kept the wound in the back open had been apparently satisfactory.

'And we've started a full morning's work,' said Hornblower. 'You have heard that we have located the wreck?'

'No. I had not heard that.'

'It's located and buoyed,' said Hornblower.

'Are you sure it is the wreck?' croaked McCullum. 'I've known some queer mistakes made.'

'It is exactly where the bearings were taken when she sank,' said Hornblower. 'It is the right size as far as the sweep can show. And no other obstructions were found by the sweep, either. The bottom here is firm sand, as I expect you know.

'It sounds plausible,' said McCullum grudgingly. 'I could have wished I'd had the direction of the sweeping, nevertheless.'

'You must trust me, Mr McCullum,' said Hornblower patiently.

' 'Tis little that I know about you and your capabilities,' answered McCullum.

Hornblower, swallowing his irritation at that remark, wondered how McCullum had managed to live so long without previously being shot in a duel. But McCullum was the irreplaceable expert, and even if he were not a sick man it would be both foolish and undignified to quarrel with him.

'I presume the next thing to do is to send your divers down to report on the condition of the wreck,' he said, trying to be both firm and polite.

'Undoubtedly that will be the first thing I do as soon as I am allowed out of this bed,' said McCullum.

Hornblower thought of all that Eisenbeiss had told him about McCullum's wound, about gangrene and suppuration and general blood-poisoning, and he knew there was a fair chance that McCullum would never rise from his bed.

'Mr McCullum,' he said, 'this is an urgent matter. Once the Turks get wind of what we want to do, and can assemble sufficient force to stop us, we will never be allowed to conduct salvage operations here. It is of the first importance that we get to work as quickly as we can. I was hoping that you would instruct your divers in their duties so that they could start now, immediately.'

'So that is what you were thinking, is it?' said McCullum.

It took some minutes of patient argument to wear McCullum down, and the grudging agreement that McCullum gave was tempered by an immediate pointing out of the difficulties.

'That water's mortal cold,' said McCullum.

'I'm afraid so,' answered Hornblower, 'but we have always expected that.'

'The Eastern Mediterranean in March is nothing like the Bay of Bengal in summer. My men won't stand it for long.'

It was a great advance that McCullum should admit that they might stand it at all.

'If they work for short intervals——?' suggested Hornblower.

'Aye. Seventeen fathoms beside the wreck?'

'Seventeen fathoms all round it,' said Hornblower.

'They can't work for long at that depth in any case. Five dives a day will be all. Then they bleed at the nose and ears. They'll need lines and weights—nine-pounder shot will serve.'

'I'll have them got ready,' said Hornblower.

Hornblower stood by while McCullum addressed his divers. He could guess at the point of some of the speeches. One of the divers was raising objections; it was clear, when he clasped his arms about his chest and shuddered dramatically with a rolling of his pathetic dark eyes, what he was saying. All three of them talked at once for a space in their twittering language. A sterner note came into McCullum's voice when he replied, and he indicated Hornblower with a gesture, directing all eyes to him for a moment. All three clung to each other and shrank away from him like frightened children. McCullum went on speaking, energetically—Eisenbeiss leaned over him and restrained the left hand that gesticulated; the right was strapped into immobility against McCullum's chest.

'Do not move,' said Eisenbeiss. 'We shall have an inflammation.'

McCullum had winced more than once after an incautious movement, and his appearance of well-being changed quickly to one of fatigue.

'They'll start now,' he said at length, his head back on his pillow. 'You can take 'em. Looney, here—that's what I call him—will be in charge. I've told 'em there are no sharks. Generally when one of 'em's down at the bottom the other

two pray against sharks—they're all three of 'em shark
doctors. A good thing they've seen men flogged on board
here. I promised 'em you'd give 'em a taste of the cat if there
was any nonsense.'

Hornblower had seen very plainly what the reactions of
these twittering, bird-like creatures had been to that horror.

'Take 'em away,' said McCullum, lying back on his
pillow.

With longboat and launch over at the far side of the Bay
for stores and water only the gig and the tiny jolly boat were
available. The gig was uncomfortably crowded but it served,
with four hands at the oars, Hornblower and Leadbitter in
the stern—Hornblower felt he could not possibly endure not
taking part in this first essay—and the Ceylonese crowded
into the bows. Hornblower had formed a shrewd notion
about the extent of McCullum's ability to speak the divers'
language. He had no doubt that McCullum made no
attempt to speak it accurately or with any attempt at
inflection. He made his points, Hornblower guessed, with a
few nouns and verbs and some energetic gestures. Mc-
Cullum's command of the Ceylonese tongue could not
compare with Hornblower's Spanish, nor even with his
French. Hornblower felt a sense of grievance about that,
as he sat with his hand on the tiller and steered the gig over
the dancing water—already the flat calm of dawn had given
way to a moderate breeze that ruffled the surface.

They reached the first of the buoys—a plank wallowing
among the wavelets at the end of its line—and Hornblower
stood to identify the others. A stroke or two of the oars
carried the gig into the centre of the area, and Hornblower
looked down the boat to where the divers huddled together.

'Looney,' he said.

Now that he had been paying special attention to them he
could distinguish each of the three divers from the others.
Until that time they might as well have been triplets as far
as his ability went to tell them apart.

'Looney,' said Hornblower again.

Looney rose to his feet and dropped the grapnel over the side. It went down fast, taking out the coiled-down line rapidly over the gunwale. Slowly Looney took off his clothes until he stood naked. He sat himself on the gunwale and swung his legs over. As his feet felt the cold of the water he cried out, and the other two joined with him in cries of alarm or commiseration.

'Shall I give 'im a shove, sir?' asked the hand at the bow oar.

'No,' said Hornblower.

Looney was sitting systematically inflating and deflating his chest, inhaling as deeply as he could, forcing air into his lungs. Hornblower could see how widely the ribs moved at each breath. One of the other two Ceylonese put a cannon-ball into Looney's hands, and he clasped it to his naked chest. Then he let himself slip from the gunwale and disappeared below the surface, leaving the gig rocking violently.

Hornblower took out his watch; it had no second-hand —watches with second-hands were far too expensive for him to afford—but he could measure the time roughly. He watched the tip of the minute hand creep from one mark to the next, from there to the next, and into the third minute. He was concentrating so deeply on the task that he did not hear Looney break water; his attention was called by a word from Leadbitter. Looney's head was visible twenty yards astern, his long thick switch of black hair, tied with a string, beside his ear.

'Back water!' said Hornblower promptly. 'Pay out that line, there!'

The second order was understood clearly enough by the Ceylonese, or at least they knew their business, for as a vigorous stroke or two sent the gig down to Looney one of them attended to the line over the bows. Looney put his hands up to the gunwale and the other two pulled him on board. They talked volubly, but Looney at first sat still on the thwart, his head down by his thighs. Then he lifted his head, the water streaming from his wet hair. Clearly he

talked about the cold—that sharp breeze must have been icy
upon his wet skin—for the others towelled him and assisted
him to cover himself with his clothes.

Hornblower wondered how he would set them to work
again, but there was no need for him to interfere. As soon as
Looney had his white garments about his shoulders he stood
up in the bows of the gig and looked about him, considering.
Then he pointed to a spot in the water a few yards away,
looking round at Hornblower.

'Give way!' said Hornblower.

One of the Ceylonese hauled in on the grapnel and let it go
again when the boat reached the spot indicated. Now it was
his turn to strip, to inflate and deflate his chest, and to take
a cannonball into his hands and drop over the side. Cannon-
balls cost money, thought Hornblower, and a time might
come when he would need them to fire at the enemy. It
would be better in the future to play in a supply of small
rocks gathered on the shore. The diver came up to the
surface and scrambled on board, to be received by his com-
panions just as Looney had been. There was some kind of
discussion among the divers, which was ended by the third
one going down in the same place, apparently to settle the
point in dispute. What he discovered led on his return to
Looney requesting by signs a further shifting of the gig, and
then Looney took off his clothes again to go down.

The divers were working industriously and, as far as
Hornblower could see, intelligently. Later on Looney and
one of his mates made a simultaneous descent, and it was on
this occasion that Hornblower noticed that Looney's legs
and feet, when he climbed in, were scratched and bleeding.
For a moment Hornblower thought of sharks and similar
underwater perils, but he revised his opinion at once. Looney
must have been scrambling about on the wreck itself. There
were decaying timbers down there, deep in the bright water,
overgrown with barnacles and razor-edged sea shells. Hornblower felt confirmed in his opinion when Looney desired to
buoy this particular spot. They anchored a plank there by a

grapnel, and then dived more than once again in the neighbourhood.

Now the divers were exhausted, lying doubled up and huddled together beside the bow thwart.

'Very well, Looney,' said Hornblower, and he pointed back to the ship.

Looney gave him a weary nod.

'Up anchor,' ordered Hornblower, and the gig pulled back towards *Atropos*.

A mile away were visible the lug sails of longboat and launch also on their return journey, coming down with the freshening wind abeam. It seemed to Hornblower as if things could never happen to him one at a time; he had hardly set foot on the deck of the *Atropos* before they were running alongside, and as the Ceylonese made their weary way forward to report to McCullum here were Carslake and Turner demanding his attention.

'The water casks are refilled, sir,' said Carslake. 'I used the little stream that comes in half a mile from the town. I thought that would be better than those in the town.'

'Quite right, Mr Carslake,' said Hornblower. On account of what he had seen in North Africa, Hornblower agreed with Carslake that a water supply that had not passed through a Turkish town would be preferable.

'What stores did you get?'

'Very little, sir, to-day, I'm afraid.'

'There was only the local market, sir,' supplemented Turner. 'The Mudir has only sent out word to-day. The goods will be coming in for sale to-morrow.'

'The Mudir?' asked Hornblower. That was the word Turner had used before.

'The head man, sir, the local governor. The old man with the sword who came out to us in the boat yesterday.'

'And he is the Mudir?'

'Yes, sir. The Mudir is under the Kaimakam, and the Kaimakam is under the Vali, and the Vali is under the Grand

Vizier, and he's under the Sultan, or at least that's how it's supposed to be—all of 'em try to be independent when they get the chance.'

'I understand that,' said Hornblower.

No one who had given any study at all to the military and naval history of the last few years in the Eastern Mediterranean could be ignorant of the anarchy and disintegration prevailing in the Turkish Empire. What Hornblower wanted to hear about was the effect these were producing locally and to-day. He turned back to Carslake to listen patiently first to his account of what had been bought and what would be available later.

'I bought all the eggs there were, sir. Two and a half dozen,' said Carslake in the course of his report.

'Good,' said Hornblower, but without any fervour, and that was clear proof that his mind was not on what Carslake was saying. Normally the thought of eggs, boiled, scrambled, or poached, would have excited him. The untoward events at Malta had prevented his buying any there for himself. He had not even laid in a store of pickled eggs at Deptford.

Carslake droned himself to a stop.

'Thank you, Mr Carslake,' said Hornblower. 'Mr Turner, come below and I'll hear what you have to say.'

Turner had apparently kept his eyes and ears open, as Hornblower had ordered him to.

'The Mudir has no force here at all worth mentioning, sir,' said Turner, his wizened old face animated and lively. 'I doubt if he could raise twenty-five armed men all told. He came down with two guards as old as himself.'

'You spoke with him?'

'Yes, sir. I gave him—Mr Carslake and I gave him—ten guineas to open the market for us. Another ten guineas to-morrow, is what we've promised him.'

No harm in keeping local authority on his side as long as possible, thought Hornblower.

'And was he friendly?' he asked.

'We-ell, sir. I wouldn't say that, not exactly, sir. Maybe

it was because he wanted our money. I wouldn't call him friendly, sir.'

He would be reserved and cautious, Hornblower decided, not anxious to commit himself without instructions from superior authority, and yet not averse to pocketing twenty pieces of gold—pickings for an average year, Hornblower guessed—when the opportunity presented itself.

'The Vali's carried off the local army, sir,' went on Turner. 'That was plain enough from the way the Mudir talked. But I don't know why, sir. Maybe there's trouble with the Greeks again. There's always trouble in the Archipelago.'

Rebellion was endemic among the Greek subjects of Turkey. Fire and sword, massacre and desolation, piracy and revolt, swept islands and mainland periodically. And nowadays with French influence penetrating from the Seven Islands, and Russia taking a suspiciously humanitarian interest in the welfare of Turkey's Orthodox subjects, there were fresh sources of trouble and unrest.

'One point's clear, anyway,' said Hornblower, 'and that is that the Vali's not here at present.'

'That's so, sir.'

It would take time for a message to reach the Vali, or even the Vali's subordinate, the—the Kaimakam, decided Hornblower, fishing the strange title out of his memory with an effort. The political situation was involved beyond any simple disentanglement. Turkey had been Britain's enthusiastic ally recently, when Bonaparte had conquered Egypt and invaded Syria and threatened Constantinople. But Russia and Turkey were chronic enemies—they had fought half a dozen wars in the last half century—and now Russia and England were allies, and Russia and France were enemies, even though since Austerlitz there was no way in which they could attack each other. There could be no doubt in the world that the French ambassador in Constantinople was doing his best to incite Turkey to a fresh war with Russia; no doubt at all that Russia since the days of

Catherine the Great was casting covetous eyes on Constantinople and the Dardanelles.

The Greek unrest was an established fact. So was the
ambition of the local Turkish governors. The tottering
Turkish government would seize any opportunity to play off
one possible enemy against the other, and would view with
the deepest suspicion—there was even the religious factor to
be borne in mind—any British activity amid Turkish posses-
sions. With England and France locked in a death struggle
the Turks could hardly be blamed if they suspected England
of buying Russia's continued alliance with a promise of a
slice of Turkish territory; luckily France, with a far worse
record, was liable to be similarly suspected. When the Sultan
heard—if ever he did hear—of the presence of a British ship
of war in Marmorice Bay, he would wonder what intrigues
were brewing with the Vali, and if Sultan or Vali heard that
a quarter of a million in gold and silver lay at the bottom of
Marmorice Bay it could be taken for granted that none would
be salvaged unless the lion's share went into Turkish hands.

There was just no conclusion to be reached after all this
debate, except for the one he had reached a week ago, and
that was to effect as prompt a recovery of the treasure as
possible and to leave the diplomats to argue over a *fait
accompli*. He walked forward to hear from McCullum's lips
how much had been learned regarding this possibility.

McCullum had just finished hearing what the divers had
reported to him. They were squatting round his cot, with all
the attention of their big eyes concentrated on his face, and
with all their clothes draped about them until they looked
something like beehives.

'She is there,' said McCullum. Apparently he had been
quite prepared to find that some gross blunder or other had
been committed, either in plotting the original bearings or
in the recent sweeping operations.

'I'm glad to hear it,' replied Hornblower, as politely as he
could make himself endure these temperamental liberties of
an expert and an invalid.

'She's greatly overgrown, except for her copper, but she shows no sign of breakingup at all.'

A wooden ship, fastened together with wooden pegs, and untouched by storm or current, might well lie for ever on a sandy bed without disintegration.

'Did she right herself?' asked Hornblower.

'No. She's nearly bottom up. My men could tell bow from stern.'

'That's fortunate,' said Hornblower.

'Yes.' McCullum referred to some pages of written notes that he held in his free hand. 'The money was in the lower lazarette, aft, abaft the mizzen mast and immediately below the main deck. A ton and a half of coined gold in iron chests and nearly four tons of coined silver in bags.

'Ye-es,' said Hornblower, trying to look as if that exactly agreed with his own calculations.

'The lazarette was given an additional lining of oak to strengthen it before the treasure was put on board,' went on McCullum. 'I expect the money's still there.'

'You mean——?' asked Hornblower, quite at a loss.

'I mean it will not have fallen through the deck on to the sea bottom,' said McCullum, condescending to explain to this ignorant amateur.

'Of course,' said Hornblower, hastily.

'*Speedwell's* main cargo was half the battering train of the army,' went on McCullum. 'Ten long eighteen pounders. Bronze guns. And the shot for them. Iron shot.'

'That's why she went down the way she did,' said Hornblower brightly. As he spoke he realized as well the implications of the words 'bronze' and 'iron' which McCullum had accented. Bronze would endure under water longer than iron.

'Yes,' said McCullum. 'As soon as she heeled, guns and shot and all would shift. I'll wager on that, from what I know of first mates in these days. With the war, any jumped-up apprentice is a first mate.'

'I've seen it myself,' said Hornblower, sorrowfully.

'But that's neither here nor there,' went on McCullum.

'Looney here says she is still, most of her, above the sand. He could get in under the break of the poop, just.'

From McCullum's significant glance when he made this announcement Hornblower could guess that it was of great importance, but it was hard to see just why this should be.

'Yes?' said Hornblower, tentatively.

'Do you think they can break in through the ship's side with crowbars?' asked McCullum testily. 'Five minutes' work on the bottom a day each for three men! We'd be here a year.'

Hornblower suddenly remembered the 'leather fuse-hoses' for which McCullum had indented at Malta. He made a hasty guess, despite the fantastic nature of what he had to say.

'You're going to blow up the wreck?' he said.

'Of course. A powder charge in that angle should open the ship at exactly the right place.'

'Naturally,' said Hornblower. He was dimly aware that it was possible to explode charges under water, but his knowledge of the technical methods to be employed was dimmer still.

'We'll try the fuse-hoses first,' announced McCullum. 'But I've little hope of them at that depth. The joints can't resist the pressure.'

'I suppose not,' said Hornblower.

'I expect it'll mean a flying fuse in the end,' said McCullum. 'These fellows here are always afraid of 'em. But I'll do it.'

The bulky figure of Eisenbeiss loomed up beside the cot. He put one hand on McCullum's forehead and the other on his wrist.

'Take your hands off me!' snarled McCullum. 'I'm busy.'

'You must not do too much,' said Eisenbeiss. 'Excitement increases the morbid humours.'

'Morbid humours be damned!' exclaimed McCullum. 'And you be damned, too.'

'Don't be a fool, man,' said Hornblower, his patience exhausted. 'He saved your life yesterday. Don't you remember how sick you were? "It hurts. It hurts." That's what you were saying.'

Hornblower found his voice piping in imitation of Mc-Cullum's yesterday, and he turned his face feebly from side to side like McCullum's on the pillow. He was aware that it was an effective bit of mimicry, and even McCullum was a trifle abashed by it.

'Sick I may have been,' he said, 'but I'm well enough now.'

Hornblower looked across at Eisenbeiss.

'Let Mr McCullum have five more minutes,' he said. 'Now, Mr McCullum, you were talking about leather fuse-hoses. Will you please explain how they are used?'

XIV

HORNBLOWER came forward to where the gunner and his mates were squatting on the deck at work upon the fuse-hose in accordance with McCullum's instructions.

'You are making a thorough job of those seams, I hope, Mr Clout,' he said.

'Aye aye, sir,' said Clout.

They had an old sail spread out to sit on, for the purpose of saving the spotless deck from the warm pitch in the iron pot beside them.

'Five seconds to the foot, this quick match burns, sir. You said one foot of slow match, sir?'

'I did.'

Hornblower bent to look at the work. The leather hose was in irregular lengths, from three to five feet; it was typical of the cross-grained ways of nature that animals could not provide longer pieces of leather than that. One of the gunner's mates was at work with a slender wooden bodkin, dragging the end of a vast length of quick match through a section of hose. When the bodkin emerged he proceeded to slip the hose along the quick match until it joined the preceding section.

'Easy with that, now,' said Clout. 'We don't want a break in that match.'

The other gunner's mate set to work with needle and palm to sew and double sew the new length to its neighbour. The joint completed, Clout proceeded to apply warm pitch liberally over the joint and down the seam of the new section. Eventually there would be a hundred and twenty feet of hose joined and pitched and with quick match threaded all the way through it.

'I've picked a couple of sound kegs, sir,' said Clout.

'Fifty-pound kegs, they are. I have bags of dry sand to fill 'em up.'

'Very well,' said Hornblower.

Thirty pounds of powder was what McCullum wanted for his explosive charge, no more and no less.

'I don't want to shatter the wreck to pieces,' McCullum had said. 'I only want to split her open.'

That was a part of McCullum's special knowledge; Hornblower could not possibly have guessed how much powder, at a depth of a hundred feet, would achieve this result. In a long nine-pounder, he knew, three pounds of powder would throw the shot a mile and a half, random shooting, but this was something entirely different, and in the incompressible medium of water, too. With a fifty-pound keg and only thirty pounds of powder it was necessary to have some indifferent substance like sand to fill the keg full.

'Send me word the moment you are ready,' said Hornblower, and turned back aft again.

Here was Turner, newly come from the shore, hovering about to attract his attention.

'Well, Mr Turner?'

Turner kept his distance, his manner indicating that he had something very private to say. He spoke in a low voice when Hornblower walked over to him.

'Please, sir, it's the Mudir. He wants to visit you. I can't make him out, but there's something he wants.'

'What did you tell him?'

'I said—I'm sorry, sir, but I didn't know what else to do—I said you'd be delighted. There's something fishy, I think. He said he'd come at once.'

'He did, did he?'

Things were bound to be fishy in these troubled waters, thought Hornblower, with a simultaneous disapproval of the style of that sentiment.

'Midshipman of the watch!'

'Sir!'

'What do you see over towards the town?'

Smiley trained his glass across the Bay.

'Boat putting out, sir. She's the same lateen we saw before.'

'Any flag?'

'Yes, sir. Red. Turkish colours, it looks like.'

'Very well. Mr Jones, we're going to have an official visitor. You may pipe the side for him.'

'Aye aye, sir.'

'Now, Mr Turner, you don't know what the Mudir wants?'

'No, sir. He wanted to see you, urgently, it seems like. "Il capitano" was all he'd say when we landed—the market was supposed to be ready for us, but it wasn't. What he wanted was to see the Captain, and so I said you'd see him.'

'He gave no hint?'

'No, sir. He wouldn't say. But he was agitated, I could see.'

'Well, we'll know soon enough,' said Hornblower.

The Mudir mounted to the deck with a certain dignity, despite the difficulties the awkward ascent presented to his old legs. He looked keenly about him as he came on board; whether or not he understood the compliment that was being paid him by the bosn's mates and the sideboys could not be determined. There was a keen hawk-like face above the white beard, and a pair of lively dark eyes took in the scene about him without revealing whether it was a familiar one or not. Hornblower touched his hat and the Mudir replied with a graceful gesture of his hand to his face.

'Ask him if he will come below,' said Hornblower. 'I'll lead the way.'

Down in the cabin Hornblower offered a chair, with a bow, and the Mudir seated himself. Hornblower sat opposite him with Turner at his side. The Mudir spoke and Turner translated.

'He hopes God has given you the gift of health, sir,' said Turner.

'Make the correct reply,' said Hornblower.

As he spoke he met the glance of the sharp brown eyes and smiled politely.

'Now he's asking you if you have had a prosperous voyage, sir,' reported Turner.

'Say whatever you think fit,' answered Hornblower.

The conversation proceeded from one formal politeness to another. This was the way of the Levant, Hornblower knew. It could be neither dignified nor tactful to announce one's business in one's opening sentences.

'Should we offer him a drink?' asked Hornblower.

'Well, sir, it's usual over business to offer coffee.'

'Then don't you think we'd better?'

'You see, sir, it's the coffee—it'll be different from what he calls coffee.'

'We can hardly help that. Give the order, if you please.'

The conversation continued, still without reaching any point. It was interesting to note how an intelligent and mobile face like the Mudir's could give no hint at all of any emotion behind it. But the coffee brought about a change. The sharp eyes took in the thick mugs, the battered pewter coffee pot, while the face remained impassive, and while the Mudir was going through the ceremony of polite refusal and then grateful acceptance; but the tasting of the coffee effected a transformation. Willy nilly, the Mudir could not prevent an expression of surprise, even though he instantly brought his features under control again. He proceeded to sweeten his coffee to a syrup with sugar, and he did not touch the cup, but raised it to his lips by means of the saucer.

'There ought to be little cakes and sweetmeats, too, sir,' said Turner. 'But we couldn't offer him blackstrap and biscuit.'

'I suppose not,' said Hornblower.

The Mudir sipped cautiously at his coffee again, and resumed his speech.

'He says you have a very fine ship, sir,' said Turner. 'I think he is coming to the point soon.'

'Thank him and tell him what a wonderful village he has, if you think that's the right thing,' said Hornblower.

The Mudir sat back in his chair—it was plain that he was not accustomed to chairs—studying first Hornblower's face and then Turner's. Then he spoke again; his voice was well modulated, well controlled.

'He's asking if *Atropos* is going to stay long, sir,' said Turner.

It was the question Hornblower was expecting.

'Say that I have not completed my stores yet,' he said.

He was quite sure that the preliminary operations of salvage, sweeping for the wreck, buoying it, and sending down the divers, had escaped observation, or at least would be quite unintelligible from the shore. He did not take his eyes from the Mudir's face as Turner translated and the Mudir replied.

'He says he presumes you will be leaving as soon as you've done that,' said Turner.

'Tell him it's likely.'

'He says this would be a good place to wait for information about French ships, sir. The fishing boats often come in with news.'

'Tell him I have my orders.'

The suspicion began to form in Hornblower's mind that the Mudir did not want *Atropos* to leave. Perhaps he wanted to keep him here until an ambush could be laid, until the guns at the fort could be manned, until the Vali returned with the local army. This was a good way to carry on a diplomatic conversation. He could watch the Mudir all the time, while any unguarded statement of Turner's could be disavowed on the grounds of poor translation if no other way.

'We can keep an eye on the Rhodes Channel from here, sir, he says,' went on Turner. 'It's the most likely course for any Frenchy. It looks as if he wants to get his twenty guineas, sir.'

'Maybe so,' said Hornblower, trying to convey by his

tone that he saw no need for Turner to contribute to the conversation. 'Say that my orders give me very little discretion.'

With the conversation taking this turn it was obvious that the best tactics would be to display a reluctance that might with great difficulty be overcome. Hornblower hoped that Turner's command of lingua franca was equal to this demand upon it.

The Mudir replied with more animation than he had previously shown; it was as if he were about to show his hand.

'He wants us to stay here, sir,' said Turner. 'If we do there'll be much better supplies coming in from the country.'

That was not his real reason, obviously.

'No,' said Hornblower. 'If we can't get the supplies we'll go without them.'

Hornblower was having to be careful about the expression on his face; he had to say these things to Turner as if he really meant them—the Mudir was not letting anything escape his notice.

'Now he's coming out in the open, sir,' said Turner. 'He's asking us to stay.'

'Then ask him why he wants us to.'

This time the Mudir spoke for a long time.

'So that's it, sir,' reported Turner. 'Now we know. There are pirates about.'

'Tell me exactly what he said, if you please, Mr Turner.'

'There are pirates along the coast, sir,' explained Turner, accepting the rebuke. 'A fellow called Michael—Michael the—the Slayer of Turks, sir. I've heard of him. He raids these coasts. A Greek, of course. He was at Fettech two days back. That's just along the coast, sir.'

'And the Mudir's afraid this'll be the next place he raids?'

'Yes, sir. I'll ask him so as to make sure, sir,' added Turner, when Hornblower glanced at him.

The Mudir was quite eloquent now that he had taken the plunge. Turner had to listen for a long time before he could resume his translation.

'Michael burns the houses, sir, and takes the women and

cattle. He's the sworn enemy of the Mohammedans. That's where the Vali is with the local army, sir. He went to head off Michael, but he guessed wrong. He went to Adalia, and that's a week's march away, sir.'

'I see.'

With *Atropos* lying in Marmorice Bay a pirate would never venture in, and the Mudir and his people were safe as long as she stayed there. The purpose of the Mudir's visit was plain; he wanted to persuade Hornblower to stay until this Michael was at a safe distance again. It was a remarkable piece of good fortune; it was, thought Hornblower, ample compensation for the freak of fate which had left McCullum wounded in a duel. In the same way that in a long enough session the whist player found that the luck evened itself out, so it was with war. Good luck followed bad—and for Hornblower that was an astonishing admission, although he was ready enough to admit that bad luck followed good. But he must on no account show any pleasure.

'It's a stroke of luck for us, sir,' said Turner.

'Please keep your conclusions to yourself, Mr Turner,' said Hornblower bitingly.

The tone of his voice and Turner's crestfallen expression puzzled the Mudir, who had not ceased to watch them closely. But he waited patiently for the unbelievers to make the next move.

'No,' said Hornblower decisively, 'tell him I can't do it.'

At Hornblower's shake of the head the Mudir actually showed a little dismay even before Turner translated. He stroked his white beard and spoke again, choosing his words carefully.

'He's offering to bribe us, sir,' said Turner. 'Five lambs or kids for every day we stay here.'

'That's better,' said Hornblower. 'Tell him I'd rather have money.'

It was the Mudir's turn to shake his head when he heard what Turner had to say. He looked, to Hornblower's searching eye, like a man quite sincere.

'He says there isn't any money, sir. The Vali took all there was when he was here last.'

'He has our twenty guineas, anyway. Tell him I want them back, and six lambs a day—no kids—and I'll stay.'

That was how it was decided in the end. With Turner escorting the Mudir back in the launch Hornblower went forward to inspect the gunner's work. It was nearly completed. A hundred odd feet of hose, carefully coiled, lay on the deck, and one end disappeared into a powder keg covered over with canvas which the gunner was smearing thickly with pitch. Hornblower stooped to examine what must be the weakest point, where the canvas cover of the keg was sewn round the hose.

'That's as good as I can make it, sir,' said the gunner. 'But it's a mighty long length of hose.'

At a hundred feet below water the pressures were enormous. A minute, indetectable pinprick anywhere in the fabric and water would be forced in.

'We can try it,' said Hornblower. 'The sooner the better.'

That was how it always was—'the sooner the better' might be found written on a naval officer's heart like Queen Mary's Calais. Man the gig, see that all necessary equipment was packed into it, herd the divers into the bows after their last-minute instructions from McCullum, and start off without a minute wasted. Drink coffee with a Turkish Mudir at one hour, and dabble in underwater explosives the next. If variety was the spice of life, thought Hornblower, his present existence must be an Oriental curry.

'Easy!' he ordered, and the gig drifted slowly up to the moored plank which marked the accessible point of the wreck underneath.

Looney knew his business. The canvas-covered powder keg lay beside him; it was bound with line, and Looney took another short length of line, secured one end to the keg, passed the line round the mooring line of the buoy, and secured the other end to the keg again. He checked to see that the free end of the fuse-hose was properly fastened to

the empty keg that was to buoy it up, and then gave a piping
order to one of his colleagues, who stood up to take off his
clothes. Looney laid hold of the powder keg, but it was too
heavy for his spindly arms.

'Help him, you two,' said Hornblower to the two seamen
nearest. 'See that the line's clear and see that the hose is
clear, too.'

Under Looney's direction the powder keg was lifted up
and lowered over the side.

'Let go! Handsomely! Handsomely!' ordered Hornblower.

It was a tense moment—one more tense moment—to
watch the powder keg sink below the choppy surface. By the
line attached to it the seamen lowered it slowly down, the
fuse-hose uncoiling after it as the keg sank. The loop of line
which Looney had passed round the mooring line of the
buoy made certain that the keg would sink to the right
place.

'Bottom, sir,' said a seaman, as the lowering line went
slack in his hands. Several feet of hose remained in the boat.

The diver was sitting on the opposite gunwale; he carried
a sheath knife on a string round his naked waist, and he took
in his hands the cannon ball that Looney gave him. Then
he lowered himself over and vanished under the surface.
They waited until he came up; they waited while the next
diver went down and came up again, they waited while
Looney took his turn too. Dive succeeded dive; apparently
it was not too easy an operation to move the powder keg to
exactly the right place under the break of the *Speedwell's*
poop. But presumably, down below the surface, the thing
was achieved in the end. Looney came up from what seemed
to be an extra long dive; he had to be helped over the gunwale and he lay gasping in the bows for some time recovering.
Then at last he sat up and made to Hornblower the un-
mistakable gesture of handling flint and steel.

'Strike a light,' said Hornblower to Leadbitter. In all his
life he had never properly acquired the knack of it.

Leadbitter opened the tinder box, and struck, and struck

again. It did not take Leadbitter more than six times before he succeeded. He bent and blew the spark on the tinder into life, took the piece of slow match and caught the fire on it, blew that into life too, and looked to Hornblower for further orders.

'I'll do it,' said Hornblower.

Leadbitter handed him the glowing match, and Hornblower sat with it in his hand for a second while he checked once more to see that all was ready. He was tingling with excitement.

'Stand by with the cask!' he said. 'Leadbitter, have the stopper ready.'

There were four or five inches of quick match hanging out of the fuse-hose; Hornblower dabbed the glowing match upon it. A second's hesitation and it took fire. Hornblower watched the spark run along the quick match and vanish down into the hose.

'Stopper it!' said Hornblower, and Leadbitter forced the wooden stopper into the end of the hose, grinding down upon the brittle ashes of the match.

At five seconds to the foot the fire was now, he hoped, travelling down the hose, down, down, far below the level of the sea. At the far end, next to the powder keg, there was a foot of slow match. That burned at five minutes to the foot; they had plenty of time—no need for feverish haste, however great the urge to hurry.

'Over with it!' said Hornblower, and Leadbitter picked up the empty cask and lowered it gently into the water. It floated there, holding up above the surface the stoppered end of the fuse-hose.

'Oars!' said Hornblower. 'Give way!'

The gig swung away from the floating keg. The spark was still travelling along the quick match, Hornblower presumed; it would be some seconds yet before it even reached the slow match down there by the wreck of the *Speedwell*. He remembered to take the time by his watch.

'Take her back to the ship,' he ordered Leadbitter; he

looked back to where the empty cask bobbed on the surface.

McCullum had said, 'I advise you to keep clear of the explosion.' Apparently the explosion of a barrel of powder, even far down under the water, created a turmoil on the surface that would endanger the gig. Beside the ship they would be a quarter of a mile away; that should be safe enough. When the bowman hooked on to the main chains of the *Atropos*, Hornblower looked at his watch again. It was exactly five minutes since he had seen the spark passing into the end of the fuse-hose. The explosion could be expected at any time from now.

Naturally the side of the ship was lined with every idler who could find a place there. The preparation of the charge and the fuse had excited gossip throughout the ship.

Hornblower changed his mind about awaiting the explosion in the gig and mounted to the deck.

'Mr Jones!' he bellowed. 'Is this a raree-show? Keep the hands at work, if you please.'

'Aye aye, sir.'

He very much wanted to see the explosion himself, but he feared to display curiosity inconsonant with his dignity. And there was the chance—a likely chance, according to McCullum—that there would be no explosion at all. A glance at his watch showed him that it was by now overdue. With an appearance of the utmost indifference he strolled forward to McCullum's bedside, where McCullum was listening to the reports of his divers.

'Nothing as yet?' said McCullum.

'Nothing.'

'I never trust a fuse-hose beyond five fathoms,' said McCullum, 'even when I handle it myself.'

Hornblower kept back an irritated answer, and gazed out towards the scene of his recent activities. In the choppy water he could just perceive at intervals the dark spot which was the keg that floated the end of the fuse-hose. He glanced at his watch again.

'Long overdue,' he said.

'Water's in that hose. You'll have to use a flying-fuse after all.'

'The sooner the better,' said Hornblower. 'How do I set about it?'

He was glad for the sake of his precious dignity that he had not waited in sight of the men.

XV

THIS time so many men were wanted for the operation that Hornblower was using the launch instead of the gig. As usual the three Ceylonese divers were huddled in the bows, but next to them in the bottom of the boat stood an iron pot of melted pitch, and beside it squatted a sailmaker's mate, and Mr Clout, the gunner, sat amidships with the powder keg between his legs. The canvas covering to the keg was incompletely sewn, gaping wide at the upper end. They dropped the grapnel and the launch rode on the little waves beside the little keg that floated with the end of the useless fuse-hose, a monument to the previous failure.

'Carry on, Mr Clout,' said Hornblower.

This was something more than exciting. This was dangerous. The divers stripped themselves for their work, and sat up to begin their exercises of inflating and deflating their lungs. There would not be any time to spare later. Clout took the tinderbox and proceeded to strike a spark upon the tinder, crouching low to shelter it from the small breeze which blew over the surface of the Bay. He caught fire upon the slow match, brought it to a glow, and looked over at Hornblower.

'Carry on, I said,' said Hornblower.

Clout dabbed the slow match upon the fuse that protruded through a hole in the end of the powder keg. Hornblower could hear the faint irregular hissing of the fuse as Clout waited for it to burn down into the hole. Among them now, in the middle of the boat, fire was creeping towards thirty pounds of gunpowder. If there were a few powder grains out of place, if the fuse were the least faulty, there would come a sudden crashing explosion which would blow them and the

216

boat to fragments. There was not a sound in the boat save the hissing of the fuse. The spark crept down into the hole. The powder keg at this upper end had a double head, the result of the most careful work by the ship's cooper. In the space between the two heads was coiled the fuse, whose farther end penetrated the inner head to rest amid the powder. Along that coil stapled to the inner head the fire was now moving unseen, creeping round and round on its way to dive down along its final length through the inner head.

Clout took from his pocket the canvas-covered stopper, and dipped it into the warm pitch.

'Make sure of it, Mr Clout,' said Hornblower.

Clout rammed the stopper into the hole in the outer head. The action cut off the sound of the hissing fuse, but everyone in the boat knew that the fire was still pursuing its inexorable way inside. Clout smeared pitch thickly about the stopper and then moved out of the way.

'Now, my hearty,' he said to the sailmaker's mate.

This last needed no urging. Needle and palm in hand, he took Clout's place and sewed up the canvas cover over the top of the keg.

'Keep those stitches small,' said Hornblower; the sail-maker's mate, crouching over instant death, was not un-naturally nervous. So was Hornblower, but the irritation caused by the previous failure made him anxious that the work should be well done.

The sailmaker's mate finished the last stitch, oversewed it, and, whipping out his sheath knife, cut the twine. There could be hardly anything more harmless in appearance than that canvas-covered keg. It looked a stupid, a brainless object, standing there in the boat. Clout was already daubing pitch over the newly-sewn end; the sides and the other end had been thickly pitched before the keg was put into the launch.

'Now the line,' said Hornblower.

As on the previous occasion a loop of line attached to the

keg was passed round the mooring line of the buoy and
secured to the keg again.

'Hoist it, you two. Lower away. Handsomely.'

The keg sank below the surface, dangling on the lowering
line as the men let it down hand over hand. There was a
sudden relief from tension in the boat, marked by a sudden
babble of talk.

'Silence!' said Hornblower.

Even though the thing was invisible now, sinking down to
the bottom of the Bay, it was still deadly—the men did not
understand that. One of the divers was already sitting on the
gunwale, a cannon-ball in his hands—that was a ridiculous
moment for Hornblower to remember that he had not
carried out his earlier resolution to get in a store of rocks for
that purpose—and his chest expanding and contracting.
Hornblower would have liked to tell him to make certain to
place the powder keg to the best advantage, but that was
impossible owing to the difficulties of language. He had to
content himself with a glance, half encouragement and half
threat.

'Bottom, sir,' announced the seaman at the lowering line.

The diver slipped from the gunwale and vanished under
the surface. Down there with the powder charge and the
glowing fuse he was in worse peril even than before. 'They've
seen one of their mates blown to bits using a flying fuse off
Cuddalore,' McCullum had said. Hornblower wanted nothing
like that to happen now. It occurred to him that if it were to
happen the launch, with him in it, would be on top of the
explosion and turmoil, and he wondered what was the
mysterious force that always drove him into voluntarily
taking part in dangerous adventures. He thought it must be
curiosity, and then he realized that it was a sense of shame
as well; and it never occurred to him that a sense of duty had
something to do with it too.

The second diver was sitting on the gunwale, cannon-ball
in hand and breathing deeply, and the moment the first
diver's head broke water he let himself slip down and

vanished. 'I've put the fear of God into 'em,' McCullum had said. 'I've told 'em that if the charge explodes without being properly placed they'll all get two dozen. An' I've said we're here to stay. No matter how long we try we get the money up. So you can rely on 'em. They'll do their best.'

And they certainly were doing their best. Looney was waiting on the gunwale now, and down he went as soon as the second diver appeared. They wanted to waste no time at all. Not for the first time Hornblower peered overside in the attempt to see down through the water, unsuccessfully again. It was clear, and the loveliest deep green, but there was just sufficient lop and commotion on the surface to make it impossible to see down. Hornblower had to take it for granted that deep down below, in semi-darkness at least, and amid paralysing cold, Looney was dragging the powder charge towards the wreck and shoving it under the break of the poop. That powder keg under water could weigh little enough, thanks to the upthrust that Archimedes discovered, twenty centuries ago.

Looney reappeared, and the first diver instantly went down to replace him. This business was for the divers a gamble with life and death, a losing lottery. If the charge were to explode prematurely it would be chance that would dictate who would happen to be down there with it at that moment. But surely it could not take long to move the charge a few yards along the bottom and into the right place. And down there, he hoped, the fire was creeping along the coils of the fuse, sandwiched tight between the two barrel-heads. The philosophers had decided that fuses were able to burn in the absence of air—unlike candles—because the nitre that permeated the cord supplied the same combustible substance that air supplied. It was a discovery that went close to solving the problem of life—a human being's life went out like a candle's in the absence of air. It might be reasonably expected soon that the discovery might be made as to how to maintain life without air.

Yet another dive. The fire was hurrying along the fuse.

Clout had allowed enough for an hour's burning—it must
not be too little, obviously, but also it must not be too much,
for the longer the keg was exposed to the water pressure the
greater the chance of a weak point giving way and water
seeping in. But Clout had pointed out that in that confined
space between the barrel-heads the heat would not be able
to escape; it would grow hotter and hotter in there and the
fuse would burn faster—the fire might even jump from one
part of the coil to another. The rate of burning, in other
words, was unpredictable.

The diver who had just appeared gave a sharp cry, in
time to prevent the next one—Looney—from going down.
An eager question and answer, and Looney turned to
Hornblower with a waving of hands.

'Get that man on board,' ordered Hornblower. 'Up
anchor!'

A few strokes of the oars got the launch under weigh; the
Ceylonese in the bows were chattering like sparrows at
dawn.

'Back to the ship,' ordered Hornblower.

He would go straight on board without looking back once;
he would not compromise his dignity by awaiting an
explosion which might never come. The tiller was put over
and the launch began her steady course towards *Atropos*.

And then it happened, while Hornblower's back was
turned to it. A sullen, muffled roar, not very loud, as if a gun
had been fired in a distant cave. Hornblower swung round in
his seat just in time to see a bulging wave overtake them,
heaving up the stern of the launch. The stern sank and bow
rose, the launch pitching violently, like a child's toy boat in
a tub. The water that surged round them was discoloured
and dark. It was only for a few seconds that the violent
commotion lasted, and then it passed on, leaving the launch
rocking jerkily.

'She's gone up, sir,' said Clout, quite unnecessarily.

The hands were chattering as much as the Ceylonese.

'Silence in the boat!' said Hornblower.

He was angry with himself because the unexpected sound had caused him to leap in his seat. He glowered at the men, and they fell into a hushed silence.

'Starboard your helm,' growled Hornblower. 'Give way!'

The launch swung round and retraced its course towards the scene of the explosion, marked by a dirty patch of water. Half a dozen big bubbles rose to the surface and burst as he watched. Then something else came up, and something else, dead fish floating up to the surface, their white bellies gleaming under the sky. The launch passed one which was not quite dead; it was making feeble efforts, just perceptible, to right itself and descend again.

'Silence!' said Hornblower again—the irrepressible chatter had broken out again. 'Easy!'

In silence the launch floated over the scene of the explosion. Dead fish, a stain, and nothing else. Nothing else at all. Hornblower felt a sick feeling of disappointment; there should be fragments from the wreck covering the surface, shattered bits of timber to show that the powder charge had done its work. The fact that there was none was proof that no gap had been blown in the wreck. His mind was racing into the future. Another charge with another flying fuse would have to be used, he supposed, and the most brutal threats would have to be employed towards the divers to make them put it into position. They had escaped the last explosion by not more than thirty seconds, he supposed, and they would be chary of running the risk again.

There was a bit of timber! No, it was the plank which had been used as a marker buoy.

'Haul in on that line,' said Hornblower to the man pulling stroke oar. There was only ten feet of line attached to the plank—the line had been broken at that point; so the explosion had effected something, at least. It was ironical that that was all—just a marker buoy torn loose.

'Put on another grapnel and line,' ordered Hornblower. They must still be close enough to the spot for the marker to be better than nothing.

Hornblower caught Looney's eye; he seemed willing
enough to all appearance. It would save time if an examination of the scant results were made now.

'Looney,' said Hornblower, and pointed overside. He had
only to point a second time for Looney to nod his agreement
and pull off his clothes again. As far as Hornblower could
remember Looney had not yet made his daily quota of five
dives yet. Looney inflated his chest and slipped in, and the
launch lay drifting. The little waves that slapped against her
sides had a different quality from usual; they had not even
the small amount of system arising from the wind that
agitated the surface—they seemed to come from all points
at once. Hornblower realized that they were the last dying
remnants of the turbulence which the explosion had set up.

Up came Looney, his slender bundle of black hair bobbing
beside his face. His white teeth showed in what might almost
be thought to be a smile, except that of course he was gasping
for breath. He struck out towards the launch, saying something to his colleagues as he did so which set them off
twittering volubly. Apparently the explosion which had torn
the marker buoy loose had not driven it any distance from
its position. They hauled Looney on board into the bows.
The chattering went on; now Looney was making his way
aft over the thwarts and between the men. He was rubbing
something in a portion of his clothing as he came—something which he put into Hornblower's hand with a broad
grin. Something disc-shaped and heavy, tarnished, encrusted,
and yet—and yet——

'God bless my soul,' said Hornblower.

It was a shilling; Hornblower could only stare at it,
and turn it over in his fingers. Every eye in the boat was
directed at it; the men were quick enough to guess even if
they could not see it clearly. Someone started a cheer, and
the others took it up. Hornblower looked down the boat at
the grinning faces. Even Clout was waving his hat and yelling.

'Silence!' shouted Hornblower. 'Mr Clout, you ought to
be ashamed of yourself.'

But the noise did not stop instantly as before; the men were too excited. But it died away at length, and the men waited. Hornblower had to think now about the next move, completely at a loss—this development had taken him by surprise and he had no idea for the moment what to do next. It would have to be anti-climax, he decided at last. For the recovery of the treasure fresh equipment would be necessary; that was certain. The divers had made nearly as many dives that day as they could. Moreover, McCullum must be informed of the results of the explosion and his decision heard regarding further steps. Hornblower even realized that there was no certainty that subsequent operations would be easy. One shilling did not make a quarter of a million sterling. There might be much further work necessary.

'Oars!' he snapped at the waiting men. The oar-looms clattered into the rowlocks and the men bent forward ready to pull. 'Give way!'

The oar-blades bit into the water and the launch slowly gathered way.

'Head for the ship!' he growled at the coxswain.

He sat glowering in the stern-sheets. Anyone seeing his face might well have thought that the launch was returning after a complete failure, but it was merely that he was annoyed with himself at not being quick-witted enough to have had the appropriate orders ready at once when that astonishing shilling was put into his hand. The whole boat's crew had seen him at a loss. His precious dignity was hurt. When he got on board he was inclined to sulk in his cabin, but common sense made him go forward soon to discuss the situation with McCullum.

'There's a cascade of silver,' said McCullum, who had been listening to the reports of the divers. 'The bags have rotted, and when the treasure room was blown open the silver poured out. I think that's clear enough.'

'And the gold?' asked Hornblower.

'Looney can't tell me as yet,' said McCullum. 'If I had

been in the launch I daresay I should have acquired more information.'

Hornblower bit back an angry retort. Nothing would please McCullum better than a quarrel, and he had no wish to indulge him.

'At least the explosion served its purpose,' he said pacifically.

'Like enough.'

'Then why,' asked Hornblower—the question had been awaiting the asking for a long time—'if the wreck was blown open why didn't wreckage come to the surface?'

'You don't know?' asked McCullum in reply, clearly gratified at possessing superior knowledge.

'No.'

'That's one of the elementary facts of science. Timber submerged at great depths soon becomes waterlogged.'

'Indeed?'

'Wood only floats—as I presume you know—by virtue of the air contained in the cavities in its substance. Under pressure that air is squeezed out, and, deprived of this upthrust, the residual material has no tendency to rise.'

'I see,' said Hornblower. 'Thank you, Mr McCullum.'

'I am accustomed by now,' said McCullum, 'to supplementing the education of King's officers.'

'Then I trust,' said Hornblower, still keeping his temper, 'you will continue with mine. What is the next step to take?'

McCullum pursed his lips.

'If that damned Dutch doctor,' he said, 'would only have the sense to allow me out of this bed I could attend to it all myself.'

'He'll have the stitches out of you soon,' said Hornblower. 'Meanwhile time is of importance.'

It was infuriating that a captain in his own ship should have to endure this sort of insolence. Hornblower thought of the official complaints he could make. He could quarrel with McCullum, abandon the whole attempt, and in his report to Collingwood he would declaim that 'owing to the complete lack of co-operation on the part of Mr William McCullum, of the Honourable East India Company's Service' the expedition had ended in failure. No doubt McCullum would then be rapped on the knuckles officially. But it was better to achieve success, even without receiving any sympathy for the trials he was enduring, than to return with the best of excuses empty-handed. It was just as meritorious to pocket his pride and to coax McCullum into giving clear instructions as it was to head a boarding party on to an enemy's deck. Just as meritorious—although less likely to achieve a paragraph in the Gazette. He forced himself to ask the right questions and to listen to McCullum's grudging explanations of what should next be done.

And it was pleasant, later, when eating his dinner, to be able to congratulate himself on his duty done, orders given, all prepared. Those words of McCullum's, 'a cascade of silver,' ran in his mind as he sat and ate. It called for little imagination to conjure up a mental picture of the wreck down there in the translucent water, with her strong-room torn open and the silver in a frozen stream pouring out of it. Gray could have written a poem about it; and somewhere in that strong-room there was the gold. Life was good, and he was a fortunate man. He slowly consumed his last mouthful of roast lamb, and addressed himself to his lettuce salad, tender young plants, sweet and delicious, the first fruits of the Turkish spring.

XVI

THE Turkish spring was not going to give way to summer without a last struggle, without calling the vanished winter back to her aid. The wind blew wildly and cold from the north-westward; the skies were grey, and the rain lashed down torrentially. It drummed upon the deck, streaming out through the scuppers; it poured in unexpected streams down from points in the rigging; even though it grudgingly gave to the crew the chance to wash their clothes in fresh water it denied them the opportunity of drying them again. *Atropos* swung fitfully to her anchor as the gusts blowing down from the surrounding mountains backed and veered, whipping the surface of the Bay into turbulent white-caps. Wind and rain seemed peculiarly searching. Everyone seemed to be colder and wetter than if the ship were battling a storm in mid-Atlantic, with the deck leaking as she worked in a sea way and the waves crashing down upon it; sulkiness and bad temper made their appearance among the ship's company along with the cold and wet—lack of exercise and lack of occupation combined with the constant drumming of the rain to bring that about.

Walking upon the quarter-deck with the raindrops rattling upon his oilskin seemed to Hornblower to be a cheerless business, the more so until this gale dropped there would be no chance of continuing the salvage operations. Boxes of gold lay over there under that wind-whipped surface; he hated having to wait through these empty hours before knowing if they could be recovered. He hated the thought of having to rouse himself from his inertia and exert himself to re-establish the good spirits of the ship's company, but he knew he must.

226

'Messenger!' he said, 'my compliments to Mr Smiley and Mr Horrocks, and I'll see them at once in my cabin.

Half an hour later both watches were assembled on deck by divisions ('Half an hour I'll give you to get it all arranged,' Hornblower had said) wearing only their duck trousers in the rain, the cold drops beating on their bare chests and feet. There was plenty of growling at the discomfort, but there was amusement among the topmen because every idler in the ship was there—'I'll have 'em all,' Hornblower had said, 'waisters and holders, gunner's crew and sailmaker's crew.' And there was the excitement always attendant upon a race; and there was the compensation of seeing the three senior watch-keeping officers, Jones and Still and Turner, climbing the ratlines to take their places in the cross-trees to see that the racing was fair. Hornblower stood forward by the knightheads with his speaking trumpet so that the wind would carry his voice plainly along the deck.

'One to get steady!' he shouted. 'Two to be ready! Three —and you're *off*!'

It was a relay race, up the rigging of each mast in turn and down again, port watch against starboard; it was the inclusion of the men who rarely, if ever, went aloft that gave spice to the proceedings. Soon divisions down on deck were dancing with excitement as they watched the slow ascent and descent of some lumbering gunner's mate or ship's corporal; until he completed the journey they were not free to dash to the next mast and start again.

'Come on, Fatty!'

The Pegasus-winged topmen to whom the ascent was a trifle leaped up and down on deck with never a thought for the streaming rain as some rival division, set free by the eventual descent of its last man, rushed joyfully along the deck to the next mast while they were forced to stand and witness the cautious movements of the slowest of their own side.

Up went the men and down, round and across. The Prince of Seitz-Bunau came shrieking round the deck, wild with excitement; Horrocks and Smiley, captains of the two sides, were croaking like crows, their voices failing them with the continual shouting as they organized and encouraged. The cook's mate, who was the last man of the port watch, was already close to the mainmast head when Horrocks, who had reserved himself to be the last of the starboard watch, began the ascent on the other side. Everyone in the ship seemed to be shouting and gesticulating. Up ran Horrocks, the shrouds vibrating with the ape-like speed of his passage. The cook's mate reached the cross-trees and started down again.

'Come on, Fatty!'

. The cook's mate did not even look to see where to put his feet, and he was coming down two ratlines at a time. Horrocks reached the cross-tress and leaped for the back stay. Down he came, sliding at a speed that must burn his hands. Cook's mate and midshipman reached the deck together, but Horrocks had farther to run to reach his place with his division than did the cook's mate. There was a final yell as both of them staggered gasping to their places, but the cook's mate was first by a full yard, and every eye was turned towards Hornblower.

'Port watch wins!' he announced. 'Starboard watch provides the entertainment to-morrow night!'

The port watch cheered again, but the starboard watch—Hornblower was observing them closely—was not humiliated. He could guess that there were plenty of men among them who were not too displeased at the thought of to-morrow exhibiting their talents to an audience and who were already planning their turns. He put his speaking trumpet to his lips again.

'Attention! Mr Horrocks! Mr Smiley! Dismiss your teams.'

Aft, beside the wardroom door, as Hornblower was returning to his cabin, there was an unusual figure, walking with slow steps under the supervision of the doctor.

'This is a pleasure, Mr McCullum,' said Hornblower. 'It's good to see you out of your bed.'

'The incision has entirely healed, sir,' said Eisenbeiss, proudly. 'Not only are the sutures removed, but I have judged it safe to remove the bristle from the wound, as the drainage was complete.'

'Excellent!' said Hornblower. 'Then that arm will come out of its sling soon?'

'Within a few days. The broken ribs seem to have knitted well.'

'Still a bit stiff round there,' said McCullum, feeling his right armpit with his left hand. He was displaying none of his usual ill temper; but a convalescent, making his first attempt to walk, and with his wound under discussion, could feel so much in the centre of the picture as to be well disposed towards humanity.

'Well it might be,' said Hornblower. 'A pistol bullet at twelve paces is not a welcome visitor. We thought we had lost you. At Malta they thought that bullet was in your lungs.'

'It would have been easier,' said Eisenbeiss, 'if he had not been so muscular. The bullet could not be felt in that mass of muscle.'

McCullum fished from his left trouser pocket a small object which he handed to Hornblower.

'D'you see that?' asked McCullum. It was the bullet which Eisenbeiss had extracted, flattened and irregular. Hornblower had seen it before, but this was not the moment to say so. He marvelled over it in suitable terms, much to McCullum's gratification.

'I think,' said Hornblower, 'that this occasion should be observed with a fitting ceremony. I shall invite the wardroom to dine with me, and I can ask you two gentlemen first of all.'

'Honoured, I'm sure,' said McCullum, and Eisenbeiss bowed.

'Let us say to-morrow, then. We can dine in comfort

before the entertainment which the starboard watch is
providing.'

He retired to his cabin well pleased with himself. He had
exercised his crew; he had given them something to think
about; he had found a suitable occasion to entertain his
officers socially; his salvage expert had returned from the
jaws of death and in a better temper than usual—all this, and
the *Speedwell's* treasure lay on the Tom Tiddler's Ground of
the sandy bottom of the Bay, with gold and silver only
waiting to be picked up. His good opinion of himself even
enabled him to endure the tedium of the concert given by the
starboard watch that night. There were the sentimental songs
which a handsome young fore-topman sang; Hornblower
found their glutinous sentimentality as wearisome to his soul
as the music was to his tone-deaf ear. 'The Flowers on
Mother's Grave' and 'The Empty Cradle'—the young seaman squeezed out every lugubrious drop from their funereal
substance, and his audience, with the exception of Hornblower, revelled in it. And an elderly bos'n's mate sang sea
songs in a thunderous bass while Hornblower marvelled that
a seagoing audience could tolerate the misuse of nautical
terms in those songs; if his 'good sail' were to 'rustle' with a
following wind, his officer of the watch would hear from
him in good round terms, and there was, of course, the
usual landsman's confusion between the sheet and the sail,
and Dibdin had never bothered to find out that a 'sheer hulk'
was still leading a useful existence thanks to its sheers—the
term did not imply a complete hulk or anything like it. And
of course the song laid stress on the statement that Tom
Bowling was dead, like the fore-topman's mythical mother
and baby. He had 'gone aloft' and everybody in the ship's
company, apparently, felt the better for it.

The hornpipes were more agreeable; Hornblower could
admire the lightness and grace of the dancers and could
manage to ignore the squeaky sweetness of the flute that
accompanist them, played by the same cook's mate whose
final effort had won the race for the port watch—his services

as accompanist were so necessary, apparently, that they were called for even though the port watch were officially the guests at the concert. To Hornblower the most amusing part of the evening's entertainment, in fact, was the difference in attitude between the two watches, the starboard watch as anxious hosts and the port watch as critical guests. He could congratulate himself again at the end of the evening on a successful piece of work. He had a willing and orderly crew, and a satisfied complement of officers.

And next morning came the real triumph, no less satisfactory in that Hornblower stayed on board the ship and allowed McCullum, his arm still in a sling, to go out with launch and longboat and all the new apparatus that had been constructed for the salvage operations. Hornblower stood at the side of the ship, warmed by the newly returned sunshine, as the boats returned. McCullum pointed with his left hand to a vast heap piled between the centre thwarts of the launch, and turned and pointed to another in the longboat. Silver! The divers must have worked fast down in the depths, shovelling the coins with their hands into the lowered buckets.

The boats came alongside, and a working party prepared to hoise the mass of silver on board. A sudden sharp order by McCullum halted the three Ceylonese divers as they were about to make their way forward to their own particular lair. They looked at him a little sheepishly as he gave a further order in their strange tongue, and he repeated it. Then slowly they began to take off their clothes; Hornblower had seen them stripping themselves so often before in the days— they seemed weeks ago—when the salvage operations had begun. The voluminous cotton garments came off one by one.

'I'll lay a bet,' said McCullum, 'they've got fifty pounds between them.'

One of the garments gave out a mysterious chink as it was laid on the deck, despite the care of the owner.

'Master at arms!' said Hornblower, 'search those clothes!'

With a grinning crew looking on the seams and folds of the clothing were emptied of coins, dozens of them.

'They never make a dive,' said McCullum, 'without trying this on.'

Hornblower could only wonder how a naked man climbing from the sea into a boat could possibly manage to convey silver coins into his clothing unobserved, but anything was possible to human ingenuity.

'That would have made them rich for life if they could have taken it back to Jaffra,' said McCullum. Reverting to the foreign speech he dismissed the divers, who picked up their clothes again and vanished, while McCullum turned back to Hornblower. 'It might be quicker to weigh this than to count it. If we get it all up there'll be four tons altogether.'

Silver by the ton! The sailmaker stitched sacks out of new canvas to hold it, and just as in the lost *Speedwell*, the lower lazarette was cleared to store it. And Hornblower found there was a profound truth in the story of Midas, who received the gift of the Golden Touch not so very far from where *Atropos* swung at anchor. Just as Midas lost his happiness at a moment when the world must have deemed him the happiest man on earth, so Hornblower lost his happiness at this moment of success. For as the silver was piled in the lazarette so he came to worry about the coins. He was in no doubt about the ingenuity and persistence and skill of the seamen under his orders; nor was he in doubt about the criminal pasts of many of them, the sweepings of Newgate Gaol. Tales innumerable were told about the remarkable ways in which seamen managed to steal liquor, but the man who stole liquor inevitably revealed himself sooner or later. This was money, English coins, and there was only a frail wooden bulkhead to keep out thieves. So, as in the *Speedwell*, the bulkheads and decks were reinforced by stout timbers nailed across them; the careful and well-planned arrangement of the stores in the hold had to be altered so that the biggest beef casks, the ones that could only be moved by block and tackle, were ranged outside the bulkheads to hinder thieves from breaking through. And even then Hornblower spent wakeful nights visualizing the situation of the lower lazarette and wondering first how he would set about breaking into it and second how he would defeat such an attempt. These feelings intensified each day as the piles of sacks of silver grew larger; and they grew ten times more intense on the triumphant day when McCullum's divers reached the gold.

McCullum knew his work, no doubt about that. One day he told Hornblower of the discovery of one of the chests of gold; the next morning Hornblower watched launch and longboat start off with strongbacks erected in their sterns, and blocks and tackles rigged on them, miles of line coiled in readiness, timbers, buckets, everything that human ingenuity could think of for use in this new task. Hornblower watched through his glass as the boats lay together over the wreck. He saw the divers go down and come up again, time after time. He saw the weighted lines lowered from the tackles; more than once he saw the hands begin to haul in on the falls and then desist while another diver went down, presumably to clear the line. Then at the end he saw the hands haul in again, and stay at work, hauling in, coiling down, until at last, between the two boats, something broke water and a yell of exultation came echoing over to the ship.

It was something quite large which was gingerly swung into the stern of the launch—Hornblower could see the stern of the launch sink and the bows rise as the weight was transferred. His calculations had already told him that a cubic foot of gold weighed half a ton—and gold was at a premium, five guineas in paper or more to the ounce. That was a king's ransom; Hornblower looked at it as the launch came pulling back alongside, a strange object lying in the bottom of the boat, half obscured by weed.

'Those must be wrought iron bars on it,' said McCullum, standing beside him while Jones fussily supervised the transfer

to the ship, 'and best Sussex iron at that. Steel would have
rusted to nothing a year ago, but some of those bars are still
whole. The weeds growing from the oak must have been a
yard long—my boys had to trim 'em off before they got the
tackles round.'

'Easy there! Easy!' shouted Jones.

'Vast heaving at the yardarm!' shouted the bos'n. 'Now,
you at the stay tackle, walk away with it!'

The chest dangled over the deck, balancing on its
supporting lines.

'Easy! Lower away, yardarm! Easy! Lower away stay
tackle! Handsomely!'

The chest sank to the deck; there were little dribbles of
water still flowing from inside it. The gold that lay concealed
inside it would have built, armed, and equipped the whole
Atropos, have filled her holds with stores for a year, have
provided a month's advance pay for the crew, and still have
left a handsome balance.

'Well, that's one of them,' said McCullum. 'I have a feeling
that it won't be so easy to get up the other two. This is the
easiest job I've ever done, so far. We've been lucky—
inexperienced as you are, you will never know how
lucky.'

But Hornblower knew how lucky he was. Lucky that
McCullum had survived a pistol shot in the ribs; lucky that
the Ceylonese divers had survived the journey all round
Africa from India to Asia Minor; lucky—incredibly lucky—
that the Turks had been so complacent, allowing him to
carry out the salvage operation in the Bay without guessing
what he was doing and without interfering. It was consideration of this good fortune that reconciled him at last to the
worry regarding the guarding of the treasure in the lower
lazarette. He was the most fortunate man on earth; fortunate
(he told himself) and yet at the same time he owed some of
his success to his own merits. He had been clever in his
handling of the Mudir. It had been a cunning move to
accept a bribe to stay here anchored in the Bay, to appear

reluctant to do the very thing he wanted most to do. Collingwood would approve, no doubt. He had recovered the silver; he had recovered one-third of the gold already. He would receive a pat on the back from authority even if McCullum should find it impossible to recover the rest.

XVII

THESE Mediterranean mornings were beautiful. It was a
pleasure to come on deck as the dawn brightened into
daylight; usually the night wind had died down,
leaving the Bay glassy smooth, reflecting, as the light
increased, the intense blue of the sky as the sun climbed up
over the mountains of Turkey. There was a refreshing chill
in the air—not enough to necessitate wearing a pea-jacket—
so that the increasing warmth of the sun brought a sensuous
pleasure with it. During a walk on deck with his mind
leisurely working out the plans for the day, Hornblower
soaked in the beauty and freshness; and right at the back
of his mind, flavouring his pleasure as a sauce might give the
finishing touch to some perfect dish, was the knowledge that
when he went below he could sit down to a plate of fried
eggs and a pot of coffee. Beauty all round him, a growing
appetite and the immediate prospect of satisfying it—at least
they brought the realization that he was a fortunate man.

To-day he was not quite as fortunate as usual, because
instead of indulging in solitary thought he had to give some
attention to McCullum and his problems.

'We'll have one more try along the present lines,' said
McCullum. 'I'll send the boys down again to-day, and hear
what they have to say. But I'm afraid that chest is out of
reach at present. I came to suspect that yesterday.

Two days ago the second of the three chests of gold had
been recovered, but only after an explosive charge had blown
a wide entrance into the wreck.

'Yes,' said Hornblower, 'that was the substance of your
report.'

'It's not easy to make 'em go down right in among the
wreckage.'

'I shouldn't think it was,' said Hornblower.

In the dimly-lit depths, under the intolerable weight of a hundred feet of water, to hold one's breath, suffocating, and to make one's way in among the tangled timbers, must be a frightful thing to do.

'The deck sloped away from the gap in the side, and I fancy the last explosion sent that third chest through and down. The whole wreck's on top of it now,' said McCullum.

'Then what do you propose to do?'

'It'll be a couple of weeks' work, I expect. I'll use half a dozen charges—with flying-fuses, of course—and blow the whole wreck to pieces. But I must inform you officially that the result may still be unsatisfactory.'

'You mean you may not recover the gold even then?'

'I may not.'

Two-thirds of the gold and nearly all the silver lay already in the lower lazarette of the *Atropos*—a good second-best, but as unsatisfactory as any other second-best.

'I'm sure you'll do the best you can, Mr McCullum,' said Hornblower.

Already the morning breeze was blowing. The first gentle breaths had swung *Atropos* round from where she lay completely inert upon the water. Now she rode to her anchor again, with a fair breeze coursing along her deck. Hornblower felt it about his ears.

And for the last few seconds something had been troubling him. Subconsciously he had become aware of something, while he had addressed that final sentence to McCullum, like a gnat seen out of the corner of his eye. He looked over at the pine-clad slopes of Ada peninsula, at the square outline of the fort on the summit. The beauty of the morning seemed suddenly to turn harsh and grey; the feeling of intense well-being was suddenly replaced by sharp apprehension.

'Give me that glass,' he snapped at the master's mate of the watch.

There was really no need for the glass; Hornblower's
powers of deduction had already reinforced his naked eye,
and the telescope merely revealed what he was sure he would
see. There was a flag waving over the fort on the peninsula—
the red flag of Turkey, where no flag had flown yesterday,
nor ever since his arrival in the Bay of Marmorice. There
could be only one conclusion. There was a garrison in that
fort now; troops must have come back to Marmorice—they
must have manned the guns of the fort. He was a fool, a
stupid, insensitive idiot, blinded by his own complacency.
Now that the revelation had come to him his mind worked
feverishly. He had been utterly deceived; the Mudir with his
white beard and his innocent anxiety had played upon him
the very trick he thought he was playing himself—had lulled
him into self-confidence, gaining time for troops to be
gathered while he thought he was gaining time to carry
out the salvage operation. With bitter self-contempt it
dawned upon him that all the work on the wreck must
have been carefully noted from the shore. Even the Turks
had telescopes—they must have seen all that was done.
They must know of the treasure being recovered, and
now they had manned the guns guarding the exit, shutting
him in.

From where he stood aft he could not see Passage Island—
Red Cliff Point lay in line with it. Without a word to the
astonished master's mate he ran forward and threw himself
into the foremast shrouds. He ran up them, gasping for
breath, as fast as any of the competitors in that foolish relay
race; back downward, he went up the futtock shrouds, and
then up the fore topmast shrouds to the fore topmast head.
There was a flag flying above the fort on Passage Island
too; the glass revealed a couple of boats drawn up on
the beach in the little cove there, showing how during the
night, or at first dawn, the garrison had been conveyed
there. The guns on Passage Island could cross their fire
with those on Ada and sweep the entrance, and could
sweep also the tortuous passage between the island and

Kaia Rock. The cork was in the bottle. He and the *Atropos* were trapped.

Not by guns alone. The easterly sun, shining behind him, was reflected back from far off in the Rhodes Channel by three geometrical shapes close together on the horizon, two rectangles and a triangle—the sails of a big ship, a Turkish ship, obviously. Equally obvious was the fact that it could not be pure coincidence that the hoisting of the flags on the forts occurred at the same moment that those sails appeared. The flags had been hoisted as soon as the lofty fort on Ada had perceived the sails; the despised Turk was perfectly capable of executing a well-planned coup. In an hour—in less—that ship would be stemming the entrance to the Bay. With the wind blowing straight in he could not hope to escape, even discounting the fact that if he tried to beat out of the entrance the guns on Ada would dismast him. Hornblower was sunk in despair as he clung to his lofty perch, glass in hand; to the despair of a man faced by overwhelming odds was added the frightful self-contempt of a man who found himself out-tricked, out-deceived. The memory of his recent self-congratulation was like the echoing laughter of a crowd of scornful spectators, drowning his thoughts and paralysing his mental processes.

It was a bad moment, up there at the fore topmast head, perhaps the worst moment Hornblower had ever known. Self-control came back slowly, even though hope remained quite absent. Looking again through his glass at the approaching sails Hornblower found that the telescope was trembling with the shaking of his hands, the eyepiece blinding him by vibrating against his eyelashes. He could admit to himself that he was a fool—bitter though such an admission might be—but he could not admit to himself that he was a coward, at least that kind of coward. And yet was anything worth the effort? Did it matter if a grain of dust in a whirlwind retained its dignity? The criminal in the cart on the way to Tyburn strove to retain his self-control, strove not to give way to his pitiful human fears and weaknesses, tried to 'die game' for the sake of his own self-respect under the gaze of the heartless crowd, and yet did it profit him when in five minutes he would be dead? There was a horrible moment when Hornblower thought how easy something else would be. He had only to let go his hold, to fall, down, down, to a final crash upon the deck and the end of all this, no need for further effort, the end, oblivion; that would be far easier than to face, trying to appear not to notice, the pity or contempt of his fellow men. He was being tempted to cast himself down, as Christ had been by Satan.

Then he told himself again that he was not that kind of coward. He was calm now; the sweat that had streamed down him lay cold upon his skin. He shut the telescope with a click that sounded clear amid the noise of the wind about his ears. He had no idea what he was going to do, but it was a healing mechanical exercise to set himself to descend the rigging, to lodge first one foot and then the other upon the ratlines, to make sure that despite the weakness he felt he accomplished the descent in safety. And, having set foot on deck, it was further good exercise to try to appear quite unruffled and unperturbed, the grain of dust unchanging in the whirlwind, even though he had a feeling that his cheeks were pale under their sunburn. Habit was a useful thing too; to put back his head and bellow an order could set his mechanism working again, as the stopped clock would start to tick again and would go on ticking after a single shake.

'Mr McCullum! Belay those arrangements, if you please. Officer of the watch! Pipe all hands. Get the launch hoisted in. Leave the longboat for the present.'

A surprised Jones came hurrying on deck at the call of all hands.

'Mr Jones! Get a hawser passed out through a stern port. I want a spring on the cable.'

'A spring, sir? Aye aye, sir.'

It was a minute compensation for his own misery to see how a glance called forth the last three words after the astonished utterance of the first three. Men who went to sea, and ten times more so men who went to sea in a fighting ship, must be ready for the execution of the most unexpected orders, at any moment, even the shattering of the routine of a peaceful morning by an order to put a spring on the cable —a hawser passed out through a stern port and made fast to the anchor cable, so that by hauling in on the spring with the capstan the ship could be swung even though she was stationary, and her guns trained to sweep a different arc at will. It happened to be very nearly the only exercise in which Hornblower had not drilled his ship's company so far.

'You're too slow, Mr Jones! Master-at-arms, take the names of those three men there!'

Midshipman Smiley went off with the hawser end in the longboat; Jones, running forward, bellowed himself hoarse through his speaking trumpet with instructions to Smiley, to the man beside him at the capstan, to the man aft with the hawser. Cable was taken in; cable was paid out.

'Spring's ready, sir.'

'Very well, Mr Jones. Hoist in the longboat and clear for action.'

'Er—aye aye, sir. Pipe "hands to quarters." Clear for action. Drummer! Beat to quarters.'

There was no marine detachment in a little ship like *Atropos*. The ship's boy who had been appointed drummer set his sticks rolling on his drumhead. That warlike sound— there was nothing quite as martial as the rolling of a drum —would drift over the water and would bear a message of defiance to the shore. The longboat came swaying down on the chocks; excited men, with the drum echoing in their ears, braced the lines about her and secured her; already the pump crew were directing a stream of water into her to fill her up— a necessary precaution against her catching fire while providing a convenient reservoir of water to fight other fires. The hands at the tackles broke off and went racing away to their other duties.

'Guns loaded and run out, if you please, Mr Jones!'

'Aye aye, sir.'

Mr Jones was startled again. In a mere exercise of clearing for action it was usual merely to simulate the loading of the guns; otherwise when the exercise ended there was the difficulty and waste of drawing wads and charges. At the cry the powder boys went scurrying to bring up from below the cartridges that Mr Clout was laying out in the magazine. Some gun captain gave a yell as he flung his weight on the tackle to run out his gun.

'Silence!'

The men were well enough behaved; despite the excitement of the moment they had worked in silence save for that one yell. Much drill and relentless discipline showed their effects.

'Cleared for action, sir!' reported Jones.

'Rig the boarding nettings, if you please.'

That was a harassing, irritating exercise. The nettings had to be roused out, laid in position along the ship's sides, and their lower edges made fast in the chains all round. Then lines from the yardarms and bowsprit end had to be rove through the upper edges. Then with steady hauling on the falls of the tackles the nettings rose into position, sloping up and out from the ship's sides from bow to stern, making it impossible for boarders to come in over the ship's side.

'Belay!' ordered Jones as the tricing lines came taut.

'Too taut, Mr Jones! I told you that before. Slack away on those falls!'

Taut boarding nettings, triced up trimly as far as they would go, might look seamanlike, but were not as effective when their function as obstacles was considered. A loose, sagging netting was far more difficult to climb or to cut. Hornblower watched the netting sag down again into lubberly festoons.

'Belay!'

That was better. These nettings were not intended to pass an admiral's inspection, but to keep out boarders.

'Boarding nettings rigged, sir,' reported Jones, after a moment's interval, to call his captain's attention to the fact that the ship's company was awaiting further orders; Hornblower had given the last one himself.

'Thank you, Mr Jones.'

Hornblower spoke a trifle absently; his gaze was not towards Jones, but was directed far away. Automatically Jones followed his glance.

'Good God!' said Jones.

A big ship was rounding Red Cliff Point, entering into the Bay. Everyone else saw her at the same moment, and a babble of exclamation arose.

'Silence, there!'

A big ship, gaudily painted in red and yellow, coming in under topsails, a broad pendant at her mainmast head and the flag of the Prophet at her peak. She was a great clumsy craft, old-fashioned in the extreme, carrying two tiers of guns so that her sides were unnaturally high for her length; and her beam was unnaturally wide, and her bowsprit steved higher than present fashions in European navies dictated. But the feature which first caught the eye was the lateen rig on the mizzen mast; it was more than thirty years since the last lateen mizzen in the Royal Navy had been replaced by the square mizzen topsail. When Hornblower had first seen her through his glass the triangular peak of her mizzen beside her two square topsails had revealed her nationality unmistakably to him. She looked like something in an old print; without her flag she could have taken her place in the fighting line in Blake's navy or Van Tromp's without exciting comment. She must be almost the last survivor of the small clumsy ships of the line that had now been replaced by the stately 74; small, clumsy, but all the same with a weight of metal that could lay the tiny *Atropos* into a splintered wreck at one broadside.

'That's a broad pendant, Mr Jones,' said Hornblower. 'Salute her.'

He spoke out of the side of his mouth, for he had his glass

trained on her. Her gun ports were closed; on her lofty
forecastle he could see men scurrying like ants making ready
to anchor. She was crowded with men; as she took in sail it
was strange to see men balanced across the sloping mizzen
yard—Hornblower had never expected to see a sight like
that in his life, especially as the men wore long loose shirts
like gowns which flapped round them as they hung over the
yard.

The nine-pounder forward gave its sharp bang—some
powder boy must have run fast below to bring up the one-
pound saluting charges—and a puff of smoke, followed by a
report, showed that the Turkish ship was replying. She had
goose-winged her main topsail—another outlandish sight in
these circumstances—and was slowly coming into the Bay
towards them.

'Mr Turner! Come here please, to interpret. Mr Jones,
send some hands to the capstan, if you please. Take in on the
spring if necessary so that the guns bear.'

The Turkish ship glided on.

'Hail her,' said Hornblower to Turner.

A shout came back from her.

'She's the *Mejidieh*, sir,' reported Turner. 'I've seen her
before.'

'Tell her to keep her distance.'

Turner hailed through his speaking trumpet, but the
Mejidieh still came on.

'Tell her to keep off. Mr Jones! Take in on the spring.
Stand by at the guns, there!'

Closer and closer came the *Mejidieh*, and as she did so the
Atropos swung round, keeping her guns pointed at her.
Hornblower picked up the speaking trumpet.

'Keep off, or I'll fire into you!'

She altered course almost imperceptibly and glided by,
close enough for Hornblower to see the faces that lined the
side, faces with moustaches and faces with beards; mahogany-
coloured faces, almost chocolate-coloured faces. Hornblower
watched her go by. She rounded-to, with the goose-winged

main topsail close-hauled, held her new course for a few
seconds, and then took in her sail, came to the wind and
anchored, a quarter of a mile away. The excitement of action
ebbed away in Hornblower, and the old depression returned.
A buzz of talk went up from the men clustered at the guns—
it was quite irrepressible by now, with this remarkable new
arrival.

'The lateener's heading this way, sir,' reported Horrocks.

From the promptitude with which she appeared she
must have been awaiting the *Mejidieh's* arrival. Hornblower saw her pass close under the *Mejidieh's* stern; he
could almost hear the words that she exchanged with the
ship, and then she came briskly up close alongside the
Atropos. There in the stern was the white-bearded Mudir,
hailing them.

'He wants to come on board, sir,' reported Turner.

'Let him come,' said Hornblower. 'Unlace that netting
just enough for him to get through.'

Down in the cabin the Mudir looked just the same as
before. His lean face was as impassive as ever; at least he
showed no signs of triumph. He could play a winning game
like a gentleman; Hornblower, without a single trump card
in his hand, was determined to show that he could play a
losing game like a gentleman, too.

'Explain to him,' he said to Turner, 'that I regret there is
no coffee to offer him. No fires when the ship's cleared for
action.'

The Mudir was gracious about the absence of coffee, as
he indicated by a gesture. There was a polite interchange of
compliments which Turner hardly troubled to translate,
before he approached the business in hand.

'He says the Vali is in Marmorice with his army,' reported
Turner. 'He says the forts at the mouth are manned and the
guns loaded.'

'Tell him I know that.'

'He says that ship's the *Mejidieh*, sir, with fifty-six guns
and a thousand men.'

'Tell him I know that too.'

The Mudir stroked his beard before taking the next step.

'He says the Vali was very angry when he heard we'd been taking treasure from the bottom of the Bay.'

'Tell him it is British treasure.'

'He says it was lying in the Sultan's waters, and all wrecks belong to the Sultan.'

In England all wrecks belonged to the King.

'Tell him the Sultan and King George are friends.'

The Mudir's reply to that was lengthy.

'No good, sir,' said Turner. 'He says Turkey's at peace with France now and so is neutral. He said—he said that we have no more rights here than if we were Neapolitans, sir.'

There could not be any greater expression of contempt anywhere in the Levant.

'Ask him if he has ever seen a Neapolitan with guns run out and matches burning.'

It was a losing game that Hornblower was playing, but he was not going to throw in his cards and yield all the tricks without a struggle, even though he could see no possibility of winning even one. The Mudir stroked his beard again; with his expressionless eyes he looked straight at Hornblower, and straight through him, as he spoke.

'He must have been watching everything through a telescope from shore, sir,' commented Turner, 'or it may have been those fishing boats. At any rate, he knows about the gold and the silver, and it's my belief, sir, that they've known there was treasure in the wreck for years. That secret wasn't as well kept as they thought it was in London.'

'I can draw my own conclusions, Mr Turner, thank you.'

Whatever the Mudir knew or guessed, Hornblower was not going to admit anything.

'Tell him we have been delighted with the pleasure of his company.'

The Mudir, when that was translated to him, allowed a flicker of a change of expression to pass over his face. But when he spoke it was with the same flatness of tone.

'He says that if we hand over all we have recovered so far the Vali will allow us to remain here and keep whatever else we find,' reported Turner.

Turner displayed some small concern as he translated, but yet in his old man's face the most noticeable expression was one of curiosity; he bore no responsibility, and he could allow himself the luxury—the pleasure—of wondering how his captain was going to receive this demand. Even in that horrid moment Hornblower found himself remembering Rochefoucauld's cynical epigram about the pleasure we derive from the contemplation of our friends' troubles.

'Tell him,' said Hornblower, 'that my master King George will be angry when he hears that such a thing has been said to me, his servant, and that his friend the Sultan will be angry when he hears what his servant has said.'

But the Mudir was unmoved by any suggestion of international complications. It would take a long, long time for a complaint to travel from Marmorice to London and then back to Constantinople. And Hornblower could guess that a very small proportion of a quarter of a million sterling, laid out in the proper quarter, would buy the support of the Vizier for the Vali. The Mudir's face was quite unrelenting— a frightened child might have a nightmare about a face as heartless as that.

'Damn it,' said Hornblower, 'I won't do it.'

There was nothing he wanted more in this world than to break through the iron serenity of the Mudir.

'Tell him,' said Hornblower, 'I'll drop the gold back into the Bay sooner than hand it over. By God, I will. I'll drop it down to the bottom and they can fish for it themselves, which they can't do. Tell him I swear that, by—by the Koran or the beard of the Prophet, or whatever they swear by.'

Turner nodded in surprised approval; that was a move he

had not thought of, and he addressed himself eagerly to the task of translation. The Mudir listened with his eternal patience.

'No, it's no good, sir,' said Turner, after the Mudir had replied. 'You can't frighten him that way. He says——'

Turner was interrupted by a fresh sentence from the Mudir.

'He says that after this ship has been seized the idolaters—that's the Ceylonese divers, sir—will work for him just as they work for us.'

Hornblower, desperate, thought wildly of cutting the divers' throats after throwing the treasure overboard; that would be consonant with this Oriental atmosphere, but before he could put the frightful thought into words the Mudir spoke again, and at considerable length.

'He says wouldn't it be better to go back with *some* treasure, sir—whatever more we can recover—than to lose everything? He says—he says—I beg your pardon, sir, but he says that if this ship is seized for breaking the law your name would not be held in respect by King George.'

That was phrasing it elegantly. Hornblower could well imagine what their Lordships of the Admiralty would say. Even at the best, even if he fought it out to the last man, London would not look with favour on the man who had precipitated an international crisis and whose behaviour necessitated sending a squadron and an army into the Levant to restore British prestige at a moment when every ship and man was needed to fight Bonaparte. And at worst—Hornblower could picture his little ship suddenly overwhelmed by a thousand boarders, seized, emptied of the treasure, and then dismissed with contemptuous indulgence for him to take back to Malta with a tale possibly of outrage but certainly of failure.

It took every ounce of his moral strength to conceal his despair and dismay—from Turner as well as from the Mudir—and as it was he sat silent for a while, shaken, like a boxer in the ring trying to rally after a blow had slipped through his guard. Like a boxer, he needed time to recover.

'Very well,' he said at length, 'tell him I must think over all this. Tell him it is too important for me to make up my mind now.'

'He says,' translated Turner when the Mudir replied, 'he says he will come to-morrow morning to receive the treasure.'

XVIII

IN the old days, long ago, Hornblower as a midshipman
had served in the *Indefatigable* on cutting-out expeditions
more numerous than he could remember. The frigate
would find a coaster anchored under the protection of shore
batteries, or would chase one into some small harbour; then
at night—or even in broad day—the boats would be manned
and sent in. The coaster would take all the precautions she
could; she could load her guns, rig her boarding nettings,
keep her crew on the alert, row guard round the ship, but to
no avail. The boarders would fight their way on board, clear
the decks, set sail, and carry off the prize under the nose of
the defences. Often and often had Hornblower seen it close,
had taken part. He had noted with small enough sympathy
the pitiful precautions taken by the victim.

Now the boot was on the other leg; now it was even
worse, because *Atropos* lay in the broad Bay of Marmorice
without even the protection of shore batteries and with ten
thousand enemies around her. To-morrow, the Mudir had
said, he would come for the treasure, but there was no
trusting the Turks. That might be one more move to lull the
Atropos into security. She might be rushed in the night. The
Mejidieh, over there, could put into her boats more men
than *Atropos* could boast altogether, and they could be
supplemented with soldiers crammed into fishing boats from
the shore. If she were attacked by twenty boats at once, from
all sides, by a thousand Moslem fanatics, what could she do
to defend herself?

She could rig her boarding nettings—they were already
rigged. She could load her guns—they were already loaded,
grape on top of round shot, depressed so as to sweep the
surface of the Bay at close range round the ship. She could

keep anxious watch—Hornblower was going round the ship himself, to see that the lookouts were all awake, the guns' crews dozing no more deeply than the hard decks would allow as they lay at their posts, the remainder of the hands stationed round the bulwarks with pike and cutlass within easy reach.

It was a novel experience to be the mouse instead of the cat, to be on the defensive instead of the offensive, to wait anxiously for the moon to rise instead of hurrying to the attack while darkness endured. It might be counted as another lesson in war, to know how the waiting victim thought and felt—some day in the future Hornblower might put that lesson to use, and, paralleling the thought of the ship he was going to attack, contrive to circumvent the precautions she was taking.

That was one more proof of the levity and inconstancy of his mind, said Hornblower to himself, bitterness and despair returning in overwhelming force. Here he was thinking about the future, about some other command he might hold, when there was no future. No future. To-morrow would see the end. He did not know for certain yet what he would do; vaguely in his mind he had the plan that at dawn he would empty the ship of her crew—non-swimmers in the boats, swimmers sent to seek refuge in the *Mejidieh*—while he went down below to the magazine, with a loaded pistol, to blow the ship and the treasure, himself with his dead ambitions, his love for his children and his wife, to blow it all to fragments. But would that be better than bargaining? Would it be better than returning not only with *Atropos* intact but with whatever further treasure McCullum could retrieve? It was his duty to save his ship if he could, and he could. Seventy thousand pounds was far less than a quarter of a million, but it would be a godsend to an England at her wits' ends for gold. A Captain in the Navy should have no personal feelings; he had a duty to do.

That might be so, but all the same he was convulsed with anguish. This deep, dark sorrow which was rending him was something beyond his control. He looked across at the dark shape of the *Mejidieh*, and sorrow was joined to an intense hatred, like some ugly pattern of red and black before his mind's eye. The vague shape of the *Mejidieh* was drawing back abaft the *Atropos*' quarter—the soft night wind was backing round, as might be expected at this hour, and swinging the ships at their anchors. Overhead there were stars, here and there obscured by patches of cloud whose presence could just be guessed at, moving very slowly over the zenith. And over there, beyond the *Mejidieh*, the sky was a trifle paler; the moon must be rising above the horizon beyond the mountains. The loveliest night imaginable with the gentle breeze—this gentle breeze! Hornblower glowered round in the darkness as if he feared someone might prematurely guess the thought that was forming in his mind.

'I am going below for a few minutes, Mr Jones,' he said, softly.

'Aye aye, sir.'

Turner, of course, had been talking. He had told the wardroom all about the quandary in which their captain found himself. One could hear curiosity in the tone of even those three words of Jones's. Resolution came to lacquer over the pattern of red and black.

Down in the cabin the two candles he sent for lit the whole little space, save for a solid shadow here and there. But the chart that he laid out between them was brightly illuminated. He stooped over it, peering at the tiny figures that marked the soundings. He knew them already, as soon as he came to think about them; there was really no need to refresh his memory. Red Cliff Point, Passage Island, Kaia Rock; Point Sari beyond Kaia Rock—he knew them all. He could weather Kaia Rock with this breeze if it should hold. God, there was need for haste! He blew out the candles and felt his way out of the cabin.

'Mr Jones! I want two reliable bosn's mates. Quietly, if you please.'

That breeze was still blowing, ever so gently, a little more fitful than might be desired, and the moon had not cleared the mountains yet.

'Now, you two, pay attention. Go quietly round the ship and see that every man is awake. Not a sound—you hear me? Topmen are to assemble silently at the foot of the masts. Silently.'

'Aye aye, sir,' was the whispered reply.

'Carry on. Now, Mr Jones——'

The gentle patter of bare feet on the deck as the men assembled acted as accompaniment to the whispered orders Hornblower was giving to Jones. Over there was the vast bulk of the *Mejidieh;* two thousand ears which might catch the slightest unusual noise—an axe being laid ready on the deck, for instance, or capstan bars being gently eased into their sockets. The boatswain came aft again to rejoin the little group of officers round Hornblower and to make his report in a whisper that accorded ill with his bulk and power.

'The capstan pawl's thrown out, sir.'

'Very good. Yours is the first move. Go back, count a hundred, and take up on the spring. Six turns, and hold it. Understand?'

'Aye aye, sir.'

'Then off you go. You others are clear about your duties? Mr Carslake, with the axe at the cable. I'll attend to the axe at the spring. Mr Smiley, fore tops'l sheets. Mr Hunt, main tops'l sheets. Go to your stations.'

The little ship lay there quietly. A tiny rim of the moon came up over the mountains, and broadened momentarily, revealing her lying peacefully at anchor. She seemed inert, incapable of action. Silent men had swarmed up the rigging and were waiting for the signal. There was a gentle creaking as the spring to the cable tightened, but there was no clank from the capstan, for the pawl had been thrown out from the ratchet; the men at the capstan bars walked silently round, and when their six turns had been completed they stood, breasts against the bars, feet braced on the deck, holding the

ship steady. Under the pull of the spring she lay at an angle
to the breeze, so that when sail should be set not a moment
would be wasted gathering stern way and paying off. She
would be under command at once

The moon had cleared the mountains; the seconds went
slowly by.

Ting-ting went the ship's bell—two bells; the signal.

Feet pattered in unison. Sheaves squealed in blocks, but
even as the ear caught that sound topsail yards and forestay
had blossomed into sail. Forward and aft came brief sullen
thumpings as axe blades cut through cable and spring—with
the sudden end of the resistance of the spring the capstan
spun round, precipitating the men at the bars to the deck.
There were bruises and grazes, but nobody paid attention
to the injuries; *Atropos* was under way. In five seconds,
without giving any warning at all, she had transformed
herself from something stationary and inert to a living thing,
gliding through the water towards the entrance to the Bay.
She was clear of the peril of the *Mejidieh's* broadside, for the
Mejidieh had no spring on her cable to swing her round. She
would have to weigh her anchor, or cut or slip her cable; she
would have to set sail enough to give her steerage way, and
then she would have to yaw round before she could fire.
With an alert crew, awake and ready for the summons, it
would be at least several minutes before she could turn her
broadside upon *Atropos*, and then it would be at a range of
half a mile or more.

As it was *Atropos* had gathered speed, and was already
more than clear before *Mejidieh* gave her first sign of life.
The deep booming of a drum came sounding over the water;
not the high-pitched rattle of the *Atropos'* side-drum, but the
far deeper and slower tone of a bass drum monotonously
beaten.

'Mr Jones!' said Hornblower. 'Rig in those boarding
nettings, if you please.'

The moon was shining brightly, lighting the water ahead
of them.

'Starboard a point,' said Hornblower to the helmsman.

'Starboard a point,' came the automatic reply.

'You're taking the west pass, sir?' asked Turner.

As sailing master and navigator his station in action was on the quarter-deck beside his captain, and the question he asked was strictly within his province.

'I don't think so,' said Hornblower.

The booming of the *Mejidieh*'s drum was still audible; if the sound reached the batteries the guns' crews there would be on the alert. And when he reached that conclusion there was an orange flash from far astern, as if momentarily a furnace door had been opened and then closed. Seconds later came the heavy report; the *Mejidieh* had fired a gun. There was no sound of the passage of the shot—but if it had even been a blank charge it would serve to warn the batteries.

'I'm going under Sari Point,' said Hornblower.

'Sari Point, sir!'

'Yes.'

It was surprise and not discipline that limited Turner's protests to that single exclamation. Thirty years of service in the merchant navy had trained Turner's mind so that nothing could induce him to contemplate subjecting his ship voluntarily to navigational hazards; his years of service as sailing master in the Royal Navy had done little to change that mental attitude. It was his duty to keep the ship safe from shoal and storm and let the captain worry about cannon-balls. He would never have thought for a moment of trying to take *Atropos* through the narrow channel between Sari Point and Kaia Rock, not even by daylight, and ten times never by night, and the fact that he had not thought of it left him without words.

Another orange flash showed astern; another report reached their ears.

'Take a night glass and go for'rard,' said Hornblower. 'Look out for the surf.'

'Aye aye, sir.'

'Take a speaking trumpet as well. Make sure I hear you.'

'Aye aye, sir.'

The gunfire from *Mejidieh* would have warned the garrisons of the batteries; there would be plenty of time for the men to rouse themselves to wakefulness at their guns, to get their linstocks well alight, so as to sweep the channels with their salvos. Turkish gunners might not be efficient, but the crossfire at East Pass could hardly miss. The West Pass, between Kaia Rock and Passage Island, would not be so efficiently swept; but on the other hand the range was negligible, and with the double turn that had to be made (*Atropos* would be like a sitting duck) there would be no chance of coming through uninjured. Dismasted, or even only crippled, *Atropos* would fall an easy prey to *Mejidieh* coming down through East Pass at her leisure. And, crippled and out of control, *Atropos* might run aground; and she was only a little ship, her scantlings were frail—a salvo from the huge stone cannon-balls that the Turks favoured, plunging from a height, could tear her to pieces, tear open her bottom and sink her in a minute. He would have to take her under Sari Point; that would double, treble the range from the guns on Passage Island; it would be a surprise move; and very likely the guns there would be trained upon Kaia Rock, to sweep the narrowest passage—their aim would have to be hurriedly changed and for a moment at least he would have the rock itself to shelter him. It was his best chance.

'Starboard a point,' he said to the quartermaster. That was the moment, like playing his King as third player to the first trick in a hand of whist; it was the best thing to do, taking all chances into consideration, and so, the decision taken, there was no room for second thoughts.

The moderate breeze was holding; that meant not merely that he had *Atropos* under full command, but also that wavelets would be breaking at the foot of Kaia Rock and Sari Point, reflecting back the moonlight visibly to Turner's night glass. He could see Ada Peninsula plainly enough. At this angle it looked as if there was no exit at all from the Bay; *Atropos* seemed to be gliding down, unhurried, as though to immolate herself upon an unbroken coast.

'Mr Jones, hands to the braces and head sail sheets, if you please.'

The gunners on Ada would be able to see the ship plainly enough now, silhouetted against the moon; they would be waiting for her to turn. Passage Island and Sari Point were still blended together. He held on.

'Breakers on the port bow!'

That was Turner hailing from forward.

'Breakers ahead!' A long pause, and then Turner's high, thin voice again, sharpened with anxiety. 'Breakers ahead!'

'Mr Jones, we'll be wearing ship soon.'

He could see well enough. He carried the chart before his mental eyes, and could superimpose it upon the shadowy landscape before him.

'Breakers ahead!'

The closer he came the better. That shore was steep-to.

'Now, Mr Jones. Quartermaster—hard a-starboard.'

She was coming round on her heel like a dancer. Too fast!

'Meet her! Steady!'

He must hold on for a moment; and it would be as well, too, for then *Atropos* could regain the way and handiness of which the sharp turn had deprived her.

'Breakers ahead! Breakers on the starboard bow! Breakers to port!'

A chain of long, bright flashes over port quarter; a thunder-roll of reports, echoing again from the hills.

'Hard a-starboard. Brace her up, Mr Jones. Full and by!'

Coming round now, with Sari Point close alongside; not merely alongside but right ahead with the hollow curve of it.

'Keep your luff!'

'Sir—sir——'

The quartermaster at the wheel was croaking with anxiety; she would be in irons in a moment. The headsails were

I

flapping. From the feel of her she was losing her way, sagging off to leeward; she would be aground before long.

'Port a little.'

That would keep her going for a moment. The black bulk of Kaia was plainly visible to port. Sari was ahead and to starboard, and the wind was in their teeth. They were creeping forward to destruction. But there must be—there *must* be—a back lash of wind from Sari Point. It could not be otherwise with that land formation. The headsails flapped again as the quartermaster at the wheel vacillated between going aground and being taken aback.

'Keep her going.'

'Sir——!'

It would be close under the land that that air would be found if at all. Ah! Hornblower could feel the transition with the acute sensitivity of the seaman; the cessation of wind and then the tiny gentle breath on the other cheek. The headsails flapped again, but in a different mood from before; before Hornblower could speak the quartermaster was turning the wheel in agonized relief. It would only be a second or two that would be granted them, small enough time in which to gather steerage way to get the ship under command again, to gain distance from the cliffs.

'Stand by to go about!'

Steerage way so that the rudder would bite; that was what was wanted now. A flash and a roar from Passage Island— Kaia Rock nearly intercepted the flash; perhaps the shot was intercepted as well. That would be the first gun to be reloaded. The others would undoubtedly follow soon. Another flash, another roar, but no time to think about them, for Hornblower's perceptions told him of the fresh alteration in the feel of the ship. They were passing out into the wind again.

'Headsail sheets!'

One moment more. Now!

'Hard a-starboard!'

He could feel the rudder bite. She was coming round. She

would not miss stays. As she emerged into the wind she was on her new tack.

'Breakers right ahead!'

That was Kaia Rock, of course. But they must gather way again.

'Stand by to go about!'

They must hold on until the bowsprit was almost touching. Wait. Now!

'Hard over!'

The wheel spun. She was sluggish. Yes—no—yes. The fore staysail was drawing. She was coming round. The yards turned as the hands came aft with the lee-braces. One moment's hesitation, and then she gathered way on the fresh tack, leaving Kaia close beside them, Sari Point ahead; no chance of weathering it on this tack.

'Stand by to go about!'

Hold on as far as possible; this would be the last tack that would be necessary. A howl close overhead. That was a cannon-ball from Passage Island.

'Stand by! Hard over!'

Round she came, the rocks at the foot of Sari Point clearly visible as she wheeled away from them. A flaw, an eddy in the wind again, but only a second's hesitation as she caught the true breeze. Hold on for safety a moment more, with Kaia close abeam. Now all was safe.

'Mr Jones! Course South by East.'

'Course South by East, sir!'

They were heading into the open sea, with Rhodes to starboard and Turkey left behind, and with a King's ransom in the lazarette. They were leaving behind a prince's ransom, so to speak, but Hornblower could think of that with hardly a twinge.

XIX

His Majesty's sloop of war *Atropos*, admittedly, was the smallest ship in the British Navy. There were brigs of war smaller then she was, and schooners and cutters smaller still, but she was the smallest ship in the technical sense, with three masts and a captain in command, that King George owned, yet Hornblower was well content with her. There were times when he looked at the captains' list, and saw below his name those of the fifty captains junior to him, and when he noted above his name the slowly dwindling number of captains senior to him—as captains died or attained flag rank—and it occurred to him that some day, with good fortune, he might be posted to a frigate or even a ship of the line, yet at the moment he was content.

He had completed a mission and was entering upon another one. He had discharged at Gibraltar two hundred thousand pounds sterling in gold and silver coin, and he had left there the unpleasant Mr McCullum and his Ceylonese divers. The money was to await shipment to London, where it would constitute some part of the 'British gold' that sustained the fainting spirits of England's allies and against which Bonaparte raved so violently in his bulletins; McCullum and his men would wait for an opportunity to travel in the opposite direction, round Africa back to India. And *Atropos* was running before a heavy westerly gale in a third direction, back up the Mediterranean to rejoin Collingwood and the Mediterranean Fleet.

She seemed to be lightheartedly free of her encumbrances as she heaved and pitched on the quartering sea; after six months afloat, with hardly six hours on land, Hornblower's seasickness was no longer apparent and he was lighthearted on that account too, along with his ship. Collingwood had seen fit to approve of his report on his proceedings at Marmorice before sending him on to Gibraltar with the treasure, and had given him, for his return journey, orders that an adventurous young captain would approve of. He was to scour the Mediterranean coast of southern Spain, disorganize the Spanish coasting trade, gather up any information he could by personal observation of the harbours, and then look in at Corsica before rejoining the Fleet off the Italian coast, where it was damming back, at the water's edge, Bonaparte's new flood of conquest. Naples had fallen, but Sicily was held intact; Bonaparte's monstrous power ended when the salt water reached the saddle-girths of his horse. His armies could march where they would, but his ships cowered in port, or only ventured forth on furtive raids, while the little *Atropos*, with her twenty-two tiny guns, had twice sailed the whole length of the Mediterranean, from Gibraltar to Marmorice and back again, without once seeing the tricolor flag.

No wonder Hornblower felt pleased with himself, standing on the plunging deck without a qualm, looking over at the serrated skyline which, in the clear Mediterranean air, indicated the mountains of Spain. He had sailed boldly in within gunshot of the harbours and roadsteads of the coast; he had looked into Malaga and Motril and Almeria; fishing boats and coasters had fled before him like minnows before a pike. He had rounded Cape de Gata and had clawed his way back to the coast again so as to look into Cartagena. Malaga and Almeria had sheltered no ships of war. That was negative information, but even negative information could be of value to Collingwood as he directed the activities of his enormous fleet, covering the ramifications of British commerce over two thousand miles of sea, with his finger on the pulse of a score of international enmities and alliances. Cartagena was the principal Spanish naval base. An examination of it would reveal whether the bankrupt Spanish government had made any effort to reconstitute the fleet shattered at Trafalgar. Perhaps a French ship or two would be sheltering there, on one stage of some adventurous cruise planned by Bonaparte to enable them to strike at British convoys.

Hornblower looked up at the straining rigging, felt the heave and plunge of the ship under his feet. There were two reefs in the topsails already—it was more than half a gale that was blowing. He considered, and then dismissed, the notion of a third reef. *Atropos* could carry that amount of canvas safely enough. Cape Cope lay on the port beam; his glass revealed that a little cluster of coasters had taken refuge in the shallows under its lee, and he looked at them longingly. But there were batteries to protect them, and this wind made any attempt on them quite impracticable—he could not send in boats in the teeth of half a gale. He gave an order to the helmsman and the *Atropos* went hurtling on towards Cartagena. It was exhilarating to stand here by the taffrail with the wind screaming round him and a creamy wake emerging from under the stern beneath his feet. He smiled to watch Mr Turner's navigation class at work; Turner had the midshipmen and master's mates around him giving them instruction in coastwise navigation. He was trying to ballast their feather-brains with good solid mathematics about the 'running fix' and 'doubling the angle on the bow' and the 'four-point bearing,' but it was a difficult task to retain their attention in these stimulating surroundings, with the wind setting the chart fluttering wildly in Turner's hand and even making it hard for the young men to hold their slates steady as it caught their inclined surfaces. ·

'Mr Turner,' said Hornblower. 'Report any case of inattention to me at once and I will deal with it as it deserves.'

That steadied the young men to a noticeable extent and made them restrain their animal spirits. Smiley checked himself in the midst of a wink at the young Prince, and the Prince's embryo guffaw was stillborn as a guilty grin. That boy was perfectly human now—it was a far cry from the stuffy German court into which he had been born to the windy deck of the *Atropos*. If ever he were restored to the throne of his fathers he would be free of the thraldom of a sextant, but perhaps he might remember these breezy days with regret. The great-nephew of King George—Hornblower looked at him pretending to study the equilateral triangle scrawled on his slate, and smiled to himself again, remembering Dr Eisenbeiss's horror at the suggestion that perhaps corporal punishment might come the way of a reigning Prince. It had not so far, but it might.

Four bells sounded, the sand glass was turned, the wheel was relieved, and Turner dismissed his class.

'Mr Smiley! Mr Horrocks!'

The released midshipmen turned to their captain.

'I want you at the mastheads now with your glasses.'

Sharp young eyes would be best for looking into Cartagena. Hornblower noticed the appeal in the Prince's expression.

'Very well, Mr Prince. You can go too. Fore topmast head with Mr Smiley.'

It was a frequent punishment to send a young officer up to the discomforts of the masthead, but it was no punishment to-day, not with an enemy's harbour to be examined, and reports made on the shipping inside. Cartagena was fast coming into sight; the castle and the towers of the churches were visible now beyond the sheltering island of La Escombrera. With this westerly wind it was simple enough to stand right in so that from the masthead a view could be had of the inner harbour.

'Deck, there! Captain, sir——'

Smiley was hailing down from the fore topmast head. Hornblower had to walk forward to hear what he had to say, for the wind was sweeping away his words.

'There's a ship of war in the outer bay, sir! Spanish, she looks like. One of their big frigates. She's got her yards across.'

That was likely to be the *Castilla*, one of the survivors of Trafalgar.

'There's seven sail of coasters anchored close in, sir.'

They were safe enough from the *Atropos* in these conditions.
'What about the inner harbour?'

'Four—no five ships moored there, sir. And two hulks.'

'What d'you make of them?'

'Four of the line, sir, and a frigate. No yards across. Laid up in ordinary, I should say, sir.'

In past years the Spanish government had built fine ships, but under the corruption and inefficiency of Godoy they were allowed to rot at their moorings for want of crews and stores. Four of the line and a frigate laid up at Cartagena was what had last been reported there, so there was no change; negative information for Collingwood again, but useful.

'She's setting sail!'

That was the Prince's voice, high-pitched and excited, screaming down. A moment later Horrocks and Smiley were supplementing the warning.

'The frigate, sir! She's getting sail on her!'

'I can see her cross, sir!'

Spanish ships of war had the habit of hoisting huge wooden crosses at the mizzen peak when action seemed likely. The frigate must be intending to make a sortie, to chase away this inquisitive visitor. It was high time to beat a retreat. A big Spanish frigate such as the *Castilla* carried forty-four guns, just twice as many as *Atropos*, and with three times their weight of metal. If only over the horizon *Atropos* had a colleague to whom she could lure the *Castilla!* That was something to bear in mind and to suggest to Collingwood in any case; this Spanish captain was enterprising and energetic, and might be rash—he might be smouldering with shame after Trafalgar, and he might be lured out to his destruction.

'She's under way, sir!'

'Fore tops'l set! Main tops'l set, sir!'

No sense in courting danger, even though with this wind *Atropos* had a clear run to safety.

'Keep her away a point,' said Hornblower to the

helmsman, and *Atropos* turned a little to show a clean pair of heels to the Spaniard.

'She's coming out, sir!' reported Horrocks from the main topmast head. 'Reefed tops'ls. Two reefs, I think, sir.'

Hornblower trained his glass over the quarter. There it was, the white oblong just showing above the horizon as *Atropos* lifted—the reefed fore topsail of the *Castilla*.

'She's pointing straight at us now, sir,' reported Smiley.

In a stern chase like this *Atropos* had nothing to fear, newly coppered as she was and with a pretty turn of speed. The high wind and the rough sea would favour the bigger ship, of course. The *Castilla* might contrive to keep the *Atropos* in sight even though she had no chance of overtaking her. It would be a useful object lesson to officers and men to see *Atropos* making the best use of her potentiality for speed. Hornblower looked up again at sails and rigging. Certainly now there could be no question of taking in a third reef. He must carry all possible sail, just as the *Castilla* was doing.

Mr Still, as officer of the watch, was touching his hat to Hornblower with a routine question.

'Carry on, Mr Still.'

'Up spirits!'

With a powerful enemy plunging along behind her the life of the *Atropos* went on quite normally; the men had their grog and went to their dinners, the watch changed, the wheel was relieved. Palos Point disappeared over the port quarter as *Atropos* went flying on into the open Mediterranean, and still that white oblong kept its position on the horizon astern. The *Castilla* was doing well for a Spanish frigate.

'Call me the moment there is any change, Mr Jones,' said Hornblower, shutting his glass.

Jones was nervous—he might be imagining himself in a Spanish prison already. It would do him no harm to be left on deck with the responsibility, even though, down in his cabin, Hornblower found himself getting up from his dinner

table to peer aft through the scuttle to make sure the
Castilla was not gaining on them. In fact, Hornblower was
not sorry when, with his dinner not yet finished, a knock at
the door brought a messenger from the quarter-deck.

'Mr Jones's respects, sir, and the wind is moderating a
little, he thinks, sir.'

'I'm coming,' said Hornblower, laying down his knife and
fork.

In a moderate breeze *Atropos* ought to be able to run
Castilla topsails-under in an hour or two, and any reduction
in the wind was to the advantage of *Atropos* as long as she
spread all the canvas she could carry. But it would call for
judgment to shake out the reefs at the right time, without
imperilling spars on the one hand or losing distance on the
other. When Hornblower arrived on deck a glance told him
that it was time.

'You are quite right, Mr Jones,' he said—no harm in
giving him a pat on the back—'we'll shake out a reef.'

The order sped along the deck.

'Hands make sail!'

Hornblower looked aft through his glass; as *Atropos* lifted
her stern he could get the *Castilla*'s fore topsail right in the
centre of the field. The most painstaking thought could not
bring a decision as to whether or not it was any nearer. She
must be exactly maintaining her distance. Then as the topsail hung dizzily in the lens he saw—he was nearly sure he
saw—the oblong broaden into a square. He rested his eye
and looked again. No doubt about it. *Castilla* had decided
that was the moment to shake out a reef too.

Hornblower looked up at the *Atropos*' main topsail yard.
The topmen, bent over the yard at that dizzy height, had
completed the untying of the reef points. Now they came
running in from the yard. Smiley had the starboard yardarm,
and His Serene Highness the Prince of Seitz-Bunau the port.
They were having their usual race, flinging themselves on to
the backstays and sliding down without a thought for their
necks. Hornblower was glad that boy had found his feet—of

course he was wild with the excitement of the flight and pursuit; Hornblower was glad that Smiley had adopted that amused paternal attitude towards him.

With the letting out of the reef *Atropos* increased her speed again; Hornblower could feel the renewed thrust of the sail upon the fabric of the ship under his feet; he could feel the more frantic leap of the vessel on the wave crests. He directed a wary glance aloft. This would not be the moment to have anything carry away, not with *Castilla* tearing along in pursuit. Jones was standing by the wheel. The wind was just over the starboard quarter, and the little ship was answering well to her rudder, but it was as important to keep an eye on the helmsman as it was to see that they did not split a topsail. It called for some little resolution to leave Jones in charge again and go below to try to finish his dinner.

When the message came down again that the wind was moderating it was like that uncanny feeling which Hornblower had once or twice experienced of something happening again even though it had not happened before—the circumstances were so exactly similar.

'Mr Jones's respects, sir, and the wind is moderating a little, he thinks, sir.'

Hornblower had to compel himself to vary his reply.

'My compliments to Mr Jones, and I am coming on deck.'

Just as before, he could feel that the ship was not giving her utmost. Just as before, he gave the order for a reef to be shaken out. Just as before, he swung round to train his glass on the *Castilla*'s topsail. And just as before he turned back as the men prepared to come in from the yard. But that was the moment when everything took a different course, when the desperate emergency arose that always at sea lies just over the horizon of the future.

Excitement had stimulated the Prince into folly. Hornblower looked up to see the boy standing on the port yardarm, not merely standing but dancing, taking a clumsy step or two to dare Smiley at the starboard yardarm to imitate him, one hand on his hip, the other over his head. Hornblower was going to shout a reprimand; he opened his mouth and inflated his chest, but before he could utter a sound the Prince's foot slipped. Hornblower saw him totter, strive to regain his balance, and then fall, heavily through the air, and turning a complete circle as he fell.

Later on Hornblower, out of curiosity, made a calculation. The Prince fell from a height of a little over seventy feet, and without the resistance of the air and had he not bounced off the shrouds he would have reached the surface of the sea in something over two seconds. But the resistance of the air could have been by no means negligible —it must have got under his jacket and slowed his fall considerably, for the boy was not killed and was in fact only momentarily knocked unconscious by the impact. Probably it took as much as four seconds for the Prince to fall into the sea. Hornblower was led to make the calculation when brooding over the incident later, for he could remember clearly all the thoughts that passed through his mind during those four seconds. Momentary exasperation came first and then anxiety, and then followed a hasty summing up of the situation. If he hove-to to pick up the boy the *Castilla* would have all the time needed to overhaul them. If he went on the boy would drown. And if he went on he would have to report to Collingwood that he had left the King's great-nephew without lifting a finger to help him. He had to choose quickly—quickly. He had no right to risk his ship to save one single life. But—but—if the boy had been killed in battle by a broadside sweeping the deck it would be different. To abandon him was another matter again. On the heels of that conclusion came another thought, the beginnings of another thought, sprouting from a seed that had been sown outside Cartagena. It did not have time to develop in those four seconds; it was as if Hornblower acted the moment the green shoot from the seed showed above ground, to reach its full growth later.

By the time the boy had reached the sea Hornblower had

torn the emergency lifebuoy from the taffrail; he flung it
over the port quarter as the speed of the ship brought the
boy nearly opposite him, and it smacked into the sea close
beside him. At the same moment the air which Hornblower
had drawn into his lungs to reprimand the Prince was
expelled in a salvo of bellowed orders.

'Mizzen braces! Back the mizzen topsail! Quarter boat
away!'

Maybe—Hornblower could not be sure later—everyone
was shouting at once, but everyone at least responded to
orders with the rapidity that was the result of months of
drill. *Atropos* flew up into the wind, her way checked
instantly. It was Smiley—Heaven only knew how he had
made the descent from the starboard main topsail yardarm
in that brief space—who got the jolly boat over the side,
with four men at the oars, and dashed off to effect the rescue,
the tiny boat soaring up and swooping down as the waves
passed under her. And even before *Atropos* was hove-to
Hornblower was putting the next part of the plan into action.

'Mr Horrocks! Signal "Enemy in sight to windward." '

Horrocks stood and gaped, and Hornblower was about
to blare out with 'Blast you, do what I tell you,' but he
restrained himself. Horrocks was not a man of the quickest
thought in the world, and he had failed entirely to see any
purpose in signalling to a vacant horizon. To swear at him
now would simply paralyse him with nervousness and lead
to a further delay.

'Mr Horrocks, kindly send up the signal as quickly as you
can. "Enemy in sight to windward." Quickly, please.'

The signal rating beside Horrocks was luckily quicker
witted—he was one of the dozen men of the crew who could
read and write, naturally—and was already at the halliards
with the flag-locker open, and his example shook Horrocks
out of his amazement. The flags went soaring up to the main
topmast yardarm, flying out wildly in the wind. Hornblower
made a mental note that that rating, even though he was no
seaman as yet—lately a City apprentice who had come

hurriedly aboard at Deptford to avoid something worse in civilian life—was deserving of promotion.

'Now another signal, Mr Horrocks. "Enemy is a frigate distant seven miles bearing west course east." '

It was the sensible thing to do to send up the very signals he would have hoisted if there really were help in sight—the *Castilla* might be able to read them or might make at least a fair guess at their meaning. If there had been a friendly ship in sight down to leeward (Hornblower remembered the suggestion he had been going to make to Collingwood) he would never have hove-to, of course, but would have gone on tearing down to lure the *Castilla* as near as possible, but the captain of the *Castilla* was not to know that.

'Keep that signal flying. Now send up an affirmative, Mr Horrocks. Very good. Haul it down again. Mr Jones! Lay the ship on the starboard tack, a good full.'

A powerful English ship down there to leeward would certainly order *Atropos* to close on *Castilla* as quickly as possible. He must act as if that were the case. It was only when Jones—almost as helpless with astonishment as Horrocks had been—had plunged into the business of getting *Atropos* under way again that Hornblower had time to use his telescope. He trained it on the distant topsail again; not so distant now. Coming up fast, and Hornblower felt a sick feeling of disappointment and apprehension. And then as he watched he saw the square of the topsail narrow into a vertical oblong, and two other oblongs appear beside it. At the same moment the masthead lookout gave a hail.

'Deck there! The enemy's hauled his wind, sir!'

Of course he would do so—the disappointment and apprehension vanished instantly. A Spanish frigate captain once he had put his bowsprit outside the safety of a defended port would ever be a prey to fear. Always there would be the probability in his mind that just over the horizon lay a British squadron ready to pounce on him. He would chase a little sloop of war eagerly enough, but as soon as he saw that sloop sending up signals and swinging boldly round on a course that challenged action he would bethink him of the fact that he was already far to leeward of safety; he would imagine hostile ships only just out of sight cracking on all sail to cut him off from his base, and once his mind was made up he would not lose a single additional mile or minute before turning to beat back to safety. For two minutes the Spaniard had been a prey to indecision after *Atropos* hove-to, but the final bold move had made up his mind for him. If he had held on for a short time longer he might have caught sight of the jolly boat pulling over the waves and then would have guessed what *Atropos* was doing, but as it was, time was gained and the Spaniard, close-hauled, was clawing back to safety in flight from a non-existent enemy.

'Masthead! What do you see of the boat?'

'She's still pulling, sir, right in the wind's eye!'

'Do you see anything of Mr Prince?'

'No, sir, can't say as I do.'

Not much chance in that tossing sea of seeing a floating man two miles away, not even from the masthead.

'Mr Jones, tack the ship.'

It would be best to keep *Atropos* as nearly straight down wind from the boat as possible, allowing it an easy run to leeward when its mission was accomplished. *Castilla* would not be able to make anything of the manœuvre.

'Deck there! The boat's stopped pulling, sir. I think they're picking up Mr Prince, sir.'

Thank God for that. It was only now that Hornblower could realize what a bad ten minutes it had been.

'Deck there! Yes, sir, they're waving a shirt. They're pulling back to us now.'

'Heave-to, Mr Jones, if you please. Doctor Eisenbeiss, have everything ready in case Mr Prince needs treatment.'

The Mediterranean at midsummer was warm enough; most likely the boy had taken no harm. The jolly boat came dancing back over the waves and turned under *Atropos*' stern into the little lee afforded by her quarter as she rode with her starboard bow to the waves. Here came His Serene

Highness, wet and bedraggled but not in the least hurt, meeting the concentrated gaze of all on deck with a smile half sheepish and half defiant. Eisenbeiss came forward fussily, talking voluble German, and then turned to Hornblower to explain.

'I have a hot blanket ready for him, sir.'

It was at that moment that the dam of Hornblower's even temper burst.

'A hot blanket! I know what'll warm him quicker than that. Bos'n's mate! My compliments to the bos'n, and ask him to be kind enough to lend you his cane for a few minutes. Shut your mouth, doctor, if you know what's good for you. Now, young man——'

Humanitarians had much to say against corporal punishment, but in their arguments, while pointing out the harm it might do to the one punished, they omitted to allow for the satisfaction other people derived from it. And it was some further training for the Blood Royal to display his acquired British imperturbability, to bite off the howl that a well-applied cane tended to draw forth, and to stand straight afterwards with hardly a skip to betray his discomfort, with hardly a rub at the smarting royal posterior, and with the tears blinked manfully back. Satisfaction or not, Hornblower was a little sorry afterwards.

XX

THERE was everything to be said in favour of keeping *Castilla* under observation for a while at least, and almost nothing to be said against it. The recent flight and pursuit had proved that *Atropos* had the heels of her even under reefed topsails, so that it could be taken for granted that she was safe from her in any lesser wind—and the wind was moderating. The *Castilla* was now a full thirty miles dead to leeward of Cartagena; it would be useful to know—Collingwood would certainly want to know—whether she intended to beat back there again or would fetch some easier Spanish port. Close hauled she could make Alicante to the north or perhaps Almeria to the south; she was close-hauled on the starboard tack, heading south, at this moment. And there was the possibility to be borne in mind that she did not intend to return to Spain as yet, that her captain might decide to range through the Mediterranean for a while to see what prizes he could snap up. On her present course she could easily stretch over to the Barbary coast and pick up a victualler or two with grain and cattle intended for the Fleet.

Hornblower's orders were that he should rejoin Collingwood in Sicilian waters after looking into Malaga and Cartagena; he was not the bearer of urgent despatches, nor, Heaven knew, was *Atropos* likely to be an important addition to the strength of the Fleet; while on the other hand it was the duty of every English captain, having once made contact with a ship of the enemy in open water, to maintain that contact as long as was possible. *Atropos* could not hope to face *Castilla* in battle, but she could keep her under observation, she might warn merchant shipping of danger, and she might with good fortune meet some big British ship of war—

in actual fact, not make-believe—to whom she could indicate the enemy.

'Mr Jones,' said Hornblower. 'Lay her on the starboard tack again, if you please. Full and by.'

'Aye aye, sir.'

Jones, of course, showed some surprise at the reversal of the roles, at the pursued becoming the pursuer, and that was one more proof that he was incapable of strategic thought. But he had to engage himself on carrying out his orders, and *Atropos* steadied on a southerly course, running parallel to *Castilla's*, far to windward; Hornblower trained his glass on the topsails just visible over the horizon. He fixed the shape of them firmly in his memory; a slight alteration in the proportion of length to breadth would indicate any change of course on the part of the *Castilla*.

'Masthead!' he hailed. 'Keep your eye on the enemy. Report anything you see.'

'Aye aye, sir.'

Atropos was like a terrier now, yapping at the heels of a bull in a field—not a very dignified role—and the bull might turn and charge at any moment. Eventually the captain of the *Castilla* would make up his mind that a trick had been played on him, that *Atropos* had been signalling to non-existent friends, and there was no guessing what he might decide to do then, when he grew certain that there was no help following *Atropos* up just beyond the horizon. Meanwhile the wind was still moderating, and *Atropos* could set more canvas. When beating to windward she behaved best under all the sail she could carry, and he might as well keep as close to the enemy as the wind allowed.

'Try setting the mainsail, Mr Jones, if you please.'

'Aye aye, sir.'

The main course was a big sail, and the little *Atropos* seemed to take wings under the tremendous pressure of it when it was sheeted home, with the tack hauled forward to the chess-trees by the united strength of half a watch. Now she was thrusting along bravely in the summer evening, lying

over to the wind, and shouldering off the hungry waves with
her starboard bow in great fountains of spray, through
which the setting sun gleamed in fleeting rainbows of fiery
beauty, and leaving behind her a seething wake dazzling
white against the blue. It was a moment when it was good
to be alive, driving hard to windward like this, and with all
the potentiality of adventure at hand in the near unknown.
War at sea was a dreary business usually, with boredom and
discomfort to be endured day and night, watch and watch,
but it had moments of high exaltation like this, just as it had
its moments of black despair, of fear, of shame.

'You may dismiss the watch below, Mr Jones.'

'Aye aye, sir.'

Hornblower glanced round the deck. Still would have the
watch.

'Call me if there's any change, Mr Still. I want to set more
sail if the wind moderates further.'

'Aye aye, sir.'

A moment of exaltation, come and gone. He had been on
his feet nearly all day, since dawn, and his legs were weary,
and if he stayed on deck they would grow wearier still. Down
below there were the two books he had bought at Gibraltar
for a badly needed guinea—Lord Hodge's 'Statement of the
Present Political Condition of Italy,' and Barber's 'New
Methods of Determining Longitude, with some Remarks on
Discrepancies in Recent Charts.' He wanted to inform himself on both subjects, and it was better to do so now than to
stay up on deck growing more and more weary while the
hours passed.

At sunset he emerged again; *Castilla* was still holding the
same course, with *Atropos* head-reaching upon her very
slightly. He looked at those distant topsails; he read the slate
that recorded the day's run, and he waited while the log was
hove again. Surely if *Castilla* intended to put back into
Cartagena she would have gone about by now. She had
made a very long reach to the southward, and any backing
of the wind round to the north—a very likely occurrence at

this season—would nullify much of her progress so far. If she did not come about by the time darkness set in it would be a strong indication that she had something else in mind. He waited as the sunset faded from the western sky, and until the first stars began to appear overhead; that was when his aching eye, straining through the glass, could see no more of *Castilla*. But at the last sight of her she was still standing to the southward. All the more reason to keep her under observation.

It was the end of the second dogwatch and the hands were being called.

'I'll have the main-course taken in, Mr Turner,' he said.

He wrote his night orders by the faint light of the binnacle; the ship to be kept close-hauled on the starboard tack; he was to be called if the wind shifted more than two points, and in any event he was to be called immediately before moonrise in the middle watch. The gloomy little cabin when he retired into it was like a wild beast's lair with its dark corners where the light of the lamp did not penetrate. He lay down fully clothed, endeavouring to keep his tired mind from continuing to try to solve the problem of what the *Castilla* intended to do. He had shortened sail, as she would probably do. If she did not, he had the heels of her and might overtake her in daylight. If she did anything else, if she tacked or wore, he was doing what was probably best to find her again next day. His eyes closed with fatigue, and did not open again until they came to tell him the middle watch had been called.

The west wind, dying away though it was, had brought a slight overcast with it, enough to obscure the stars and deprive the small moon, almost in its last quarter, of most of its light. *Atropos*, still close-hauled, was now, in the lessening wind, only flirting with the waves that came on to her starboard bow, meeting them elegantly like a stage beauty extending her hand to a stage lover. The dark water all around seemed to fall in with the mood and to murmur pretty conventionalities. There seemed no imminence of blazing death. The minutes passed in warm idleness.

'Deck there!' That was the masthead lookout hailing. 'I think I can see something, sir. Right away on the starboard bow.'

'Get aloft with the night glass, youngster,' said Turner, who had the watch, to the master's mate beside him.

A minute passed, two minutes.

'Yes, sir,' came the new voice from the masthead. 'It's the loom of a ship. Three miles—four miles—fine on the starboard bow.'

The night glasses trained round more forward.

'Maybe,' said Turner.

There was a tiny patch of something darker than the surrounding night; Hornblower's night glass could tell him no more than that. He watched it painstakingly. The bearing of it seemed to be altering.

'Steer small!' he growled at the helmsman.

For a moment he wondered if the patch was really there; it might be something his mind suggested to his eye—a whole ship's company could sometimes imagine the same thing if the idea was once put in their heads. No, it was undoubtedly there, and drawing across *Atropos'* bows, more than could be accounted for by any wavering of her course with bad steering. It must be *Castilla;* she must have swung round at midnight and come hurrying down wind in the hope of pouncing on her prey by surprise. If he had not shortened sail she would be right on him. The Spanish lookouts were not up to their work, for she was holding on her course.

'Heave-to, Mr Turner,' he said, and walked across to the port side to keep the *Castilla* under observation as *Atropos* came up into the wind. *Castilla* had already lost most of the advantage of the weather gage, and in a few minutes would lose it all. The slowly-moving clouds overhead were parting; there was a faint gleam of light through a thin patch, further darkness, and then the moon shone through a gap. Yes, that was a ship; that was the *Castilla*, already far down to leeward.

'Deck, there! I can see her plainly now, sir. On the port quarter. Captain, sir! She's wearing round!'

So she was. Her sails gleamed momentarily bright in the moonlight as they swung round. She had failed in her attempt to surprise her enemy, and was making a fresh one.

'Lay her on the port tack, Mr Turner.'

The little *Atropos* could play catch-as-catch-can with any big frigate in this sort of weather. She swung round and headed into the wind, her stern to her pursuer again.

'Masthead! What sail has the enemy set?'

'She's setting her royals, sir. All plain sail to the royals.'

'Call all hands, Mr Turner. Set all plain sail.'

There was still enough wind for the addition of courses and royals to lay *Atropos* over and send her flying once more. Hornblower looked back at *Castilla*'s topsails and royals, silhouetted now against clear sky below the moon. It did not take very long to determine that now *Atropos* was gaining fast. He was pondering a decision regarding shortening sail when he was saved the trouble. The silhouettes narrowed again abruptly.

'Deck there!' hailed the masthead. 'Enemy's hauled her wind, sir.'

'Very well! Mr Turner, wear ship, if you please. Point our bows right at her, and take in the fore course.'

The terrier had evaded the bull's charge and was now yapping at its heels again. It was easy to follow the *Castilla* for the rest of the night, keeping a sharp lookout during the periods of darkness lest she should play on them the same trick as *Atropos* had played once. Dawn, rising ahead, revealed the *Castilla*'s royals and topsails an inky black before they changed to ivory white against the blue sky. Hornblower could imagine the rage of the Spanish captain at the sight of his pertinacious pursuer, dogging him in this fashion with insolent impunity. Seven miles separated the ships, but as far as the *Castilla's* big eighteen-pounders mattered it might as well be seventy, and moreover the invisible wind, blowing direct from *Atropos* to *Castilla*, was an additional protection, guarding her from her enemy like the mysterious glass shield that turned the hero's sword in one of the Italian epics. *Atropos*, seven miles to windward, was as safe and yet as visible as the Saracen magician.

Hornblower was conscious of weariness again. He had been on his feet since midnight, after less than four hours' rest. He wanted, passionately, to rest his legs; he wanted, hardly less, to close his aching eyes. The hammocks had been brought up, the decks swabbed, and it only remained now to cling to *Castilla's* heels, but when any moment might bring the need for a quick decision he dared not leave the deck—odd that now he was safely to windward the situation was more dynamic than yesterday when he had been to leeward, but it was true. *Castilla* might come to the wind at any unforeseen moment, and moreover the two ships were driving into the blue Mediterranean where any surprise might be over the horizon.

'I'll have a mattress up here,' said Hornblower.

They brought one up and laid it aft beside the weather scuppers. He eased his aching joints down on to it, settled his head on his pillow, and closed his eyes. The lift and send of the ship were soporific, and so was the sound of the sea under the *Atropos'* counter. The light played backward and forward over his face as the shadows of sails and rigging followed the movement of the ship. He could sleep—he could sleep, heavily and dreamlessly, while the ships flew on up the Mediterranean, while they called the watch, while they hove the log, even while they trimmed the yards as the wind came a little northerly, moving round ahead of the sun.

It was afternoon when he woke. He shaved with the aid of a mirror stuck in the hammock nettings; he took his bath under the washdeck pump and put on the clean shirt that he sent for; he sat on the deck and ate cold beef and the last of the goodly soft bread taken on board at Gibraltar, somewhat stale now but infinitely better than ship's biscuit; and the fresh butter from the same source, kept cool so far in an earthenware crock was quite delicious. It struck seven bells as he finished his last mouthful.

'Deck there! Enemy's altering course.'

He was on his feet in a flash, his plate sliding into the scuppers, the telescope in his hand without conscious volition on his part. No doubt about it. *Castilla* had altered to a more northerly course, with the wind abeam. It was not very surprising for they had run a full two hundred miles from Cartagena; unless the *Castilla* was prepared to go right up the Mediterranean far to leeward of all Spanish bases, it was time for her to head north to fetch Minorca. He would follow her there, the terrier harassing the bull, and he would give a final yap at the bull's heels outside Port Mahon. Besides, the *Castilla's* alteration of course might not portend a mere flight to Minorca. They were right on the track of convoys beating up the Mediterranean from Sicily and Malta.

'Port your helm, Mr Still, if you please. Maintain a parallel course.'

It was only sensible to stay up to windward of *Castilla* as much as possible. The intense feeling of wellbeing of five minutes ago was replaced now by excitement, a slight tingling under the skin. Ten to one the *Castilla's* alteration of course meant nothing at all, but there was the tenth chance. Eight bells; hands mustered for the first dogwatch.

'Deck there! There's a sail ahead of the enemy, sir!'

That was it, then.

'Get aloft with you, Mr Smiley. You can go too, Mr Prince.'

That would show His Serene Highness that a punishment cleared the record in the Navy, and that he was being trusted not to risk any more monkey tricks. It was a detail that had to be borne in mind despite the flood of excitement following the masthead report. There was no knowing what that sail over there, invisible from the deck, might imply. But there was a chance that it was a British ship of war, fair in *Castilla's* path.

'Two sail! Three sail! Captain, sir, it looks like a convoy, dead to leeward.'

A convoy could only be a British convoy, and a convoy meant the presence of a British ship of war ahead there in *Castilla's* path.

'Up helm and bear down on the enemy. Call all hands, Mr Still, if you please. Clear for action.'

During all the long flight and pursuit he had not cleared for action. He had not wanted action with the vastly superior *Castilla*, and had been determined on avoiding it. Now he hoped for it—hoped for it with that tremor of doubt that made him hate himself, all the more so as the repeating of the order brought a cheer from the men, the watch below pouring on deck for duty with expectant grins and schoolboy excitement. Mr Jones came bustling up on deck buttoning his coat; apparently he had been dozing comfortably through the afternoon watch. To Jones would fall the command of the *Atropos* if any accident should befall him, if a shot should take off his leg or dash him into bloody fragments. Odd that the thought of Jones becoming responsible for handling *Atropos* was as disturbing as the rest of it. But all the same Jones must be brought up to date on the situation and told what should be done. He did it in three sharp sentences.

'I see, sir,' said Jones, pulling at his long chin. Hornblower was not so sure that he did see, but there was no more time to spare for Jones.

'Masthead! What of the convoy?'

'One sail has tacked, sir. She's standing towards us.'

'What d'you make of her?'

'She looks like a ship of war, sir. I can only see her royals, sir.'

'Mr Horrocks, make the private signal and our number.'

A ship standing towards *Castilla* could only be a ship of war, the escorting vessel. Hornblower could only hope she would be one of the larger frigates, able to meet the big *Castilla* on something like equal terms. But he knew most of the frigates Collingwood had—*Sirius, Naiad, Hermione*—thirty-two gun twelve-pounder frigates most of them, hardly a match for *Castilla's* forty-four eighteen-pounders unless well handled, and unless *Castilla* fought badly, and unless he himself had a chance to intervene. He strained his eyesight staring forward through his glass, but the British ship was not yet in sight from the deck, and *Castilla* was still running boldly down before the wind. Clearing for action was nearly completed; they were casting loose the guns.

'Signal, sir!'

Horrocks was ready with the book as the masthead reported the flags.

'Private signal correctly answered, sir. And her number. She's *Nightingale*, sir, 28, Captain Ford, sir.'

Almost the smallest of the frigates, with only nine-pounders on her maindeck. Please God Ford would have the sense not to close with *Castilla*. He must out-manœuvre her, keep her in play, and then when *Atropos* came up there could be some pretty tactics until they could shoot away some of *Castilla's* spars and take her at a disadvantage. Then they could rake her and weaken her before closing in for the kill. The captain of the *Castilla* was showing proof of having grasped the essentials of the situation; caught between two hostile ships so that he could not avoid action if it were forced on him he was plunging down at his best speed to the attack on the one most accessible to him; he was still carrying all sail to bring him most quickly into action before *Atropos* could intervene. He could well hope to batter *Nightingale* into a wreck and then turn on *Atropos*. If he succeeded—oh, if he succeeded!—it would be a terrible problem for *Atropos*, to decide whether or not to accept action.

'Ship cleared for action, sir,' reported Jones.

'Very well.'

Now his glass picked her up; the distant sail, far beyond *Castilla*. As he looked, as the top gallants appeared below

the royals, the royals disappeared. *Nightingale* was shortening down to 'fighting sails' ready for action. Hornblower
knew a little about Ford. He had the reputation of a good
fighting captain. Please God he had discretion as well. Ford
was far his senior in the Navy list; there was no possibility
of giving him orders to keep clear.

Castilla was still hurtling down upon *Nightingale*.

'Signal, sir. Number 72. "Engage the enemy more
closely!" '

'Acknowledge.'

Hornblower was conscious of Jones's and Turner's eyes
upon him. There might be an implied rebuke in that signal,
a hint that he was not doing his best to get into action. On
the other hand it might be a mere signal that action was
imminent. *Nightingale's* topsails were over the horizon now;
close-hauled, she was doing her best to come to meet
Castilla. If only Ford would hold off for half an hour—
Atropos was steadily gaining on *Castilla*. No, he was still
hurrying to the encounter before *Atropos* could arrive; he
was playing *Castilla's* game for her. Now *Castilla* was clew-
ing up her courses; she was taking in her royals, ready for
the clash. The two ships were hastening together; white sails
on a blue sea under a blue sky. They were right in line from
where Hornblower stood staring at them through his glass;
right in line so that it was hard to judge the distance between
them. Now they were turning, *Nightingale* paying off before
the wind as *Castilla* approached. All the masts seemed
blended together. Ford *must* keep clear and try to shoot
away a spar.

A sudden billowing of smoke round the ships; the first
broadsides were being fired. It looked as if the ships were
already close-locked in action—surely it could not be. Not
time yet to take in courses and royals; the sooner they got
down into action the better. Now, heavily over the blue
water, came the sound of those first broadsides, like the
rumbling of thunder. The smoke was blowing clear of the
fight, drifting away from the ships in a long bank. More

smoke billowing up; the guns had been reloaded and were
firing away, and still the masts were close together—had
Ford been fool enough to lock yardarms? Again the long
rumble of the guns. The ships were swinging round in the
smoke cloud; he could see the masts above it changing their
bearing, but he could not distinguish ship from ship. There
was a mast falling, yards, sails and all; it must be *Nightingale's* main topmast, hideous though the thought was. This
seemed like a lifetime, waiting to get into action. Cannon
smoke and cannon thunder. He did not want to believe the
glass was really revealing the truth to him as he looked, the
details becoming clearer as he approached. The two ships
were locked together, no doubt about it. And that was
Nightingale, main topmast gone. She was lying at an angle
to *Castilla's* side, bows towards her. The wind was still
turning the two ships, and it was turning them as if they
were one. *Nightingale* must be locked against *Castilla*, bowsprit or possibly anchor hooked into *Castilla's* fore chains.
All *Castilla's* guns could bear, practically raking *Nightingale*
with every broadside, and *Nightingale's* fire must be almost
ineffectual. Could she tear herself loose? There went her
foremast, everything, over the side; almost impossible to
tear herself loose now.

The men at the guns were yelling at the sight.

'Silence! Mr Jones, get the courses in.'

What was he to do? He ought to cross *Castilla's* bows or
stern and rake her, come about and rake her again. Not so
easy to fire into *Castilla's* bows without hitting *Nightingale;*
not so easy to cross her stern; that would put him to leeward
and there would be delay in getting back into action again.
And the two ships were still swinging considerably, not only
with the wind but with the recoil of their guns. Supposing
that as he took *Atropos* to lie a little clear they swung so that
Nightingale intercepted his fire and he had to work back
again to windward to get back into action? That would be
shameful, and other captains hearing the story would think
he had deliberately stayed out of fire. He could lay his ship

alongside *Castilla* on her unoccupied side, but her slender scantlings would bear little of *Castilla's* ponderous broadside; his ship would be a wreck in a few minutes. And yet *Nightingale* was already a wreck. He must bring her instant, immediate relief.

Now they were only a mile from the locked ships and running down fast. Years of experience at sea told him how rapidly those last few minutes passed when ships needed each other.

'Muster the port side guns' crews,' he said. 'Every man, gun captains and all. Arm them for boarding. Arm every idler in the ship. But leave the hands at the mizzen braces.'

'Aye aye, sir.'

'Pikes, pistols and cutlasses, lads,' said Hornblower to the eager men thronging round the arms chests. 'Mr Smiley, muster your topmen for'rard by No. 1 gun. Starboard side. Stand by for a rush.'

Young Smiley was the best fighting man of them all, better than the nervous Jones or the stupid Still or the aged Turner. It was best to give him the command at the other end of the ship. Aft here he would have things under his own eye. And he realized he was still unarmed himself. His sword—the sword he had worn at the court of his King—was a cheap one. He could guess its temper was unreliable; he had never been able to afford a good sword. He stepped to the arms chest and took a cutlass for himself, drawing it and dropping the scabbard discarded on the deck; looping the knot over his wrist he stood with the naked blade in his hand and the sunlight beating down in his face.

Now they were closing on *Castilla;* only a cable's length apart and it looked closer. It called for accurate judgment to come close alongside.

'Starboard a point,' he said to the helmsman.

'Starboard a point,' came the repetition of the order.

Discipline kept the helmsman entirely attentive to his particular duty, even though *Castilla's* port side gun ports were opening, even though at that close range the gun muzzles were glaring straight at them, and the faces of the gunners could be seen through the ports looking along the guns. Oh God, it was just coming!

'Now, starboard slowly. Bring her gently round.'

Like the end of the world that broadside came, ripping and smashing into the ship; there were screams, there were frightful crashes, the sunlight was full of dust particles flung up by the hurtling cannon-balls as the splinters whizzed through the air, and then the ship sidled into the powder smoke jutting forth from the gun muzzles. But he must think about only one thing at this moment.

'Now! Hard a-port. Braces there! Back the mizzen tops'l!'

There was a tiny gap between the sides of the two ships, closing by inches. If she struck violently she might rebound and open the gap again; if her forward way was not checked she might scrape forward and swing. In the loftier sides of the *Castilla* the gun ports were above the level of those of the *Atropos*. The dish-shaped *Atropos* had no 'tumble-home' to her sides. Her bulwarks would make contact—he had been counting on that.

'Starboard side! Fire!'

The infernal crash of the broadside; the smoke whirling round, the orange-painted side of *Castilla* torn by the carronade balls; but not a moment to think about it.

'Come on!'

Up over *Castilla's* side in the eddying smoke pierced by sunbeams; up over the side, cutlass in hand, wild with fighting madness. A distorted face looking up at him. Strike, swinging the heavy blade like an axe. Wrench the blade free, and strike again at this new face. Plunge forward. Gold lace here, a lean brown face gashed by a black moustache, a slender blade lunging at him; beat it aside and strike and strike and strike with every ounce of strength, with all the speed possible to him; beat down the feeble guard and strike again without pity. Trip over something and recover again. The terrified eyes of the men at the wheel looking round at him before they ran from his fury. A uniformed soldier with white cross-belts extending his arms in surrender; a pike appearing from nowhere beside him and plunging into the soldier's unprotected breast. The quarter-deck cleared but no time to breathe; shout 'Come on' and plunge down on to the maindeck.

Something hit his cutlass blade and sent a numbing shock up his arm—a pistol bullet, most likely. There was a crowd of men massed round the main mast, but before he could reach it a surge of pikes from the side broke it up into fleeing fragments. Now a sudden rally on the part of the enemy, pistols banging, and then suddenly opposition ceased and Hornblower found himself glaring into a pair of wild eyes and realized that it was an English uniform, an English face although unknown to him—a midshipman from *Nightingale*, leading the boarding party which had stormed into the *Castilla* along *Nightingale's* bowsprit.

He could stand there now amid the wreckage and the dead with the madness ebbing out of him, sweat running into his eyes and blinding him; and yet once more he had to clear his mind and brace himself. He had to stop the killing that was still going on, he had to organize the disarming of the prisoners and the herding of them against the ship's side. He had to remember to say a word of thanks to Smiley, covered with blood and smoke, when he met him on the gangway forward. Here was the huge hulk of Eisenbeiss, chest heaving, the bloody cutlass like a toy in his vast hand. The sight roused his wrath.

'What the hell are you doing here, doctor? Get back on board and attend to the wounded. You've no business to neglect them.'

A smile for the Prince, and then his attention was demanded by a thin-nosed, long-faced rat of a man.

'Captain Hornblower? My name's Ford.'

He was going to shake the proffered hand, but discovered that first he must slip the cutlass lanyard from his wrist and transfer the weapon to his other hand.

'All's well that ends well,' said Ford. 'You arrived in time, but only just in time, captain.'

It was no use trying to point out to a senior the senior's errors. They shook hands there, standing on the gangway of the captured *Castilla*, looking round at the three ships clinging together, battered and shattered. Far down to leeward, drifting over the blue sea, the long trail of powder smoke was slowly dissipating under the blue heaven.

XXI

THE church bells of Palermo were ringing, as always, in the drowsy heat of the morning. The sound of them drifted over the water of the bay, the Conca d'Oro, the golden shell which holds the pearl of Palermo in its embrace. Hornblower could hear them as he brought *Atropos* in, echoing round from Monte Pellegrino to Zaffarano, and of all musical noises that was the one that annoyed him most. He looked over at the senior ship, impatient for her to start firing her salute to shatter this maddening sound. If it were not for the church bells this would be almost a happy moment, dramatic enough in all conscience. *Nightingale* under her jury rig, the clear water gushing out of her as the pumps barely kept her afloat, *Atropos* with the raw plugs in the shot holes in her sides, and then *Castilla*, battered and shot torn, too, and with the White Ensign proudly flying over the red and gold of Spain. Surely even the Sicilians must be struck by the drama of this entrance, and for additional pleasure, there were a trio of English ships of war at anchor over there; their crews at least would gape at the proud procession; they at least would be sensitive to all that the appearance of the newcomers implied; they would know of the din and the fury, the agony of the wounded and the distressing ceremony of the burial of the dead.

Palermo looked out idly as the ships came to anchor, and as the boats (even the boats were patched-up fabrics, hurriedly repaired after being shattered by shot) were swung out and began new activities. The wounded had to be carried ashore to hospital, boat-load after boat-load of them, moaning or silent with pain; then the prisoners under guard —there was pathos in those boat-loads of men, too, of a proud nation, going into captivity within four gloomy walls,

under all the stigma of defeat. Then there was other ferrying
to be done; the forty men that *Atropos* had lent to *Nightingale* had to be replaced by another forty. The ones that came
back were gaunt and hollow-cheeked, bearded and dirty.
They fell asleep sitting on the thwarts, and they fell asleep
again the moment they climbed on board, falling like dead
men between the guns, for they had laboured for eleven days
and nights bringing the shattered *Nightingale* in after the
victory.

There was so much to do that it was not until evening that
Hornblower had leisure to open the two private letters that
were awaiting him. The second one was only six weeks old,
having made a quick passage out from England and not
having waited long for *Atropos* to come in to Palermo, the
new base of the Mediterranean Fleet. Maria was well, and
so were the children. Little Horatio was running everywhere
now, she said, as lively as a cricket, and little Maria was as
good as gold, hardly crying at all even though it seemed
likely that she was about to cut a tooth, a most remarkable
feat at five months old. And Maria was happy enough in the
Southsea house with her mother, although she was lonely
for her husband, and although her mother tended to spoil
the children in a way that Maria feared would not be
approved by her very dearest.

Letters from home; letters about little children and
domestic squabbles; they were the momentary lifting of a
curtain to reveal another world, utterly unlike this world of
peril and hardship and intolerable strain. Little Horatio was
running everywhere on busy little legs, and little Maria was
cutting her first tooth, while here a tyrant's armies had swept
through the whole length of Italy and were massed at the
Straits of Messina for an opportunity to make another
spring and effect another conquest in Sicily, where only a
mile of water—and the Navy—opposed their progress.
England was fighting for her life against all Europe combined
under a single tyrant of frightful energy and cunning.

No, not quite all Europe, for England still had allies—

Portugal under an insane queen, Sweden under a mad king, and Sicily, here, under a worthless king. Ferdinand, King of Naples and Sicily—King of the Two Sicilies—bad, cruel, selfish; brother of the King of Spain, who was Bonaparte's closest ally; Ferdinand, a tyrant more bloodthirsty and more tyrannical than Bonaparte himself, faithless and untrustworthy, who had lost one of his two thrones and was only held on the other by British naval might and who yet would betray his allies for a moment's gratification of his senses, and whose gaols were choked with political prisoners and whose gallows creaked under the weight of dead suspects. Good men, and brave men, were suffering and dying in every part of the world while Ferdinand hunted in his Sicilian preserves and his wicked queen lied and intrigued and betrayed, and while Maria wrote simple little letters about the babies.

It was better to think about his duties than to brood over these insoluble anomalies. Here was a note from Lord William Bentinck, the British Minister in Palermo. 'The latest advices from the Vice-Admiral Commanding in the Mediterranean are to the effect that he may be expected very shortly in Palermo with his flagship. His Excellency therefore begs to inform Captain Horatio Hornblower that in His Excellency's opinion it would be best if Captain Horatio Hornblower were to begin the necessary repairs to *Atropos* immediately. His Excellency will request His Sicilian Majesty's naval establishment to afford Captain Horatio Hornblower all the facilities he may require.'

Lord William might be—undoubtedly was—a man of estimable character and liberal opinions unusual in a son of a Duke, but he knew little enough about the workings of a Sicilian dockyard. In the three days that followed Hornblower succeeded in achieving nothing at all with the help of Sicilian authorities. Turner was voluble to them in lingua franca, and Hornblower laid aside his dignity to plead with them in French with o's and a's added to the words in the hope that in that manner he might convey his meaning in

Italian, but even when the requests were intelligible they were not granted. Canvas? Cordage? Sheet lead for shot holes? They might never have heard of them. After those three days Hornblower warped *Atropos* out into the harbour again and set about his repairs with his own resources and with his own men, keeping them labouring under the sun, and deriving some little satisfaction from the fact that Captain Ford's troubles—he had *Nightingale* over at the careenage—were even worse than his own. Ford, with his ship heeled over while he patched her bottom, had to put sentries over the stores he had taken out of her, to prevent the Sicilians from stealing them, even while his men vanished into the alleys of Palermo to pawn their clothing in exchange for the heady Sicilian wine.

It was with relief that Hornblower saw *Ocean* come proudly into Palermo, vice-admiral's flag at the fore; he felt confident that when he made his report that his ship would be ready for sea in all respects in one day's time he would be ordered out to join the Fleet. It could not happen too quickly.

And sure enough the orders came that evening, after he had gone on board to give a verbal account of his doings and to hand in his written reports. Collingwood listened to all he had to say, gave in return a very pleasant word of congratulation, saw him off the ship with his invariable courtesy, and of course kept his promise regarding the orders. Hornblower read them in the privacy of his cabin when the *Ocean's* gig delivered them; they were commendably short. He was 'requested and required, the day after to-morrow, the 17th instant,' to make the best of his way to the island of Ischia, there to report to Commodore Harris and join the squadron blockading Naples.

So all next day the ship's company of *Atropos* toiled to complete their ship for sea. Hornblower was hardly conscious of the activity going on around *Ocean*—it was what might be expected in the flagship of the Commander-in-Chief in his ally's capital. He regretted the interruption to his men's work when the admiral's barge came pulling by, and still more

when the royal barge, with the Sicilian colours and the
Bourbon lillies displayed, came pulling by to visit *Ocean*.
But that was only to be expected. When the flaming afternoon
began to die away into the lovely evening he found time to
exercise his men in accordance with the new station and
quarter bills—so many had been the casualties that all
the organization had to be revised. He stood there in the
glowing sunset watching the men come running down from
aloft after setting topsails.

'Signal from the flag, sir,' said Smiley, breaking in on his
concentrated thought. ' "Flag to *Atropos*. Come on board!" '

'Call my gig,' said Hornblower. 'Mr Jones, you will take
command.'

A desperate rush to change into his better uniform, and
then he hurled himself down the ship's side to where his gig
awaited him. Collingwood received him in the well-remembered cabin; the silver lamps were alight now, and in the
boxes under the great stern windows were strange flowers
whose names he did not know. And on Collingwood's face
was a strange expression; there was a hint of distress in it,
and of sympathy, as well as something of irritation. Hornblower stopped short at the sight of him, with a sudden
pounding of the heart. He could hardly remember to make
his bow properly. It flashed through his mind that perhaps
Ford had reported adversely on his behaviour in the recent
action. He might be facing court martial and ruin.

At Collingwood's shoulder stood a large elegant gentleman in full dress, with the ribbon and star of an order.

'My lord,' said Collingwood, 'this is Captain Horatio
Hornblower, I believe you have already had correspondence
with His Excellency, Captain. Lord William Bentinck.'

Hornblower made his bow again, his feverish mind telling
him that at least this could not be anything to do with the
action with the *Castilla*—that would not be the Minister's
business; on the other hand, in fact, Collingwood would
keep strangers out of any scandal in the Service.

'How d'ye do, sir?' asked Lord William.

'Very well, thank you, my Lord.'

The two Lords went on looking at Hornblower, and Hornblower looked back at them, trying to appear calm during those endless seconds.

'There's bad news for you, Hornblower, I fear,' said Collingwood at last, sadly.

Hornblower restrained himself from asking 'What is it?' He pulled himself up stiffer than ever, and tried to meet Collingwood's eyes without wavering.

'His Sicilian Majesty,' went on Collingwood, 'needs a ship.'

'Yes, my lord?'

Hornblower was none the wiser.

'When Bonaparte conquered the mainland he laid hands on the Sicilian Navy. Negligence—desertion—you can understand. There is no ship now at the disposal of His Majesty.'

'No, my Lord.' Hornblower could guess now what was coming.

'While coming out to visit *Ocean* this morning His Majesty happened to notice *Atropos*, with her paint all fresh. You made an excellent business of your refitting, Captain, as I noticed.'

'Thank you, my Lord.'

'His Majesty does not think it right that, as an island King, he should be without a ship.'

'I see, my Lord.'

Here Bentinck broke in, speaking harshly.

'The fact of the matter, Hornblower, is that the King has asked for your ship to be transferred to his flag.'

'Yes, my Lord.'

Nothing mattered now. Nothing was of any value.

'And I have advised His Lordship,' went on Bentinck, indicating Collingwood, 'that for the highest reasons of state it would be advisable to agree to the transfer.'

The imbecile monarch coveting the newly-painted toy. Hornblower could not keep back his protest.

'I find it hard to believe it necessary, my Lord,' he said.

For a moment His Excellency looked down in astonishment at the abysmal junior captain who questioned his judgment, but His Excellency kept his temper admirably all the same, and condescended to explain.

'I have six thousand British troops in the island,' he said in his harsh voice. 'At least, they call them British, but half of 'em are Corsican Rangers and Chasseurs Brittaniques—French deserters in British uniforms. I can hold the Straits against Bonaparte with them, all the same, as long as I have the goodwill of the King. Without it—if the Sicilian army turns against us—we're lost.'

'You must have heard about the King, Captain,' interposed Collingwood, gently.

'A little, my Lord.'

'He'd ruin everything for a whim,' said Bentinck. 'Now Bonaparte finds he can't cross the Straits he'd be willing to reach an agreement with Ferdinand. He'd promise him his throne here in exchange for an alliance. Ferdinand is capable of agreeing, too. He'd as lief have French troops in occupation as British, and be a satellite—or so he thinks at present—if it would mean paying off a score against us.'

'I see, my Lord,' said Hornblower.

'When I have more troops I'll talk to him in a different fashion,' said Bentinck. 'But at present——'

'*Atropos* is the smallest ship I have in the Mediterranean,' said Collingwood.

'And I am the most junior captain,' said Hornblower. He could not restrain himself from the bitter comment. He even forgot to say "my Lord."

'That is true as well,' said Collingwood.

In a disciplined service an officer was only a fool if he complained about treatment received on account of being junior. And it was clear that Collingwood disliked the present situation intensely.

'I understand, my Lord,' said Hornblower.

'Lord William has some suggestions to make which may

soften the blow,' said Collingwood, and Hornblower shifted his glance.

'You can be retained in command of *Atropos*,' said Bentinck—what a moment of joy, just one fleeting moment! —'if you transfer to the Sicilian service. His Majesty will appoint you Commodore, and you can hoist a broad pendant. I am sure he will also confer upon you an order of high distinction as well.'

'No,' said Hornblower. That was the only thing he could possibly say.

'I thought that would be your answer,' said Collingwood. 'And if a letter from me to the Admiralty carries any weight you can hope, on your return to England, to be appointed to the frigate to which your present seniority entitles you.'

'Thank you, my Lord. So I am to return to England?'

He would have a glimpse of Maria and the children then.

'I see no alternative, Captain, I am afraid, as of course you understand. But if Their Lordships see fit to send you back here with your new command, no one would be more delighted than I.'

'What sort of a man is your first lieutenant?' demanded Bentinck.

'Well, my Lord——' Hornblower looked from Bentinck to Collingwood. It was hard to make a public condemnation even of the abject Jones. 'He is a worthy enough man. The fact that he is John Jones the Ninth in the lieutenants' list may have held him back from promotion.'

A wintry twinkle appeared in Bentinck's eye.

'I fancy he would be John Jones the First in the Sicilian Navy List.'

'I expect so indeed, my Lord.'

'Do you think he would take service as captain under the King of the Two Sicilies?'

'I should be surprised if he did not.'

That would be Jones's only chance of ever becoming a captain, and most likely Jones was aware of it, however he might excuse himself for it in his own thoughts.

Collingwood entered the conversation again at this point.

'Joseph Bonaparte over in Naples has just proclaimed himself King of the Two Sicilies as well,' he remarked. 'That makes four Sicilies.'

Now they were all smiling together, and it was a moment before Hornblower's unhappiness returned to him, when he remembered that he had to give up the ship he had brought to perfection and the crew he had trained so carefully, and his Mediterranean station of honour. He turned to Collingwood.

'What are your orders, my Lord?'

'You will receive them in writing, of course. But verbally you are under orders not to move until you are officially informed of the transfer of your ship to the Sicilian flag. I'll distribute your ship's company through the Fleet—I can use them.'

No doubt about that; probably every ship under Collingwood's command was undermanned and would welcome a contingent of prime seamen.

'Aye aye, my Lord.'

'I'll take the Prince into my flagship here—there's a vacancy.'

The Prince had had seven months in a sloop of war; probably he had learned as much in that time as he would learn in seven years in an Admiral's flagship.

'Aye aye, my Lord.' Hornblower waited for a moment; it was hard to go on. 'And your orders for me personally?'

'The *Aquila*—she's an empty troop transport—sails for Portsmouth immediately without convoy, because she's a fast ship. The monthly convoy is assembling, but it's far from complete as yet. As you know, I am only responsible for their escort as far as Gibraltar, so that if you choose to go in a King's ship you will have to transfer there. *Penelope* will be the escorting vessel, as far as I can tell at present. And when I can spare her—God knows when that will be— I shall send the old *Temeraire* to England direct.'

'Yes, my Lord.'

'I would be glad if you would choose for yourself, Captain. I'll frame my orders in accordance with your wishes. You can sail in *Aquila*, or *Penelope*, or wait for *Temeraire*, whichever you prefer.'

Aquila was sailing for Portsmouth immediately, and she was a fast ship, sailing alone. In a month, even in less with fair winds, he could be setting foot on shore half an hour's walk from where Maria was living with the children. In a month he might be making his request to the Admiralty for further employment. He might be posted to that frigate that Collingwood had mentioned—he did not want to miss any opportunity. The sooner the better, as always. And he would see Maria and the children.

'I would like orders for *Aquila*, if you would be so kind, my Lord.'

'I expected you would say that.'

So that was the news that Hornblower brought back to his ship. The dreary little cabin which he had never had time to fit out properly seemed sadly homelike when he sat in it again; the sailcloth pillow supported once more a sleepless head, as so often before, when at last he could force himself to go to bed. It was strangely painful to say good-bye to the officers and crew, good characters and bad, even though he felt a little spurt of amusement at sight of Jones, gorgeous in the uniform of a captain in the Sicilian Navy, and another at sight of the twenty volunteers from the ship's company whom Jones had been permitted to recruit into the Sicilian service. They were the bad characters, of course, laughed at by the others for exchanging the grog and hardtack of old England for the pasta and the daily quart of wine of Sicily. But even to the bad characters it was hard to say good-bye— a sentimental fool, Hornblower called himself.

It was a dreary two days that Hornblower waited for *Aquila* to make ready to sail. Bentinck had advised him to see the Palace chapel, to take a carriage out to Monreale and see the mosaics there, but like a sulky child he would not. The dreamlike city of Palermo turns its back upon the sea, and Hornblower turned his back upon Palermo, until *Aquila* was working her way out round Monte Pellegrino, and then he stood aft, by the taffrail, looking back at *Atropos* lying there, and *Nightingale* at the careenage, and the palaces of Palermo beyond. He was forlorn and lonely, a negligible passenger amid all the bustle of getting under way.

'By your leave, sir,' said a seaman, hastening to the peak halliards—a little more, and he would have been elbowed out of the way.

'Good morning, sir,' said the captain of the ship, and instantly turned to shout orders to the men at the main topsail halliards; the captain of a hired transport did not want to offer any encouragement to a King's captain to comment on the handling of the ship. King's officers would only grudgingly admit that even admirals came between them and God.

Aquila dipped her colours to the flagship, and *Ocean* returned the compliment, the White Ensign slowly descending and rising again. That was the last memory Hornblower was to have of Palermo and of his voyage in the *Atropos*. *Aquila* braced round her sails and caught the first of the land breeze, heading boldly northward out to sea, and Sicily began to fade into the distance, while Hornblower tried to displace his unaccountable sadness by telling himself that he was on his way to Maria and the children. He tried to stimulate himself into excitement over the thought that a new command awaited him, and new adventures. Collingwood's flag lieutenant had passed on to him the gossip that the Admiralty was still commissioning ships as fast as they could be made ready for sea; there was a frigate, the *Lydia*, making ready, which would be an appropriate command for a captain of his seniority. But it was only slowly that he was able to overcome his sense of loss and frustration, as slowly as the captain of the *Aquila* made him welcome when he was taking his noon sights, as slowly as the days passed while *Aquila* beat her way to the Straits and out into the Atlantic.

Autumn was waiting for them beyond the Straits, with

the roaring westerly gales of the equinox, gale after gale,
when fortunately they had made westing enough to keep
them safe from the coast of Portugal while they lay hove-to
for long hours in the latitude of Lisbon, in the latitude of
Oporto, and then in the Bay of Biscay. It was on the tail of
the last of the gales that they drove wildly up the Channel,
storm-battered and leaky, with pumps going and topsails
treble reefed. And there was England, dimly seen, but well
remembered, the vague outline to be gazed at with a catch
in the breath. The Start, and at last St Catharine's, and the
hour of uncertainty as to whether they could get into the lee
of the Wight or would have to submit to being blown all
the way up-channel. A fortunate slant of wind gave them
their opportunity, and they attained the more sheltered
waters of Spithead, with the unbelievable green of the Isle
of Wight on their left hand, and so they attained to Portsmouth, to drop anchor where the quiet and calm made it
seem as if all the turmoil outside had been merely imagined.

A shore boat took Hornblower to the Sally Port, and he
set foot on English soil again, with a surge of genuine
emotion, mounting the steps and looking round him at the
familiar buildings of Portsmouth. A shore loafer—an old,
bent man—hurried away on twisted legs to fetch his barrow
while Hornblower looked round him; when he returned
Hornblower had to help him lift his chests on to the
barrow.

'Thank'ee, cap'n, thank'ee,' said the old man. He used the
title automatically, without knowing Hornblower's rank.

No one in England knew as yet—Maria did not know—
that Hornblower was in England. For that matter no one in
England knew as yet about the last exploit of the *Atropos* and
the capture of *Castilla*. Copies of Ford's and Hornblower's
reports to Collingwood were on board *Aquila*, in the sealed
mailbag in the captain's charge, to be sent on to the Secretary
of the Admiralty 'for the information of Their Lordships.'
In a day or two they might be in the Gazette, and they might
even be copied to appear in the Naval Chronicle and the

daily newspapers. Most of the honour and glory, of course, would go to Ford, but a few crumbs might come Hornblower's way; there was enough chance of that to put Hornblower in a good temper as he walked along with the wooden wheels of the barrow thumping and squeaking over the cobbles behind him.

The sadness and distress he had suffered when he parted from *Atropos* had largely died away by now. He was back in England, walking as fast as the old man's legs would allow towards Maria and the children, free for the moment from all demands upon his patience or his endurance, free to be happy for a while, free to indulge in ambitious dreams of the frigate Their Lordships might give him, free to relax in Maria's happy and indifferent chatter, with little Horatio running round the room, and with little Maria making valiant efforts to crawl at his feet. The thumping of the barrow wheels beat out a pleasant rhythm to accompany his dreams.

Here was the house and the well-remembered door. He could hear the echo within as he let the knocker fall, and he turned to help the old man lift off the chests. He put a shilling into the shaky hand and turned back quickly as he heard the door open. Maria was there with a child in her arms. She stood beside the door looking at him without recognition for a long second, and when at last she spoke it was as if she were dazed.

'Horry!' she said. 'Horry!'

There was no smile on her bewildered face.

'I've come home, dearest,' said Hornblower.

'I—I thought you were the apothecary,' said Maria, speaking slowly, 'the—the babies aren't so well.'

She offered the child in her arms for his inspection. It must be little Maria, although he did not know the flushed, feverish face. The closed eyes opened, and then shut again with the pain of the light, and the little head turned away fretfully but wearily, and the mouth opened to emit a low cry.

'Sh—sh,' said Maria, folding the child to her breast again, bowing her head over the wailing bundle. Then she looked up at Hornblower again.

'You·must come in,' she said. 'The—the cold. It will strike the fever inward.'

The remembered hall; the room at the side where he had asked Maria to marry him; the staircase to the bedroom. Mrs Mason was there, her grey hair untidy even in the curtained twilight of the room.

'The apothecary?' she asked from where she bent over the bed.

'No, mother. It's Horry come back again.'

'Horry? Horatio?'

Mrs Mason looked up to confirm what her daughter said, and Hornblower came towards the bedside. A tiny little figure lay there, half on its side, one hand outside the bedclothes holding Mrs Mason's finger.

'He's sick,' said Mrs Mason. 'Poor little man. He's so sick.'

Hornblower knelt beside the bed and bent over his son. He put out his hand and touched the feverish cheek. He tried to soothe his son's forehead as the head turned on the pillow. That forehead; it felt strange; like small shot felt through velvet. And Hornblower knew what that meant. He knew it well, and he had to admit the certainty to himself before telling the women what it meant. Smallpox.

Before he rose to his feet he had reached another conclusion, too. There was still duty to be done, his duty to his King and Country and to the Service and to Maria. Maria must be comforted. He must always comfort her, as long as life lasted.